By ELLE E. IRE

Vicious Circle

STORM FRONTS
Threadbare

Published by DSP PUBLICATIONS
www.dsppublications.com

ELLE E. IRE

VICIOUS CIRCLE

DSP PUBLICATIONS

Published by

DSP Publications

5032 Capital Circle SW, Suite 2, PMB# 279, Tallahassee, FL 32305-7886 USA
www.dsppublications.com

Trade Paperback ISBN: 978-1-64405-444-4
Digital ISBN: 978-1-64405-443-7
Library of Congress Control Number: 2019950113
Trade Paperback published January 2020
Second Edition
v. 2.0
First Edition published by Torquere Press Publishers, November 2015.

Printed in the United States of America

This paper meets the requirements of
ANSI/NISO Z39.48-1992 (Permanence of Paper).

To my wonderful spouse, who has driven, inspired,
and supported me in more ways than I can name.

ACKNOWLEDGMENTS

MANY THANKS to this book's original editor, Deelylah Mullin, for answering a million questions, and my editors at Dreamspinner: Rose Archer, for catching every misplaced comma imaginable, and Yv and Brian. Thank you to Kris Norris for the fabulous cover art she had to do twice over because, reasons. Credit also goes to my crit partners: Joe, Amy, Alina, Jennye, and Mark, as well as all the Celebration Writers Groups under Jan's fearless leadership. Thanks to author Jodi Meadows for her feedback, and authors Linnea Sinclair, John Pitts, and Gini Koch for blurbs and advice. Thank you to Torquere Press for initially believing in my work and Dreamspinner Publications for continuing to believe in it. Special gratitude goes to my current critique group, Facebook buddies, and workmates for letting me talk out endless plotlines and keeping me from despair and discouragement. And last but not least, thank you to my family for their support, and my parents who taught me to never give up. If I've forgotten anyone, I offer my sincerest apologies. This book has been a long time coming.

ELLE
E.IRE

VICIOUS
CIRCLE

CHAPTER 1

I SHOULD have been dead by now.

A wall of stone blocked the tunnel entrance. Instead of colliding with rock, I walked through the illusion, leaving the dark cold Sardonen desert behind. My arrival activated the string of flickering lights overhead.

I had to be crazy to come back.

Thin, brittle bones protruded from the hard-packed earth. They lined the walls from the dirt floor up to the tunnel's ceiling. Skeletal fingers reached for me, clawing their way free from their rocky prison with each tremor and landslide that had plagued this world for hundreds of years. They caught on sleeves and pant legs wherever the passage narrowed, drawing the living to the deceased one thread at a time.

It was a barbaric way to dispose of our dead. In an age of disintegrators and molecular recyclers, the masters of the Assassins' Guild held steadfast to their traditions; tradition taught lessons to those who came after.

Like me. I'd learned this lesson: Assassins who erred died young.

I swear, under penalty of death, to uphold the rules of the Guild, to protect its secrets, to defend the defenseless, to take a life only when deemed necessary by the Guild Leader, or in self-defense, or in defense of the Guild, to fulfill the contracts I accept.... Until now. The oath echoed in my head, pounding against my brain in painful pulses. Guilt and fear vied with rage, tearing at my intestines.

No, I could do this. I could state my case, defend it, work something out. They wouldn't hold me to the death penalty. They couldn't. My breath came in heavy puffs. I sealed my black flight jacket with one quick jerk of the zipper and plowed onward. Anger and determination carried me. I needed to ride that wave before it crested and evaporated.

Ahead, the light grew brighter. I slowed, then stopped at the entrance to a wide man-made chamber. I snapped the leather strap closed over the grip of the laser pistol at my side and tucked the hilt of my knife farther into my right boot. Reaching behind my head, I unfastened a matte black clasp and tucked it into my jacket pocket, letting my hair fall in a flow of inky darkness. It settled on my shoulders, heavy, thick, and straight.

Someone like me couldn't present a less threatening appearance, short of wearing a dress. I hadn't willingly worn a dress in all my twenty-nine years.

Absently, I rubbed at the cuff over my left wrist. The Guild tattoo itched incessantly, no matter how often the others told me it was all in my head. I stepped into the light.

The greeting chamber extended before me. If I squinted, I could make out the domed ceiling above, higher than a two-story building and shrouded by shadow. An irregular opening in the center let in minimal starlight and allowed smoke from the fire to escape. Ornate columns carved from local stone prevented the roof from caving in despite regular seismic tremors. The circular space could hold the entire Guild, all ninety-nine of us, ten times over. Low temporary dividers separated it into work, eating, and rest areas.

This had all been above ground before quakes decimated a rocky desert outcropping and buried the structure. Evidence of windows and blocked doorways remained in the fractured walls. No one knew its former purpose, but a cracked marble altar stood at one end, suggesting possible religious significance.

Ironic—a place of worship had become a training ground for murderers.

I bit my lower lip hard enough to taste blood—anything to prevent the shedding of tears. The term "murderers" never would have occurred to me before five days ago.

The flames thrived and danced in the central firepit, fed by a team of apprentices morning, midday, and night since the origination of the Guild. The oldest records and journal entries described the smoke as a constant annoyance. Later generations installed the metal ventilation shaft above the pit, drawing the smoke to the ceiling aperture, where it would release into the desert. Hundreds of steam geysers dotted the sandy surface—one of the many sources of seismic instability. Despite a slight variance in color, the assassins' smoke went unnoticed. Assassins needed to have a camouflaged safe haven, and its isolation added to its invisibility.

Micah waited by the altar, his stance deceptively casual. The loose black training tunic hung over brown trousers to his upper thighs and covered muscles I'd once traced with my fingertips. Bright blue eyes under thick dark hair bore into my soul, seeing everything: my failures, weaknesses, and needs. "Come in, Corianne." His use of my birth name tightened the muscles around my mouth. Nothing so melodious should apply to a master assassin. Everyone called me *Cor*. Micah's voice was little more than a whisper, but those who stood behind the altar could be heard in every part of the open area—even speaking at low volume. Such were the acoustics of this room. Useful for training purposes.

While he crossed to the fire and stood beside it, I scanned the other sections of the only home I could remember. At least a dozen of the masters inhabited the Guild at any given time, and twice as many apprentices. The sleeping area should have been dotted with rolled-out smart mattresses that conformed to and cushioned tired bodies. Murmured conversation should have drifted from lowered heads around the docken-wood dining tables while masters consumed bowls of vegetable stew and mugs of ale.

Micah and I were alone. That realization raised the hairs at the nape of my neck. My hand dropped to rest on the grip of my holstered pistol. His eyes followed the motion, as I knew they would. The folds of his tunic hid his hands from my view.

A grinding noise jerked my attention to the entrance, where a steel door slid into place. I'd known of its existence. I'd seen it used before, but I'd clung to foolish hope Micah's affections would prevent its use on me.

"You have a purpose. State it." The commanding tone carried his words in echoes that bounced off the chamber walls. If I reached out far enough, I could touch his anger. It filled the room and threatened to suffocate me.

My jaw muscles clenched so tightly, I could barely force the words from my lips, but I spat them like tossed coins at a beggar's feet. "I renounce my master's status. I resign from the Guild." There. Done. The speech sealed my fate. Whatever the next few minutes brought, there was no going back. It hurt more than I imagined.

Even from this distance, I saw his shoulders slump. He'd wished for a different outcome, maybe hoped I'd agree to go back and finish what I'd started. Not going to happen. Nice to know our relationship counted for something, though. Maybe I could use that.

My musing almost cost me my life as he drew a tiny pistol from a hidden wrist holster. He fired once, the beam of energy slashing the air between us. I lunged to the right and felt the tingling in my skin that always followed near-death. The burst struck the wall with a flash that threw sparks from the stone.

I'd gotten lucky. Micah rarely missed.

A dive to the left carried me over the closest divider and into the sleeping area. Several mattresses softened my landing, and I rolled to crawl back and peer over the partition. Micah had gone the opposite direction, into the dining section. He ducked under a table, then flipped it on its side as a barrier. Docken wood was partially petrified, prized for its hardness. I snapped the strap off my much larger, more powerful laser and drew it into the palm of my hand, fingers wrapping around the custom grip.

A standoff meant my eventual defeat. The other Guild members wouldn't stay away forever. If I pursued Micah, he would shoot me. Instead I fired two shots, one at the ventilation shaft, knocking it askew, and another into the fire itself. It surged and roared, scattering embers and bits of wood in every direction. Billows of smoke poured from the enraged flames, carrying into other sections and obscuring vision. Stifling a cough with my free hand, I plunged into the ashy cloud cover and lost myself.

My eyes burned and teared as I circled the pit, hoping to approach Micah from behind. Pockets of drifting smoke floated like lost spirits— the ghosts of my victims, rising to seek their revenge.

A blur of motion launched from the smoke, tackled me to the ground, and slammed my gun hand against the polished marble floor. My bruised fingers released, and the weapon skittered across the smooth surface, disappearing into the shadows.

That's it. I was dead. No real disgrace. He was Guild Leader for a reason. So why hadn't he shot me already?

Micah's weight pressed me down. He struck me hard enough across the face my vision blurred for a second, and I felt the shock wave run down my spine. "Why?" he demanded, breath hot against my cheek. I smelled the red wine he preferred in overabundant amounts. His decision to carry out Guild law had not come easily. Maybe he still had feelings for me.

I pictured fresh-faced, blue-eyed innocence under a mane of curly blond hair—my last assignment—and the bile rose in my throat. My Guildmates nicknamed me the Core of Sardonen, a play on my name, because they claimed I was the heart of the Guild. That heart cost me everything.

I spat in Micah's face while I struggled to think of something else to say. The saliva ran down the side of his wide nose. "You sent me to kill a child." The growl made my voice unrecognizable, even to me.

"A tyrant. His rulings have ended thousands of lives. You should have fulfilled the damn contract. Coming back here... you've left me few choices."

Conversation equaled distraction. I drew my legs up to place my feet flat on the floor and thrust with my hips, twisting my torso. The sudden motion knocked him off-balance, and we rolled toward the edge of the firepit. His hand came down on a chunk of burning kindling. His cry of pain tore at me.

I looked sideways at him. Micah still gripped me with his left hand, but his opposite sleeve and the skin of his gun hand were aflame. He flung the tiny pistol, its metal superheated. It vanished into the fire. We shoved apart. Micah beat his burning clothing against his hip. My head met the stone floor, creating sparkles at the edges of my already spotty vision, but I rocked back for momentum and gained my feet in one move, panting. A flash of fabric caught my eye as Micah's tunic disappeared behind another partition.

"He was a puppet, Mic!" I drew breath to continue but expelled the air in a wracking cough. My eyes streamed tears from the ash, and more. "The Gibran council made the decisions. His guardian pulled the strings." I slipped the knife from my boot and strained my ears, listening for any cue that would give away Micah's exact position. No human sound carried to me, only the crackling of burning wood and the creak of the ventilation shaft swinging overhead where I'd half detached it from its moorings. Micah taught me everything I knew about stalking prey. I didn't expect to detect—

An arm wrapped around my shoulders and across my chest. I threw my weight forward, tossing him over my back to land with a thud and a grunt and a stirring of dust.

In an instant I'd straddled him. Memories of the two of us in similar positions under much more pleasant circumstances threatened to break my concentration. I shook my head once, viciously, and held my knife at his throat.

His gaze met mine. My hair brushed his cheeks. I noticed the stubble there, and this close I could see the shadows beneath his eyes. How long had he known of my refusal? Three days' transit by star freighter from Gibran to Sardonen, another day to cross the desert in my aircar and refuel at the oasis city of Weathered Palms, then an hour to the Guild's hidden base of operations. He'd had plenty of time to consider this moment.

My voice softened. "The Guild can't know everything, Micah. Even you make mistakes. Admit it, dammit. Admit you were wrong. Let me walk away." As I'd been taught, as *he* taught me, I'd returned to face my fate with honor. I'd resigned. If he admitted his personal error in accepting the contract for the Guild, my loss of status and livelihood would be punishment enough for me. Of course, it would also end him as Guild Leader.

What worth did he place on loyalty? On love, even love long lost? Time ceased to pass while I awaited his response.

"We are bound by the contracts we accept, Cor." His breath wheezed in his chest.

What pieces of my heart he'd left me plummeted to the soles of my boots.

No doubt now where his priorities lay. I'd thrown myself on his mercy. I wouldn't throw myself on his sword. Rigid adherence to Guild rules ended our relationship. That same rigidity would end one of our lives. More bones for the corridor walls. I'd been a fool to think I could depend on our relationship to convince him not to kill me. "I don't kill kids." My tone dropped to a whisper. "You couldn't have done it. He was younger than an apprentice—thirteen at most. We do what we do to protect the innocent. It's the only thing that makes this profession tolerable. You asked me to become a monster."

"Thirteen…." Micah's eyes closed. He drew a shuddering breath and released it.

A horrible understanding dawned.

Too easy. He realized what he'd done—no doubt after the fact—but he knew. With one order he'd destroyed everything I'd trained for, everything I was. My home, my friends, my livelihood—he'd taken them all with his one bad decision as Guild Leader to send me after that child. He knew. And he regretted it.

By coming back, I'd forced him to choose. My life and his humiliation or my death and his eternal guilt. But there was a third choice I'd initially failed to see.

No witnesses. He'd dismissed everyone so he could let me win this fight. Avoiding that first attack with the pistol shot hadn't been luck. He'd missed intentionally. No other explanation made any sense. Micah trained me himself. Even drunk, he would always best me in combat. Besides some minor scrapes and bruises, I was unharmed.

He hadn't sealed the entrance to keep me in. He'd locked it to keep others out, in case they returned ahead of schedule. Ahead of me killing him and getting away. Of course, even if I escaped, they'd hunt me. But I'd be alive and free, and he'd die a hero's death.

The realization shook me, along with another, deeper epiphany.

I didn't care. I didn't care about Guild law or losing my status. And I wouldn't make him a martyr to preserve his precious ego.

Few assassins lived to twenty-nine, even fewer to Micah's thirty-five. I'd taken enough lives. Time to start living my own—by my rules, not theirs.

Little by little, I eased my blade away from my former lover's throat. We could reach a compromise that would permit us both to live. Would my infliction of a severe enough beating allow him not to lose face for failing to kill me? Maybe if I drugged him first. "Micah—"

In a swift movement worthy of a master, he seized my wrist in his left hand. One slice and he'd drawn the knife across his own jugular. My scream echoed off the walls of the chamber, bouncing back to me in taunting waves of agony.

I couldn't remember the last time I'd screamed.

Yes, I could—in pleasure. With Micah.

Blood poured, drenching my hands in sticky warmth. The weapon slipped from my wet fingers. I jerked away from the gaping wound, hideous like a macabre smile. My eyes went to Mic's face, but life had already left him. His head lolled, and a dark pool formed on the stone. The scent of iron overpowered the smoke.

I gagged once, swallowed, then gagged again and lost the battle, vomiting until my abdomen ached. I continued to dry heave, my intestines wrenching like the wringing of a wet towel.

I'd been exposed to plenty of blood and gore in my profession. This certainly wasn't the first friend I'd seen die. But it was the first time I'd held the weapon.

I screamed again, putting all my rage and frustration behind the sound. "You bastard!" The words strangled from my tightened throat while my open palms slammed the stone floor. Micah had stolen my choices from me. Again.

Time passed, I'm not sure how much, but breathing grew more and more difficult as smoke filled the room. Knees shaky, I staggered to my feet, then nearly fell when the chamber tilted and swam. Oxygen deprivation. I needed to get out.

Despite the urgency, I stumbled to the sleeping area, locating the lockers built into the partition. Tears blurred my vision, and I found my storage space by feel and habit. It took three tries to enter the release code on the keypad, one of the few evidences of modern technology in the Guild house. When it snapped open, I dumped its contents and clawed through them for whatever I could easily carry: a spare pistol and back holster, another knife (I wasn't retrieving my favorite one), a holocube. I could have used the change of clothes, another set of working gear. However, I'd left my satchel in the aircar on the surface. I cut a strip from a shirt and wrapped it around my mouth and nose.

Now for the door. I weaved my way to Micah's corpse, aware of my unsteady limbs. My thumping heart reverberated in my chest and head, building to a migraine crescendo that finally dropped me to my knees beside the body. The impact clicked my teeth together in an audible snap.

I made the error of glancing at his face one last time, but this slack, lifeless mask wasn't the man I'd loved, the man who'd saved me and given me a purpose in life.

It had been months since he'd been that man, almost a year since he'd chosen the Guild over me.

I forced myself to look away.

Like detached things, my hands slid beneath his tunic, fumbling for his belt and the door release I'd find there. The lingering warmth of his skin seeped into my fingertips, renewing my nausea, but I fought it down. No more time. Darkness encroached on the edges of my vision.

I closed my grip around the device, found the signal switch, and flipped it. The shriek of metal on stone sent my headache to new heights of agony, and I blinked repeatedly before standing to face the door.

Three master assassins blocked my exit.

At least I thought there were three. The way my eyesight was distorted, I could have been mistaken. Three or ten, it didn't matter. One would best me in my current condition.

I'd watched my lover kill himself, nearly asphyxiated on smoke, gotten the door open, and I still wasn't going to get away. Part of me wanted to shatter.

The masters glanced from me, wavering and covered in blood not my own, to Micah. It gave me time to identify them: Benn, Alek, and Yesenia. Benn, whom I'd always considered a friend, hesitated. Yesenia shouted with rage. I had a half second to react before she and Alek drew their knives and flung them.

I dive-rolled behind the firepit, where the smoke clung thickest and the flames roiled. One of the blades missed, but the second drove into my back, just below my right shoulder. I smothered a shriek of pain beneath a choked sob and crouched, considering my options. There were frighteningly few, and judging from all the motion in the room, Benn had decided to join the attack against me. I swallowed my hurt and surprise. Assassins had no permanent friends.

One thing in my favor—all three wore training clothes, not working gear. I'd have the only laser in the room, not that I could aim it with my head swimming, but it was something. Micah must have planned this, sent them out on some minimalist survival expedition so if they returned early, I'd have a small advantage. Small consolation, knowing he wanted me to live, but better than nothing.

A trickle of sweat, or maybe blood, ran down my back. It traced odd patterns beneath my clothing, reminding me of nights Micah had done the same with his fingertips. I shook myself, earning an agonizing burst of pain for my efforts. Since the blade didn't feel terribly deep, I reached over my shoulder with my left hand, grasped the knife hilt, and yanked once, hard. The weapon slid from skin and muscle with a sound like a baby suckling. This time I did cry out, though the crackling flames drowned it.

The masters approached with caution. They needn't have bothered. My right arm hung useless; my head spun. I've never been much for religions or gods, but I turned my face upward, toward the ventilation hole in the chamber ceiling. Before I could offer up a random prayer, I froze, staring.

My fingers scrabbled at my belt, drawing the thin grappling line from its pouch a meter at a time so the wire zinged; I cringed at the noise, but I didn't have time for quiet action. The duroclamp at its end activated with the press of a button, and I hurled it, straight up into the billowing smoke. It continued to unwind from its container, homing sensors searching for something to dig into, built-in impellers carrying it farther than my waning strength could throw. I worried it might not have enough length, when it went taut.

Its powerful miniaturized motor activated instantly, and I was jerked off the floor by the waist before I had a chance to grip the line with my good hand. Flailing like a fledgling bird, I presented an easy target to my former comrades. Another knife embedded itself in my thigh, then went deeper when I collided with the exterior of the ventilation shaft, clanging up along its outer casing like some deranged bell-ringer until the duct work stopped two meters short of the ceiling. I sucked air through my teeth and willed myself to remain conscious. At last I finally managed to wrap my fingers around the cord and pull my torso upright.

I rose higher, the ground swirling dizzyingly below, and hit the overhead stone surrounding the hole. The grapple motor strained to finish retrieval of the line. Contorting myself, I bent at the waist to fit my body through the opening. I tore several holes in my clothing squeezing through the tight space and forced the knife in another several centimeters until its blade no longer showed. Blood ran in a river from the wound.

One-handed, I clawed at the sand around the jagged aperture, finally grasping a rock to aid the grapple in its job. I flopped on the dirt like a dying fish, ripped the fabric from my face, and gasped air through my mouth and nose in delicious gulps.

I couldn't imagine moving, but I wasn't out of this yet. Below, I could barely make out shouting, and in the distance, an aircar engine roared to life.

Wonderful.

The chain of events had been set in motion. Phantasmic shapes drove through the midnight fog, blending with the natural phenomenon and hiding themselves amongst it. The grotesque and distorted faces of the ancient dead, stretched and twisted in the tendrils of haze, remnants of corporeal forms trailing behind in elongated strands of white.

The ephems, as He-Who-Had-Created-Them named the creatures, let themselves be carried by the air currents, multiple mouths open in silent death-throe shrieks. The wind blew in the desired direction, so they conserved their demonic energy for later deeds. They flew across great expanses of ocean waves, over narrow docks and harbored boats, above corrugated rooftops and wooden-frame houses—so peaceful. So vulnerable.

They intermingled and fought, struggling for dominance, attempting to tear one another's tenuous forms apart. Then they separated. He-Who-Had-Created-Them would disperse them for such behavior. They had a purpose. They bore on toward their final destination, though the life forces in each human home tempted.

The mansion rested atop a low rise at the edge of the village. Oblivious inhabitants slept within, windows thrown open wide to cool rooms using gentle ocean breezes. The specters hovered at first one ledge, then another, at last drawn inward by the unmistakably bright, delicious aura of the bedroom's single occupant.

Like magnets to metal, the white light surrounding the sleeping young man drew the entities closer. Succeed, and they would live off his sustenance for days, perhaps weeks. Fail, and the energy would dissipate and destroy them, returning them to the realm of nightmares from which they'd been called.

They had no choice. Retreat meant destruction assured. The master did not accept failure.

Swirling about the bed, they sought entry. The sleeper had a beige blanket pulled all the way up to his chin, but it left his face exposed, expression beatific in slumber.

The spirits' expressions formed demons and death's heads in the misty fog. They surged into the young man's nostrils, driving deep into his soul on a single intake of breath.

The sleeper awoke, choking and sputtering, sitting bolt upright in the double bed. He coughed and wheezed as he struggled to draw air into his lungs. While those vital organs fought to sustain life, he squeezed his eyes tightly shut and therefore did not see the flare of bright white light that emanated from his body and lit the comfortably appointed bedroom.

It flashed through the open window, streaking across the mansion's manicured lawn and arcing over the village below. Late-night revelers at the town tavern would tell tales of it for weeks to come. None of them believed.

It thrust the specters out, hurling them in rolling balls of distortion until they gathered themselves and recoalesced at the harbor's edge. The fog helped, thickening the air and providing additional weight and substance. Without it, they might have been torn apart beyond reconstitution.

They could not return to He-Who-Had-Created-Them. Not with the task unfinished.

Heat lightning flashed, arcing from the sky to the waves and sizzling on impact. The spirits drew on its energy, taking in as much power as they dared to regain a semblance of physical form. Dead bodies walking the streets might bring retaliation, but the lightning alone did not provide strength enough. They needed a different sort of vitality.

It was a simple matter to seek out thoughts of grief, loss, and mourning amongst the living, and a child's emotions ran closer to the surface than those of adults. The ephems took those thoughts, crafting and shaping them into pale representations of familiar corporeal shapes.

Side by side, the elderly couple, a white-haired man and woman, shuffled up the cobblestone street of the sleepy island town. In the flicker of old-fashioned streetlamps, the few passersby did not discern their bloated bodies or the blue tint to their skins. This was how the child imagined them, how she saw them in her nightmares, and therefore, these were the images their natures forced them to adopt.

The sweet tang of sorrow drew them off the main thoroughfare to a cottage surrounded by gardens of white chella flowers. At one time, four wrinkled hands had carefully tended the blooms, husband and wife laughing and chatting back and forth, but the plants had grown wild in recent weeks, creeping over the paving stones leading to the whitewashed porch.

One of those hands, gray and bloodless, tried the door. When he found it locked, he knocked a dull, steady, insistent rhythm.

The porch light sprang on, and the ephems in their assumed bodies shied from it, stepping from its cast circle of warmth into the shadows of the covered porch. The door creaked open on salt-air-rusted hinges, and a sleepy face peered into the night.

Wide blue eyes struggled to pierce the darkness, to see the faces of her visitors, whose figures seemed so familiar. "Grandma? Grandpa?"

She reached a hand to rub the granules from her eyes. Tearstained cheeks crinkled as she beamed a smile. "Grandma! Grandpa!"

The little girl threw herself upon the closer figure, the "woman," tiny arms wrapping around her grandmother's ample waist, unable to meet behind her.

"The boat! They said you'd drowned. I knew they were wrong. I knew!" She sobbed and laughed as one, a joyous yet heart-wrenching sound that would have brought human onlookers to tears of their own.

On the ephemerals, it had no effect.

They stared down at the child, faces expressionless, eyes sunken into their sockets, eaten—as the girl had dreamed—by the many carnivorous creatures that roamed the planet's seas.

"Felicia?" An adult woman's voice, tinged with concern, carried from within the cottage.

At the same moment, the girl recognized a wrongness in how her grandmother felt, in her lack of response to her only grandchild. Felicia looked up, mouth dropping open in shock and horror.

Reverting to their spirit forms, the ephems poured down the girl's open throat.

It took seconds to drain her.

Vitality restored, they drove their way toward the mansion once more, this time selecting a different window for entry, one a little less brightly lit.

Far behind them, in the village below, a woman screamed as only a mother who'd lost her child could.

CHAPTER 2

THEY'D FOUND my aircar, despite holographic shielding and camouflage nets. I recognized the grinding in the motor I had ignored for months. I'd never been one of those my-aircar-equals-my-baby types.

I raised myself on my left elbow. The right arm had no feeling, and I suspected nerve damage or worse—poison. The Guild only allowed the use of fast-acting toxins, labeling all others as inhumane, but that didn't stop a few of the grittier assassins from sneaking in a vial or two and keeping a knife coated in some torturous concoction. But to use it on me…. Well, I was a traitor now, wasn't I? Looking across the desert surface, I scanned the base of the rocky outcropping hiding the cave entrance. A pair of headlights glowed like a predator's eyes.

My first attempt to gain my feet ended with me flat on my face, spitting sand and biting back a sob. In my delirium, I'd forgotten the blade protruding from my thigh. I ran my fingers along the exposed bit of hilt, tracing small, smooth pieces of shell used as decorations. I knew this weapon and its owner—Alek. Dread drove the remaining warmth from my body. Master Alek preferred a serrated edge. Removing it would rip my leg apart, and I'd bleed out. Given I was still alive, it was better to leave it in.

Enough of this.

I braced myself and stood, placing most of my weight on my right leg. Even the slightest pressure on my left drove the breath from me in a ragged gasp.

The aircar's motor revved higher, and the vehicle rocketed toward me. I reached across my body and drew my pistol from its holster, leveling it at the motor, not the driver. Even now I couldn't bring myself to take a former comrade's life. Between the glare of the headlights and the surrounding darkness, I couldn't see who sat at the controls, but I knew everyone in the Guild.

My mouth twisted in a humorless smile. They knew me too. Didn't seem to matter to them.

A big part of why you're leaving, a little voice reminded me.

The first shot from my laser went wide, scorching the sand and turning it to molten glass. The second reflected off the front grill, and the driver ducked lower.

Good. Stay down.

Narrowing my eyes, I focused my concentration. My target range record was almost as good with my left hand as my right, but I missed the comfort factor. At least the cleaner air cleared my vision. When I could read the falsified ID numbers on the front plate, I fired and dropped flat in the dust.

The aircar passed over me, bathing my body in its superheated cushion of air and raising blisters on the exposed skin of my hands and the back of my neck. Instead of simply burning out as I'd planned, the engine's whine rose to a keening screech. I had a sickening premonition of what was about to occur. Lifting my head, I watched the nose of the car plow into the desert floor. Then the vehicle flipped up and over to land on its passenger cab.

The impact churned up a wave of sand and debris, and for a long moment, I could see nothing. Then a fireball exploded from the wreck, and I ducked to avoid being impaled by shrapnel. Hot pieces of metal whistled over my head as they flew and embedded themselves in the dunes, sizzling wherever they landed. One tiny chunk hit the back of my thigh, burning a hole through my pant leg before I could shake it off—one more small voice to add to my chorus of pain.

I clung to the hope the driver somehow escaped the inferno until the dust settled and all movement ceased. Maybe I hadn't killed Micah, but I'd certainly ended the aircar operator's life. Strange to regret killing someone hunting me, but the driver thought I'd murdered the Guild Leader. In his place, I would have done the same, and that knowledge brought guilt and pity.

The ground shifted under my feet, another of the frequent quakes famous in this region. Forcing myself upright, I jolted to the left. A steam geyser erupted from a new fissure in the distance. Another opened, and I hobbled faster, trying to put distance between myself and the uncertain ground around the smoldering aircar. A piece of the vehicle's door, flung by the explosion, served as my crutch, but the heated debris raised new blisters on my fingertips.

More things to worry about. An assassin without fine motor skills wouldn't be much of an assassin at all. Wouldn't be much of anything.

The ground rumbled again. In my years with the Guild, I'd encountered nothing I feared more than nature itself. The violent tremors bred in me a healthy phobia of live burial. Hurricanes and volcanic eruptions were predictable. A person could see them coming and at least try to get out of the way, but when your enemy lived in the very earth you stood on….

Hand beams caught my attention, and my adrenaline spiked as I altered course away from them. Almost no one ventured out here except Guild members and the Fatal Force mercenaries who used the area for training. So far, the mercs hadn't located our underground hiding place. I tried to remember if this was their season to be on Sardonen. They might help, for a price, but I couldn't identify them by hand lamps and wasn't desperate enough to take chances… yet.

Making it to the closest city, Weathered Palms, seemed beyond my current physical ability. Maybe I could get to the mercenaries' camp, but I had to evade the other assassins Micah sent out on some manufactured exercise. Scanners might pick up my bio-signs, but despite the harsh environment, the desert housed plenty of distracting wildlife. Besides, with the fire I'd started, the aircar crash, and the minor quake, the Guild had other things to attend to beyond finding me. I tried to convince myself my efforts weren't for nothing.

I traveled several kilometers, my training and fitness prior to this fiasco paying off, but eventually collapsed. The chill in my body stemmed from more than the nighttime desert temperatures. If I didn't get to a hospital soon, I'd bleed to death. If I didn't get the antidote for Alek's poison, and by now I was certain I *had* been poisoned, it would kill me. If the sun came up, I'd dehydrate. If the Sardonen sand lizards found me—I could hear them croaking to one another behind the dunes—they'd pick my bones clean before I needed to worry about the sun.

A hysterical laugh escaped me. I tried to swallow it down, but it burst from my throat and multiplied until I couldn't breathe, and tears again bathed my cheeks. My crutch lay beside me, discarded, and I wrapped my good arm around myself, unable to stifle my insane mirth.

The laughter released some tension. I crawled forward on two functional limbs, my right arm more like a lifeless stick and my wounded leg dragging a line in the sand, and hoped I continued in the right direction.

I'd gone beyond delirium by the time I entered the tent circle of the Fatal Force mercenaries' survivalist training camp. The weapons they pointed at me aroused no fear or concern. Pain, sorrow, and self-pity wound together in a tight ball in my gut. At that moment, I would have welcomed death.

The mercenaries' demands for my identity went unanswered. I'd lost the capacity for speech. One pulled at my sleeve, revealing my Guild tattoo, respected and feared throughout the settled worlds. The five or six men and women surged back from me, then laughed at themselves for their foolishness. I was clearly harmless. I hadn't been harmless in a long time.

They muttered to one another. One man suggested they return me to the Guild. Another, a woman, said only a master assassin could succeed in doing this kind of damage to another master. They'd sign my death warrant by returning me. A spark of self-preservation kindled, and I jerked and twisted, making a faltering attempt to crawl a few more pitiful meters away and failing with a belly flop in the sand. More muttering. Something about exacting payment for my rescue. A second male voice said there might be a contract on my head, a bounty they could collect.

"We aren't bounty hunters. We're mercs." The woman again, clearly their leader. "We don't sell injured people to their attackers. We don't kill defenseless women, either, even if they are assassins."

My opinion of mercenaries in general rose several notches.

They carried me into one of their tents. An hour later, their shuttle carried me off-world.

In the mansion bedroom adjacent to the one they'd previously entered, movement was easier, the currents of life force a little thinner, though admittedly not much so.

The bed's occupant, a female this time, lay uncovered upon the mattress. Her white satin nightgown shimmered in the moonlight where it had ridden up around her thighs. Her breasts rose and fell with each slow, deep breath of her dreams. Red-and-gold hair fell across the pillow in gentle waves.

Beneath the gown, she wore nothing.

If wisps of vapor could leer, these would have. They seeped into the crevice between her legs, sifted through the soft covering of pubic hair, tickled and teased the delicate skin.

The girl exhaled on a moan. Her tongue moistened her lips. Her heart rate increased.

Urged on by her response, the ephemeral beings doubled their efforts, increasing speed, flickering over her most sensitive areas in feathery touches only an ephem could produce. They drew from the chill of the night air pouring through the open shutters, blowing it over her skin, raising the tiny hairs and hardening her nipples to points beneath the gown. They flowed through the moisture they created, spreading it to greater effect.

"Mmm." The vibration of pleasure rippled through her lithe frame.

The ephems used her slickness as a conduit. She opened to their gentle but persistent pressure, and they slid up and in as her wetness poured down. Her hips rocked, increasing the flow and threatening to expel them, but curling into themselves, they held on and waited.

Without their stimulation, her body calmed, breathing and heartbeat returning to normal, skin flushed and lips swollen with unsatisfied need. Distracted by the pleasure, the light of her aura never flared. Her invaders settled in, establishing a firm hold.

Sensing their victory, one drew away from the other, keeping an end of its wispy self in place while it extended throughout the girl's body, moving upward toward the brain. The other remained near the center of her pleasure, compressed and waiting.

The first mingled with the energy of her thoughts, abstract and indistinct in dream-state, now tinged with desire and frustration. It tweaked the electrical impulses of her synapses, sent signals to her mind and body, woke her.

Unlike her brother, now recovered and returned to sleep in the adjacent bedroom, she neither choked nor sputtered, but her eyes darted about, searching for what disturbed her sleep. She sat bolt upright, and the shift in position drew attention to the dampness of the sheets.

A tentative hand slipped between her thighs. Confusion faded as her lips turned up in a half smile.

The specter sensed the tumult of her thoughts, the need for completion while her fingers moved. With one painful redirect of energy, it put a stop to that, and the girl removed her hand to press fingertips to her forehead.

She stood on shaky limbs, headed for the bathroom and the painkillers she kept on a shelf above the sink, but her steps took her elsewhere. Before she realized it, she navigated the stairs to the lower floor, crossed the hall, and entered the expansive kitchen. Her hand opened the cutlery drawer, drawing forth a cutting knife of the finest quality her family's credits could buy. Its sharpened edge glinted in the moonlight from the kitchen windows, but her eyes saw nothing.

Padding soundlessly in her bare feet, she returned to the second floor. At her brother's door, she hesitated. Her gaze darted to the blade, blinking in wonderment at its presence. She shook her head to clear it. The evil in her brain sent a signal along its own length, down through her body to its counterpart. The second ephem swirled over her pleasure center, rubbing and stroking, sending her staggering against the wood-paneled wall.

A tendril stifled the cry that rose in her throat. By the time her orgasm subsided, the dual entities had diverted her attention enough to reestablish their control.

She opened the unlocked door. She crossed to stand over the sleeping figure in the beige-blanketed double bed. She raised the knife high over his chest.

It helped that her own will wasn't totally opposed to the coming result. It facilitated muscular direction.

What she opposed was the act itself. The hand holding the blade froze. The tip of the weapon trembled. A rigid belief system fought the urge to bring the weapon down. No matter how the entities coerced and encouraged, they could not control this action. She would not kill him herself. They would need to use her to find another, more willing puppet.

Still in her somnambulant state, she returned to her own room where the knife slipped out the open window for confused gardeners to find it in the morning. When asked, she had no idea how it had come to be there.

She pulled a suitcase from beneath her bed and set about packing. She had a sudden desire to travel.

Poets might find sunsets worthy of verse. I found them annoying—an aftereffect of the poison.

I'd recovered a great deal since my frantic escape from Sardonen three months prior. The mercenaries had well-stocked medical supplies and a trained doctor in their camp. On their shuttle, and later at a secure asteroid base, he treated me for shock, blood loss, and burns. He saved my right arm and my left leg. He administered the antidote for Alek's poison.

A little too late.

The chemicals affected my nervous system, targeting muscle control and eyesight. Even after two surgeries, I still limped. And the quality of light at dusk made it difficult for me to see in the accursed shadows. At least full daylight and dark weren't issues yet.

I was born paranoid. Guild training exacerbated it. Now the sense of constant pursuit haunted my every waking thought and many of my worst nightmares.

I hobbled down the alleyway between the bar and the brothel, careful to avoid garbage from an overflowing dumpster, and numerous puddles. Deluge was a wet world, one of the central settled planets, as different from the deserts of outer rim Sardonen as I could find, and I couldn't afford to ruin my good pair of boots. The Guild froze all my professional accounts, but I had private ones under a variety of false names. And I'd converted a great deal to hard currency. However, I'd spent much of my savings repaying the mercenaries for the medical treatment and passage off-world. Owing people favors wasn't my style.

My few attempts to find work had gone less than well. I had no résumé, no references. Legitimate businesses couldn't hire me as security without them. My residual injuries and handicapped vision made me unsuitable for the one profession I knew. Local clubs wouldn't even consider me for a bouncer.

I'd have to settle for something else, and soon. The Eternal Rest biodisintegrator down the street was looking for an assistant to help with the bodies. How ironic would *that* be?

Coming out of the alley, I turned right and entered the bar— Flagon's Flood. The last place I needed to be was here, spending credits on booze, but here I was. The bartender knew me by now and nodded a greeting. I had no desire to exchange pleasantries, but I returned the nod to be civil. There was no use in antagonizing one of the few humans who didn't want me dead.

Though they hadn't found me yet, the entire Guild had orders to kill me on sight—standard punishment for murdering the Guild Leader. Micah committed suicide. Of course, no one knew but me. Hunter to prey. What an insane reversal I'd undergone.

A trio of merchants, identifiable by their coveralls and company logos, occupied my regular booth. I stood over them, glaring and silent, drawing aside my jacket to reveal the straps of my back holster. They shifted to another table. The assassin still rose to the surface when I wanted her to.

I took some comfort in that and slid into the wooden booth in the back corner of the establishment. From there I could watch both the front door and the kitchen exit to the alley. If I couldn't run, I'd damn well better be vigilant.

The barmaid arrived to take my order. Bar*maid* tasted like acid on my tongue, but looking at the girl, I knew nothing else could adequately describe her. I glanced at her nameplate—Kila. Never could keep that straight, even though she waited on me every time I came here. A few months ago, I could have recited the names of several dozen people after a quick glance at their IDs. The Guild trained us to remember monikers and faces. I couldn't keep *much* straight these days.

Young, pert, pretty, and nauseatingly cheerful, Kila never ceased in her efforts to evoke a smile from me. She hadn't succeeded yet. I growled out my usual request, and she tucked the touch pad order screen into the front pocket of her tight-fitting black skirt. Her blouse, no doubt designed by management, strained across her breasts. From the way she always crossed her arms over her chest, I suspected it made her uncomfortable. She hurried away.

This evening, when she returned with the mug of ale brewed in a small distillery right up the street, she took extra care wiping the table, the seat backs, even the bench beside me. "Raining again. Don't need weather reports on Deluge, just a recording of wet, wet, and more wet." Kila laughed at her own flippancy. I took a long, calming sip of my ale. "We're having a special on some of their other varieties," she said, indicating my drink. "Two for one. Interested?"

I growled something noncommittal.

"Well, just let me know, okay? Say, have you seen that new vid, *Poured Passion*? I think Tess is going to run away with Terry."

I thumped my mug on the spotless wood surface, letting the ale slosh onto the table. When she went to clean it again, I grabbed her wrist and held it immobile.

The girl squeaked. Assassins moved fast. Nice to know I retained a few skills. She turned wide green eyes to meet my gaze.

"Go away."

"But—" She indicated the spill with her free hand.

"It's clean enough. Customer's always right. Go away." I reserved that tone for my targets, on the rare occasions I faced them head-on. It didn't faze her. The moment I let her go, she swiped the surface one last time, soaking the ale into the towel she carried. Then she actually winked at me.

Kila smiled, and it was the brightest thing in the room. She tossed her auburn-blond hair over her shoulders and turned away. "Nobody likes a mess!" I heard her say, though she faced the opposite direction. Then she giggled—the girl had a death wish.

She began humming an unfamiliar tune, her steps in time with its melody as she made her way to another table and then to the bar. My mood lightened in spite of myself.

A pang of regret clenched my chest. No matter how I treated her, Kila made overtures of friendship. I neither needed nor wanted friends. Friends were liabilities, innocent pawns for enemies to use against me in a struggle.

At least I tipped well.

I took another sip, letting the beer roll down my throat and warm the pit of my stomach.

With a mind of its own, my hand slipped into the pocket of my black pants and removed the holocube I'd saved from my locker in the Guildhall. I placed it on the table before me, staring at it for a long minute before swiping my thumb over the print reader on its side.

A three-dimensional hologram of a much younger Micah appeared atop the cube. He stood, one fist on his left hip, the other clutching an ancient handbook of Guild law, in full lecture mode, prepared to deliver a lesson on honorable deaths and the avoidance of unnecessary suffering to a team of intermediates, including me.

Oh, the irony.

It was before our brief relationship, but I'd loved him even then, both of us full of righteous conviction everything the Guild did was for the greater good. Micah's faith in Guild law let all the apprentices sleep at night. I'd admired his strict adherence to the code. He wasn't Guild Leader yet, but his mere presence painted the vibrant colors of leadership upon him in broad strokes, making him the perfect instructor. His guidance provided safety and security. The Guild gave us purpose.

Now I saw his conviction for what it was—a blind following of things black and white with no room for the gray, no room for mistakes or deviations from his path.

No room for his own failure.

No room for me.

I swallowed a lump in my throat. Telling myself I didn't care about all I'd lost was one thing. Believing it while living in this hole was another.

Micah never knew I'd captured the holo with a portable cam. When he taught, he focused all his attention on the instruction. We weren't even supposed to own the cubes, but like the slow-acting poisons some members used, we all had our little quirks and secrets. Our tattoos marked *what* we were, but *who* we were was another story. Our physical appearances we played down. We didn't draw unnecessary attention to ourselves. We didn't pose for holos. But during those long missions, on cold, isolated nights, I'd wanted a piece of Micah with me. And I'd always felt a sense of pride in getting away with something he didn't know about.

Once he became Leader, he earned access privileges to all the storage compartments. Common practice didn't include invading each other's privacy, but still, I wondered if he knew and let me keep it anyway. I wanted to believe he had.

The *one* rule he'd allowed me to break without consequences.

I rubbed the smooth surface again with my thumb, and the image disappeared. I returned the cube to the safety of my pocket. The surface of the table looked darker and dingier, and it wasn't due to the absence of the holocube's projector light.

My left leg ached. I propped it on the opposite bench, hiding it beneath the table where no one could note the occasional tremors in the knee joint and detect my weakness. One major drawback of living on a wet world—the humidity affected my injuries. A dull, throbbing pain took up residence in the limb and my right shoulder whenever it rained, and it always rained on Deluge.

As if on cue, a rhythmic pattering sounded on the pub's corrugated metal roof. I sighed, downed my ale in a few gulps, and ordered another with a wave of one hand in the general direction of the bar. At least this time Kila kept her mouth shut when she delivered it. I didn't look at her, fixing my eyes on the new mug with the condensation beading on its sides. The droplets ran like tears.

Patrons came and went—merchants, local work crews, smugglers, slavers. I could always tell the legals from the lawbreakers. Legals sat in the center at the separate round tables that dotted the floor of the pub. They chatted noisily so their conversations carried to other, less-interested listeners. Smugglers and slavers kept to the walls, watched the doors, and spoke in whispers. The slavers paid particular attention to the young men and women who passed. Their lascivious glances raised the hackles at the back of my neck.

I sat in a corner booth, alone, and wondered if the other professionals could tell my occupation as easily by my habits as I identified theirs. Maybe I should start alternating corner booths.

My fingers twitched at the sight of a group of slavers getting drinks at the bar. One cupped Kila's breast as she placed their mugs on the counter. Another grabbed her ass when she turned to go back on the floor. I silently counted to ten and washed down my disgust with ale. As a profession, slavers ranked well below assassins. Among what we called "shadow occupations," assassins topped the hierarchy. On many worlds governments sanctioned the practice of necessary assassinations. They hired us. Most civilized beings found slavery in general a foul, inhumane, and outdated practice. Uncivilized individuals labeled it lucrative in the extreme. On a personal level, I despised them with every cell in my body.

As the largest spaceport town on the planet of Deluge, Six Rivers tended to draw as many unsavory characters as law-abiding ones, which made it easier to lose myself among them and avoid the Guild. When they clashed, almost nightly, the bar could get noisy, but as my tab and intoxication grew, the arguments and broken glassware faded into a hazy oblivion.

Good way to get yourself killed, an internal voice reminded me.

"Do I really care?" I whispered to my empty mug.

My younger self would never have permitted this nonchalance. As a Guild member, I drank little outside of the assassins' stronghold. Alcohol dulled the senses, reduced accuracy and perception.

My younger self needed to shut up.

I could have gotten drunk in the basement studio apartment I now called home. That would have been safer. But without the camaraderie of the Guild, I felt desperate for some kind of human connection, even a distant one.

The pain in my thigh reasserted itself, igniting a fuse cord that burned down to my heel and up to my hip. I sucked air through my teeth, then focused on even breathing until the aftershocks—sequentially decreasing throbs of torture—ebbed. In my jacket pocket, two small bulges pressed against my side, a constant enticement. If I concentrated hard enough, I could discern their shapes in detail, the smooth, rounded glass of the vial with the chipped plastic cover I'd taped to avoid leakage, and the fabric pouch of wrapped, sterile auto-injectors. The weight in that pocket had diminished considerably over the past few weeks.

The next pain wave caught me off guard. It shot like a laser along the nerves in my leg. At the same moment, my shoulder injury joined the attack, sending white-hot agony across my chest. The two met somewhere around my rib cage, and I doubled over the edge of the table with a groan.

This was bad, very bad, the worst I'd had since the damage occurred, and without some relief, I wasn't walking out of here.

"Are you all right?"

My spine snapped straight, causing me more torment, and I took in Kila's concerned expression. Though I hadn't asked for it, she'd come to deliver my bill. Guess she figured I'd had enough. She placed the slip on the table with delicate, uncallused fingers. Her manicured nails clicked against the wood surface. Somewhere, in the liquor-dulled recesses of my mind, a niggling sensation of wrongness gnawed at me. I shoved it back under its alcoholic shroud.

"I'm fine," I managed, convincing no one. Blinking, I cleared the moisture from my vision.

She frowned, lips pressing together, but said nothing more.

I drew a few coins and a couple of wadded bills from my pocket and tossed them next to the check, purposely aiming one to bounce and hit the floor. While she turned away to pick it up, I used the table to brace myself and gained my feet without falling. This favorite table of mine sat next to the unisex lavatory—the perfect escape from her sympathy and sickening pity. I ducked inside and locked the door behind me before she straightened.

Physical pain tasted almost as sweet as grief, and the ephems drank of the dark-haired woman's pain, drawing it in through Kila's pores like water through a strainer. It took effort. Almost more effort than they could manage after so much time spent dormant. For weeks they'd let her search, lying in wait within the girl, leading her to this world of legal edge-walkers.

This woman. This woman might be the one, broken as she was, who could complete their task. She'd come and gone, each time a little darker, the scent of her more desperate as her dependencies grew.

They could use this woman. She was the one.

Auto-lights came on as I entered the restroom, startling the glossy-shelled beetle in the sink and sending it skittering down the drain. Maybe no one liked a mess, as Kila said, but the staff hadn't cleaned the single-person lavatory in some time. My boots stuck to the tile, creating a sound like peeling tape with each step, and a layer of grime painted the toilet bowl a brownish-beige. The odor of bodily fluids thickened the air and turned my stomach, already queasy from not enough food and days of too much alcohol. I convinced myself I didn't need to use the facilities.

Instead, I braced myself in front of the cracked mirror, placing one palm on each side of the ceramic sink and clamping my fingers in place. These days, I tended to avoid my reflection, but I forced my head up to look. I didn't recognize the person in the glass. Her sunken, bloodshot eyes met mine, the shadows around them so dark they looked blackened from a fistfight. Her hair hung around her face in lifeless strings, her complexion resembling that of a corpse.

I knew how I'd come to this state and hated myself for it, but that didn't stop one hand from releasing the sink and snaking into my jacket to withdraw the vial and injectors. Holding the glass container to the overhead light, I measured the remainder with my eyes. Two, maybe three doses left. More would be hard to acquire.

Palotrin was an illegal narcotic. That didn't concern me. In this neighborhood, finding a dealer meant stepping into the nearest dark alley. But the cost… I should tough it out, conserve my resources.

A shiver of pure need and delicious anticipation passed through me, bordering on erotic. I filled the injector.

I hated needles. This device minimized my discomfort, needing only to be held over bare skin to activate. I rolled up my sleeve and for a moment was transfixed by the Guild brand permanently embedded in my wrist. Once tattooed, nothing could remove the mark—crossed blades in a circle with a single thread binding them to each other. I yanked the cuff down and shoved up the other one.

This arm, my right, bore half-healed scars of previous injections. They ran in an uneven line from my wrist to the crook of my elbow. Biting my lip, I picked an unblemished spot and held the injector over it, not quite in contact. The needle shot from the device, pierced my flesh, drove the palotrin into my bloodstream, and retracted, all in a blur too fast for the eye to follow. I dropped the used injector into the waste disposal unit and listened to its grinding whir while I waited for the drug to take effect.

Experience told me that wouldn't take long. The chemical traveled through my system, leaving iciness in its wake. I had about twenty minutes before I needed to be prone. After that, my muscles would go numb and I'd lose myself to the drug's oblivion. Palotrin eased pain in even the worst sufferers, and that easing lasted a full standard day, but it also caused hallucinations and physical impairment, especially when mixed with alcohol.

None of this presented an immediate problem. I lived a block away, a five-minute walk even with my limp. Normally I'd never take even this risk, but with the pain coming harder and more frequently than usual tonight, I doubted I would have gotten home *without* using the drug.

I took a tentative step toward the exit, noting with satisfaction I could put weight on the leg without any pain.

Something heavy slammed into the door from the opposite side, shaking the handle and the frame. A muffled grunt carried from the bar. I gradually became aware of distant shouting and breakage. Someone screamed; I thought it might be Kila. Then I heard the whine of a fired ripper and ducked to the side as the blast blew the old-fashioned wooden door inward, showering me with splinters. Rippers were brutal weapons, banned by the Guild and favored by those with fewer concerns about clean kills and causing pain.

I leaned to peer through the new gap and went cold as I spotted one of the slavers attempting to drag Kila through the alley exit. He wasn't having much success. The barmaid kicked and scratched like a wild feline. Her long nails dug into the man's stubble-covered face, leaving a blood trail along his cheek. I smiled at his shout of pain. My grin faded when the slaver clubbed her in the side of the head with the butt of his gun. She slumped over his arm. Elsewhere in the main room, merchants slugged it out with the slaver's friends. Kila was popular with the locals, and the attack started a minor riot in the Flagon's Flood.

The last thing I needed right now was to involve myself in a bar fight. Micah always warned me my soft spot for the innocent and helpless would get me killed. *Stay within the parameters of the contract. You can't save everyone.* Tonight might prove him correct. I didn't have much time before numbness set in. I could almost feel it as the drug slowed my circulation and deadened nerve endings.

I reached beneath my jacket and drew the pistol from my back holster. One quick check of the indicator noted the firearm as fully charged. Taking a deep breath, I stepped through the jagged opening in the door and joined the fray.

CHAPTER 3

THE FIRST drunken idiot to spot me ignored my weapon and attempted a headfirst charge. A sidestep sent him plowing through the remains of the bathroom door. I risked a glance over my shoulder to see him sprawled on the tile floor, passed out.

One good thing about a bar fight—alcohol leveled the playing field somewhat. But even drunk I could shoot better than most, and my hand-to-hand combat skills remained superior. Of course, having more feeling in my hands would have helped.

I managed to fire my pistol once, taking down a slaver holding a wooden chair over his head ready to smash on a cowering local businessman. The shot caught him in the chest, throwing him backward against the bar. The chair dropped from his hands and clattered to the floor. He fell, legs twitching. Down and permanently out.

I felt no remorse over the slaver's death. The Guild trained its apprentices in detachment, one of the first lessons learned. The twinge of pleasure and satisfaction, however, surprised me. Usually I experienced no emotion at all. One more psychological rip to sew up later. I shook it off.

The slaver had Kila halfway through the alley door. She'd regained consciousness but appeared dazed, making only halfhearted attempts to get away. I turned in their direction, ducking when a bottle flew over my head and shattered against the wall. Bits of broken glass showered me, catching in my hair, and fragments clung to my clothing. The movement was pure instinct. My peripheral vision sucked in low-lit bars.

An explosion took a chunk out of the ceiling, dropping hot metal and plaster on the combatants while rain poured through the new hole. None of the other fighters paused or even noticed. I followed the source to the bar, where the bartender held a blast rifle and shook his head in disgust. We made eye contact, and I shrugged. Blast rifles caused more damage than they were worth. The weapon fired a pulse of energy that would leave a gaping hole in a wall or a body.

The alley door swinging closed got my attention again, and I saw Kila and her attacker had vanished. I took a step to follow, but something dropped at my feet. Glancing down, I discovered my own pistol on the floor, and I stared at my empty hand.

Attempts to tighten my right fist failed. The drug was taking hold, affecting my extremities first. I could close the fingers of my left around the weapon's grip just long enough to return it to my back holster, but I felt like a fumbling toddler with undeveloped motor control.

Well, there was more than one way to win a fight.

Using my hip, I shoved through the door and stepped into the alley and the pouring rain.

The area around the exit smelled of vomit, though the rain had washed visible evidence away. The water soaked through my trousers. My jacket's material would resist the moisture a little longer. I used a sleeve to swipe strands of wet hair from my face and eyes. My vision was bad enough. I didn't need additional impairments.

Exterior lights illuminated the alley in splotches. The slaver had reached the far end with Kila. Her assaulter held her immobile while he leaned into the busier cross street, probably to check for bystanding do-gooders.

"Let her go!" I shouted over the storm. I stood between two of the circles of lamplight and extended an arm outward as if holding a weapon. Discerning otherwise should have proved impossible in the dark.

Thunder rumbled in the distance. A flash of lightning bathed the entire alley in its yellow glare, revealing my empty hand and my ridiculous pose.

I lowered my arm and rolled my eyes to the traitorous heavens. The slaver laughed, a grating sound that carried on the rising wind. Instead of escaping with his prize, he dragged her toward me, smirking and chuckling. The rain pasted Kila's blouse to her skin, and she shivered, though whether that was cold, fear, or both, I couldn't tell.

"You have to be the worst merc in the history of the profession," he said when he got close enough not to bellow. Unsure of my ability to walk, I let him continue his approach. One meaty arm wrapped around Kila's chest over her breasts; the opposite hand clutched another bullet-thrower. He couldn't seem to decide where to point it, at my head or my torso, and I realized he'd imbibed as much, if not more, than I had, not that it gave me any advantage with my other problems.

"I'm not a merc," I snarled. Mercs didn't have my training or discipline—well, former discipline—no matter what they believed. The alleyway swayed, or maybe that was me, and I shuffled my feet farther apart for balance. My left boot kicked something that clanged, a piece of discarded metal piping.

Kila watched with wide, frightened eyes. In the downpour I couldn't discern tears from raindrops, but I suspected she was crying.

Whatever happened tonight, I was not letting him take her.

"What are you, then? Boozer? Addict? Idiot?" He took another step, then another. He wanted to be sure of his aim. With his slurred speech and the way he rocked when standing still, I couldn't blame him.

When we stood a mere two meters apart, I went into motion. The toe of my boot slid under the pipe, then kicked it up and out. I had no delusions of actually hitting my target, and I didn't want to hurt Kila, but I got close enough. Besides, even if the bar did hit her, it wouldn't do any permanent damage. The metal rod passed to the side of the slaver's head within centimeters, near enough to distract him and force a dodge.

At that moment, I threw myself forward, slamming into both of them with my shoulder. All three of us hit the pavement hard and separated. I heard metal skittering on concrete, and my eyes frantically sought the source.

"Get the gun!" I shouted. My roll sent me careening into a damaged auto-recycling bin. The lid popped, and overflowing garbage buried me. I shoved away soiled papers, half-eaten food, and empty containers with my shoulders and knees. My arms had gone numb from the elbows down. My feet tingled. Toes didn't exist. Rolling, then rocking back and forth for momentum, I managed to end up on my rear.

Kila stood over the slaver, holding his gun to his head. Dramatic but acceptable. He glared at me. I didn't like what needed to happen next, but I could think of no alternative. I couldn't think of much at the moment. Dark, shadowy things crawled at the edges of my vision. For now, I recognized them as the drug-induced hallucinations they were. I ignored them since they weren't real to me. At least not yet.

"Club him or kill him," I said, my voice soft. Training apprentices didn't bother me. They volunteered to learn the assassin trade. This girl embodied innocence. No one should force another to do violence, but I had no choice.

Kila's ragged breath caught at my command. The hand that held the weapon trembled. She backed away from the slaver, never diverting her aim, and she didn't look at me, but she ended up by my side. "I can't," she whispered.

The slaver watched us, eyes darting from my face to hers. If he saw an opportunity to attack or escape, he'd take it. The rain continued to pour from above. I should have felt cold, but I felt little. "Neither can I." My chest tightened. Confessing to weakness chiseled one's headstone. I glanced at the slim figure beside me and sighed. At this point I had no choice but to trust her. I wasn't getting home under my own power. "Palotrin."

Her shoulders stiffened, but she didn't turn from the slaver. Working in the bar, she would have seen plenty of addicts, even though she'd begun her employment there only shortly after my own arrival on Deluge. And she'd certainly seen me stagger out once or twice, or, well, more.

"Sooner or later, his friends in the bar are going to show up."

Kila gave me one last hopeless glance, which I faced head-on. Limbs jerking mechanically, she moved to the man's side, then behind him. He closed his eyes. She closed hers and swung the butt of the gun at his head. It made an audible crack when it impacted with his skull. He toppled, and I cringed. The kid had no idea how to gauge a knockout blow. That strike fractured the slaver's cranium. I knew by the sound. If he didn't die from the injury, he'd certainly have brain damage. I peered into the shadows, trying to detect the rise and fall of his chest, and saw no motion.

If grief and pain were sweet like dessert, then death was the main course.

Unable to resist, the ephems surged from Kila's body, flowing out her nostrils in a puff of chilled breath, then clinging low to the asphalt to resemble rain-induced mist.

A touch of life force hung about the slaver, too weak to offer any resistance to the invading entities. They surged into his gaping mouth, the tongue lolling to one side, drops of bloody drool coming from one corner to spatter the pavement and wash away in the downpour. No breath to aid the ephems here. They traveled down his throat under their own power.

Deep in his chest, the man's heart gave a few final beats. Resuscitation might even have been successful, if done immediately. Sirens approached. There was a chance.

The ephems wrapped around the crucial muscle and squeezed—squeezed until it burst and the blood flow from the slaver's mouth turned from droplets to a small stream. Then they soaked up the energy, the essence, dividing it between them and restoring depleted reserves.

Exiting the way they'd come, they returned to Kila on the girl's next shuddering gasp.

She'd done it. She'd taken life, albeit unintentionally. Accident or not, once meant she could do it again. Perhaps they had been too hasty in seeking another killer.

But the killer had been found. The assassin. The Guild member. The perfect choice to carry out their master's orders. A bit damaged but still useful. And dependent on Kila, on them.

Dependency built companionship. Companionship built trust. Trust built compliance.

And it never hurt to have an additional weapon on hand.

Kila stared at the body. The gun dropped from her fingers. Our first break of good fortune kept it from misfiring. In the dim light, I watched the blood drain from her complexion. She trembled from head to foot, and I feared she might pass out. "Come here!" I ordered, using the voice I reserved for unruly apprentices.

Her muscles jerked in response.

"Now!"

When she crouched beside me again, I issued orders in rapid-fire succession, giving her no time for further contemplation. "Get me on my feet. Get us out of here. My apartment is—" A wave of dizziness assaulted me, and I sagged against her. Physical contact with any relative stranger set off screaming sirens in my head and made my skin crawl. But I hadn't the strength to pull away.

In the distance, alarms sounded and came closer with each passing second—local authorities responding to the bar brawl at last. Kila threw one of my arms across her shoulders and hauled me upright. She possessed more strength than I would have expected from her delicate frame.

If I stared at my boots and willed them to take steps, I could manage it, but every third one resulted in a stumble. We weaved down the alley, and I nudged her toward home.

"Thanks for saving me," she said just loudly enough to be heard over the storm. When I looked into her eyes, I saw a mixture of hero worship and something else I couldn't quite place.

My shrugging off her gratitude caused us to career into a wall. "You saved me as much as I saved you," I admitted, pushing off the brick surface to lean on her again. But it felt good to be helping someone. I'd missed that aspect of Guild membership the most.

All the way home, the dark things followed us. They crept from shadows and peered around corners. They hid behind the sheets of rain. A bolder one touched my shoe, and I kicked at it, almost sending both of us tumbling to the street. Kila followed the motion and frowned up at me, her face glistening with rain and tears. "There's nothing there," she whispered.

The hallucinations had worsened. Soon I'd need to switch to some other drug. I tried to shake my head to clear it, but it ended up more like a loll. "Yeah, I know."

By now the wet chill seeped through all our clothing to the skin, and we shivered together. She held me as tightly as she could against her side, and I didn't argue. Our minimal shared body warmth kept me going. The quiet of the late night calmed me. Nocturnal and solitary by nature, I thrived in the dark, though I preferred to explore it alone. At this hour, with the city almost silent around us, I came to life. At least I used to.

We reached the front steps of the building I lived in. Run-down and made of crumbling stone shored up with more modern materials, it wouldn't win any city beautification awards. I'd never been so glad to see a place in my life.

Kila hesitated. She shifted my weight, preparing to attempt the stairs, but I held my position. "Around the corner," I directed her. My words slurred, and I could barely get my lips and tongue to form them.

Maybe she thought I was having a different hallucination. She checked my eyes for confirmation before helping me into another alleyway that ran between my building and the warehouse next door. A stairway led down to my basement apartment. The entrance to my studio beckoned, but there, I froze.

Whether I was an assassin any longer or not, old habits died hard. I'd taken different routes home from the Flagon's Flood each time I'd gone there, and I had two other bars I frequented randomly to mix up my routine. Now, for the first time in my life, I'd escorted a stranger to my door. Well, she'd escorted me. We stumbled more than walked down the short flight of stairs.

"Keycard. Right side."

Kila propped me against the metal railing, which sapped the last of the warmth from my body. Her fingers slipped inside my jacket pocket and hesitated. She'd found my retractable blade.

"Don't touch the slider on the handle." If she did, she'd cut herself, or worse, stab me. I had enough problems.

The reddish-blond head nodded. She retrieved the card and slipped it into the door slot. Three audible clicks sounded as electronic and mechanical locks disengaged. The landlord provided one. I installed the other two and linked all three to the card. I liked to think of it as *home improvement*.

"Lights!" I called, my voice hoarse. The interior illuminated in harsh white light from two tacky, cracked overhead fixtures. The glare hurt my eyes, but I could do nothing to shield them. Kila hauled me into the space and eased me onto my double bed against the right-hand wall. It folded up into a recess in that same wall, but I never bothered. I didn't get visitors.

Why I cared, I didn't know, but a part of me felt relief that I kept the place clean. The paint peeled from all surfaces and the furniture was secondhand, but I'd dusted the solitary table and chair, emptied trash bins, and cleared my minimal wardrobe from the couch with the stuffing sticking out between the seams. I'd stacked the dishes and cookware in the washer this morning. The Guild had expected neatness.

Kila stood in the center of the single room, watching me.

I blinked. "Is that blood?"

She glanced down at her white shirt, where a red stain marked the fabric. Kila took a quick and comical look into her blouse, which almost earned that smile she'd been after. "Not mine," she confirmed, then came to sit beside me. "Your arm."

Indeed, blood soaked through the black material of my jacket. Between the rain and the dark color, I hadn't noticed, and the palotrin dulled the pain. A jagged tear in my left sleeve indicated the point of entry, and when Kila rolled it up, she revealed an equally ragged slice in my forearm. She winced at the awful sight.

Some of the Guild members used large concentrated doses of palotrin on their weapons. The drug numbed the skin on contact. By the time a target noticed the wound, he'd already lost a fatal amount of blood. Judging from the width of the stains, I wasn't quite that far gone yet, but there was more on my shirt and hers than I would have preferred.

"Must've gotten the gash when I hit the recycler," I slurred, then repeated it when she cocked her head in confusion. My tongue felt swollen—probably was. I let myself fall against the pillows. "Med-kit's in the bathroom." My eyes closed of their own volition. I hoped she didn't fear blood as much as she did violence.

Her footsteps crossed the room. A door slid open and shut. I dozed, and the dark things came for me. They swarmed behind my eyelids, crawled across my chest. They slithered over my arm, peeling my wet jacket and shirt off my shivering form. I jerked and twisted but could not escape.

A weight settled on my chest. Weakness prevented further struggle. Gentle fingers brushed damp hair from my forehead. "It's just me. Take it easy."

Kila. I exhaled and cracked open an eye. She had her arm across my rib cage, holding me down. Once she saw I recognized her, she lifted herself and set to work on the cut.

The med-kit rested on the blanket beside me. She'd hung my jacket, shirt, and back holster over the single chair. With the exception of my athletic bra, I was naked to the waist.

Apprentices to the Guild discarded modesty shortly after their arrival in the hall. Once in a while, a master would catch a first-year sneaking into the tunnels for privacy to change into training robes. Second-years would drag the unfortunate young person out in his or her state of undress to finish the operation standing upon the altar.

Nudity, at least mine, bothered Kila, though. The poor girl flushed a deep shade of pink. She fixed her eyes on the injury and the kit while humming that little tune of hers. My muscles relaxed. One by one, with meticulous care, she removed the items she'd need: sterile gauze, antiseptic, and sealant gel. I had to tell her nothing. She knew. Again, I felt that nagging sense of wrongness in her actions, but since my life depended on her aid, I said nothing.

Kila wiped away the excess blood, then cleaned the wound with antibiotic spray. That should have stung like a thousand insects, but the palotrin continued to deaden all pain. She picked up the gel to close the gash and lifted my arm by the wrist, turning it for a better angle.

Kila froze.

Her eyes darted to my face, then back to my wrist. She'd discovered my Guild tattoo.

CHAPTER 4

THE ROOM spun. I couldn't fight unconsciousness much longer. Kila disliked violence—that much I knew from her encounter with the slaver. Did that abhorrence extend to me now? Would she commit an aggressive act to eliminate someone more violent than herself? This line of thought was overly paranoid. I knew but couldn't stop it. The palotrin stole my rationality. Maybe she'd leave me here, helpless, blood soaking into my sheets until my body was drained dry. When I joined the Guild, I vowed never to allow myself to be this vulnerable. Never again.

So much for youthful vows.

I watched, bleary-eyed, as she traced the indelible mark with one finger. I felt nothing, but she followed the entire pattern, from the crossed blades to the binding tie to the encompassing circle.

A tremor rocked me. The areas of skin I could still detect prickled from the room's chill. My landlord did not believe in the luxury of heat.

My movement shook Kila from her contemplation. She grabbed the sealant gel and squirted it into the wound, which closed in its wake. The chemicals in the gooey clear substance matched my skin composition, forming a layer over the injury. She unfolded the comforter lying at the foot of the bed and wrapped me in its soft warmth.

Cocooned and exhausted, I fell into a narcotic-induced sleep filled with nightmares of childhood memories.

Sleep always improved control. The mind at rest made manipulation simpler. No active thoughts to interfere with the ephemerals' goals.

While Kila dozed in a chair, the pair of ephems separated, one remaining wrapped around her brain tissue, the other seeping out through her open mouth on a soft snore.

The aura around the assassin woman hung dark and heavy, a black cloak with scattered shafts of silver piercing its thickness, holding her conscience and moral sanity together by threads thinner than she likely realized. The former Guild member walked a fine line between good and evil, skirting an edge into an inescapable abyss, sometimes dangling a toe over and dipping it in to test the brackish waters.

Entering the assassin's body caused the ephem no trouble or resistance. Injury and exhaustion, combined with the mind-numbing drugs, had taken their toll. It slipped in through an ear, unrepelled by the woman's weakened life force.

The entity tapped her consciousness to reveal her thoughts. She considered herself "even" with Kila. They saved each other and owed each other nothing. While the assassin had developed a faint liking for the girl and even a grudging respect, she saw no need for the complications of friendships in her life. The ephem sensed her intention to cut Kila loose at the soonest opportunity that wouldn't endanger the girl. Not acceptable.

Dark magic and the realm of nightmares coexisted in close proximity. Casting a tendril deep into the assassin's brain, the ephem sought the perfect memory to accentuate, to bring to the forefront of the dream state and remind her what life had been like once before on her own, and how much she needed the company of others.

I was dreaming. I knew it. And nothing I could do would stop the old nightmare's progress.

The storeroom smelled of urine, feces, and rotten food. If the slavers came in now, they'd find me for certain. I tried to tally the number of days I'd been in hiding, anything to distract me from rising panic, but I'd lost count.

Cor, you've initiated the stupidest escape plan ever.

Not that my previous attempts had been works of genius. Since taking me from a group home three months prior, the slavers foiled two other tries—the first a failed play on a young slaver's sympathy, and the second swapping places with another girl who'd rather be held than sold. She'd thought fondling from an eighty-year-old was a fate worse than death. I figured at that age he couldn't do much more than fondle, and it would be easier to get away from him. I didn't know he'd insisted on a blond.

Despite my previous belief, teenagers didn't know everything.

This time I tried hiding.

The captives worked the storage areas, all six of them, on a regular basis. We stacked boxes and crates, fed livestock kept in interior pens,

cleaned tanks of fresh seafood, and moved goods to the central kitchen—
any menial tasks the slavers wouldn't lower themselves to do.

I prepared my bolt-hole with meticulous care. I found a cache of
twelve large containers of porridge mix collecting dust at the rear of
storeroom six. To the best of my knowledge, none of the slavers ate
the foul-tasting crap, nor fed the fattening breakfast food to the girls. I
assumed it had been ordered by mistake. No one ever went near it.

Shifting them into a different configuration, I managed to circle the
boxes around an empty space, then used four to make a sort of bridge
over the top. If I stayed in the center, it would hide me from view on all
sides, or so I hoped.

A substantial portion of the large storage space contained pens of
soon-to-be-slaughtered animals including hoofers from Chalice, furrials
from Deluge, and a coop of flyziers whose squawks sounded like nails
scraping slate, drowning out any noise I might make. They would fool
heat sensors if the slavers looked for me here, and their smell might mask
my own. I empathized with the animals' captivity and wished I could do
something to free them.

I couldn't even free myself.

I stocked my hiding place with packaged self-heating meals I'd
filched and an empty plastic container for relieving myself. Then one
evening, I "disappeared." Pulse racing, I pulled the last box into place to
conceal my entry and effectively vanished.

They searched. At one point, Reva, the slaver leader, came prowling
through storeroom six, calling my name in a singsong sarcastic tone.
"Corianne… if you come out I might not kill you…. Corianne…."

I didn't fear death. Besides, he couldn't sell a corpse. But what he
might do to me as punishment scared me shitless. I stayed put and kept
quiet. Eventually I figured they'd all give up, let their guard down.

Days passed. Other slave girls came and went. I suspected some
figured out I was there, and I spent sleepless nights staring through the
cracks, waiting to be hauled out, but no one sounded the alarm. They
owed nothing to the slavers. They held pointed conversations about my
supposed whereabouts just outside my self-made prison. They discussed
the girls who'd been questioned. The search continued outside but
remained confined to the grounds. The slavers didn't think I'd escaped
the compound.

At one point I became so desperately lonely I almost revealed myself to them, but I bit my lip until it bled. For now they could honestly say they knew nothing. If I involved them, I gave the slavers something to dig out during interrogation. At night, to ease the depression, I'd crawl out and play with some of the animals. I became rather close to the hoofers and furrials. The flyziers had sharp beaks and a tendency to bite, so I avoided them.

After almost two standard weeks, I could bear it no longer. I vowed to surrender myself the next time someone entered the room.

I didn't count on it being Reva.

He stepped into the storage area. I watched him through the cracks between containers, heart in my throat and threatening to choke me. After some shuffling by the entrance, he found the shaker of spice he wanted. Then he paused.

"Corianne!" His false cheer fooled no one. He eased a knife from his belt. "You've been a bad girl, Corianne, far more trouble than a skinny thing like you is worth. Offer's changed, Corianne. I will kill you when I find you. The longer it takes, the slower I'll be."

He was fishing for a response, didn't really know I was there, but that knowledge didn't ease my nerves. Cringing, I pressed myself into the farthest corner of my makeshift refuge, but it wouldn't help if he found me. Sweat beaded on my forehead and dripped into my eyes, stinging painfully, but I didn't dare move to wipe it away.

I heard his approach, boots crunching on spilled animal feed. When he reached my crates, he stopped and sniffed, then sniffed again. I'd been dumping my urine and excrement with the animals' each night, but I'd still accumulated some that day, and my body odor was unmistakable. A moment later, he kicked aside the boxes I'd so carefully stacked. They tumbled around and on top of me, bruising my arms and legs with their corners. He upended my waste, spilling the contents in a puddle that soaked into my shapeless tunic and pants. The stench suffused the entire room. I tried to scramble away but was blocked at every angle.

When Reva grabbed my hair, I screamed, then screamed louder as his head exploded, spattering my soiled clothing with blood and brain matter. The hand gripping me tightened in a death spasm, then released, and we fell together to the concrete floor. Animals screeched, hooted, and growled in panic, throwing themselves against fencing to escape the newcomers.

A set of polished black boots stood before my eyes, where my face pressed the cold surface. Knees replaced them when the owner crouched, his gun in a gloved hand. I looked into the man's eyes, gentle in a face hardened by harsh experience. "I won't hurt you. You're free to go," he said—Micah's first words to me, perhaps the most beautiful words I'd ever heard.

The sounds of laser and ripper fire echoed throughout the slaver compound. I raised myself to sit without aid and turned to the entrance. Two teenagers, maybe three or four years older than I, skidded into the room and froze, sniffing and gagging.

"Whew! Did he void his bowels after you shot him? I hate that. It's worse than all the beasts." The male covered his mouth and nose with a free hand. His other held a pistol, barrel glowing from recent firing.

The girl punched him in the arm. "You are *such* a first-year. That's waste from… ew." I guess she spotted me. Despite my shock and terror, I flushed with embarrassment.

Micah pulled me to a standing position, and I struggled to remain on my feet. My food supplies had run low, and I'd weakened from rationing what remained. He holstered his weapon and spread his hands apologetically, shooting a glare over his shoulder at the teens. "We don't usually bring *apprentices* on assignments," he said, spitting their designation like a curse, "but our employer wanted all the slavers dead, and we needed the manpower. Besides, it's good field training." He indicated I should precede him to the door. A sharp gesture with his right fist sent the two teenagers scrambling to take point.

Impressive obedience. Judging from the way the man carried himself, I didn't doubt the reason for it.

I had an overwhelming desire to stay on this man's good side, to impress him.

"I'll see that you get home to your parents."

Apprentices, deaths, field training. It didn't take me long to put it all together with stories I'd heard. And if I was wrong, it didn't matter. From the moment I saw him, I was determined he wouldn't leave me behind, anywhere.

I turned back to him, jaw set and eyes focused on his. In my filth, I must have looked ridiculous, but his lips didn't so much as twitch. "My parents are dead. The slavers took me from a group home on Chalice." I put my hands on my hips, wincing as they squished in the wet fabric of my pants. "My name is Cor Sandros. I submit myself to you for apprenticeship." The formal statement sealed our first contract.

The ephem released Cor's mind. The moment it did so, powerful invisible walls rose to crush it against the interior of the assassin's skull. The woman clawed her way toward consciousness, fighting the drugs, exhaustion, and injuries, intent on regaining control.

Despite the darkness of her soul, which should have made influence easier, her sheer will dwarfed any the ephem previously encountered. She would not allow herself to be controlled, would not be manipulated except under the most extreme mental and emotional duress. If she took the path of evil, it would be her own choice, not that of an outsider.

Cor's will pressed and pressed, flattening the entity to an almost impossible thinness. The ephem began to separate, lose cohesion. If that occurred, it would cease to exist.

Desperate to escape, it slithered and slid, seeping and seeking an outlet, searching out the ear canal through which it entered the assassin's body. It wrenched itself free in one final tearing motion, leaving behind a tendril—which withered and dissipated to nothingness.

With great haste, it darted inside Kila's dozing body, twirling itself in thick cords around its fellow and vibrating like a plucked string.

I awoke, warm, drowsy, and disoriented. Judging from the slant of light coming through the two slit windows near the ceiling, the sun had almost reached its zenith. The beams cast odd shadows about the single room. I followed their path to a figure kneeling on the stained beige carpeting.

My first reaction tightened the muscles I could feel, which weren't damn many of them. The palotrin wouldn't wear off until a complete twenty-four hours passed from the time of injection. That meant well after sunset. Whoever the intruder was, I was at her mercy.

The events of the previous night rushed through my muddled brain, and I relaxed against the pillow. A return to sleep beckoned, but the sight of Kila held me transfixed. Even as I watched, the shifting sunlight caught in her hair and lit the blond strands, making them glow. She must have used my shower to clean herself up. Her thick mane flowed down her back, almost to her waist, in rivulets of red and gold.

A faint buzzing sound carried from her small figure, and I identified it as humming, though this time I couldn't detect a tune. In her hands she held a book, an honest-to-goodness book with real paper and a tattered animal-hide cover. The pages had yellowed, and I could make out some torn corners. The artifact had to be hundreds if not thousands of years old, no doubt preserved with modern chemicals to survive this long. It would bring a small fortune in the antiquities trade. No one read paper books anymore. Comps stored all written material. I wondered what a barmaid wanted with such a thing and how she could possibly have afforded it.

That prompted another question. Where the hell had she gotten it? She didn't have it with her when we left the Flagon's Flood. A sense of foreboding settled in the pit of my stomach. I knew the answer, but I had to ask anyway.

"You went back to the bar, didn't you?"

She glanced in my direction. The humming ceased. "To get my belongings." Kila pointed to a carryall shoulder bag on my kitchen table. "I lived there, in the storeroom. Under the circumstances, I felt I should resign." She wrapped her arms around the book, clutching it to her chest. When she spoke again, I could barely hear her whispered words. "Did I kill that man who tried to take me?"

I closed my eyes. The image of the unmoving figure lying facedown in the alley rose behind my eyelids. *Yes*, I thought. "No," I said.

Kila's shoulders slumped with relief. She exhaled, then drew a long, slow breath. "The body was gone. I didn't know…."

The slaver's friends would have disposed of him, or the authorities might have gotten to it first. The odds of her finding out the truth were slim. I didn't own a vid-viewer, so even if the local news cared about a dead slaver, she wouldn't hear about it in my apartment. And besides, I had bigger things to worry about.

I tried to raise myself on my elbows but fell back, exhausted. Undisturbed, I would have slept a full standard day on the palotrin. I required more rest, but the need for self-preservation sent my adrenaline levels soaring. "Did anyone see you? Were you followed?"

She blinked green eyes at me. "I don't think so. I took a different road coming back."

Regardless, this naive girl wouldn't detect a tail if it attached itself to her backside. I groaned. "When I can move again, we'll have to leave— get off-world." We? I'm not sure what formed that thought, but I'd voiced it aloud. I'd already saved her life, and she'd saved mine. Guild law stated saving an assassin's life incurred a life debt. I'd be bound to protect her until death, hers or mine. But I was no longer Guild. We owed each other nothing. We should go our separate ways. And yet, having had time to consider, I continued to speak. "I have some savings, enough for passage elsewhere." No matter how bad things got, I always kept enough funds in my account for a shuttle ticket. If I sold everything except clothing and weapons, I could afford two. Nothing would convince me to leave the girl at the mercy of the slavers' friends.

Kila rose, carried the book to her bag, and slipped it inside the crude sacking material. She placed her hands atop the satchel's exterior and closed her eyes for a long moment. Then she crossed to stand beside me. I thought I detected tears at the tips of her lashes, but she blinked them away before I could be certain.

She smelled like my cheap shampoo, and though she'd tried to wash it, her damp shirt bore the pinkish tinge of my blood. "I can pay my own passage."

I smiled. "Not on a bar waitress salary."

"I have money."

More alarm bells went off. The previous night I'd been drunk and drugged. Today I was still drugged, but without the alcohol, I could think more clearly, and I put together the things that bothered me about Kila. No calluses marked her perfect hands. She knew more than basic first aid. She carried this expensive artifact. She had credits to spend.

Kila might not pose a threat, but she was not what she appeared to be.

She pulled the covers from me and examined the wound on my arm. It showed no signs of infection. She'd done a good job, a better job than a barmaid should have.

My eyelids grew heavier. The room became dim, and I blinked to clear my vision. "You've had medical training."

"You could say that." She wrapped the blankets around me and tucked them in like a mother for her child. Something about her made me feel warm and safe. I fought to shake it off.

"What *else* could I say? Who are you?" I demanded.

She smiled cryptically. "I'm the least important member of my family. Not like you."

I scowled at her. "What the hell is that supposed to mean?" My voice rose and fell in my ears, echoing in a disconcerting manner.

She turned away from me, instead facing my table, the bag, the book. "You are Corianne Sandros, the Core of Sardonen. And I want to hire you to kill my brother."

I tried to ask how she knew me, what she wanted, why she'd want her brother dead, but it all slipped away when she began that infernal humming. The haunting melody wove a tapestry of sound that weighed upon my eyes until I had no choice but to close them. It followed me into sleep, carrying me farther and farther from her slim figure, and yet, she remained beside me. I felt her presence like a tangible thing, soothing and easing my fears, and against my will, I let go.

CHAPTER 5

KILA THE barmaid turned out to be Mistress Kila T'ral of Lissex. That much I gathered from her in a public aircar on the way to the port, which added a lot more sense to the slavers' actions. A prize like that would bring a healthy price, or an exorbitant ransom. She'd gone to work in the Flagon's Flood based on its reputation for attracting customers in the shadow professions, customers like me.

As for identifying me, she found my name on my universal ID when she went through my jacket. My tattoo told her my profession. How she'd gotten my nickname, I had no idea.

She knew a lot more about me than I did about her. I didn't care for that at all.

I'd awakened well after sunset, my limbs having returned to somewhat normal function while I slept. It took me minutes to pack my few possessions. Using her credit chit and my comm, Kila secured passage for us on an outbound shuttle—passage to her home world. Destination didn't matter to me. Someone else choosing would make the Guild less likely to find me. And if I didn't take Kila's contract, I had my emergency savings to book a shuttle elsewhere.

The buildings of Deluge flashed past the aircar's windows, distorted by rainwater on the glass. I stared at the blocky gray blurs, not really seeing them, instead contemplating my new circumstances. Fate knew I needed a job, but I'd require a good deal more information before accepting Kila's offer.

I pieced together the parts I already had. I knew Lissex. I'd traveled there on assignment for the Guild several years before. A woman in one of the ruling families, not the T'rals, wanted a kidnapper killed. The man stole her three-month-old baby from his nursery, asked for ransom, collected the money, and then killed the child. He'd done it before, to other families on other worlds. I didn't lose any sleep over that job.

That likely explained how Kila had come to know of me. Jobs like that built one's reputation. Potential clients identified the Core of Sardonen as the assassin for the sensitive contracts, the emotional ones. I didn't kill monarchs; I killed molesters. The Guild sent me in to eliminate baby-dealers and school bombers. I came to think of myself as an avenger for the young and innocent.

It made Micah's mistake all the more painful.

I cleared my thoughts with a breath and focused on my current tentative contract.

Settlements on Lissex consisted of strings of islands. A different family owned each string, and the various clusters specialized in certain trade goods. Larger islands practiced farming and raised livestock. Smaller ones focused on fishing or craftwork. All very symbiotic, despite the isolation. Getting to the kidnapper had proven quite the challenge. A fortress surrounded by water was a fortress indeed.

I glanced at Kila beside me on the plastic-covered seat. She stared straight ahead, focusing on nothing, but when she felt my eyes on her, she gave me a gentle smile.

The corner of my mouth twitched, but I repressed the urge to return it. She'd had ulterior motives from the start. She must have suspected *what* I was, even if she hadn't known *who*. All her overtures of friendship had been ploys to earn my trust, to encourage me to take her contract on her brother. I had a thousand questions, but one didn't discuss my type of business in a public car. My inquiries would have to wait.

She watched my eyes, and I wondered what she saw there because her smile turned sad, and she looked away.

We arrived at the shuttle port, and I paid the driver. Together, we ducked inside the flat-roofed single-story terminal, each clutching a bag of belongings. The rain drenched us both before we could get under cover.

Even at this hour, passengers milled about the terminal. Others sprawled asleep on the hard metal seats, and some vagrants cowered in the doorways to avoid the downpour. Announcements of arrivals and departures blared from overhead speakers and flashed on vid-screens hanging from the ceiling. As one of the central worlds, Deluge received ships well into the night.

I paused and scanned a screen, then set off, limping, for the access gate. Of course it had to be the farthest one. My leg ached, and until I settled myself in a new, safe location, I couldn't take palotrin or any other mind-altering drug. As it was, as soon as the buildup of the addictive chemicals began to wear off, I would suffer the withdrawal. Regular painkillers had proven useless against the poison's effects, like drinking water when you needed caffeine.

If I hadn't intervened on Kila's behalf, I'd have my home, such as it was, and at least the illusion of security.

And no income. And a growing addiction. And self-imposed isolation.

I heard my boots thumping in their uneven rhythm across the linoleum floor, and I pulled up short. I had no right to my anger. The last standard day provided more activity and diversion than I'd seen in three months. I couldn't foresee the future, and I couldn't hate Kila for that.

On cue, she plowed into me from behind, then froze like cornered prey when I whirled on her. I stared at her terrified expression for a long moment before breaking into genuine laughter.

"Come on. We'll miss our launch."

Eyeing me as a psychiatrist would a patient, she followed.

Security gave us no problems. My satchel had signal scramblers built into its lining, making it seem harmless even though it brimmed with weapons and equipment befitting my profession.

A shuttle carried us to the orbital station. During the layover, I had a light meal and snoozed while Kila shopped. She returned with four overstuffed bags of who knew what.

From there we boarded a small but elegant passenger liner bound for Lissex. That's when I discovered what traveling with a nobleman's daughter entailed.

The ship carried a maximum load of two hundred passengers and fifty crew. The sleek little vessel boasted first-rate engines that would shave a full day off the usual four-day voyage to the outer rim. Traveling in Weiss-space, named for the inventor of faster-than-light engines that pushed ships through the alternate reality, made transport between worlds feasible and practical.

Staff would deliver meals to the staterooms; there was no public dining hall. The central gathering lounge served premium wines and liquors. As we went to locate our cabin, uniformed attendants eyed my working clothes and Kila's stained garments but addressed each of us as "mistress." I snickered every time I heard that title.

Our two-bedroom suite defined luxury. The decor resembled what one might find on a planetside oceangoing vessel, right down to a viewport that could be switched to reflect a three-dimensional image of rolling waves, among other vista choices.

I ignored the call of the sleeping area, instead easing my tired muscles onto an overstuffed couch that dominated the suite's sitting room. Kila took one of two armchairs opposite me and leaned forward with her elbows on her knees. I noted the dark smudges under her eyes and wondered if she'd slept since this whole ordeal began.

"So," I started, letting my head rest against the back of the couch, "why do you want your brother dead?"

She blinked at my bluntness.

Despite training, I didn't read people as well as I would have liked. I could judge when someone would strike, run, or scream for help, but I had no clue when they lied or told the truth. Assassins didn't negotiate. But it would have come in handy now. I watched the emotions playing over Kila's face, her expression shifting from sad to determined to angry and settling on uncomfortable.

She fixed her gaze on her fingernails, rubbing her thumb over a broken one that had snapped all the way to the quick. "Jaren, well, he…." Her eyes met mine, pleading and shining with unshed tears.

Without her needing to say another word, I could guess what her brother had done. However, I didn't end people's lives on guesswork. If she wanted me to kill him, she'd have to spell it out. A subtle rumble in the starship's frame signaled the engines powering up. That vibration would continue throughout the voyage. It made me sleep like an infant during interstellar travel, which meant placing a proximity sensor at my bedroom door. The alarm it would give off would wake the deepest of sleepers.

Kila took a steadying breath. "He… touched me. He forced me to touch him."

"By touch, you mean rape." I kept a cold, even tone. Emotions could not play a part in business.

"Yes." Her voice shook.

"Say it like it is, then." Something twisted inside me. My fingers clenched into fists, and I fought to uncurl them, laying them flat on my thighs. Control. Control and objectivity. No personal involvement. This response felt alien to me. I prided myself on detachment. Where was this coming from? I had to judge this like any other case or potential contract. "How many times?"

Her gaze narrowed. Her eyebrows raised. "Does it matter?"

"How many times?" I repeated.

She made a sound of disgust. Throwing her arms wide in exasperation, she stood and paced the plush maroon carpeting. Her shoes sank into the centimeters-thick material, leaving indentations as she walked. "Six? Seven? Maybe I should have made notches in the headboard!" Kila spun, green eyes blazing. Anger gave her a kind of raw beauty, an edge to the innocence. "I'd like to forget." She returned to her seat, spine rigid against its cushions. I saw her hands trembling and fought the sudden urge to cover them with one of my own.

I supposed I owed her an explanation for my callousness. "A person who does something once can sometimes be rehabilitated through punishment or counseling." Not always true, but often enough. I followed Guild standards here, not my personal beliefs. I had to, because I personally wanted to rip some strange boy apart, organ by internal organ, leaving the brain for last so he'd be aware of every torturous moment. I couldn't recall ever feeling that kind of rage, and I fought to dampen it. Maybe the palotrin had side effects unknown to me. Every life deserved a chance at justification, and I'd justify her brother's, if I could identify any reasonable chance of redemption. "A repeat offender is usually a lost cause—at least with that kind of offense."

Kila stared at me. "Rape is rape. It can't be undone, even once."

"Neither can death." Now I was the one who was angry. "I don't kill for pleasure—mine or yours." She opened her mouth, but I cut her off. "I don't kill for revenge, either." Not entirely true. Many of my assignments could have been described as vengeful. I, however, preferred to think of them as preventives. I placed my palms flat on the table between us, drawing her eyes to mine, because I wanted, needed, her to understand. "I don't do it for the money. There's no price tag on my conscience—because when it's done, I have to live with myself." Images of the boy I'd almost murdered flashed in my mind. "I kill for the betterment of the majority, and I have to account for every potential benefit and repercussion." I paused, hoping she would consider the ramifications and look beyond whatever had been done to her, no matter how awful. "Do your parents know?"

She shook her head.

"Have you thought about telling them?"

Kila turned her body to face the bulkhead. "He's the eldest son, set to inherit and manage the family fortune and its affairs." Her voice grew softer, and some of the life left her eyes. "They won't jeopardize the succession, not for me, not for anyone. And once he inherits, there'll be no stopping him."

And if she contacted the authorities, they either wouldn't believe her, or their intervention would ensure she lost her inheritance and whatever else she would gain from her family. Maybe a small price to pay for personal security, but she shouldn't have to buy peace of mind and body….

I considered the situation, sadness weighing on me like wet leather. Stupid, backward, chauvinistic outer rim worlds, leaving women like Kila with few options beyond hiring someone like me. They weren't all that way. Sardonen culture was forward-thinking for outer rim. No one treated me differently because of my sex.

I allowed myself an ironic grin, which I hid from Kila under the guise of rubbing my face. Yes. The Guild was as willing to kill me as any man who violated its rules.

I had a few more questions. Most could wait. We had three days together on this liner, but the way she leaned forward, the way her expression pleaded, I sensed Kila needed as much assurance as I could give her.

"How old is he?" If he were too young, I wouldn't do it. I'd report him myself and try to find Kila a safe house somewhere. She'd forgive me eventually. Maybe.

"Nineteen. Twenty in three standard weeks. Same as me. We're twins. Twenty is considered an adult on Lissex, old enough to manage the family affairs."

Old enough to kill.

"Why didn't you simply petition the Guild? Why go to Deluge in the first place?"

She looked down at her hands in her lap. "I have access to funds, but my parents know where I spend them. They think I'm off seeing the stars before settling down. If I transferred that many credits, my family would trace it."

I snorted. "If they could. The Guild scrambles all account transfers. We're pretty discreet." I caught myself. *We*? Not *we* anymore. "*They* take customer privacy seriously." Leaning back against the cushions, my body registered my exhaustion. All I wanted was sleep. "So, you found yourself a second-rate assassin, me, someone who would work for cheap. Is that it?"

It was *her* turn to hold *my* gaze. "I found someone I thought I could befriend and trust."

Well, shit.

"And how do you intend to get me into your household?" I indicated my game leg and shrugged my bad shoulder, then grimaced at the pain the movement caused. "I'm not the person I was the last time I visited Lissex. Infiltrating those islands will take someone abler than I am or a very good plan."

Kila smiled, and in that moment, I would have done anything for her. Had to be the addiction. I gave myself a mental kick.

"I have a plan," she said and went to her bedroom. She left the door open. I thought she was fetching something to show me, something that would define this plan of hers. A minute later, her light went out.

My eyebrows rose. I remained on the couch a little longer before soft snoring carried through the open doorway.

The plan, apparently, would wait.

I settled into my own bed, luxuriating in the thick smart-mattress that conformed to my body and eased my aches and pains. The soft blankets warmed themselves, adjusting to my skin temperature. The vibration of the ship and the distant engine hum lulled me. It wasn't until I was drifting off I realized Kila hadn't said she had a *good* plan. Well, if I didn't like it, I could come up with something of my own.

KILA PROVIDED me with appropriate clothing to wander the ship, products of her shopping spree during our layover on Deluge's orbital station. The latest fashion on the outer rim worlds—like I would have any clue—was the "military look." I turned my limited wardrobe over to the ship's laundry and slipped into the camouflage pants and black shirt. The false gold epaulets on the shoulders seemed gaudy and ridiculous, but I removed them, taking great pleasure in dropping them in the recycler one by one. Otherwise I appreciated that they fit, didn't smell, and didn't involve a skirt or dress.

Apparently Kila didn't care about or follow trends, either. She flowed out of her room in a forest green ankle-length dress, cinched at the waist with a brown rope belt. The colors set off her eyes. Her hair fell in soft waves over her shoulders, with a dark green headband keeping it out of her face. She wore no jewelry, but she didn't need adornments. Her natural beauty was stunning enough.

We had slept almost a full day. Attendants apparently left meals in our sitting area on the low table. One sat there cooling now. We devoured the meal in silence, interrupted only by the clinking of silverware and sounds of appreciation. I noticed Kila left the meat untouched. No surprise there. Many cultures opposed to violence also promoted vegetarianism.

Full almost to bursting, I craved a good workout but knew my leg wouldn't hold up. If I kept eating like this and living in such opulence, I'd double my size in a year. I announced my intention to take a walk, and Kila chose to accompany me. I didn't protest. If she was with me, I could keep an eye on her. Besides, I'd never admit it out loud, but this high-society liner intimidated me just a little.

I hid a sad smile. Micah would have found anything that could intimidate me incredibly funny.

Kila and I proceeded to the central lounge, an unusual pair. At least the other passengers and crew no longer stared at our attire. Now they simply stared at us, and I wondered what they thought.

I ordered an ale from the white-coated bartender. He listed ten possibilities, and I randomly chose one, which he immediately dubbed a "good choice." Kila selected a dry white wine, another "good choice," and I muffled my snort with a sip from my frosted glass. A bottle would have served me just as well but would have appeared too common, I supposed.

Other patrons mingled about the open space furnished with low couches and a few more secluded booths for couples. Some guests sported the trendy military look, elderly women in wrinkles and faux fatigues, men clothed in dress uniforms, their paunches overhanging their cummerbunds. The flashy, flimsy fabrics gave them away as posers when their lack of physical fitness didn't. I tried to focus on the decor rather than the passengers, afraid I'd spit my ale in a sputter of laughter.

The lounge's blue and gold color scheme pleased the eye. The view of endless white through the solid duraglass making up one entire bulkhead was stunning, even to my jaded self. Weiss-space was beautiful and terrifying. Our ship sped through a dimensional shift that looked white to the human eye. No stars or planets broke up the monotony, and yet it possessed an aesthetic attraction all its own.

I'm not one for mingling with strangers. Standing alone in a lounge invited others to approach. So I stayed with Kila, content to share the view and the unobtrusive company.

A few drops of ale sloshed on the toe of my right boot. At first I thought the ship made a sudden course correction, but glancing around, I saw none of the other passengers disturbed. A sinking feeling settled in my chest. I extended my right hand, holding the glass out in front of me. It remained steady for a few seconds. Then a violent and uncontrollable muscle spasm sent more liquid to leave a stain on the navy carpeting. The tremors were internal, not external.

Palotrin withdrawal.

I knew the symptoms. When I started on the drug, I researched the effects and aftereffects. I loathed myself enough not to care how terrible they could be. Seizures and searing nerve pain would plague me throughout the next standard day as my body relearned how to function without palotrin. If I ever took it again, the effects would be worse. The plan had been to switch to another drug once these withdrawals got bad. Unaccustomed to narcotics use in general, I'd apparently waited too long.

I turned to Kila, prepared to take my leave and suffer the consequences alone in my sleeping quarters. She stared out the view window, oblivious to my presence. The solitary tear running down her cheek startled me.

Reaching out, I brushed her sleeve with my fingertips. Kila turned, her face flushing while she wiped the tear with the back of her hand. Then she blinked at me. I guess I looked as bad as I felt.

"Are you all right?" she asked.

"I need to leave." Taking great care, I set my ale on the nearest table. She followed and placed her wineglass beside it.

"I'll walk with you." We'd made it to the center of the room.

Weakness made me uncomfortable. An audience of even one would intensify that discomfort. "You don't need—"

The ship's proximity alarm cut me off midsentence. The high-pitched rise and fall startled everyone, and several more liquors and wines splattered the carpet. A shudder in the vessel's frame indicated the Weiss engines shutting down, and the view returned to that of normal space.

A large vessel shimmered into existence off the passenger liner's starboard side, dropping out of its own Weiss-field. To identify and accurately arrive at a point so close to our own ship's current position had to have taken a brilliant astronomical navigator, dumb luck, or great stupidity. The slightest miscalculation and we would have merged in a violent explosion. I suppressed a shudder. We wouldn't have known what hit us.

The lounge occupants pressed themselves to the duraglass, gaping at the massive ship. The crew members clustered, whispering and muttering into their handheld comms, likely communicating with the bridge staff.

While the sheer size of our visitor prevented a complete view, one thing was certain. Engineers designed her for war. Weapons bristled from the side facing us—high-intensity laser turrets and at least one missile launch tube. She'd been in some action of late. Long black score marks streaked her hull, and several antennae had been sheared off, leaving their bases behind. She'd seen better days. A crew doing well wouldn't leave damage unrepaired. The vessel's name became visible as her trajectory shifted to pace us—*Regiment 1*.

One side of my mouth curled upward. I knew this ship and the pirates who crewed her. And I knew her captain.

CHAPTER 6

GRABBING KILA by the arm, I pulled her down the corridor to our quarters. The tremors were kind enough to hold off, and I burst into her bedroom and dug through her bags until I located her barmaid blouse. "Here," I ordered, thrusting the stained shirt and a pair of clean dark pants into her arms. "Put these on. Find some flat shoes."

She opened her mouth, took one look at my face, and closed it again. Instead, she removed her clothing. She was half naked before I remembered her modesty issues and turned away. Once dressed, she disappeared to find some suitable footwear.

My current attire was acceptable enough, but I stashed a blade in my boot, snapped my gun belt around my waist, and fastened on my back holster and second pistol. My jacket covered the extra firepower. Crews set the temperatures on starships notoriously cold, anyway. The pirates would know I carried weapons, but I didn't need them seeing exactly where or how many.

Kila hadn't appeared, so I paced our sitting room, flexing both hands, desperate to prevent further muscle spasms. They wouldn't hold off forever, and I needed to be fully functional if I was going to keep the two of us alive. I always did have rotten timing.

The passenger liner vibrated as a docking tube connected to the outer hatch. Our captain apparently decided to hold position—smart under the circumstances. Running would have resulted in a lot more damage to our vessel.

Kila emerged, her cloth bag over her shoulder. Her confused but trusting expression shook me, but it was too late to alter course now. I grabbed my own satchel and left our suite, knowing she'd follow.

"Where are we—?"

Without looking back, I held up a hand to stop her questioning. She shut up.

Chaos filled the corridors. Two young stewards now armed with shock sticks patrolled the passage, urging the guests into their rooms and keeping them there. I doubted the kids with the sticks even knew how to use them. They carried them like babes in arms rather than stunning devices.

While they paused to calm an elderly woman sobbing in her doorway, I slipped my pistol from my thigh holster. No time for talking. They didn't spot us until Kila and I stood a meter away. Then they turned in unison and angled their weapons in our direction.

Kila's steps froze behind me, but I kept advancing until the end of one shocker touched my chest. Despite its nonlethal nature, I could feel the weapon trembling in its owner's arms. I stole a quick glance at the other. He hadn't unlocked the safety on the underside of the metal tube.

"Get out of the way," I commanded, putting years of training and experience into the words.

"You are to return to your staterooms and remain there until the captain gives the all clear." The teenager's voice wavered as badly as his weapon. I almost felt sorry for him. He couldn't have been more than eighteen, with just the hint of a mustache appearing on his upper lip.

One quick move wrenched the stick from his grasp. I flipped it neatly, single-handed, and tucked it under my arm with the end pointing at him. The other steward attempted to ignite his to take me down with a wave of crackling energy, then groaned when he saw the engaged safety. Before he could release it, I had my pistol pointed at his head.

I smiled without mirth. "Have you ever seen what kind of damage a gun like mine can do to a bulkhead?" Other passengers clustered in their stateroom doorways, watching the interaction with fearful expressions. I raised my voice. "If you miss your intended target, you can blow a hole through to open space… lose all your breathable air." I made eye contact with an older couple and a gentleman in his forties. "Kill everyone onboard." They stepped inside their rooms and sealed their doors. Up and down the corridor, I heard other hatches closing. My smile broadened. I returned my attention to the two would-be guards. "I'm pretty sure of my targets, but whether I missed or not, you'd die. Now, move."

They stepped aside. I took the second shocker and handed it to Kila. She shook her head at first, but a glare from me got it into her grasp. Even then, she held it away from her body, touching as little of its metal surface as possible. So defensive violence disturbed her as well. Her actions with the slaver on Deluge seemed even more impressive now.

"Are you working with the boarders?"

A fair question. I'm sure it looked that way. This close, I could read the crewman's name badge. McGinan. "No, I'm not." Not yet. "But as incompetent as all of you are, I'd be better off than getting pinned down here." I slung the carry strap of the shock stick over my shoulder, snapped the comms off both the stewards' belts, and smashed them under my boot. Then I headed down the corridor at a trot, Kila's footfalls sounding on the deck plates behind me.

When we rounded the next corner, she came up alongside. "Won't they just contact the bridge from one of the rooms?"

I kept going. "The captain will have disconnected internal comms. Otherwise, passengers would overload all the available channels with panicked questions." I glanced sideways at her. "That's assuming the captain is thinking at all. Either way, I'm not heading for the bridge."

Though I hadn't had much time to explore, the liner's configuration resembled any number of other ships I'd traveled on, and I always tried to pay attention. In my profession, I never knew when I'd need to get from point A to point B, fast. And when we made one wrong turn, the clanks and groans of someone forcing an airlock hatch told me where to go. The smartest action for the captain would have been surrender, but instead he'd chosen to seal up and arm the crew. Stupid.

One curve from the lock, I put out an arm and halted Kila beside me. Scanning her from head to foot, I took her hands and placed them in the proper positions on the shocker she still carried. I yanked the headband from her hair and tossed it aside, then tousled the auburn-blond locks until all sense of styling vanished. I grabbed a handful of her shirt and untucked it from the waistband of her dark brown trousers, letting the faded bloodstain show. Then I surveyed the results.

Not too bad. Nothing I could do on such short notice would make the girl into a fighter, but at least she'd lost that privileged look.

"What, exactly, do you expect me to do with this?" she whispered, begging me with her eyes to take the weapon from her.

"Not a damn thing. The safety's on. Just carry it. Try not to act like you're afraid of it."

She bit her lower lip, then straightened, pulling her shoulders back. "I'll try, but I *am* afraid of it." All the blood drained from her complexion. Her breathing came fast and short.

A strand of hair fell into her eyes. With her hands on the stick, she tried to blow it aside. I took it between my fingertips and tucked it behind her right ear. "I know you are. I won't ask you to use it. Just calm down, and—" I sucked in a sharp breath as a new spasm hit and threw my arms out to brace myself against the bulkhead. Every muscle from right wrist to shoulder tightened into painful twisted knots. I didn't drop my pistol, but instead clenched it in a death grip. I couldn't maintain my position and ended up rolling my body so my spine instead of my forearms pressed against the metal wall.

Squeezing my eyes shut, moisture seeping from beneath the lids, I willed each muscle to relax, one by one. I tried to control my breathing, but the agony persisted, and I gasped harshly.

The sound of metal hitting the floor carried over my own panting. Kila grabbed my midsection, and she held me upright. She didn't possess the physical strength but made up for it with leverage, extending one leg behind her to provide more support.

The seizure passed. I allowed myself to lean on her for a few more seconds until I knew I could carry my own weight. Exhausted, I let my chin rest on the top of her head and breathed in the scent of berries and flowers that made up whatever shampoo the liner provided among the toiletries. She hummed softly against my chest, tuneless but soothing.

"Well," boomed a voice from the turn in the passage, "this explains why you showed no interest in me!"

Kila hushed and stiffened, and I raised my head slowly to meet the wicked gleam in the newcomer's eyes. In the years since I'd last seen him, the captain of the *Regiment 1* had changed little, in personality or appearance. I holstered my pistol, extending my free hand in a gesture of surrender. The pirate shouldered his rifle, then indicated the two crewmen with him should do the same.

"Cor!" he shouted, wrapping both his hands around mine. The size of his palms swallowed my fingers until all five were hidden from view. "Woman, you look like shit!"

"So do you, Derrick." The thready quality of my voice surprised me. I shifted Kila to one side, keeping a casual arm around her shoulders like we'd known each other for years. It stunned me to realize it felt that way too.

Derrick Vargas released me to place his hands on his hips. He looked down at himself, surveying his impressive biceps, broad muscular chest, and tree-trunk legs. He wore a loose-fitting white shirt, probably tailored for him, but his sculpted musculature stretched the seams of his tan vest.

The black animal-hide trousers left nothing to the imagination. "What are you talking about? I look the same as I always have."

"Exactly," I said, letting my lips turn up in a grin.

I watched the two pirate lackeys' eyebrows rise.

Vargas burst out in a blast of uncontrolled laughter, the sound resonating off the metal walls. He ran one palm over the two days' worth of stubble shadowing his cheeks and chin. "Knew I should have found a way to convince you to stick around, Cor, for the amusement factor alone." His lascivious gaze wandered over my curves. "And other things."

"We got each other out of a tight spot. That's all. I'm not a pirate, Vargas."

"Not exactly an assassin anymore, either."

I froze. How much did he know about my removal from the Guild and how much was fishing?

Vargas turned from me to Kila, then back again. I felt Kila's piercing eyes but kept my own carefully forward. As far as she knew, I'd left the Guild due to injury. "So, what are you now?" he asked, striving for casual.

Another tremor shook me, not as violent this time but noticeable. Derrick's expression showed genuine concern, and I struggled with embarrassment. "I'm tired of standing around in this hallway. How about giving a couple of gals a lift?"

I didn't expect him to take me literally, but I should have known better. Captain Vargas took my shock stick and slung it over his own shoulder, then scooped me into his arms. I attempted a protest, which fell on deaf ears. He gave orders to his men to "follow the usual routine," and stomped his way through the airlock and into the *Regiment 1* still carrying me. Over his shoulder, I saw Kila trailing behind. She'd retrieved her weapon and bag from the floor. She had my satchel as well, though I didn't remember dropping it.

A dozen or so armed pirates passed us en route to take the liner, strip her passengers of all valuables, and leave the ship a floating derelict, with a long-range emergency beacon blaring a call for help. Some of them nodded to me, showing deference and recognition. In my current position, I felt ridiculous returning the serious nods, but I did so anyway.

I knew the *Regiment 1* well. She'd been my ride home on a two-week voyage from one side of the outer rim to the other. I held privileged guest status, which meant I had free run of most of the ship, including the bridge, mess, infirmary, engine room, and Vargas's quarters, if I'd desired.

I hadn't.

That's where he took us, though, pounding down the central corridor on the primary deck. The ship had become shabby since my last tour on her. Open access panels, exposed wiring, loose housings—all marks of bad times. His cabin abutted the bridge, and the door opened at his approach. I lost a few skin cells as he squeezed the pair of us through the hatch. Then he laid me on a wide couch in his lounge with more care than I would've given him credit for.

Captain Vargas's accommodations were tacky in every way the liner's staterooms had been tasteful. Red velvet covered each seating surface: the couch, two chairs, and, of all things, a love seat. I blinked twice, checking for hallucinations. Nope. The love seat remained. Kila sat on it, crossing her legs in front of her and leaning the shock stick against it. She placed our bags next to her on the seat.

Pictures of naked women decorated the bulkheads, some with artistic merit, some plainly erotic. Kila stared at one, tilted her head from side to side as if analyzing the positions, caught my amused expression, and blushed redder than the velvet. She turned her attention to her fingernails, picking at one that had torn during our exodus.

Despite the tasteless opulence, the furnishings showed as much wear and tear as the rest of the ship. A piece of underlining hung from the base of one of the chairs. Scratch marks marred the central table. The couch springs squeaked with every shift of my weight.

I pushed myself upright, unwilling to be treated as an invalid, and planted my boots flat on the thick black carpeting. *Well, at least it doesn't show bloodstains.* Derrick removed the shocker he'd taken from me and hung it on a hook embedded in the wall. He sat in an armchair, resting his palms flat on his knees.

"So, what brings a master assassin and her...." He gestured in an abstract manner toward Kila.

"Apprentice," I filled in.

Vargas's eyebrows rose, and a smile played about his lips. "So, that's what you're calling her, eh?" He winked.

I shot a quick glance at Kila, but she remained unperturbed. Either the innuendos went over her head or the idea of the captain believing us to be a couple didn't bother her. Even with her innocence, I suspected the latter, and my pulse jumped a little at the thought. Maybe it was just the spasms.

I really didn't know what to make of Kila. Nudity sent her into embarrassed fits of blushing, but not same-sex pairings. Well, some cultures had very open ideas of acceptable partnerships, even on the outer rim. I hadn't had time to investigate the nightlife the last time I traveled to Lissex. Chauvinism *and* homosexuality, though, made for an interesting combination.

As for me, I'd go with whatever story kept us alive. The particulars didn't matter. "I don't share my *apprentices*," I added with more force than necessary to make my point clear.

The captain nodded, all seriousness now. He understood my unspoken message—mess with my friend and earn yourself an enemy. When, exactly, Kila had become my friend, I couldn't say, but the title fit well enough, so I let it ride.

"And where are you and your apprentice headed?" Tenacious as always, he'd keep asking until he received an answer.

No point in lying. He could check the liner's itinerary if he wanted to know badly enough. "Lissex." Another look to Kila, who stared straight ahead. "For a job."

"Then, ladies," Vargas said, "you're in luck, because that's exactly where the *Regiment 1* is going."

Now, what would a bunch of space-bound pirates want with a collection of islands inhabited by noble families? They might be accomplished at commandeering and robbing other space vessels, but planet-bound thieving involved a different skill set.

I opened my mouth to ask, when the mother of all seizures hit. It snapped my spine straight, jerked my arms and legs rigid, and sent my head back to slam against the bulkhead behind the couch. My teeth clamped down hard, biting my tongue. I tasted blood and spit it in a hoarse curse. "Oh shit."

Both Derrick and Kila scrambled to reach me, the pirate captain grabbing my arms and sitting on my legs with half his weight. Kila placed a throw pillow behind my head to protect it from further injury. My vision blurred, and I suspected I had a concussion. The pain made me writhe, but I couldn't escape it. It felt like someone cut open my fingertips and was pulling out my muscles one centimeter at a time.

I could hear Vargas demanding to know what afflicted me. Kila's response was beyond my ability to comprehend. Speech left me altogether. I managed a low groan.

The next spasm sent me into blissful unconsciousness.

CHAPTER 7

"IF YOU distract the guard, I can get us out of here." I paced the length of my cell and back. At this rate, I'd wear a groove in the stone floor. The old-fashioned metal bars striated my view of the adjacent holding area, but I could see the other prisoner.

The burly man whom a guard called "Vargas" looked up from his cot, then rubbed his palm over the stubble covering his face. Either he was naturally hairy or he'd been in here a lot longer than the single day I had. "And how, exactly, do you think you'll manage that, little girl?"

I smiled and watched him reevaluate me. From experience, I knew the effect my smile had on others. It didn't stem from warmth or humor and didn't inspire those emotions in anyone who saw it.

"Who are you?"

I stopped pacing, went to the hole in the corner of my prison, skimmed down my black pants, and peed. My captors hadn't seen fit to provide anything to clean myself with, so I yanked my trousers up and returned to the bars. The man watched the proceedings with raised eyebrows, refusing to turn away. I didn't care. I had bigger problems. Like getting out.

I gripped the cold metal with both hands and forced eye contact by sheer will. The chill of the bars sapped the warmth from my palms and added to my constant trembling. Grission authorities kept the temperatures in their holding cells at just above freezing. To them, cold promoted complacency. Irrational discomfort pissed me off.

"You can call me Cor. And you?" I already had part of it but wondered if he'd share.

He hesitated a moment. Names gave power. But I'd given him mine, and he couldn't appear less brave than the "little girl." "Captain Derrick Vargas."

I scanned his tight-fitting trousers, ship boots with magnetic-reactive soles, white shirt, and dark vest and made an educated guess. "They don't tolerate piracy on this side of the outer rim, Derrick." He blinked impassively. "And they do things in the old ways." I flicked one of the bars with a fingernail, producing a dull clang like a cracked bell. "Bars and beheadings. Gotta love these backwater yokels."

That got his attention. A lost look drained his features of all energy, the look of a man who knew his fate and resigned himself to it. He stood and crossed to his own bars so only the two-meter wide cross-corridor separated us. "They hang prostitutes."

All right, my clothes fit snugly. The enforcers, the same ones whose boss hired me, by the way, took my jacket when they hauled me in here. My dark brown tank top might have been cut a bit low. However, no one would mistake me for a woman who sold her body to whomever could pay. I opened my mouth for a scathing retort.

Vargas winked.

He'd baited me. And won the reaction he'd sought. Two points to the pirate.

"What's the plan?"

I glanced up the corridor, toward the closed door at its end. No one in sight. So far I'd only seen four of the locals, two on the day shift and two on the night, all of them idiots. Idiots with guns. I'd searched every inch of my cell for viewing and listening devices—under my bare mattress on the metal cot, in crevices between the cinder blocks making up the walls—and found none. That didn't mean the enforcers hadn't installed them in the corridor somewhere, but worlds employing metal bars and guillotines didn't favor high-tech bugs.

"At our next feeding"—I growled the word. The gray sludge they'd brought us barely qualified as food—"make a grab for him through the bars. Make it obvious."

Vargas nodded slowly. Then the guard would throw himself back, colliding with the steel blocking my exit. "Why don't *you* reach for him?" The pirate cracked his massive knuckles. The message was clear: "I'm the man. I have muscles. I'm better suited for this." Except he wasn't.

I shook my head. "Did you watch them at lunch? They won't come near my cell. They'll kick the tray to the bars and let me stretch for the food. They know what I am, and they're a lot more afraid of me than of you."

He eyed me again. His gaze lingered on my hips and breasts, too distracted by my femininity to use logic. "What are you?"

Raising my left hand from the bars, I let him see my bare forearm. Even at this distance and with the impaired view, he should clearly discern the Guild tattoo. To my satisfaction, he blinked twice. "Do you know how to twist a man's neck at just the right angle so it snaps before he can scream?" I asked him, voice emotionless and even.

"I'm in."

My stomach rumbled, and I pressed one hand to my abdomen to quiet it. The sound of several locks disengaging carried along the corridor to the cells. Turning, I retreated to the cot and sat upon it. I let my shoulders slump and my head hang but kept watch on the passage through a curtain of my hair.

"Shouldn't you be—?" Vargas began but hushed as the door flew open and one of the guards marched in.

He carried a single tray bearing two bowls of inedible crap. As predicted, he set the tray down in the center of the aisle, took one container off, and pushed the tray and remaining bowl in front of my cell with his boot. When he carried the second to Vargas, the pirate made a sudden grab for his throat. The guard threw himself backward.

I was up and at my bars before the guard made contact. My arm went through the narrow space and around his neck. One twist and a sickening wet crunch and the enforcer dropped at my feet. I glanced at Vargas while pawing through the guard's uniform. The pirate looked ill.

"Don't tell me you've never killed anyone before," I snarled, coming up with the keys. Deftly, I inserted them in the exterior lock and let myself out.

Derrick Vargas puffed out his broad chest. "Certainly. But I've never seen a woman do it with her bare hands."

This time I had the wicked gleam. "You haven't associated with the right women." I hesitated a moment before unlocking his cell. He might prove more trouble down the line, but he'd done his part, and I owed him. I turned the key.

"Clearly not," he said, stepping out. "May I now consider you my associate?" He reached a hand as if to rest it on my shoulder, then thought better of it and lowered it to his side.

"I'm not your enemy." The pirate relaxed visibly at my words. "As long as you don't touch me without permission." He stiffened again, and I smirked, belatedly realizing I'd left a half-open door with that statement. Bending, I took the enforcer's gun and turned it over in my hands. The bullet-thrower felt awkward and heavy compared to my confiscated laser, and the barrel had rusted. I hoped it would fire if I needed it to.

I stepped over the body, feeling no remorse. The locals petitioned the Guild and hired me to rid them of a nasty serial killer. "Set a murderer to catch a murderer," they'd quipped. I wasn't some random psychotic—I was a trained professional. But I'd held my tongue.

When I finished the job and delivered the corpse, the head enforcer claimed his government lacked the funds to pay me. Given the primitive state of the colony world, I wasn't entirely surprised.

What did surprise me was when they convicted *me* of murder and used that as their excuse for not paying. They locked me up and set the date for my public beheading. Which made them a threat to my life. Which nullified our contract. Which gave me a whole slew of new Guild-approved targets.

Never piss off an assassin.

Extending the guard's gun before me, I pushed open the door at the end of the corridor. The remaining enforcer sat at a ramshackle desk covered in hard-copy files in actual paper folders. He glanced up when I entered, eyes widening when he saw his two prisoners in the doorway. I put a bullet between those widened eyes, spattering the wall behind him with his brain matter. It ran down the rough stone surface in gray gobbets. At least the archaic piece of hardware worked. Behind me, I heard a choked gag.

Vargas swallowed audibly. "Remind me not to make you angry."

"That *was* your reminder." I moved to the main entrance of the otherwise empty jail building and peered outside. The hour was late, the sun having long set, and the street stood empty. In the distance, I heard sirens. Someone had called in the sound of gunfire.

"We'll have to get to the landing field, steal a shuttle." Avoiding the gore, Vargas took the second enforcer's weapon. "If we can make orbit, my ship will pick us up."

I stood aside. "I'm thinking this is more your area of expertise, then." He took point as we stepped into the street.

THE DARK things swarmed me. They crawled over and under my skin, humming and buzzing, making me shiver from the inside out. I'd never heard them make noises before, but the insectoid sounds traveled through the very marrow in my bones. Working their way from my feet to my face, they enveloped my legs, hips, torso, and mouth. I choked as they entered my nostrils and slid down my throat. I coughed and gagged. My chest heaved. I couldn't draw air. They pressed in harder, filling every centimeter of space, suffocating me.

Horrible way to die, and I wasn't going down easy. I writhed, trying to dislodge the shadowy creatures. The pressure continued to grow, and with one final tremendous effort, I let loose a horrific scream, expelling the dark things from my lungs.

Panting, I sat up on the doublewide bunk, eyes wide and darting about the small cabin. A force pulled at my shoulders, drawing me down on the mattress, where the shadows could better smother me again.

I threw my left fist up and back, connecting with something soft and pliant that cried out in pain. Twisting, I swung my legs over the side of the cot, turning to face my attackers.

Kila stared up at me from where she knelt on the deck plates. One hand covered her mouth. A trickle of blood ran from beneath it, down her chin.

Ah, hells.

Reality crashed in, and I sagged, closing my eyes for a moment to regain my bearings and gasping with relief. I was on the *Regiment 1*. Derrick must have moved us to guest quarters after I blacked out. I opened my eyes and scanned the room. A single table and two chairs rested in the center. Our bags lay atop the table.

Judging from the rumble of the ship's engines, we were already underway to Lissex, and I wondered how long I'd been out. My head pounded, and I tentatively touched the bump at the back of my skull, remembering my impact with the bulkhead. I turned my attention to Kila. She hadn't moved.

I stood and the room spun, but I wasn't giving in to the raging headache. Glancing at the two hatches, one on each side of the cabin, I took a guess and walked through the right-hand one into the sanitary facility. There, I splashed icy water in my face, then soaked a towel and returned to Kila. When I crouched beside her, she flinched away from me.

I couldn't blame her, but it hurt nonetheless.

"I'm sorry," I whispered. "I didn't know."

She nodded but didn't remove her hand from her face. I had to pry it away gently.

Jaw set, I surveyed the damage I'd caused. Not too bad. My fist had driven her lower lip into her teeth, cutting the flesh just inside her mouth.

Her lip would swell, was beginning to already, but it would heal without leaving any permanent marks.

I used the towel to clean the blood from her chin, then wrapped her fingers around the wet cloth and pressed her hand to her lip. "Keep it there. It'll reduce the swelling." I shifted my weight to seat myself more comfortably on the metal floor with my back against the cot. It felt good to rest my head against the mattress. I couldn't look at her anymore. "I'm sorry." I was unaccustomed to asking for forgiveness and had no other words.

Her free hand closed around one of mine, squeezing it twice before letting go. I took that as acceptance of my apology. Something inside me unclenched its grip around my heart. Maybe it was the last of the dark things.

CHAPTER 8

WHEN I woke again, the darkness of the cabin sent me into near panic before I remembered. Deep breathing helped me relax. That peace evaporated when I sensed movement in the room.

Fingers flexed, reaching to my belt for a knife that wasn't there. I willed my body to stillness, listening, waiting for my eyes to adjust to the dimmed lighting. The cabin's furnishings revealed themselves bit by bit: the double-wide mattress I lay on, my boots and two bags—mine and Kila's—on the deck, the single table and two chairs in the center of the room, my jacket and weapons on one of them, and Kila seated in the other with that ancient book laid out before her. Her continued presence surprised me but shouldn't have. A pirate vessel wouldn't house many guest quarters, and from the impression I'd given Vargas, he would have bunked us together.

With my face turned to the side and half-hidden by a pillow, I watched Kila. She pored over the text, one finger tracing the lines of writing across the page and back again. The other hand held a narrow-beam penlight. She'd changed into a simple gray dress of warm woven material. It hugged her curves, accenting her breasts and trim waist. I could never have worn anything like that. With my muscular upper arms and legs, I'd look like someone carved me from stone and wrapped me in knitting.

She must have felt my stare. Her head came up, and she met my gaze, eyes sparkling with tears. Whatever the book contained, it wasn't light reading.

"Tell me again why we're traveling with pirates?"

I blinked twice, surprised by the directness of her question. Her words slurred, and if I squinted, I could make out the cut on her lip. The swelling didn't seem as bad as before. That didn't dissolve the rock of guilt in my gut over the injury and the situation. She hadn't questioned my decisions before now. I supposed I owed her an explanation.

"I haven't told you a first time," I quipped, stalling.

The silence of our quarters hung like a thick curtain between us, broken only by our breathing, the rumble of the engines, and the faint whooshing of air through the vents.

"We're on this ship because otherwise we'd be stranded. I didn't know they were headed for Lissex." I paused, considering. "Don't know why they *would* be, either." Vargas conducted his business in space, especially after that incident on the Grission colony. I'd kept loose tabs on him over the years. A contact like Derrick could prove useful. We'd traded information by comm on a few occasions. All of us traveling to Lissex was one hell of a coincidence. I've never cared for coincidences— or surprises, for that matter.

Kila closed the book, the pages falling together with a dull thud. She made some sort of intricate hand gesture over the cover before resting her palms on her thighs. I cleared my throat.

"Right. Well, I can tell you Captain Vargas always pillages a ship in the same way. He robs the passengers, disables the engines, and leaves an SOS beacon screaming on its hull. If we'd stayed on the liner, we'd be stuck for days." A jaw-splitting yawn caught me off guard. Sitting up, I scrubbed my face with both hands, wiping the sleep from the corners of my eyes. At least my body responded to my commands with no trace of spasms or tremors. The headache remained but had dulled to a mere annoyance. No concussion, then. Thank fate for small favors.

"He doesn't kill the crew and passengers?"

Ah yes, that violence issue. "As pirates go, he's pretty tame. Don't get me wrong," I hastened to add. "I wouldn't trust him as far as I could throw him, and even with my training, that wouldn't be far." I smiled at the image that conjured up. "But I've never seen him murder people indiscriminately."

Kila's shoulders relaxed. I hadn't noticed how rigidly she'd been holding herself. It was like I'd pierced an air mattress.

I searched for a change of subject and gestured toward the book with a vague wave. "Is that some sort of religious text?"

It was her turn to blink. She turned to the volume, set the penlight beside it so it lit the entire table, and placed both her palms upon its weathered cover of animal hide. "It's the Generational," she intoned, a slight frown crossing her face, "of the Givers of Life." As if that explained anything.

Religions didn't interest me. Not that I discounted those of others. If believing in deities and an afterlife gave people comfort, and the idea of eternal punishment prevented others from doing harm, then I was all for them. I wouldn't even label myself an unbeliever. The universe functioned in far too orderly a manner to be pure happenstance. But organized religions weren't for me.

Too many unworthy individuals profited off the charity of the faithful. Too many advocated widespread death and destruction in their names. Besides, if there were a great omniscient force in the universe guiding everything, it would have to focus on the big picture. I doubted it cared about little, insignificant me.

"Interesting belief system you have. It prohibits violence and killing?"

Kila smiled and nodded.

"But you can hire others to do your killing for you." The sneer slipped into my tone, though I hadn't intended it. I liked Kila, considered her a friend when I had few others. But I lacked respect for people unwilling to do my job themselves. I understood a lack of training, a physical incapacity, even squeamishness, but a moral objection? What a bunch of hypocrites.

I watched Kila's smile falter, then fade like a light on a dimmer switch, and I hated myself for blowing the fuse. People rarely favored me with smiles, and I'd come to appreciate them from my traveling companion.

"In extreme cases, we can employ those outside the faith to commit violence on our behalf," she said, so softly I almost missed her words.

Repeated rape must qualify as an extreme case.

The tears welling in her eyes began to fall in earnest, dripping on the book's cover and soaking into the material. Kila sucked in a ragged breath and wiped them away with her sleeve. She sat back, continuing to cry in silence, her small frame trembling.

Give me a battle to fight, a target to track, a victim to protect. Don't drop a sobbing nineteen-year-old girl in my lap and expect me to know what to do.

I stood and crossed to her, noting the stiffness in my limbs. Not enough exercise and too much lying down. If I was going to pull off this job, I needed to get back on some kind of workout routine. The past few months put me out of shape.

Reaching out, I let my hand hover over her, drew it back, then reached again and lay it on the soft fabric covering her shoulder. The sympathy undid her. She doubled over in heart-wrenching sobs that almost dragged tears of pity from my own eyes. What must all this have been like for her, the sexual abuse, leaving her home, searching for someone like me? Not to mention the needs my less-than-optimal physical condition placed on her, and then the pirate raid.

I shifted closer, coming alongside her chair, and drew her against me. Kila buried her face in the curve above my hip, her tears soaking through the material of my black T-shirt and marking it with darker damp splotches. I stroked her long hair in what I hoped was a soothing gesture. I'd seen it in vids, but no one had ever done it for me. Not even Micah.

"I'm sorry." I'd said that more times in the past week than the past five years. Master assassins did not apologize. They made mistakes, but they self-corrected without admitting to them. Again, Micah's face flooded my memory.

Given where that particular character trait led him, and now me, it was no longer a characteristic I wanted to emulate.

With Kila, the words of apology needed to be spoken and believed by the speaker, and her need dragged them from me, one awkward syllable at a time, as many times as they needed to be said.

THE NEXT two days of transit proceeded without incident. The *Regiment 1* didn't have the sleek engines of the starliner we'd left, so we'd regained the day we'd shaved off.

Few things bored me more than space travel. After all the recent excitement, I should have welcomed boredom, but within one standard rotation, I felt like climbing the walls of the tiny cabin.

While working with the Guild, I'd book passage on anything headed in the right direction. That usually meant a merchanter with no amenities beyond a lounge, some out-of-date hologames, five-year-old vids, and an inadequate gym. The pirate vessel wasn't much better, though I could add an impressive supply of intoxicants and pleasure-enhancing drugs to the offerings. Close-knit crews on small ships that spent a lot of time in space did not aspire to monogamy. They adopted an open-hatch policy when off shift. If a hatch stood open, one took it as an invitation to share sleeping arrangements, and in a tight group like this, no one was picky.

For the most part, Kila and I ignored the extracurricular activities. We offered to pitch in wherever Vargas needed an extra pair of hands on the chore roster. I was no spacer, but I knew enough about weapons—both light and heavy—to be of some assistance in their repair efforts.

Kila lent her skills to the ship's mess. She had a way with spices that earned her the crew's admiration. With her skills, I'd thought she'd volunteer in the infirmary, but she avoided it, even going so far as to change the subject when I suggested working in there.... I didn't mention it again.

We let ourselves be "inconveniently" assigned to opposite shifts, and I groused about it enough people heard. If we slept at different hours, sharing a bed became unnecessary.

We didn't see much of Vargas, other than passing him in a corridor on his way to one section or another. While he remained courteous, I had the feeling other concerns occupied his attention. On our last night prior to arrival, however, we gathered in the mess hall for what Vargas declared to be a farewell feast for his guests.

He'd dug into the ship's stores to put on a spread that included five different meats, fish, fowl, a number of green and starchy vegetable dishes flavored with Kila's spice combinations, bowls of fruits from half a dozen worlds, and an endless flow of potent ales.

I hadn't had a chance to finish a drink since I left Deluge, and since drugs no longer appealed and I continued to hurt, I needed something to take the edge off. Besides, at some point during our flight, the remaining vial of palotrin vanished from my jacket pocket, along with the infuser. I suspected Kila but said nothing. If she'd taken and disposed of them, she'd done me a favor.

Vargas placed Kila and me on either side of him at the end of the table running the length of the mess hall. Each dish was accompanied by another mug, a different brew from a different world to accent each taste. Vargas always did like his ales and prided himself on a fine collection of them. The first mate started a round of pirate ditties, some of which I knew, and I lent my alto to the tenors, basses, baritones, and a couple of sopranos around me. Derrick didn't recruit many women. In the midst of a dozen pirates, battle talk, bawdy humor, and drinking songs, I lost track of the number of beverages I'd consumed.

I did notice Kila's disapproving glare and shot her one of my own. She might be my employer, but even that remained unsettled. Kila certainly didn't control my actions, and giving me public looks of reproach was taking things too far. She didn't birth me. Likely wouldn't matter if she had. Dear old Mother dumped me in a group home at the age of six, then died in an aircar accident three weeks later. Of course, she'd been drinking at the time. I shifted in my seat, then looked Kila straight in the eye, took a long swig from my mug, and smiled sweetly. She broke eye contact and sipped her water.

By dessert, I was thoroughly inebriated and furious with myself for it. The mess hall rocked at the edges. I heard my voice louder than it should have been, though no one else noticed. When I stood to return to our cabin, I had to brace my palms on the massive wooden table to steady my balance.

Kila caught my arm. I hadn't seen her leave her seat. Her very touch annoyed me, and I shoved her away. No one needed to babysit me. My continued existence for so many years testified to my ability to take care of myself, albeit poorly. Her stricken expression and pout pulled at me, but I stomped those emotions down. Irritation and self-loathing tore me in opposite directions.

Vargas's arm around my shoulders nearly sent me over the edge. He glanced from me to Kila, an amused grin on his wide face. "Looking for a different kind of company tonight, Cor? A change of pace?" His hand slid lower, under my jacket, settling on my waist. His breath in my ear smelled as ale-laden as mine but sent little trickles of pleasure down my neck and spine.

No doubt about it. The alcohol affected my judgment. Otherwise I'd never consider Derrick as a partner. But I hadn't had sex in almost a standard year, not since Micah broke off our relationship. Frustration ran high in assassins, higher when we experienced life-threatening situations, and I'd had several of those recently. Self-gratification never satisfied enough. Without some kind of serious relief, I'd take that stress out on the wrong person, in the wrong way.

Like I'd just done with Kila.

I shifted in Derrick's grasp, letting my body curve against his and my breasts brush his chest. As usual, his tight-fitting wardrobe outlined everything, including his arousal, which seemed as large as the rest of him. I suppressed a shiver. This might be fun after all.

"I'm willing to experiment," I replied, voice sultry and low. Inside I laughed. Let him think he's my first male partner. The ego boost will shoot him through the hull.

The pirate's grin broadened, eyebrows rising in surprise, and he turned to guide me from the hall. "Sleep well, little girl!" he called back to Kila, standing alone where I'd pushed her, staring after us. His hand cupped my ass, and I didn't protest. My heart rate increased with the anticipation of events to follow.

I tried not to notice the disappointment in Kila's eyes. I hated myself enough already.

Through Kila's eyes, the ephems noticed details she missed, interpreted unusual crew orders, analyzed odd glances between this Captain Vargas and his first officer.

Before he and the assassin could abandon the feast, the pair of entities separated. One remained deep within Kila, soothing hurt feelings with strokes on her pleasure center, tiny tweaks to calm and distract. Jealousy and betrayal were powerful forces, useful in many situations but capable of great damage to their current mission.

The other ephem allowed itself to be expelled from Kila's body on an exhaled breath, snaking into the ship's ventilation system before it could be spotted by any of the drunken revelers. It traced the ductwork, following the metal shafts, turning at sharp angles, until it arrived in Captain Vargas's darkened quarters. Under the bunk it waited, but not for long. The laughing couple came through the hatch and paused in the sitting area, not bothering to raise the lights. Vargas pressed the assassin against the bulkhead for a fierce kiss. She in turn rolled him so she held the controlling position. They groped at each other's clothing in the shadows cast by the dimmed recessed lighting.

Various fabrics hit the floor, some kicked onto the furnishings, others remaining where they fell. Soft grunts, whispers, and sighs followed.

The ephem left its hiding place and darted around the one called Cor, attracted by her tempting drunkenness and the tang of lust but wary after its last encounter with the assassin's powerful mind. Unwilling to risk oblivion, it entered the pirate captain instead and set about tapping into Vargas's thoughts and plans.

Distracted by Cor's darting tongue and stroking hands, Vargas's hidden agenda lay unprotected against the ephem's search.

Deviousness and betrayal tasted sweeter than intoxication. Vargas proved to be a being worthy of admiration in that regard, one to be introduced to He-Who-Had-Created-It under other circumstances.

But not now.

The ephem found itself in the unlikely position of undoing misdeeds, or at least attempting to do so. It tried to alter Vargas's mind, change his course, but other factors more threatening than anything the spirit could fake were involved. If the pirate captain changed his path now, he would be punished by outside forces, perhaps to the point of death.

The ephem could not convince him to take suicidal steps. Man's will to live overrode all else. Unless Vargas already had a death wish, he could not be coerced to place himself in assured mortal danger.

Instead of affecting Vargas, the ephem would have to work with Cor. But it couldn't risk entering her again.

By now the twosome had reached the bedroom and flopped onto the wide, thick mattress. They rolled, vying for the top position, slick skin sliding and breaths coming fast. Cor won the dominant seat, straddling the wide girth of the pirate captain and lowering herself to sheath him within her. She braced herself with her palms flat against his hairy chest while he rocked his hips upward in a gentle rhythm. Cor's groan of pleasure rippled through all three of them, including the entity within Vargas.

Somehow, Cor needed to gain an advantage. Between her drunkenness and the physical exertion, she'd sleep hard and sound for hours after their lovemaking. She'd be weakened and oblivious to the actions around her.

Vargas was not nearly as inebriated as he appeared. The ephem knew he'd taken an antitox tablet before the feast, reducing the effects of the alcohol he'd consumed. Regardless of the sexual activity, which currently looked like it might last hours, he'd awaken and be fully functional long before Cor.

A plan formed in the ephem's consciousness. It found Vargas's memories, sorted through them, and sent specific images to the forefront of the pirate's mind: a time he'd walked in on his heavyset mother, naked; a painful three days he'd spent recovering from a sexually transmitted disease that left red lesions on his penis; the time his religious and overly strict father caught him masturbating in a storage closet.

To his credit, Vargas tried to bluff his way through it, but after a few more pumps of his hips, he groaned in exasperation, and his flaccid member fell from within its sheath. Through his eyes, the ephem watched Cor's face, a mask of annoyance, frustration, and disappointment. She rolled off, mumbled slurred words of insincere condolence, and attended to her own needs with a few strokes of her deft fingers. Then she sank into a deep sleep.

Vargas cursed into his pillow and slept as well, first setting an earbud alarm to wake him in two hours without disturbing Cor.

Satisfied Cor now had at least a fighting chance of getting enough rest to be alert when she needed to, the entity abandoned Vargas's snoring figure and seeped back into the ventilation system to rejoin its companion in Kila's body.

A bump and shudder in the *Regiment 1*'s frame woke me. At first, I thought we'd docked with an orbital station.

Intercourse with Vargas proved short and unsatisfying. Contrary to popular belief, size wasn't everything. Since little time passed, intoxication still muddled my brain. I tried to concentrate on my surroundings and failed. Warning bells sounded in the back of my head, but I couldn't identify the cause.

I rolled over, muscles sore from Derrick's weight, though I hadn't let him be on top long. The dim cabin lights cast everything in shadows, but it didn't take much time to figure out the captain was gone. Sirens screamed in my subconscious.

I threw off the thick coverlet, as black as the carpeting. The ventilation system blew chilled air over my naked form, sending shivers through me. I padded out of the sleeping area, steadying myself on the doorframe. Disjointed images of hasty stripping, fevered kisses, and frantic groping floated in my mind's eye, and I groaned. What the hell had I been thinking? My clothes lay scattered about—pants on the chair, shirt on the love seat, boots, jacket, socks, and undergarments on the floor.

My weapons were missing.

I double-checked everything. I hadn't worn my pistols to dinner, but Vargas found the knife I'd had in one boot, just in case, and another concealed in the lining of my jacket. The concerns dulled by the alcohol snapped into clear focus. Lissex didn't have an orbital station. It rested too far out to warrant such an extravagance. That bump I'd felt earlier meant we'd docked with another ship.

I grabbed my clothes, yanking them on in jerks and fits, trying to maintain my balance as I stagger-stepped into my pants and pulled at my boots. All the while I fought blurred vision and a growing nausea. Suspicion gnawed at me, and I wondered if Vargas drugged my ale. Not that he'd needed to with the amount I'd drunk, but I felt unsteadier than I should with adrenaline pumping through my veins.

Moving to the hatch accessing the central corridor, I palmed the opener pad. Nothing. I tried the internal comm system by the door and tapped in a request for a connection to the guest quarters. Static blared from the tiny speaker.

Shit.

I scanned the room, searching for something I could use. One of the erotic paintings hung askew. I grabbed it with both hands, wrenched it from the wall, then brought it down over the back of an armchair, shattering its glass and its frame. My old arm wound ached, but I ignored it.

My breath came hard and fast. I dropped to my knees and sifted through the debris, coming up with a long shard. Standing, I dug it under the control panel for the hatch, barely noticing when I sliced open my palm and blood ran down my arm. The protective covering snapped free, and I threw it across the room to clang off the bulkhead. The glass I tucked under my belt. It was the only weapon I had besides my bare hands, and although those could be formidable, until the ales wore off, my martial arts skills were more than suspect. Burying my wrists in the wall, I grasped handfuls of conduits and dragged them out where I could examine them.

"Lights!" I shouted, then almost sobbed when even those failed to brighten from the dim glow of ship's night. Dammit, now he wasn't playing fair.

This wasn't another raid on some new unsuspecting passenger liner. I could think of no reason why Vargas would drug and disarm me and lock me in his cabin. No reason, except one.

Cold dread pressed against my rib cage. I'd underestimated Derrick, but it made sense now—the shabbiness of the ship, the need for repairs, the lack of funds, our chance encounter in the first place.

Someone tipped him that I was on the passenger liner. Someone like the slavers, or perhaps another contact of his on Deluge. Derrick sold me out. He'd contacted the Guild.

The Guild had arrived.

CHAPTER 9

HOT-WIRING A door always looks easier in the vids. Usually I used this skill for entering, not escaping—not that it made much difference. Even with Guild training, it took me longer to open the hatch than I would have preferred.

I forced myself to stare into the bright corridor lights until my eyes adjusted. All the while my heart raced, and my muscles stretched taut for action. When I could see, I slipped out of the captain's cabin, keeping close to the wall and getting as far from the bridge as fast as I could.

Kila. What had that traitorous bastard done with Kila?

If he'd left her in the guest quarters, I could retrieve her, pick up my spare weapons, and try to get us both to an escape pod. With the Guild, I'd built up a tolerance to many knockout drugs, and since I'd left, my stamina for alcohol had increased. It was quite likely I'd recovered consciousness faster than Derrick expected. Maybe he hadn't bothered to move my new friend.

I listened to the ship's vibrations, felt them through the deck plates. The engines idled, at low use for station-keeping. We'd reached orbit around Lissex. A pod wouldn't need to travel far to safety.

Nice, neat plan. Nothing is ever that easy.

My path would take me past the airlock. I couldn't accurately estimate the amount of time that passed since I'd felt us bump another ship, but the Guild representative or representatives had to be aboard by now. The question was, where?

Silence hung heavy in the corridor. I slid by several open cabin doors, their dark interiors like mouths straining to engulf me. From some of them, I heard snoring, at others, moans and cries of pleasure. The crew had drunk as much as I had or more, which didn't explain Vargas's resilience. I could only guess he'd taken an antitox tab before attending the feast. Right now I'd kill for one of those. In fact, I even knew *whom* I'd kill.

I tried to think like a pirate as I continued to move. My headache returned full force, and a bead of sweat trickled down my forehead. I brushed it away with a swipe of my sleeve. Vargas would want payment before turning me over to the assassin. The best place to conduct business on the *Regiment 1* was the lounge, located amidships. I stood two meters from its hatch now, and it was open, flooding the corridor with additional light. Shadows crossed back and forth, as if one of the occupants was pacing impatiently. If I controlled my breathing and held still, I could make out voices.

"Everything is in order. The transfer is complete." Alek, one of the three masters who'd found me with Micah's body. The one who'd gotten me in the leg with his poison-dipped blade back on Sardonen. Unlike most of us, Alek enjoyed killing, not for the good it did others, but for the act itself. He hid it well, but I saw it in his eyes, in his very being on the couple of assignments we'd worked together before I refused to work with him again. A shudder passed through me, and my thigh ached at the memory.

"It's half what we agreed." Vargas. Rage burned inside me, boiling the acid in my stomach and creating a bitter taste in my throat. Up until this moment, I'd clung to some hope they'd tricked or coerced him, but no. It all centered around credits, and I was an idiot. I hoped it was a lot of credits, at least.

"You'll get the rest beamed to your account when my ship is clear. You've incapacitated her?"

Derrick snorted. I winced. "She did it to herself. Quite the habit she's acquired since you parted company."

I didn't think I could feel any smaller. I was wrong.

"I want two-thirds up front," the pirate continued.

"The Guild does not negotiate."

Heh. If Derrick Vargas had been Guild, this would never have happened. I'd saved Vargas's life when I released him from that jail cell. In Guild terms, I'd incurred a life debt from him. Save an assassin's life and he owes you his eternal loyalty.

Save a pirate's life, you get screwed.

I heard someone large cross the floor and the creaking of furniture as he sat. Had to be Vargas. Assassins don't weigh much, and Alek was no exception. "You'd better *start* negotiating," the pirate countered. "You're alone on my ship with my crew. I don't appreciate alterations to the original deal." After a prolonged silence, the pair began to haggle over my ownership.

The wall held me up, because my knees wouldn't have. Somehow I had to get past the open hatch, find the only friend I had, and steal a pod, and all I could think about was how I would prevent myself from vomiting and giving away my location.

Approaching footsteps jerked my head up and cleared the disorientation, at least for the moment. I drew the piece of glass from my belt, prepared to defend myself with it as best I could. The shallow cut on my palm had ceased bleeding, but gripping the jagged shard reopened the injury, and I swore under my breath at the stinging pain.

I couldn't afford a close-in fight. That would bring the lounge's occupants running, and they'd outnumber me three to one. However, I could throw the glass like a dagger. Something flying that fast across the doorway might go unnoticed, and the right hit would drop the new arrival with minimal noise, if I were very, very lucky.

I raised the makeshift weapon, prepared to hurl it with as much force as I could muster.

Kila rounded the curve in the corridor, both our bags over one shoulder. I'd underestimated Vargas, but he'd underestimated my friend.

Stopping the throw brought physical pain. Every muscle in my arm tightened with the effort. I threw my free hand out in a halting gesture, nodding with satisfaction when she froze in place. I raised a finger to my lips, then pointed to the open hatch. A wave of dizziness hit, and I pressed the cool, smooth side of the glass to my forehead.

Kila set the two bags down against the wall on her side of the door. She reached in the pocket of her skirt—Kila had changed clothes as soon as I'd let her discard the ruse of being my apprentice. No one believed it anyway, and our other charade worked just as well, perhaps better, for putting the pirates off guard. A tiny item flew in my direction, above the top of the hatchway. I caught it by reflex, closing my hand around the smooth capsule. Opening my fingers, I stared first at the antitox tablet, then at Kila, who shrugged one shoulder and grinned. At that moment, I could have kissed her.

I downed the pill in one dry gulp, then suppressed a groan of relief as the rapid-release meds shot through my bloodstream. The tab's chemicals scoured the remaining alcohol from my system, cleared my head, and quelled the nausea. The adrenaline component heightened my awareness to a fever pitch. I felt supercharged, though it wouldn't last long. Whatever I was going to do, I'd better do fast.

"What's the penalty for people who break Guild rules?" Vargas asked. His voice carried into the hallway. He had to know they planned to kill me. Maybe he wanted the grisly details.

I figured Alek would think himself above answering, but the master assassin went for the scare factor. "She murdered the Guild Leader. That requires a public execution, stripped naked in front of the entire Guild, the apprentices, the masters, and the new Leader, as a lesson to all." Yes, assassins loved their traditions.

Kila's eyes widened at Alek's pronouncement. I locked gazes with her, shaking my head slowly and firmly. Whether she believed my innocence or not, I couldn't tell, but her posture relaxed.

Before I could do a thing to stop her, she stepped into the open doorway.

"Captain Vargas," she called, no trace of tremor in her voice but a little higher pitched than her norm. "I was looking for Cor. Have you seen her?" She walked into the lounge. "I'm sorry to interrupt."

Assassins don't kill innocents, I reminded myself, swallowing hard. Newly formed sweat ran down the back of my neck. The hand clenching the glass trembled. I couldn't see her, couldn't help her, couldn't do a damn thing except listen to her soft steps crossing the room. I offered a prayer to whatever omniscient beings others believed in, any deity that might help her now.

"Oh, is that your ship?" She padded farther away. Her flat sandals slapped on the deck plates.

It was a distraction. She drew their attention away from the door. I blurred past the hatch opening. When no sound of alarm rose from within, I knelt by the bags Kila left and pawed through mine, trying to identify the items while making as little noise as possible. I dropped the piece of glass and replaced it with a proper knife in my belt. A blackout bomb went into my pocket. I fastened on my belt holster and checked the charge on the pistol tucked snug within it. I eased the safety off the laser, muffling the click with my thumb.

Standing, I took three deep breaths, letting each one in and out as slowly as my racing heart could manage. I listened to the voices, pinpointing each person in the room. They clustered together, presumably at the viewport on the far side. Judging from the muffled conversation, they faced away from the entry.

Gun in hand, I stepped through the doorway.

Taking a shot with a laser on a starship involves great risk. Even a tiny hole in a hull results in atmospheric loss, and my pistol packed some serious power. With both my targets and Kila against the viewport, the concerns outweighed the advantages.

Alek sensed me before I opened my mouth to speak. He turned to face me, Vargas following suit a moment later. I watched with some satisfaction as the blood drained from the pirate captain's face. Kila tried to ease away, but Vargas seized her by the wrist, holding her firmly in front of him.

Wonderful. Now they had a hostage.

The barrel of my pistol did not waver, but Alek's expression was unconcerned. He looked from me to the viewport and back again, shaking his head. Before I could close the gap, he had his own laser out of its holster. I dove behind one of the four low couches in the lounge as he opened fire. Facing away from the hull, he could do so without much concern.

Everything erupted at once. Alek's first shot splintered the armrest of the couch and sent stuffing flying. My targets took cover as well, Vargas and Kila behind the bar and Alek behind a second couch. I kept moving, my head low and my body in a painful crouch. Every few seconds I popped up to fire at my former Guild mate. We were effectively dismantling each other's barriers, taking the seating apart piece by piece with every blast.

The sound of breaking glass drew my attention to the bar counter. Vargas used the arm not wrapped around Kila to swipe away bottles and glassware. Then he leveled his pistol on the counter's surface and started his own barrage on my position. For him, I guess siding with Alek was the lesser of two evils. The Guild wouldn't pay him what they owed him. I, on the other hand, planned to kill him slowly for his betrayal, and Vargas knew it.

This plan was beginning to suck, and if my next move didn't work, we were all going to die.

I had the layout of the room memorized: four couches, the bar, two chairs, a pair of tables, the viewport, and the hatchway to the corridor. I leaned around the edge of the couch, aimed, and fired into the pile of broken liquor bottles on the floor.

They ignited, trailing fire wherever the alcohol had spilled in vicious tendrils that snaked up the bar, behind it, and across the hard flooring of the lounge. I felt a pang of regret for the loss of good ale.

"You're insane!" Vargas shouted, fleeing the bar with Kila in tow. I shot a beam of energy directly in front of him, and he threw himself flat behind a table, dragging Kila down hard.

Maybe I *was* crazy. Fire in space meant nowhere to go and posed just as much threat as the loss of atmosphere, because if it weren't extinguished, the flames would *consume* the atmosphere, but the standoff was getting me nowhere, and the crew wouldn't sleep forever.

Alarms blared from overhead speakers. Suppression foam poured out of the ventilation system. It would suck the oxygen from the space, extinguishing the fire. It would also smother us if we didn't get out of here.

A computer-generated vocal countdown began, overlaying the alarms. "Thirty seconds to compartment seal-off, twenty-nine, twenty-eight…." An amber light above the hatch flashed its strobe across the room.

I coughed, harsh and rasping, and heard the others doing the same. *What is it with me and fire, anyway?*

The scenario trapped us in a fatal game of head-on. The question was, who would blink first? Anyone making for the door got shot. Anyone staying in the lounge burned or suffocated. Having done this before, and fairly recently, I had a good idea of how long I could remain conscious. I hoped the others had less experience.

The air grew thinner. My lungs tightened.

Vargas broke for the door first, the only one of us who could do so without serious risk as long as he had Kila. I couldn't let him disappear with her, couldn't let him reach the rest of the crew, who were no doubt on their way. Those alarms would wake the dead.

Alek and I rose at the same moment, our weapons leveled at each other's heads while the smoke flowed around us. My free hand palmed the blackout bomb. My gun arm trembled. I'd trained Alek, watched him grow from an orphaned teenager, not so different from myself, to this young man of twenty-two. We'd shared meals, a sleeping area, complaints, and conversation. I didn't approve of his attitude or eagerness, but I'd already caused the death of one comrade and watched Micah kill himself. Dammit, I didn't want more blood on my already stained conscience.

Kila. I didn't have time for this. I had to get to Kila. And take care of Vargas. No conscience problems there.

I threw the blackout bomb, aiming it for the center of the lounge. It exploded against the floor, its automated internal signal activating and transmitting to switch off every light in the room and the adjacent corridor.

Alek fired a split second before I did. I suspected he'd already moved by the time my shot crossed the space between us, and if he hadn't, well, he should have. I dive-rolled for the corridor, pleased when I didn't collide with the hatch rim instead of tumbling into the hall.

Pain throbbed in my leg on impact, but I gained my feet and turned left, toward the crew quarters. Shouting echoed back to me, Vargas's voice. Lights flared in open hatchways, casting pools of white into the hallway. The corridor would stay dark for another two to three minutes.

I had no time but paused anyway, feeling in the dark beside the lounge entrance until my hand wrapped around the woven fabric of Kila's bag. Maybe I had no use for religions, but the Generational held more meaning for her than anything I'd ever believed in. I'd dragged her into this particular mess. Saving the book was the least I could do. I threw it over my shoulder and ran down the hall into the shadows.

The ship's engineer staggered from his cabin, bleary-eyed and blinking. I caught him with a backhanded fist to the chin and sent him sprawling backward before he could block my path.

A roundhouse kick took out a second crewman. He fell against the bulkhead, skull connecting with the metal and knocking him cold prior to hitting the floor. I kept expecting a laser or ripper to pierce my back, ending this little flight, but none came. Where the hell was Alek?

Where the hell was Kila?

A fire team charged around the corner, carrying gear and heading for the lounge. I started to raise my weapon, but a wave from the second officer stopped me. They didn't know. They didn't know about Vargas's betrayal. I waved back and ran on.

A left turn brought me to the lifepod alcove, a short hall with four small hatches, each leading to an escape pod that would provide life support for three. Here, there were working lights, and I blinked to clear my vision. Derrick stood outside pod one, trying to push a struggling Kila ahead of him through the hatch. I raised my weapon. When he saw me, he yanked her out and pressed the barrel of his gun to her head. Her whimper carried the length of the corridor.

"Let us go, Cor. I'll release her on Lissex."

No, he wouldn't. He'd keep her as insurance until he found a way to kill me. Otherwise, I'd hunt him until I found him.

I strained my ears for any hint of Alek but heard nothing behind me. "You'd abandon your ship and crew?"

The pirate smiled without humor. "If you don't shoot me, the other assassin will."

Well, he had that right. Alek wouldn't forgive him for this fiasco of a botched bounty collection.

I eyed the pair of them. It was a very risky shot. Kila blocked a good portion of Vargas's body with her own—everything except his massive, hairy head. Anything less than a fatal wound would give him the opportunity for retaliation.

I calculated the odds. I weighed the consequences, fully aware Kila's assessment of balance and counterbalance might not match my own.

I fired.

CHAPTER 10

MY SHOT caught him just above the right eyebrow. Kila screamed as gore spattered her top and skirt, tangled in her hair with bits of bone, and ran down the bare skin of her arms. In shock, she touched the droplets with trembling fingers, smearing them across her paleness.

Derrick's body spasmed, jerking his wrist up and tightening his finger on the trigger of his own weapon. It fired. I'm certain Kila felt the searing heat of the laser as it passed centimeters in front of her face. She threw herself back, colliding with the lifepod hatch and slamming it against the wall with a resounding clang. The energy of the blast hit the interior of the hull, leaving a scorch mark and a neat round hole. A high-pitched whistling indicated the sound of escaping air.

The corpse toppled at Kila's feet, limbs jerking in a macabre rhythm. It blocked her path, and I thought she'd claw her way through the metal trying to escape it. Her screams died to a continual whimpering. Her breath came in hyperventilated gasps.

I jogged to her, holstered my gun, and grabbed her shoulders. Hauling her bodily over the dead man at our feet, I thrust her through the open escape pod hatch. Her forehead caught the rim, and I winced in sympathy at her cry but didn't let up until she disappeared inside. "Sit down!" I ordered, knowing she could hear me and hoping my words would register. I yanked her bag off my arm and tossed it in the pod after her.

She must have managed to obey my command. An automatic countdown to hatch closure began, triggered by someone strapping into one of the three chairs. In thirty seconds, the pod would seal itself, and the tiny escape vessel would rocket away from the pirate cruiser seeking the closest life-supporting world, which would be Lissex.

Thirty seconds. I braced myself in front of the open hatch, feet apart for greater stability. The air continued to suck into space, in a narrow stream through the hole. Alarms blared, drowning out the hissing and whistling. I had to prevent anything from interfering with the launch for the next thirty seconds.

Before I could draw my gun again, Alek stepped into view at the end of the short corridor.

Why in all the worlds and fates is nothing ever easy?

"Twenty-one, twenty, nineteen—"

"Bitch," my old comrade snarled. He gripped his upper right arm with his left hand, and I spotted the scorch mark between his fingers. I hit him with that wild shot-in-the-dark in the lounge. His right hand still clung to his pistol, but he couldn't seem to raise it past my abdomen.

No matter. A shot there would be lethal enough.

"Ten, nine—"

Alek showed no sign of hearing the countdown. His focus was all on me, not the soft voice coming from within the pod. He edged closer, probably wanting to be sure of his aim. A faint popping noise carried to me over the wailing of klaxons. An emergency bulkhead, basically a large slab of metal, dropped from the ceiling and sealed off the escape pod access corridor from the rest of the ship. It effectively cut off the crew from half their means of survival if they needed to abandon the *Regiment 1*. In order for the ship's computer to take such a drastic precaution and trap us, things had to be about to get very, very bad.

I risked a quick look. Hairline fractures appeared in the metal around the hole from Derrick's shot. They spread out like earthquake fissures. An indentation formed, the plating sucked outward.

Oh shit.

I wondered why the auto-sealant didn't pour from the overhead vents and plug the hole while it was still small. Maybe with the fire suppression system operating, it couldn't handle both at the same time. Or maybe this was one more of the *Regiment 1*'s damaged systems Vargas hadn't had credits to repair. Regardless of the reason, I was in serious trouble.

At least Kila was safe within the pod. I didn't give a damn about Alek.

Using my own body to cover my actions, I snaked my left hand back and wrapped my fingers around the pod hatch's handle. My grip tightened until my knuckles cracked.

Alek took another step toward me. At this distance, I could see his arm trembling violently. He'd miss me if he weren't standing within a meter.

He struggled to raise the gun higher, to my chest. His finger on the trigger twitched.

"Four, three—"

Everything happened at once. The panel blew out, creating a gaping hole, and anything not bolted down went flying. Derrick's body began a gradual slide over the floor, his immense dead weight preventing faster suction. Alek slid toward the opening, boot soles squeaking on the deck. He fired. The shot passed so close I smelled the odor of burned human hair. Then his gun slipped from his grasp, whirled end over end, and disappeared into the blackness of space.

"One, zero." The hatch moved, and I moved with it, still gripping the interior handle. Motors and gears shrieked, trying to close the door against the sucking of the vacuum. Muscles strained to draw myself inside before the sealing hatch crushed my arm between the door and the bulkhead.

I wasn't going to make it. I didn't have the strength to pull my weight into the escape pod. My arm stretched to its fullest extension and beyond. I felt a tearing pain in my shoulder, but I somehow retained my grip on the metal handlebar.

Alek slammed into the bulkhead, his torso blocking the opening where the panel ruptured. He splayed out his arms and legs flat against the wall, desperately holding himself in place. The tendons in his neck and arms stood out under the pale skin. He screamed.

The force of the vortex sucked the assassin, a man of almost two meters in height, through a hole half that size. The sound of his spine and neck snapping as his body bent into unnatural and impossible angles carried over the howling of the atmospheric loss and the wailing of alarms. Making use of the obstruction, I gained some ground, managing to get half of my body inside the escape pod before the gale returned to full strength.

Derrick Vargas's body completed its journey across the hall, then up the metal wall. His muscular form blocked the opening for a few vital seconds, again cutting down on the sucking force.

I moved.

Taking full advantage, I dove into the escape pod, banging my shin on the base of one of the three seats and my head on the opposite side of the egg-shaped emergency vessel. The hatch clanged shut, and air hissed through overhead vents as the pod's own systems provided oxygen from its separate, onboard storage tanks.

I snaked my hand up and over the rim of the forward control panel, feeling for the transparent plastic covering I knew would be there. After flipping it up, I pressed my palm down on the launch button—incredibly dangerous in my position, but we'd run out of time. The entire section of hull on the starboard side of the *Regiment 1* was at risk. If the crew didn't arrive with a patching system, more panels would blow out. And the repair team would have to get through the emergency seal-offs first.

My stomach wrenched inside out as we dropped away from the *Regiment 1*, driven by miniature thrusters designed to get us far from a damaged ship as quickly as possible. I left the deck, and my spine connected with the ceiling. Below, Kila stared up at me, pale and shaking, her frail figure pressing against the restraining straps of her seat.

I was bruised and nauseated, my shoulder likely dislocated, and it wasn't over yet. I closed my eyes and tried to breathe despite the compression of my lungs. The seconds ticked off in my head, and I listened to each of the pod's systems initiating.

Several blips and bleeps sounded from the control panel, which lit up in an array of telltale greens and a couple of flashing reds. Sensors scanned the surrounding solar system for habitable planets. This part wouldn't take long. Judging from travel time, we emerged from Weiss-space close to Lissex. I couldn't see the beautiful, mostly aqua-blue world. Engineers built escape vessels with practicality in mind, not aesthetics, so we didn't have the luxury of a viewport, but I cringed in anticipation.

The pod's engines ignited. Their rumble shuddered through the vessel's frame. I tried to brace myself, but there was nothing to grab on to, and my left arm was useless.

"Cor?" Kila's voice wavered. Her breath came in short gasps. I recognized the symptoms of panic and hyperventilation, but I had my own problems.

The engines flared to full power. Acceleration kicked in a heartbeat later, flinging me into the rear of the compartment and landing me in a heap against the built-in storage lockers, my face plastered to the floor.

I tried to push myself up to a seated position and failed, my arm buckling at the elbow and dropping me again. Could the universe conspire to batter me any further today? There was, I supposed, a slight chance the *Regiment 1* would pursue and shoot us down, but with their captain dead and repairs to make, it seemed unlikely.

A groan escaped my throat before I could swallow it. I let my cheek press against the cold metal flooring and closed my eyes. The ship rumbled around me, vibrating through my skin in unpleasant waves. I endured several minutes before concluding it wasn't the ship but me, shaking with the aftershock and adrenaline depletion. With the pod's tiny engines, it would be hours, perhaps eight or nine, before we reached Lissex's surface. Another attempt to rise failed, and I decided spending the trip there on the floor wasn't such a bad idea.

Kila had other thoughts. A cabinet opened to my right. I heard shuffling and the slap of fabric being shaken out. Then a warm blanket dropped over me. I cracked open an eye to watch her slide down the bulkhead and seat herself on the deck. She looked awful, pale and shaky. Reaching, she popped open another storage compartment and dragged out the med-kit. The injection of painkillers elicited a sigh, and the fogginess that settled in my brain suggested a sedative as well.

Drawing me closer with one arm, she let my head rest on her thigh—a far cry more comfortable than the floor. She stroked my hair, paused at the singed bits, and continued following the strands down my back, her fingers working out the knots and tangles. Her attempt at humming failed, her voice too tremulous to carry the tune with any success.

"You could use a sleep aid too," I murmured, my words almost unintelligible with my mouth pressed to the material of her skirt. "Everything's automated from here down." The sensation of floating wrapped itself around me. My body felt weightless, though I knew the gravity functioned fine. Exhaustion pulled at my eyelids, sealing them shut.

"What if we hit the ocean?"

A fair question. Lissex consisted of mostly water and scattered islands. "We won't. It's programmed to find a landmass, no matter how small, and it prioritizes by population—" My words drifted off. I couldn't think of what I wanted to say next. "—size."

"Let yourself rest, Cor." Her hand rubbed my back, careful to avoid the injured shoulder.

I didn't have much choice. The drugs sent me into a deeper sleep than I'd had in days.

I ROSE naked from the sleeping pallets Micah and I had hidden in an access tunnel. He'd appropriated a spare holograph projector from the

Guild's stores. To anyone passing along the cross corridor, the entrance to this side cave looked like a solid rock wall. No one would discover our secret. That is, unless our moans and cries of pleasure gave us away. Silently, I donned my clothing.

Watching him continue to sleep, his chest rising and falling steadily, I smirked. Last night we'd made considerable noise and hadn't concerned ourselves. The apprentices roamed the surface in teams, foraging for food, avoiding the sand lizards, and constructing shelters from native materials in one of Micah's survival exercises. The other masters busied themselves with loud practice drills or were off Sardonen on assignment per Micah's orders. As Guild Leader, he had the authority to make sure no one would hear us.

As I pulled on my boots, my smile faded.

My lover had changed since Farn's death, then his promotion to Leader. The brushes of his hand or knee against mine under the dining tables, the stolen kisses in shadowy alcoves, the "accidental" drape of his arm over my body while we slept on adjoining pallets—all ceased. He'd said nothing, and it hurt, but he continued to meet me here whenever circumstances permitted. When I questioned him, he'd go silent or change the topic.

Guild rules forbade our relationship from the start, though such affairs happened with some frequency. They didn't last long, and Leaders generally overlooked them.

Ours lasted more than two years. And now he was the Leader.

Micah's eyes opened, and we looked at each other for a long minute before he rose and spoke. Expression, posture, and tone told me before words this night had been our last together. I'd seen this coming but hadn't wanted to admit it.

"I have to set an example," he told me.

My shoulders stiffened. My fists clenched at my sides, and I willed the fingers to uncurl. Emotion wouldn't convince him to change his mind. Logic might. "You've always set an example. You train apprentices and first-years. It's never concerned you before." No anger, just a statement of fact.

"The Guild is my life." He reached for his discarded clothing, the pants and tunic, the sash that identified him as Leader. It gave him an excuse not to meet my eyes.

"The Guild doesn't know." We'd hidden it this long. We could continue to do so.

"Farn knew."

I blinked in surprise.

"He told me to end it. He threatened to remove my name as successor from the records. If he hadn't died...." His voice caught. Micah and Farn had been close, like brothers. Farn's death affected us all, but Micah the most. "Nothing can supersede devotion to the Guild." He turned to me, and his gaze softened. "Nothing and no one. Not even you. We've become too attached—dependent, even. Our enemies could use us against each other. If one of us were captured...."

My dream-self observed the proceedings without the emotional bindings of the moment, hovering outside my body like an invisible ghostly voyeur.

If I'd been captured on some assignment and used against him, he'd have sacrificed me for the greater good. I hadn't believed that then. I certainly believed that now. And I also knew, now, he'd sacrifice himself in order to preserve the image of perfection he'd worked so hard to craft and mold.

I watched myself kick a loose stone, bouncing it off the wall. "Will ending it change that? Will you care less about me if we're not having sex?"

His shoulders slumped. He looked away. "Over time, yes."

I swallowed hard against the lump in my throat. "Time will not change how I feel about you."

But it had. Part of me hated him now, and hated myself for hating him.

Pushing past him, I walked through the holographic wall, then ran down the corridor before he could see my tears, my weakness.

Things worsened between us after that. Little hints indicated Micah hadn't given up all sexual activity. He'd just given it up with me. Maybe he'd found someone he could be more casual with. Someone he wouldn't accidentally show feelings for in public. Someone who wouldn't interfere with his devotion to the Guild.

CHAPTER 11

A CHOKED sob woke me—my own. I hauled in a breath, but the tears fell, a few at first, then an outpouring of emotion I hadn't allowed myself since Micah's death.

Kila held me, rocked me, and made soothing noises against my hair. What must she think about me? Calculating assassin, psychological wreck. The catharsis ended, and my sobs died down to the occasional hiccup. I couldn't look at her. I didn't want to see the concern and pity I would find in those expressive green eyes.

"Who's Micah?" she asked, voice almost lost in the rumble of the pod's engines. Guess I talked in my sleep. Good thing I was an assassin and not a spy.

I waited until I had complete control before answering, which took longer than I would have liked. "Savior, friend, lover, Guild Leader." At least the sleep restored a little of my strength. Pulling away from her, I stood and shuffled across the narrow space to the trio of seats at the control console. "Stubborn bastard," I muttered.

"What?"

"Nothing."

One mistake. One admitted mistake and Micah and I would both be living our lives in the Guild. He wouldn't be Leader. But he'd be alive.

And all the death that followed his would never have been necessary.

My dislocated shoulder throbbed, but the physical pain distracted me from the emotional ones.

"This was the Guild Leader who died?"

"Yes." I checked the console displays. All systems functioned within normal parameters. We would land on Lissex within an hour. I'd slept hard.

"The one that other assassin said you killed?"

I drew a stilling breath, letting the anguish drain. "Yes," I sighed. Kila stood behind me, so close her breath moved strands of my hair.

"I'm sorry."

Shifting in the confined space, I faced her. I gripped her forearm with my good hand. "I didn't kill him." I needed her to believe. No one else in the universe would. I was the only living being who knew Micah ended his own life. Someone else's affirmation would go a long way toward ending my nightmares.

Kila's eyes bore into mine, searching, searching. "I know."

The atmospheric alarm sounded—a welcome interruption. "Strap in." I led by example, seating myself in the nearest chair and fastening the restraint across my waist. The shoulder straps proved impossible without help. Kila drew the stretch bands down for me and snapped them into place, keeping things snug around my injury to minimize jolts. "Thank you," I told her, and tried to convey more than gratitude for her assistance with the restraints.

She smiled, and my heart lifted.

Sitting side by side, we watched the altimeter count down to zero, the braking thrusters pushing us against our seats. I gritted my teeth at the agony the pressure caused but didn't black out. We hit and bounced twice. No landing gear on something this small. The pod rolled on its side, then righted. We'd arrived on Lissex.

As I predicted, the pod's onboard scanners and sensors landed us on the largest of the inhabited islands, imaginatively named Paradise. Local time was midmorning, and the tropical sun beat down on us upon our emergence from the escape vessel.

The craft rested in a field of green plants bearing violet fruit that hung heavy off the stems. In the distance we could see the coastal village—one couldn't call it a city—of Wayfarer's Wharf, according to Kila. Sun glinted off metal rooftops, and pastels dominated the color scheme.

We walked in companionable silence toward the waterfront town. Kila tugged one of the globes off the vine and popped it into her mouth, then passed a couple to me. I bit through the purple skin, letting the sour juices quench hunger and thirst simultaneously. A rumble from my stomach reminded me we hadn't eaten since the previous evening, and I grabbed a few more of the ripe round fruits to consume on our journey.

By the time we reached Wayfarer's Wharf, the sun had climbed to its zenith. I sweated heavily in my jacket, and my hair clung to my forehead in wet strands. Kila showed signs of wear as well, with her heavy bag over her shoulder. I'd left mine back on the *Regiment 1*, but I'd pulled my best weapons from it before the fight with Alek and Vargas. Those were my only possessions that mattered.

Here in the village, we caught the breeze of Lissex's endless oceans, and the temperature grew cooler. Front porches with rocking chairs and swirling fans beckoned. Visitors and residents reclined on lounges, sipping tall drinks from glasses coated with condensation. I would have searched for an inn or rest house to recuperate for a night, but Kila caught my arm and guided me toward the docks.

We passed slip after slip housing the most beautiful seagoing vessels I'd ever seen. Granted, I'd spent a great deal of my life in the desert of Sardonen, but I'd traveled extensively and visited many worlds. These graceful, elegant boats with their flowing sails and traditional wooden hulls painted in bright colors drew my eye away from everything else. They evoked a festive air, a cheeriness in harmony with the sun, the warmth, and the pleasant chatter of locals strolling the boardwalk. It was easy to see how such a world produced someone like Kila.

I glanced sideways at her. She'd changed clothes before we left the pod, exchanging her brain-spattered top for an off-the-shoulder white blouse that left her midriff bare above the waistband of her skirt. Compared to the natives, she was pale, but she'd been off-world for some time. Her hair shone red and gold in the sunlight.

Kila noticed me staring and flashed a smile. I turned away quickly. My blush caught me by surprise, and I covered my discomfort with a cough.

My guide came to a halt at slip 179. The yacht docked there surpassed all others in its grandeur. The hull glowed cheerfully in a glorious yellow with aqua trim. Three masts rose from her polished light wood deck. Judging from the size, it had to contain several cabins, a mess, and who knew what else. Someone had painted *T'ral's Triumph* across the side, also in aqua, T'ral for her family name and Triumph for obvious reasons.

"What's it doing here?" I asked, wondering how many knew Kila's whereabouts and how they *could* know.

"It's mine. Right where I left it before heading off-world. This is the largest island with the largest population. The spaceport is located on the opposite side."

"Ah." My blood pressure lowered.

"All aboard!" she announced, swinging onto the deck by grasping a rigging line and giving a little jump.

I possessed plenty of athleticism, but with one good arm and a lack of familiarity, I looked awkward and unbalanced compared to her on that boat. I tried to gauge the motion, even as slight as it was here in dock, in order not to stagger while boarding. I almost managed the maneuver without a stutter-step. Hopefully I'd make a better show of it next time.

We passed through a wooden door, then down a short flight of stairs to the area below deck. Though everything was neat and orderly, the air here smelled stale and musty, and a thin layer of dust coated everything. Kila ran her hand over the paneled walls, the counters, the brass doorknobs leading into the cabins. The beatific smile on her face reminded me of someone greeting a long-lost friend or lover. I watched her caress each surface and a strange warmth flooded the pit of my stomach.

Shaking it off, I followed her to the forward-most compartment and stepped over a raised threshold. What met my eyes surprised me. I could have been on the bridge of a starship with the amount of technology this little room held. One chair dominated the center of the space, an interface panel embedded into its armrest.

"No crew?"

"Nope," she said, dropping her bag on the deck and seating herself. I moved to stand behind her. "The computer actually runs everything." She pressed her thumb to a scanner. The panel lit up in green. A screen on the forward bulkhead activated, showing the dock to the right and the ocean extending out to the horizon. "Take us home, *Triumph*."

"Aye, aye, Kila," an automated woman's voice responded through overhead speakers.

Hidden motors vibrated to life within the bowels of the yacht, and I heard the repetitive patter of underwater propellers. "It's not wind driven."

Kila shook her head. "Too unreliable. The sails are for show, though they can function in an emergency. Lissex loves its traditions, and we perpetuate them for the tourist trade, but in the early days, hundreds of ships and their crews were lost to the sea." She made some minor adjustments, setting our speed and turning on the stabilizers to counteract the motion of the waves.

I hid a sigh of relief. I'd traveled on many starships and had no tendency toward spacesickness, at least not anymore. Seasickness was something else entirely, and I had already shown far too many inadequacies on this journey.

"How long will the trip take?"

"We're a full day and a couple of hours out. Plenty of time for me to acquaint you with the pleasures of ocean travel." She grinned, and for a second I wondered if she had something in mind other than sun and sea.

I gave myself an internal kick. Kila was my employer, and I hoped she considered herself my friend. Anything beyond was more than I needed or wanted at this point in my likely-to-be-short life. I didn't even understand where the thoughts came from. My feelings about Kila blindsided me. While I appreciated attractiveness in both men and women, my partners to this point had all been male. That didn't mean I wasn't open to other options. Fate knew I'd had less than stellar success with men. But I was not experimenting with this sheltered, impressionable, very young girl of nineteen. Resolutely, I focused on our departure.

The journey would give me time to recuperate and rest. I would have preferred longer, but with her brother's coming-of-age ceremony approaching, we couldn't afford the luxury of dawdling.

I glanced at the viewscreen so I wouldn't have to look at Kila. The *Triumph* puttered its way to the edge of the inlet. The roar of the motors increased, and I felt the acceleration upon entering the open sea.

"Pleasure will have to wait," I told her. "There's something I need to fix first."

THE YACHT boasted an impressive little infirmary, tiny but well-stocked and the equipment first-rate. I rifled through a cabinet of vials until I came up with the appropriate local painkiller and injected myself just below the dislocated shoulder. The area around the injury went numb, though I knew it was temporary relief.

Scanning the room, I chose a bare patch of wood-paneled wall and stepped up to it. I took several deep breaths to steel myself.

"Cor, what—?"

Before Kila could intervene, I slammed my shoulder into the wall, forcing the joint back into place with a sickening wet pop. Even with the local anesthetic, the pain tore through me. The edges of my vision darkened and fragmented. My body swayed from more than the ocean's waves. Breathing steadily and evenly, I lowered myself to one knee so I'd have less distance to fall if I passed out. Kila assisted in getting me there, easing me down by my elbow.

"Are you truly insane?"

"I'll let… you know… in a minute." I put my head down below my bent knee and continued to breathe. The fog rolled in and out of my brain, then receded altogether. Cautious and tentative, I tested my arm's range of movement. It hurt like blazes but seemed to have good mobility. I rose, keeping one hand on the wall, just in case the blood rushed to my head. "Not insane," I said to Kila. "At least not yet."

"Can you walk?"

I nodded. I felt steady enough. In fact, I hadn't noticed much aching in the leg since we arrived on Lissex, despite the long hike. Even with the humidity, the warm climate no doubt helped.

Kila led me above deck, where the smell of the salt air assailed my nostrils, and the wind whipped my hair around my face so hard it stung my cheeks. I pulled a hair tie from my jacket pocket and made a tail of the dark strands. Overhead, the metal fasteners holding the furled sails in place clanged like bells against the mast or boom or whatever seafaring people called it. I scanned the sea in all directions. Behind, I could make out the hazy outline of Paradise, receding with every second. To the sides and in front, there was only open water, waves cresting with whitecaps and not another ship or landmass in sight.

Though I'd never told anyone, space travel made me a bit nervous—trapped on a ship in the middle of nowhere, with an unfamiliar crew and passengers. This was completely different, calming and peaceful. This kind of isolation felt safe.

"You can stow the jacket here." Kila pointed to a wooden box attached to the decking. She drew out a pair of heavy body-length towels and, with some difficulty from the breeze, managed to spread them out flat. Little weights attached to the corners kept them there.

I put my hands on my hips. "You aren't serious." After all we'd been through and still had ahead of us, she wanted to sunbathe?

She giggled, actually giggled. "Completely." Placing her hands on her own hips, she did a fair impression of my stance and mimicked my voice. "I'm in charge. I'm the captain of this vessel, and I order you to dump the jacket and the weapons in the locker and relax for a few hours." She dropped my persona with a laugh. "Besides, the heat will help keep your shoulder from stiffening up again."

Good point. I stripped off the jacket and my side holster and pistol and tossed them into the box along with my belt knife. I reached between my shoulder blades before remembering my back holster and spare gun were lost aboard the *Regiment 1*. After removing my boots, I placed them up against the cabin as far from the spray as possible. I tucked my socks inside them.

I seated myself on the towel, rolled my pants to my knees, and tucked the sleeves of my T-shirt under my bra straps. I tugged the material from the waistband of my slacks and curled it under the bottom of the bra, exposing my abdomen to the warm sun.

Kila lay down, her skirt around her thighs and her eyes closed. She began humming that nameless tune, its melody familiar to me by now. The song held no particular rhythm and yet kept time with the gentle rocking of the boat and the thrum of the vessel's engine.

I reclined, sighed, and drifted with the waves. Aches and pains faded with each successive verse of Kila's tune. The sound of her voice lulled me into a dreamlike state. It was more peace than I'd felt in a lifetime.

NIGHTMARES OF Micah's death startled me awake, dispelling the peace I'd finally achieved, and I focused on regulating my breathing before opening my eyes. I lay facedown, my cheek rubbing the thick white towel. I didn't remember rolling over but thanked fate I had. The formidable Lissex sun could no doubt burn with prolonged exposure, and I had no idea where Kila stored the sunblock.

That sun had set, and judging from the height of the three-quarter moon, the hour was quite late. The *Triumph*'s computer lit the yacht with soft incandescent lamps strung around the topside cabin. The effect gave it a celebratory air, and I could picture well-dressed citizens strolling the deck, sipping drinks, while whatever music the upper class currently favored played softly in the background.

I faced Kila, watching her sleep. Her parted lips and the complete relaxation in her expression erased years from her. Again I fought down seething rage over what she'd endured at her brother's hands.

My stomach growled. I stood and padded barefoot to the door leading inside. The supplies in the galley consisted of instameals and a preparation unit, though there was empty storage for fresh produce and other goods. I heated a vegetarian casserole and carried it to the bridge.

"Greetings, guest." The automated voice startled me, and I fumbled but caught my fork. "How may I assist you?" The viewscreen lit up, showing a moonlit ocean and millions of stars.

I sank into the cushioned central chair. "ETA to home port?" I mumbled around a mouthful of food. The flavors tasted unfamiliar but pleasant, with a touch of spiciness that tingled on my tongue and made me wish I'd grabbed a drink as well.

"Eighteen hours, nine minutes at current speed."

I munched another bite and swallowed. "Any vessels nearby?" So much for my peaceful state. Once paranoid, always paranoid.

"One commercial vessel, the *Louise*, seven leagues astern."

Okay, I knew astern meant behind us. Spaceship terminology borrowed heavily from nautical terms. And a league was pretty far, though I wasn't familiar with exact calculations of distances at sea. Seven of them sounded like we had the area to ourselves. "Thanks. Nothing further."

The screen went dark.

I finished my meal and tapped my fingers on the armrest. Like space travel, ocean travel could be boring. My arm swung down by my side and brushed something made of fabric—Kila's bag. Without looking, I felt my way inside and touched the cover of the Generational.

Slowly, I drew the large volume into my hands and rested it on my lap. The script on its cover, embossed in gold, was faded so much as to be almost illegible. I hesitated. Assassins might share sleeping and eating quarters, but they respected privacy. I did not want to alienate Kila by invading hers. But maybe a glimpse into her religious beliefs would help me analyze her unusual words and confusing gestures toward me. Maybe the book contained a commandment instructing believers to treat all others as potential lovers.

I opened the book and very carefully turned to random pages. She'd never forgive me if I damaged the sacred tome. The paper felt brittle, and some sections had detached from the binding, though none appeared out of order. Inside, the writing remained clear and dark enough to read, although the arcane form of our Standard language caused me to pause and review numerous passages to grasp their meanings. Ornate hand-drawn pictures amazed me with their detail and beauty. One in particular, a temple with a domed roof and sculpted exterior columns, caught my attention and held it. Light flared from its oval windows, casting beams across the page to each of the four corners. It apparently appealed to Kila as well. The binding showed more creasing here than in other parts of the Generational, and she'd left a small plastic chip between the pages to mark this place. "And the Giver of Life shall return to the sacred temple where He shall disseminate His gifts to the worthy, the innocent, and the pure, and He shall be protected by an army of steadfast warriors granted leave to take life on His behalf. His army shall defend Him in eternal strife against the ephemeral minions of the bringer of death."

Interesting. And completely meaningless out of context.

At least I could relate to the whole bringer of death part, but ephemeral minions?

I snorted and turned to the front and back of the book. Of course, it didn't contain a glossary or table of contents. If one were reading this text, it was assumed one should know its organization and precepts.

I looked for other thin plastic place markers and found one toward the front. Scanning, I located a passage on the page, more worn than others, as if someone traced her finger across it, time and time again. "At the turn of the second decade, He shall come of age, and His Gifts be granted in full by the true Powers. He of the line is both blessed and cursed."

Uh-huh. My mind shifted the words, but without further perusal, I couldn't form meanings. Maybe I could find some way to ask Kila about it, though why I cared, I couldn't fathom. What mattered to her mattered to me now too. In a way, she'd become my new Guild.

I reached to replace the book where I'd found it, but gentle hands pulled it from my grasp.

CHAPTER 12

"THANK YOU," Kila said. Her tone implied gratitude for more than the return of the book. Her mouth formed an amused smile. Her eyes crinkled at the corners.

"You're not angry?"

Kila's eyebrows rose. "For caring enough about me to be curious?" She placed a gentle hand on my shoulder, and the skin beneath my shirt heated.

"Oh." Interesting perspective. I would have been angry.

Kila put away the book, turned, and left the bridge.

I spent the rest of the night and early morning flat on my back in a bunk in one of the guest cabins. Sleep eluded me, no matter how hard I tried to recapture it. I counted the slats in the ceiling overhead, actually the underside of the above deck. Forty-eight slats. I double-checked.

The decor of the cabin suited the warm climate—lots of pastels in the furnishings and frills on the curtains over the porthole. It was a girly room, with a mirrored dresser and a settee for applying makeup.

It was all alien to me.

In the adjacent bath, I'd opened each of the delicate glass containers on the sideboard, trying to identify soap. I selected the one that smelled the least flowery. For all I knew, I'd rubbed mouthwash over my hands.

What would my life have been like if I'd grown up a normal girl in an average family? Would the violent tendencies have surfaced if I hadn't been a slave?

I didn't understand Kila. I certainly wouldn't want to suffer the negative aspects of her life. But part of me envied her.

And I couldn't get her out of my mind.

Dawn broke over the ocean's surface, and the glow outside the porthole turned a pinkish orange. I found myself gripping the sides of the bed frame, just to keep myself from going to her cabin.

Something needed to give in the tension between us. Otherwise the distraction would get me killed.

"IT'S TIME you told me what the plan is." I seated myself opposite Kila in the yacht's galley. The long wooden table would have held at least six. She took an empty plate and scooped rehydrated fruits and breads on it, then passed it to me. My long shower worked wonders. I hardly noticed her delicate fingers or the way her off-the-shoulder top exposed the skin around her neck. Fates save me. This was worse than I'd been as a teenager around Micah.

She didn't meet my eyes, and I got a sinking feeling. Whatever her plan, Kila didn't expect me to like it.

"I think—" She paused, cleared her throat, and started again. "I think I'll tell my family that you are my consort."

I covered my mouth with my hand and stared at the table. The silence dragged out between us. The first chuckle surprised me. It grew to genuine laughter, and soon I had tears rolling down my cheeks from my mirth.

Everything made perfect sense now. This plan had been in her head since we left Deluge. Her touches and gestures? All part of a performance. Whether conscious or unconscious, she'd been preparing for my introduction to her relatives and my reason for being on her estate.

Relief flooded me, dampened only by a touch of disappointment I quickly smothered with a bite into my bread roll. Once I managed to control myself, I looked up and signaled with a wave for her to continue. My hand froze midgesture. Her stricken expression tore at my soul.

Maybe I'd hurt her feelings, finding so much humor in her plan.

Or maybe my hypothesis was wrong.

Kila pushed away from the table and left the room. I heard her cabin door slam. The sound echoed along the short hallway.

With nothing to do but wait for her to calm down, I returned to my own cabin. I paced to the wall and back, trying to relieve the frustration. We couldn't afford this crap. In a few hours, we would dock at her family's island. Private security would ask questions that needed answers. Assassins didn't work undercover, at least not this one. I hunted my targets and killed them. My acting ability sucked.

Another long shower helped. The boat had a top-of-the-line system with plenty of pressure and hot water. I let it pour over me, luxuriating in its warmth, washing my anger down the drain.

When I emerged, I found a smart-pack on my bed. That explained how Kila managed to store so much in her single shoulder bag even with its large size. Lifting it in my hands, I let my finger run along its airtight seal. It released, and the neatly folded and compressed clothing within it burst a little through the open seam.

I removed a skirt and blouse in blue and green jewel tones and shook them out over the bed. My size. Wonderful.

When I donned the outfit, the transformation stunned me. I stared at my reflection in the mirror, marveling at how much feminine clothing softened me. The green skirt hung in a circled flare halfway between knees and ankles. The shirt hugged my curves and enhanced my breasts. A bejeweled headband drew my hair away from my face, accenting my cheekbones and high forehead. A keen observer would detect the hardness, the wear and tear in the shadows beneath my eyes, but it would no longer be the first thing someone noticed.

It would never convince me to "go girlie." For one thing, I couldn't strap on a holster to carry a pistol. Well, a thigh holster would work, I supposed, but I didn't have one, and the single blade in my boot didn't comfort enough. Secondly, I *liked* my hardened, intimidating appearance. I needed it.

I twirled once, watching the skirt whirl around me and feeling silly even as a smile crossed my face.

This was a nice temporary change, though.

Judging from the open admiration on Kila's face when I found her in the galley, she liked it too. She made no reference to our earlier topic of conversation, and I didn't bring it up.

"Sit!" she ordered me.

I obeyed with a raised eyebrow, and she took a small case off the counter behind her. When she opened it, I leaned as far away from her as I could in the confining chair. "Oh no you don't," I warned.

Weapons drawn, she came at me, prepared to leave marks. I would have slid the seat back, but iron fasteners bolted it to the deck.

She had me. At the first touch, I wrinkled my face in disgust. The makeup felt wet and sticky and smelled funny.

"Quit scrunching like that. You're making this harder. I'll mess up." Kila finished slathering beige crap on my cheeks, forehead, nose, and chin. She put one brush away and grabbed another.

"It's all a *mess up*," I grumbled, my words garbled while I tried to hold my mouth still.

She finished lips and eyes, and I grabbed a mirror from her kit.

I hardly recognized my reflection. The last time I'd studied myself this thoroughly, I'd been gaunt and pale, drunk and hooked on palotrin. Now my exposure to the Lissex sun had returned the tan I'd lost when I left Sardonen. Even living and working in the caverns there, Guild members couldn't avoid the intense sunlight of the desert world entirely. I didn't realize until now how much I'd missed the healthier look.... Kila's artistry brought out my eyes, hid minor imperfections and a few early lines around my mouth, and subtracted another couple of years. I analyzed her appearance more closely. Her personal makeup choices added to her maturity. By doing so, she'd narrowed the apparent age gap between us, making us appear more like contemporaries.

"Just one more thing."

I opened my mouth to protest, but she caught my hand and extended my arm out straight. Rolling up my sleeve, she revealed the Guild brand. To this, she applied a generous amount of beige cover until the marks vanished beneath the goop.

"Just in case." Kila patted my shoulder.

Strange emotions flooded me. Officially, I hadn't belonged to the Guild in months, but the brand signified so much more. On assignments, I wore long sleeves or jackets, which had the benefit of preventing unnecessary identification and unwanted questions and kept me from scaring every stranger I met. But in general, I wasn't *trying* to hide. Intentionally covering the symbols felt, well, wrong, and very final in a way I couldn't define. To my immense embarrassment and surprise, my eyes filled with tears.

Kila continued to admire her artistry, scanning from my wrist up to my face. We locked gazes. For the first time, I felt no need to hide my emotions from someone, and it was like she could read my thoughts. "Oh!" Her smile faded, and she caught me up in a hug. We stayed that way for several seconds before she pulled back and met my eyes again. Her serious expression had all my attention. "I'm sorry, Cor. I didn't think how this might affect you, especially that." She inclined her head toward my wrist.

"It's the smart thing to do." More dependable than jewelry or even long sleeves. My voice came out hoarse. I cursed myself silently.

"I'm not trying to change you. I just want to protect you."

That brought a snort from me. No one protected me. Well, no one since Micah, and even he failed that test in the end, choosing his reputation over my exoneration. "I thought that was *my* job. You've got it backward."

"Arriving at destination." The boat's computer voice sounded through the internal speaker system and interrupted the awkwardness. Standing, I skirted around Kila. "Welcome to Triumph!" I fought not to roll my eyes and failed. They named the boat after the T'ral family island. Like it or not, the plan was in progress.

Topside, I noticed the large volume of boats, yachts, and merchant ships in dock. Though we still floated well off shore, I could see the dozens, if not hundreds, of flags in a rainbow of colors flying atop the masts in the glow of the late-afternoon sun.

Triumph didn't look to be a very large island. I could discern the curve of the shoreline even at this close distance. Unless it extended directly away from us, thus hiding length, it was actually a pretty small place.

Our computerized captain cut the engines to one-quarter power, then further as it delicately maneuvered our vessel in and among the others. Closer in, it appeared boats filled every slip of the long wooden dock. Some ships anchored themselves in the calm bay, ferrying in crew and passengers via rowboats that lined a strip of beach near the working docks. Family vessels took priority, though. One last empty space awaited us at the end of the wharf closest to the sprawling village and affording the shortest walking distance.

As we docked, underwater lines extending automatically to connect with receiving ports on shore, I noticed the crowded streets of traditional cobblestone. In some places people had to turn sideways in order to pass one another.

"Is it always like this?" I turned to Kila. She stared out at the scene, a frown pulling at her lips and concern in her eyes.

"No. This is at least five times our normal population." Graceful as ever, she snagged her bag and hopped over the side onto the boardwalk. "They're here for my brother's inheritance ceremony." Her tone sounded low and flat.

I swung a borrowed carry sack containing my weapons over my shoulder and followed. She trudged ahead, almost stomping in her anger, brushing between shoppers and tourists with no regard for their complaints at her brusqueness. I spotted different sorts as well, military types, mercenaries, and a number of unsavory characters, all of them incongruous in this sun-kissed vacation destination. Even stranger, many carried modern copies of the Generational religious text. Some were plastic-sheeted hard copies with the name emblazoned on the covers in garish gold. Others held smaller digital versions, but I could still read the title on their cases. Kila shoved between them, oblivious to all while I nodded, smiled, and mumbled apologies. Even disguised in my current costume, the last thing I wanted was to draw attention to myself.

I suppose I couldn't blame Kila for her frustration. Celebratory banners hung in doorways and from second-floor balconies, all bearing the T'ral family colors of yellow and teal. Her brother raped her, and the town was throwing him a party.

Best to let it get out of her system before we reached the mansion rising above the smaller structures at the edge of town. No one bothered with aircars in a community this small, and the little seaside village seemed to cultivate quaintness and a lack of technology as an affectation for visitors, so I trudged after her, heading for her family home.

CHAPTER 13

THE PROSPECT of meeting Lord and Lady T'ral made me as nervous as if I really were Kila's consort seeking their approval. Maybe more so, since completing my assignment depended on them accepting me in the household.

Getting past the security contingent at the gate provided the first obstacle. No fewer than six guards flanked the wrought-iron bars surrounding the three-story mansion. Their teal uniforms with yellow trim gave them an almost clown-like appearance, but their piercing eyes and professional demeanor discouraged any antics.

I presented one of my many false identification chips. When inserted into their netreader, it would bring up a headshot and my name—Corianne *Enara* from Deluge—along with the address of my below-street-level apartment. Kila introduced me as a *friend*, slipping her hand in mine with such comfortable ease I blinked twice before smiling. Her grip felt warm. My own palm sweated, and I resisted the urge to pull away and wipe it on my clothing.

Her small gesture warmed the head guard's attitude. His sun-weathered craggy face cracked a grin as he looked from Kila to me and back again. "Good to have you home, Mistress." He nodded to me. "And nice to see you with someone."

"Thank you, Willen." Kila stood on tiptoe to plant a quick kiss on the guard's cheek.

The older man flushed an impressive shade of red, and his smile broadened. He winked. Swinging out an arm, he indicated the other five sentries. "I must say, some of these lowlifes had a pool going on whether you would Bond at all."

I glanced at Kila, raising an eyebrow. Her cheeks turned as pink as the guard's. She managed an embarrassed giggle. "No one's Bonding with anyone *yet*." The slight emphasis on the last word made my breath catch, and I swallowed hard.

Willen stepped back, examining me from head to foot and resting his gaze on my face. His gray-blue eyes searched mine for several long moments, and my muscles tensed, thinking I'd been found out. Then he smiled, nodded with approval, and waved us through the gate.

Halfway up the front-walk stepping stones, a row of tall bushes obscured us from the sentries' view. I took the opportunity to drop my hand from Kila's, though she seemed reluctant to let go. Not wanting to offend her, I smoothed the wrinkles from my long skirt as an excuse. "What's all this about Bonding? You're only nineteen."

"Practically an old maid on Lissex. Average marriage age is seventeen. I'm almost twenty." That thought sobered her.

Right. Twenty. And her brother as well.

Instead of ringing the classic brass announcement bell hanging from a post outside the entry, Kila placed her palm against the lock panel. The massive wooden door swung open without a sound, but a uniformed butler stood just inside. Archaic decor and accouterments, but the T'rals employed modern-day technology and security cameras. I scanned the bushes and the exterior of the house, spotting nothing. Good equipment if I couldn't see it.

"You've been announced" was all the butler said, but Kila thanked him anyway. Despite the pomp and circumstance, wealth and privilege, Kila treated everyone we met with respect and friendliness.

I followed her to a set of dark wood double doors that slid into wall pockets as we approached. Years of stress-control training fled as I faced the individuals seated in stiff-backed chairs behind those sliding panels. My heart rate picked up. Kila greeted her parents and said my name, but my lips couldn't form words. The smile I managed felt forced and unnatural.

Lord T'ral stood and circled me, a frown deepening the lines on his face. He smoothed the strands of his neatly cropped gray hair with the palm of his hand. "Does she talk?"

Ah, he'd kept all the pretentiousness for himself. My nervousness left as fast as it came. I was here to kill this man's rapist son, a son he would support over Kila, despite those horrible acts. I found my voice. "Yes, she does," I answered, keeping the tone friendly to lighten my not-so-subtle rebuke.

A grilling worthy of military interrogators followed, questions about my family and upbringing, financial status, and age. Years of mingling with lawbreakers taught me plenty about responding. Give truths whenever possible and lie only when necessary to minimize my chances of getting caught in those lies.

"I assume you are a Believer?" Lord T'ral bowed his head on the last word.

Kila's sharp look alerted me to tread with care, but I didn't need the warning. Religion clearly meant a great deal to this family, and I had prepared the answer to this question. "I admit I was unfamiliar with your beliefs before meeting Kila. However, her deep devotion has prompted me to begin reading the Generational." True enough. Her father's frown evaporated as he nodded acceptance.

Throughout the session, Lady T'ral said nothing, but I watched her appraising Kila. The woman seemed weary, worn into submission, but she smiled at her daughter and rose to take my hand briefly before my dismissal.

In the hallway again, I paced in front of those now closed doors, listening to voices as they rose and fell—Lord T'ral's demanding, angry, and sharp; Kila's strong, logical, and adamant.

When Kila emerged, she nodded once and left it at that. Her struggle with her father had drained her of all energy, and her shoulders slumped as I followed her up a wide, winding wood staircase. I hurried to catch her, taking her hand in mine. She clearly needed a little space, but we had an illusion to maintain, and she managed a smile for me.

A long hall at the top of the stairs went left and right. To the left, a pair of guards flanked a door at the end of the corridor. Kila stared at them a long moment. Then she turned right and entered a cheerful suite in blues and whites with a sunny view overlooking the bay in the distance and the town below.

At first I thought this was a guest room, but the personal touches— holos of Kila sailing with friends, riding some kind of six-legged animal, and a couple of formal portraits—identified the space as hers. A couch and table rested in the foreground, with a double bed and a door leading to the bath at the rear. A kaleidoscope of colored pillows covered the bed, and my host threw herself facedown among them, scattering some to the deep blue carpeting.

"I take it I'm allowed to stay?" I asked, pulling her bag from her and laying it on the couch with my borrowed one beside it. I seated myself next to her on the bed and let one hand rest on her back. Her breath made her spine rise and fall under my touch. I felt her heart beating, faster than I thought normal.

"Mm-hmm."

"What's with the security in the hall?"

Kila rolled without warning, and my hand brushed her left breast through her blouse before I got out of her way. If she noticed, she didn't comment, but heat ran from my fingertips to my shoulder and down into my own chest. I drew air in and let it out slowly. This girl would be the death of me yet.

"That's my brother's room." She sighed.

"Your brother has armed guards?" My assignment just became a whole lot more difficult.

Kila groaned. "He didn't when I left."

"Right." I thought through my options. "When would be a good time for me to go into town on a *shopping* trip? I'll need extra equipment if I'm going to pull this off." I glanced down, suddenly uncomfortable. "And credits. My account is pretty dry." My discomfort confused me. Kila hired me. She would expect to cover my expenses and pay a hefty fee beyond. Friends or not, I didn't work for free. But after all we'd been through, it felt strange asking her for payment. Usually we settled all this with our clients well beforehand. In the quiet moments we'd had, my mind had been on other things, things it shouldn't have.

She seemed to sense my awkwardness. Moving to her dresser, she opened a compartment to reveal a computer built into the piece of furniture. She entered several codes on a keypad, then spoke quietly into a voice pickup. A moment later, a slot expelled a small credit chit. Kila handed it to me. "This should take care of the finances, but let me know if you require more."

I examined it. Standard-issue, no personal signatures. Dangerous to leave lying around since anyone who picked it up could use it. Safe for me. Unless a person had significant technological know-how, it would never be traced back to either Kila or myself. I slipped it in the pocket of my borrowed skirt.

"Tomorrow morning would be the best time," she added. "But finding what you need might be difficult on Triumph. We're a fishing village and a tourist destination. Sun, beaches, not weapons." She stood and crossed to her bag, slipped the Generational out and placed it on the table by the couch. Her movements jerked like a robot's while she put away her few other belongings in a cabinet and chest of drawers.

"Weapons, I have," I said, indicating my own carry sack. "But I can't exactly walk down the hall, sweet-talk my way past the guards, and stroll in to kill your brother. I'll need to do it from the exterior. I assume he has a window like yours?"

Kila looked out at the expansive panorama. "A bigger one. Double panes opening inward, and a cushioned window seat inside."

"And electronic security? Surveillance systems? I know you have a camera on the front door. That butler was waiting for us."

"My family believes in human protection, not machines. The front is on camera for efficiency, not security."

I snorted at her disdain. "Perfect. Good and fallible." The window wouldn't have been my first choice, but at least I wasn't contending with computer-monitored alarms. "Don't worry," I told her, rising to stand at her side. "I'm trained to improvise. Besides, I have a couple of thoughts on where I can get what I need." I put an arm around her shoulders, then withdrew when she stiffened. Her sudden aversion to my presence surprised me, but I attributed it to guilt and nerves. This wasn't some stranger or neighbor I was killing. It was her brother. And family bonds ran deep, regardless of a sibling's behavior. As an only child—as far as I knew—I needed to remember that.

"Just make certain you return in time for the ceremonial dinner."

"The what?"

The wicked gleam in Kila's eye assured me she'd regained her good humor. "Don't worry. I'll take care of your attire."

I SPENT a restless night on the too firm couch with a couple of neon-pink throw pillows under my head. In the darkness, the house creaked and groaned with each gust of wind off the bay, and I wondered how many generations of her family had lived here. Kila left the window open, and the smell of salt air carried on the breeze. Desert-raised as I was, the ocean attracted me as any novelty would, and I strained my ears to hear each lapping wave against the village docks.

The moonlight shining through the shutters lit the entire suite in shades of bluish white. Kila's shadowy form tossed and turned on her wide mattress, and I resisted the urge to go to her and offer comfort from her nightmares. After all, there was a good chance my upcoming mission here caused them. She might reject or resent my concern. At last she settled and snored lightly in a most endearing manner.

I strangled in my own needs, inner voices of reason and desire arguing among themselves until I wanted to shout them down regardless of waking the household. What in all religions' hells was I thinking, anyway? Suppose Kila did want me, with all my violent traits and psychological failings. Suppose I slipped into bed beside her right now. What then? I came to do a job. Though I didn't intend to be seen or get caught, once that job ended, I couldn't exactly take off with the girl in tow. She didn't deserve a life of running with me, hiding from the Guild's punishments.

And I certainly couldn't stay on Lissex.

Could I?

For years, I belonged to the Guild. They provided a sense of family and stability. I needed that, wanted that, and hadn't had it since I'd left. Lord and Lady T'ral might accept me if I proved myself to them. It was just another type of trial, not so unlike those the Guild subjected me to. Less painful, less physical, but no less challenging.

I stood and paced in the darkness, bare feet sinking into plush carpeting. I'd lost my mind. I couldn't stay here. Kila wouldn't want me after I killed her brother, no matter how much relief that act gave her. I'd still be a painful memory. And what if the Guild found me here? They'd out me as an assassin, make it obvious I was the one who killed her brother. They'd ignore Kila. They didn't harm innocents. But she'd watch them hunt and capture me, perhaps kill me before they could haul me back to the underground fortress to execute me there. I didn't want her to see that.

Throwing myself on the couch again, I buried my face in the pink pillows and covered my head with my arms.

I rose with the dawn. Brief rummaging in Kila's closet produced a long-sleeved blouse that fit and didn't clash with the only skirt I owned. In the lavatory, I did a passable job of recreating Kila's makeup masterpiece. Then I slipped out the door and closed it behind me.

I nodded to the guards, different ones from the night before. At some point, I'd missed a shift change. These acted friendlier, returning my nod and cracking knowing grins over the steaming cups they held. It gave me a chance to check out their weaponry—high-quality stun pistols in thigh holsters and shock sticks in their belts.

No one stopped me when I left the house, though the gate security asked after my destination.

"Shopping for the young lord's birthday," I told him, flashing a smile.

"Ah." The older guard nodded. "He appreciates woven art and classic Hibrin music."

Whatever that was. I thanked him for his suggestions and flounced out the gate, even giving my long hair a toss for good measure. Adding a little more hip sway than usual to my walk, I made my way down the path and caught more than one whistle from the other guards on duty.

That changed once I turned between two buildings and lost myself in their cover. I ducked into an alley and double-checked the pistol I wore under my full skirt. A few extra tightening holes, added with my knife, turned my belt holster into an adequate thigh holster. It would take some doing to reach the weapon, but I felt better knowing I had it with me. The blades in each of my boots pressed against my ankles in a comforting manner.

I headed away from touristy areas, keeping to backstreets and alleyways. If a seedy side to Triumph existed, my knack for locating trouble would find it.

Well out of view of the ocean, I located a boarding house, run-down and shabby. Several large men lounged on the rickety porch, drinking ale from chipped mugs and exchanging bawdy jokes. The subject matter shifted when they spotted me, and I became the topic of conversation while they vocally pondered what I charged and which positions I preferred.

"I'm more interested in acquiring some climbing gear, wall exterior, stone and wood." I'd bet my Guild training these men were mercs. What they wanted here, I had no idea. I guess even hired guns needed vacations. Identification of my intended target didn't concern me. Every building on the island of Triumph appeared to be made of stone and wood. I stepped through a swinging gate that hung by one hinge and stood at the foot of the porch.

Derisive laughter met my request, and I flushed with anger before remembering my costume. "Hasn't your sergeant taught you not to judge by appearances?"

The largest of the men, round-faced with red hair, stuck a thumb in his chest. "*I* am the sergeant." He burped a curse at me, and the odor of stale brew carried the meter between us. The others laughed and speculated on whether I could handle all three of them in bed at one time.

I'm not sure what possessed me at that moment. I hadn't slept well, my sexual frustration levels neared an all-time high, and for a change, my leg and shoulder weren't bothering me in the slightest. I also hadn't had a drink in a couple of days, which made me edgy. In short, I was itching for a good fight, and if that earned their respect, maybe I could accomplish other goals. "I'll tell you what, I take you out, you sell me what I need." My stance indicated I wasn't referring to escorting them on a date.

Their expressions shifted from amusement to surprise to disbelief. The sergeant got up and swaggered to my side. He swayed where he stood, the alcohol getting the better of his balance and judgment.

"Come on, pretty girl. Don't fight. There's better things to do with all that energy." He laid one paw on my shoulder.

Big mistake.

I grabbed his arm with both my hands and wrenched it behind his back. Something snapped, and he howled with pain, then tumbled forward, staggering on the uneven walkway and hitting the ground on his knees. His buddies hooted with laughter.

"Don't just sit there!" The sergeant's command brought the others to their feet.

This was getting interesting.

The pair of younger mercs hopped the porch railing, flanking me on either side. I kept them in my peripheral vision, while I watched their leader stand once more. Scanning them for weapons, I spotted a couple of knife hilts but no guns. Didn't mean they weren't packing them under jackets, but those would take more effort to reach. As long as they didn't pull anything, I planned to remain unarmed as well. Fighting with honor produced fewer conscience problems.

Women were generally born with less strength and muscle, but I made up for it with greater agility and quickness than my male opponents. When one of the mercs charged me, I dodged him, letting the man plow into his comrade on my opposite side. They crashed against the fence, uprooting several posts from the sandy earth and snapping others at their bases. The impact drove splinters into bare arms and faces, and one merc shouted in pain. When his head swiveled toward me, I spotted a shard of wood protruding from beneath his right eye, and blood streamed over his cheek. His buddy tried to remove it and received a scream for his efforts.

I used the distraction to seize a fence post and club the uninjured merc over the head with it. He dropped to the ground, unconscious.

"If your squad medic is on the property, he can probably save the eye," I offered, always helpful. The half-blind soldier clambered to his feet and half walked, half crawled up the steps into the rooming house.

The sergeant watched the man abandon him, then cursed me in at least three languages, two of which I understood. Something about my privates, my father's parentage, and a piece of rotting meat. I appreciated his creativity and smiled in response, which seemed to unnerve him. He shifted his weight from one foot to the other, shooting quick glances at the inn's closed door.

"He'll need surgery. No one's coming back anytime soon." My words caught his full attention. "How about I give you a list of things I want and we go see your supply master?"

Out came the knife. He turned the long wicked-looking blade from side to side, letting the steel catch the sunlight. Its polished metal would have blinded me with the glare if I'd stared directly at it.

I let out a dramatic sigh. So much for my nice, tension-relieving yard brawl. A few bruises I could live with and hide. If this was going to be an all-out knife fight, it had become more than I could risk while residing in Kila's house.

I reached down and pulled up my skirt to reveal well-formed calves. Not what the sergeant expected. His eyebrows rose, though he didn't stop brandishing the knife. While his thoughts wandered higher, I drew my own blades from my boots so I gripped one in each hand.

I took a quick glance around the property. One of the wooden porch support beams sported a knothole in its white-painted surface. I pointed the tip of one blade at it. "See that dark spot?"

The merc turned sideways a fraction so he could see where I indicated and still keep an eye on me. Scrunching up his face, he squinted at the pillar. "What of it?"

I drew back and threw the knife from my right hand. It flew in a blur of motion, end over end, landing its point in the center of the tiny knot. The hilt twanged, quivering where it extended from the weathered wood. The merc gaped at the feat. I breathed an inner sigh of relief. I excelled with throwing weapons, but weeks had passed since my last target practice.

Raising the second knife, I faced him. "Next one between your eyes."

The sergeant's blade dropped to land with a dull thud in the dead grass and sand at his feet. He extended his arms, palms outward in surrender.

"I'd like to buy some climbing gear for wood and stone," I said, addressing him as I would any shopkeeper or merchant behind a counter.

"Who are you? A thief?"

"What's available, and how much will you charge?" My real identity would remain secret. He had my physical description, of course, but all of us in the shadow professions tended to keep quiet about one another. Sort of a professional courtesy between loosely connected comrades. Which made Captain Derrick Vargas's betrayal even more painful. My stomach clenched at the memory. My smile hardened.

The sergeant grunted in response. "Let me check in with my supplier."

An hour later I had everything I needed, or thought I might need, tucked into a large carry sack I'd also procured from the mercs.

I went from the boarding house to the tourist district—quaint inns, an inviting pub, a few outdoor eateries, and a row of shops selling homemade arts and crafts. The open doors of the alehouse beckoned. The sun hung high overhead, beating down and making sweat bead on my forehead. The bag of gear weighed heavily on my shoulder. I could hear clinking glassware and jovial conversation inside the pub, and a cool drink would have gone down nicely. It took great effort to turn away.

Between buildings, in a side alley, I spotted three men hunched together in the shadows. They haggled for a few moments, then exchanged credits for something small and reflective. A duraglass vial.

Despite the heat, I shivered. Cold sweat replaced the hot sheen on my skin. I closed my hand around the anonymous credit chit in my skirt pocket, then turned the plastic over and over between my fingertips.

I had no way of knowing if the dealer was selling palotrin, but whatever was in that vial, my body wanted it.

I felt no pain. Except for occasional aches, the leg and arm had given me little trouble in recent days. Didn't matter. The draw of the drug pulled at me, urging me to step away from the side of the building I leaned on and walk into that alley. My arms and legs trembled with need—nothing violent, but annoying and anticipatory. I'd been naive in the extreme to think I'd conquered a growing addiction so easily.

My gaze darted up and down the thoroughfare, searching for any kind of distraction. Some of the shoppers cast concerned looks in my direction. One older well-dressed gentleman asked if I needed help, but I managed a faint smile and waved him away. As he left, I spotted a more modern copy of the Generational tucked under one arm.

At last I noticed a sign advertising blankets and wall hangings, just the thing the gate guard suggested Kila's brother might like for his birthday, and I couldn't return from my supposed shopping trip without some sort of gift.

I thrust myself away from the wall with a shove of pure will. After crossing the street on jerky limbs, I pushed through a swinging door and set off a set of tinkling bells. Inside, fans circulated the ocean air, drying the sweat and cooling my body temperature by degrees. It took me a long moment of closed eyes and deep breaths standing in that doorway before I moved another centimeter. When I felt I'd regained control, I raised my eyelids.

Rows of racks held a veritable rainbow of woven artwork. Some consisted of colored patterns in primaries or pastels while others had been threaded into very realistic depictions of seascapes, starfields, and local wildlife. I spotted one of the type of beast Kila had ridden in that holo in her room. Another displayed a field of the purple fruits we'd consumed on our journey. Everything reminded me of her and made it harder to think about the drug dealers in the alley. I released the breath I'd held and set about selecting something for her brother.

In the end, I purchased two pieces—an abstract weaving of sunset colors for the young lord and a patchwork of pastels for Kila. After all, as twins, it was her birthday as well. She'd been left out quite enough in this monarchy.

When the elderly woman shopkeeper rang up my purchases, I caught a quick glimpse of the balance remaining on the chit. It took some effort not to gape at her screen and choke on the small mint I'd selected from a bowl of complimentary hard candies. Kila had transferred thousands of credits in the standard currency onto the small piece of plastic. It covered my expenses, the as-of-yet-incomplete assassination, and a generous bonus besides.

If I fretted over her trust in me and my ability to complete this assignment, this laid all my worries to rest.

I headed back toward the T'ral home, but singing and chanting drew me to a domed structure on the outskirts of town.

The wooden temple boasted fieldstone finishings, though the materials seemed wrong somehow. Granite or marble would have been more appropriate for such an ornate building, with its carved exterior curlicues and intricate patterns.

Despite my distrust of religions, curiosity pulled me to the heavy wooden double doors. I cracked one open, wincing as it creaked, but none of the hundred or so seated within seemed to hear it over the hymns.

At first, the parishioners appeared as no more than huddled shadows, but as my eyes adjusted to the dimmer lighting, I discerned more detail. The templegoers knelt upon colorful pillows scattered about the wood floor, facing an altar at the far end. The seating had no particular order, no rows or plan. They seemed to drop wherever they felt comfortable, and indeed, a bin of cushions stood just within the door to my right. I didn't take one.

Instead, I leaned against the interior wall next to a stand bearing an offering plate that overflowed with local currency. Good thing I wasn't a thief as the mercs suggested. I dropped my purchases lightly on the floor beside me and watched.

Sconces holding flickering candles ran in two lines up the walls toward the altar, and scented smoke wafted from each one, creating a thick haze in the sanctuary. I inhaled, identifying the smell. Therix wax. Mildly narcotic. Completely legal in small amounts, though the parishioners were pushing it with so many candles. They produced a soothing effect, reduced tension. I'd tried using one as a sleep aid shortly after my arrival on Deluge but quickly discovered a need for something stronger. Besides, I hadn't liked the side effect of suggestibility.

I glanced again at the brimming offering plate. Explained a lot.

I took in the temple with a more critical eye, noting its cleanliness but some signs of disrepair—fraying edges on the pillows, cracks in the stonework. My cynical side wondered where all that money was going.

Kila might be devout. Didn't mean everyone who professed belief was equally so, including the local religious leader.

Each worshipper held a copy of the Generational in both hands. From it, the congregation recited or sung passages selected by the "leader," for want of the appropriate name. This white-robed figure stood behind the altar, expressive face and energetic hands conveying his message. His dark hair was close-cropped and neat, his angled cheekbones and a thin mustache adding to his distinguished appearance.

I peered closer at him. Bright, almost feverishly intense eyes roved over the congregation and back to the altar where he presumably kept his own copy of the Generational. No sign of narcotic dullness. An antitox tab taken before each service would do the trick. He was slight of build but full of stage presence, and his charismatic voice carried to the gathered assembly without the use of any sort of amplification technology. I marveled at the acoustic architecture, appreciating a simplistic solution to a problem dating back hundreds or thousands of years.

"...and the Guardian shall protect the Chosen from those sent to do Him harm. In defense of Him, the Guardian's life is forfeit."

In response, the parishioners chorused, "May the Guardian be found."

"And in return, the Chosen shall bless the Guardian, empowering the Guardian with all His gifts of life."

"May the Guardian be found."

It was all complete and utter nonsense, and yet a small part of me envied these simple, happy people and their unwavering beliefs. Faith for me came from the barrel of a laser or the tip of a blade. Those were my gifts of life. But it would be nice, for once, not to have to fight for it.

Prior to meeting Kila, I'd considered religious types gullible, perhaps less intelligent, and the potential corruption here added a bit to that. But Kila had no lack of intelligence. Though she was inexperienced, I would never name her gullible either.

What instilled faith in some but not others? Was I too damaged to ever truly believe?

In the coolness of the temple, I listened to the religious service and tried to understand, hoping to better understand Kila, herself.

At its conclusion, and no better enlightened than I'd been going in, I followed the congregation from the temple. Apparently tradition dictated the worshippers follow their religious leader to his abode after a service. They followed him, and I followed them.

We arrived at a pleasant boarding house in yellow with white trim, overlooking the ocean. The structure had weathered many a storm, and a few missing roof tiles and some chipped paint attested to that, but it was a far cry from the run-down inn the mercs occupied, and in a much better part of town. Still, these lodgings didn't account for the missing temple's funds.

Maybe they gave it all away to charities. I mentally kicked myself for my earlier uncharitable thoughts.

The pastor, priest, whatever this religion called him, stood at the entry and shook hands warmly with each parishioner before he or she departed into the village. With some, he stopped to exchange a few words, a sympathetic smile, a touch on the shoulder.

Curiosity placed me at the end of the lineup, and when the preacher got to me, he froze, then fluttered one hand up to smooth his thin mustache. His handshake was firm, but his fingers were cold, colder than they should have been after shaking with so many others. I wondered if I had blown my cover somehow.

"Is something wrong?" I asked, keeping my tone light and pleasant.

His faltered smile righted itself. "No, my dear, nothing at all. You simply reminded me of someone." His gaze darted about, searching the now empty yard of the boarding house, though what he looked for, I had no idea. "New here?" he asked.

I nodded. "Passing through. Sampling cultures." I favored him with a rare smile. "I hope that's all right?"

"Of course. Of course. Curiosity can make for many a convert."

I got the impression he was quoting the Generational, though I hadn't read that particular passage.

"And you live here year-round, I presume?"

To my surprise, he laughed. "No, I'm almost as much of a transient as you. I stay here on worship days, to conduct the services, but my permanent home is on a smaller island, privately owned. Much solitude is a requirement for proper meditation."

Of course it was.

Private island, huh? Something like that would cost a small fortune.

CHAPTER 14

UPON MY return to the T'rals', I tossed the climbing gear in its sack over a secluded area of fence, behind the mansion and among some trees. Then I strolled through the front gate with the woven art I'd picked up as my diversion for the guards. I'd had some concerns about retrieving the gear, but my worries proved pointless. The house bustled with activity: caterers, florists, and well-dressed individuals coming and going in a constant stream. I could have sneaked around with a blast cannon and no one would have noticed.

After removing a comforter and sheets from the chest at the foot of Kila's bed, I stored the gear within it, then placed the coverings on top and closed the lid. My formal attire lay spread across the mattress, a floor-length gown of shimmering silver and shoes to match. I showered and slipped into the dress, which fit me like a blade's sheath. The sparkling material contrasted with my dark hair, setting it off nicely.

The costume provided no place to hide a weapon. I couldn't fit anything between myself and the fabric. A slit up the side went halfway up my right thigh, leaving little to the imagination, and the back and front dipped low enough to make even me a bit self-conscious of the amount of exposed skin. At least the full-length sleeves hid my Guild brand, though I'd cover it with the beige goop to be safe. I wondered what Kila had been thinking when she selected this for me. My mind wandered to thoughts of what *she* might be wearing this evening, and I wrestled it back to more pressing concerns.

I spent time applying makeup and fastening my shoes, and still Kila had not returned. I practiced walking in the high heels, back and forth across the floor, until I could do so with grace. Natural agility helped, though I wondered if wearing them for any length of time would aggravate my former leg injury. During my pacing I spotted a small handwritten note on the armrest of the couch:

Expected at dinner. Will meet you there. Can't wait to see you in the dress. And a smiley face. Instead of rolling my eyes, I smiled down at it.

Armed with nothing more than my good looks, I ventured forth. I noted the hallway guards' absence as I made my way down the stairs.

Sounds of clinking tableware drew me to a large banquet hall complete with a parquet dance floor at one end. Elegant couples in various combinations swirled over the glossy surface to the lilting music of a live string quartet. About a dozen circular tables were laden with expensive crystal and hand-painted dishes. Servants in white jackets bore tureens of soup, bowls of exotic fruits, and trays of roasted vegetables that caused a rumbling in my empty stomach. Rays of the setting sun flowed through long rectangular windows overlooking the bay, the village, and the gated grounds.

A huge stack of wrapped and unwrapped presents made a pyramid against one wall, and for a moment, I regretted leaving the woven art in Kila's suite. The regret faded fast. I had a different gift in mind for Kila's rapist brother.

I scanned the crowd for Kila's face but couldn't spot her. Instead, my eyes fell upon the head table, situated at the front of the room adjacent to the dance floor. Five of its six seats sat empty, and a pair of guards stood behind its single occupant.

I got my first look at the young man I'd come to kill. He was nothing like I expected.

The resemblance between him and Kila showed in every feature, from the delicate cheekbones to the thick gold-and-auburn hair. His hung shorter, in fashion with other men of Lissex, just below his earlobes, but he had the same gentle innocence of his sister.

A mask for his depravity, I reminded myself. Somewhere in the T'ral line, genetics had failed, producing this sweet-faced monster.

Unseen, I moved to a corner beside a temporary bar serving beverages from all the settled worlds. From there I watched him while he nodded and smiled, exchanged pleasantries with passing guests, and nibbled at the food on his plate. His friendliness seemed forced and false. The smiles didn't reach his eyes, and I wondered if I imagined my interpretation or if he couldn't fully suppress his guilt and shame.

Interesting also were the reactions of others toward him. Men bowed. Women curtsied. Some kissed his hand or clutched his fingers to their chests with tears glistening in their eyes. That preacher from town was here too. No surprise there. Every village leader seemed to be present. He greeted Kila's brother Jaren, then appraised him with an intensity of gaze that seemed to bore through the younger man. Finally, he nodded and moved on. The display sickened me, and I understood Kila's hopeless position more than ever. If the villagers worshipped Jaren now, how would they interact once he took over control of the family affairs in another couple of days? His father would retire, and he would be in charge. Of everything. And everyone.

The bartender offered to pour me a drink, suggesting something pale blue and sparkling, and I politely refused. When I turned back, the young lord stared right at me.

He studied me with piercing green eyes uncomfortably like Kila's, nodding in appreciation at whatever he saw. Then he smiled... a genuine smile.

I blinked twice and walked in the opposite direction, unsure of my destination and not caring so long as it carried me away from him. Was that approval? Did he know who I was, or at least who I was supposed to be? Or was he simply scoping out a new conquest?

This undercover nonsense discomfited me. On occasion, Guild members had to play parts and infiltrate large groups of people to get to their targets. Didn't mean I had to like it. I had no desire to pursue an acting career. Give me a straight hunt-and-shoot any day.

Add to that the personal and emotional nature of this particular assignment. This was not going to be easy.

Blinded by fury and confusion, I collided with Kila before I focused on her. She stumbled on her own heels, and I caught her before she fell, wrapping my arms around her warm bare shoulders. Heat flooded me, spiraling outward from the middle of my stomach up to my face and down to places I tried, without success, to ignore.

Kila's giggling laughter brought me around, and I examined her flushed cheeks and glassy eyes with practiced expertise. "How many have you had?" I whispered, leaning to speak into her ear. She shivered in my arms as my warm breath passed over her neck. I watched the little hairs on her skin rise and swallowed hard at the response.

"I lost count," she complained, pouting pink lips at me. "I was only going to have one, you know, for courage." She blushed. "They keep filling up my glass before it's empty." Kila indicated the long-stemmed crystal she held, despite the near fall. The liquid within, more of the blue sparkling wine, sloshed onto the floor, but some remained. At least the spill missed the lacy white dress draping her in tiers like cascading water. A stain would have ruined her angelic appearance. She giggled again.

"I thought you didn't drink."

"I don't. Not really. At least not until today."

Wonderful.

"I'm sorry." She was too. I heard it in her voice and wanted to hug her. And as someone unpracticed who hadn't planned to drink, she hadn't thought to take an antitox tab. I hadn't either, but I knew my tolerances, and despite recent events on Vargas's ship, I was working and had no intention of getting drunk tonight.

"Don't worry. We'll deal with it." In keeping with our performance, I hooked my arm in hers and led her to an empty pair of seats at one of the tables farthest from her brother. "Let's get some food into you." A drunken Kila might give me away. One slip and the entire contingent of guards would have me cut off from any possible escape. I eyed the uniformed men stationed at each exit from the banquet hall, then signaled a server to bring my companion a plate.

While we ate, Kila kept one hand on my thigh, beneath the stark white tablecloth. Not part of the show, since no one could see it. I considered shifting position, but her fingers trembled, and I figured she needed the contact. The alcohol was playing her emotions through their entire repertoire.

"Calm down," I breathed.

She managed a smile but accepted another refill from a passing servant.

I suppose I couldn't blame her. She'd been off-planet for weeks. Now she occupied the same room as the man who'd raped her multiple times. That had to wear on her stability. I watched her throughout the meal.

Another couple joined us, tuxedo-clad gentlemen, fit and attractive, wealthy shopkeepers from the village specializing in foodstuffs and spices imported from other worlds. Their constant chatter about taxes, exotic molds, and root vegetables saved both me and Kila from having to speak a word. I nodded and smiled and tried to look interested while keeping an eye on my friend and how much she drank—at least two glasses during the main course, and fate knew how many prior to my arrival. I considered cutting her off, but ordering about a member of the ruling household might start a scene.

They'd filled my own glass twice, and the potency of the beverage surprised even me. Kila didn't weigh much, so she had little body mass to absorb the alcohol. If I didn't get her out of the party soon, she'd be too intoxicated to walk.

Clearing my throat, I interrupted a debate between the two men over the rising costs of preservatives in shipped goods. "If you'll excuse us?" I drew Kila up to stand beside me. She wavered, catching herself with one hand on the back of her chair.

"Of course!" one of the shop owners said, rising as well. He winked.

"We understand completely," his partner assured us, eyes gleaming and a lascivious grin spreading across his face.

Their responses played right into our drama. I didn't care what they thought, as long as I could escort Kila to her bedroom before she embarrassed herself or I had to carry her.

I put an arm under hers for support, concerned by her dependence on me to remain upright. Turning her in a gradual motion so as not to add to her disorientation, I pointed Kila in the direction of the main doors… and came face-to-face with her brother and his two guards.

CHAPTER 15

HERE. THEIR master was here. Through Kila's eyes they had seen him, though she knew him not for the great creator he was. And now, even as they came face-to-face with their target, their master was moving away, blending into the shadows, letting matters run their own course.

A shiver of what passed for trepidation passed through the ephems. Intelligence of noncorporeal beings had limitations, but if He-Who-Had-Created-Them had seen fit to attend this gathering, then their exalted master had lost faith in the ephems' ability to carry out their task.

And put other plans into motion.

Prophecy dictated without the Guardian, their master would achieve eminence. But a multitude of different paths could lead to that favorable outcome. And some might not be so favorable for the ephems.

"Jaren!" Kila stumbled backward until she connected with the table, setting dishes to rattling and knocking over at least one glass. A servant appeared as if from nowhere to clear the mess.

He wasn't the only one to appear from nowhere. I cursed my lack of vigilance.

Jaren moved as if to embrace his sister, and instinctive protectiveness placed me between them. The guards frowned. I tried to cover my actions by extending my hand to take his. "We haven't met. I'm Corianne." My full name sounded strange coming from my lips.

The young lord recovered quickly, wrapping strong fingers around mine in an affectionate press. I tasted bile in my throat.

"A pleasure!" he exclaimed, his voice as melodious as his sister's and equally soothing.

I shook my head as a sudden fogginess filled my vision. Perhaps I, too, had lost track of the wine refills.

Jaren's eyes sought Kila behind me. "I'm so glad. You deserve someone so attractive—and strong!"

I realized my grip had tightened and released him. He flexed his fingers with a sheepish grin. "I would have come to see you sooner, but with all the preparations for the final ceremony...." Jaren's hand swept the room, including tonight's festivities. His grin faltered, and I had the distinct impression the evening and all the attention weighed upon him.

Poor thing.

"I would love to hear all about the two of you. Mother says you're well matched. Will we be planning a different sort of ceremony soon?" His genuine enthusiasm stunned me. He was quite the performer himself.

"Jaren," came Kila's voice from over my shoulder, "you don't understand."

Uh-oh. Had the alcohol weakened her resolve? Too risky to let her continue, I cut her off. "We haven't made any long-term plans. And we were just leaving. Kila's not feeling well."

His concern seemed equally real. "Should I contact the physician?" This time he managed to pass me, placing his hands on Kila's arms and forcing eye contact. I tried to reinsert myself, but one of the guards cleared his throat and shook his head. I obeyed the electrablade he carried more than the subtle command and remained where I stood. A better time for this confrontation would present itself.

"It's nothing, too much celebration." The firmness of Kila's voice reestablished my emotional balance. Her gaze met mine and held it. I watched with heightened admiration as she embraced her greatest nightmare in a warm hug. "Nothing a few hours' sleep won't cure."

"You'll miss the presentation of the gifts," Jaren mumbled. His delicate chin rested on Kila's shoulder. "I think some of them are even for you."

"I know. Forgive me. Please."

I saw her fingers press more deeply into the material of his formal jacket. The tone of her words carried heavier weight than a simple apology. Jaren noted the change as well. His head came up, and he scrutinized her face.

Time to go. "Well, off to bed, then!" I laughed, feigning a bit of unsteadiness on my own feet, and managed a half fall that bumped them apart. One guard caught me by the elbow, helping, not hindering, while Jaren stabilized his sister's balance. I recaptured Kila's arm and maneuvered her out of his grasp and through the double doors.

In the hallway, I sagged against the wall with relief, pulling Kila against me for a moment before attempting the stairs. She didn't look at me, didn't speak, but when I kicked off my heels, she followed my lead, carrying the shoes to manage the climb to the second floor. Even so, we collided with the banister numerous times, and our steps weaved to her bedroom suite.

I wasn't intoxicated, not in the slightest. The close call with Jaren drove away the mild buzz I'd gained from a few glasses of the sparkling blue liquid. But keeping Kila upright presented a challenge.

After depositing her on her mattress, I turned and threw open the window to let in the cooler night air. Holding her had raised my temperature to an uncomfortable level. Kila flopped on the pastel sheets with a contented sigh and appeared to pass out. I moved to stand beside her, checked her breathing, rolled her on her side, then covered her with a light blanket.

Returning to the window, I cooled myself in the ocean breeze and let my heart rate slow to normal speed. The moonlight reflected off the silver material of my dress, casting rainbow patterns on the walls, ceiling, and rug. I watched them shift and shimmer with every breath I took.

Despite the late hour, I detected quite a bit of activity in the little seaside village. Hand lamps bobbed and weaved along the walkways, the tiny lights dancing and disappearing between buildings. I appreciated the island's desire to remain low-tech, using it as a tourist attraction. It kept things quaint.

My sensitive hearing picked up shouting and what might have been gunfire. A bar brawl spilling into the streets, perhaps. Regardless of the cause, additional security guards emerged from a side entrance and formed a human wall at the T'ral mansion's gates. The island's first family didn't take chances.

Then again, they'd let me in.

I stepped away from the window with purpose, stripped the formal wear off my body and retrieved my work clothes from Kila's dresser. Each familiar snap and fastening fortified me. The feel of the knife in my hand before I sheathed it reminded me of who I was. With or without the Guild behind me, I was a master assassin, not some arm ornament for a wealthy debutante.

I stood before the full-length mirror, scanning my appearance from boots to face. When my eyes met my own reflected gaze, I knew I wouldn't return to this room. Until now, I'd fantasized about completing the job and sliding back into my consort persona, remaining in the household to comfort Kila through her inevitable psychological trauma, despite being half its cause.

I'd comprehended little of the religious service I'd attended, but I understood one thing for certain: Kila didn't need someone like me. She needed a gentle soul, a lover and protector unencumbered by a dark past and a tormented future. She'd be better off without her brother. She'd be better off without me.

What I needed didn't matter.

I waited until I heard voices in the outer hall, male voices. Then I held off an additional hour to give my target a chance to fall asleep. At the end of that time, I pulled Kila's gift from where I'd hidden it with my clothing and draped it over the back of the couch. At least she'd have something to remember me by, if she wanted to.

Maybe she'd burn it instead.

I collected the climbing gear from the storage chest and leaned out past the shutters, my dark-clad form one more shadow against the stone wall. Jaren's room lay two doors down the hallway, so I counted windows and guessed at the distance to his.

I held the round auto-extender, careful to keep my palms flat, and ran my thumb over a dial embedded in its surface until the measurement numbers on its tiny viewscreen matched my estimation. Then I aimed for the recessed area around Jaren's window and depressed the release.

A self-guided pair of lines a meter apart shot from the ball and angled outward, flying across the expanse between my target destination and myself. Powerful adhesive tips at their ends impacted with Jaren's window frame and locked into place with a squish. I held my breath, but the sound carried away on the wind and the crash of distant waves.

Next, I pressed the extender ball against the stone wall just outside Kila's window. After a few seconds of applying pressure, the device's malleable material adhered itself to the rock and secured my end of the wires. Now I had two taut cords, each capable of holding five times my weight, stretching from one window to the other.

I slapped grip soles to the bottoms of my boots and prepared to pull on a pair of climber's gloves, when I heard the rustle of Kila's sheets.

"Cor?"

As if compelled by some unseen force, I rose from the windowsill, leaving the gloves behind, and crossed to stand over her. The grips on my shoes made sucking sounds with each step, and I winced at the noise shattering the peace of the moment.

At some point during my preparations, Kila had rolled onto her back and wriggled free of the coverings. Her filmy dress gathered around her thighs, and the paleness of her skin shone in the light cast by the moon. I could see her eyes were open, but her exposure kept drawing my gaze lower.

Backlit, I must have appeared as no more than a silhouette—a silhouette in assassin gear.

She extended a hand to me, and I reached out to grasp it, letting her draw me to sit beside her on the bed. The mattress exhaled with the addition of my weight, a soft sigh of escaping air.

Kila didn't release me, but rather drew me closer, then closer still until our faces were centimeters apart. With a slight lift of her head, she closed her lips over mine.

I forgot to breathe. I forgot to think. Her petal-soft touch drifted away, making me wonder if I'd imagined the contact. I leaned my other palm onto the mattress to prevent my body's collapse. Part of me wanted to fall, to press myself against her, but I locked my arm in place. If this was going to happen, she had to lead.

Reading my thoughts, Kila took the hand she still held and placed it over the thin fabric between her breasts. Her heart pounded so hard I wondered I couldn't hear it in the near-silent room. The pulse drove through the skin of my wrist and traveled up my veins, maddening me with its echo. My own heart rate raced to catch up.

The outer edges of my fingers brushed the sides of her breasts. Keeping my palm firmly in place, I moved my fingertips ever so slightly over her soft curves. Her body arched, pressing her more firmly against my hand. Kila's breath caught. Mine came more heavily.

All pretense of resistance fled. I leaned down and caught her mouth with my own, my tongue teasing her lips and tasting the fruity blue sparkling wine. Kila released my hand to run hers through my hair, allowing me to explore her body more freely. I strummed my fingers from her waist up her rib cage and over one breast, then across to the other and down the opposite side. Her sharp inhalation broke our kiss.

Every piece of clothing I wore felt too restrictive. Despite the open window, the room sweltered. Kila captured my hand again, this time bringing it to her uncovered thighs. The heat of her soft skin seared me. Her perfume of flowers and spice dazed me more than any alcohol or drug.

Unsure of myself, I hesitated, drawing a tiny whimper from her. I knew what *I* liked. I had no experience with other women. Very slowly, then a little faster, I ran my fingertips in a feathering touch up and down the crease where her legs pressed together, encouraging her to part them. I hoped I might give her a pleasurable memory to blot out her brother's aggressive acts.

My hand stilled.

In her intoxicated state, how was this any better than what Jaren had done?

I wanted her. My desire rivaled what I'd had with Micah at the height of our affair. A desperate groan escaped me as I sat up on the bed and drew my arm away.

Kila wrapped both her hands around my wrist. "Please stay."

I forced a smile, hoping she could see it in the darkness. "Ask me again when you're sober." I pulled from her grip and brushed strands of hair away from her face, thinking the gesture might soften my refusal.

"You won't want me then." Kila rolled onto her side, facing the wall. The bed shook as she trembled.

What in all hells did that mean? Did she know I didn't plan on coming back? By the time the alcohol wore off, I'd be long gone. Was that it? I opened my mouth to argue with her, but there was no argument for truth and nothing more to be said.

I returned to the window and slipped on the climbing gloves, trying to ignore the muffled sobs emanating from the pile of pillows and blankets behind me. Swinging my legs over the sill, I planted the grip soles of my boots on the lower wire and clutched the upper one with both hands. Then I edged my way along the exterior of the T'ral mansion.

Even through my clothing, the cold stone sapped the arousal heat from my body and enabled me to focus on the job. Down below, in the adjacent village, the shouting had risen in volume, and more gunfire resonated along its streets. Something had turned the sleepy town into a shooting gallery, likely all the mercs and other visiting military types, but I couldn't concern myself with any of that right now. The job mattered, nothing but the job, because that was the only thing keeping me from climbing back through the window and into Kila's bed.

All the windows on the second floor were dark. The one on the guest room between the siblings' suites was closed. Jaren's, however, hung open, and every scrape I made against the exterior wall accelerated my pulse. As I arrived at his ledge, clouds obscured the moon and plunged me into absolute darkness. The lights in his suite were extinguished, but as I seated myself on the sill, I heard faint snoring coming from within and knew the young lord had retired for the night.

I found the window seat Kila described and used it to climb into the room. I removed the grip soles and placed them in my pocket but kept the gloves to avoid leaving fingerprints on anything. Then I waited.

The moon appeared from behind the clouds, lighting the room. The layout of the furnishings matched Kila's, though the specific decorative choices reflected a more masculine taste. The light wood dresser and chairs bore sharp angles rather than rounded edges. Darker fabrics instead of pastels covered the couch and the bed. As expected, woven art pieces hung from the walls. I couldn't make out their themes or subjects in the shadows, but their rough fringes identified them.

Padding across the carpet, I moved to stand about a meter from my target. Jaren lay face-up. He slept shirtless, and the low-lying covers exposed his neck and pale, hairless chest. His expression was beatific in the innocence of sleep.

I slid my blade from its sheath, then grabbed a muffling throw pillow from those scattered on the floor. Before I could cross the last few steps between us, the young lord snorted, then coughed and inhaled deeply.

Hells.

Instead of going back to sleep, Jaren sniffed, then sniffed again. My heart stopped. The perfume. Kila's perfume. I'd grown accustomed to it, enveloped in it as I'd been, but now I could smell it on my clothing and in my hair from when she'd touched me.

Jaren smelled it too.

"Kila?" he muttered, eyelids fluttering as he attempted to focus in the dark room.

Of course he recognized the owner of the scent. He'd been close enough to it.

Jaren shoved the blankets the rest of the way off and sat up, calling for the automatic lights.

We stared at each other in the lamps' glare.

Jaren didn't shout. Instead, he looked from my face to the blade in my hand and back again. I watched comprehension dawn in his changing expressions. He appeared more saddened than afraid.

"I really hoped she'd found someone," he whispered, almost too low for me to hear.

"Why?" I snarled. "You like threesomes? Not going to happen."

Jaren's face twisted in a mixture of disgust and confusion. He swung his legs over the side of the bed and stood in loose-fitting pajama pants, then reached for a robe tossed over a nearby chair. My muscles tightened. I shifted my weight to the balls of my feet and turned so I could see both him and the door where the guards would enter.

The young lord drew on the robe one casual sleeve at a time, the long, soft brown material falling around his too thin frame. I wondered, with his lack of physical build, how Kila hadn't managed at least once to fight him off and get away. She abhorred violence, yes, but to defend herself from rape? Maybe she'd seen it as pointless to resist the inevitable.

Or maybe something was wrong with this whole scenario. And still, Jaren didn't call for help or make a move to stop me.

Queasiness formed in the pit of my stomach, a subtle churning that made me regret the meal I'd consumed in the banquet hall.

"You do care for her. I could see it at the party. Will you leave her, once this is done and over with?" Jaren finished tying a sash around his waist.

A buzzing took up residence in my ears, a distraction I didn't need with everything falling apart around me. I reached up with my free hand to viciously rub the left side of my head. It didn't help. The buzzing continued like insects swarming my brain. Something told me if I killed him, it would stop, but I had to sort this out first.

"What happens between me and Kila doesn't matter to you. You won't be around to worry about it." I took an unsteady step forward. What in hells was the matter with me?

With one long stride, he stood before me, and there was no breaking from his intense gaze. "What happens to Kila matters to me. It matters to me very much."

I believed him.

Wrong. All wrong. All of this. Everything.

The nausea increased tenfold when he bared his chest to my blade. An incomprehensible compulsion to kill him warred with my absolute certainty this was a mistake. "It's time. Finish it. Just promise me you won't leave her alone."

In my profession, squeamishness and nerves over a potential kill weren't things I generally worried about, but the queasiness in my stomach didn't relent and finally became unmanageable. I staggered to the corner of the bedroom and gagged, then vomited.

CHAPTER 16

WHEN MY stomach had emptied itself, I straightened, wiping my mouth on the back of my glove. Jaren tried to assist me, supporting my arm, but I flinched away as if burned. "You never raped her." It wasn't a question.

The young lord's eyes flew wide. The buzzing in my ears abruptly stopped. Weird. "Raped who? Kila?" Now he was the one to look ill. "I've never raped anyone. I'd never *hurt* anyone."

No, he wouldn't. Not this soft-spoken young man with the sad green eyes and a longing for death.

Kila played me, lied to me from the beginning, used her false friendship to gain my trust and more, spun her rape story to convince me to end Jaren's life. And I'd come so close to finishing it, so close, just like with the child Micah assigned me to kill. Sooner or later, I was bound to take an innocent life. I caught the armrest of a chair and pulled myself into it. My legs would no longer support me.

You won't want me then. Kila's last words echoed in my head. She must have thought I'd figure out what I'd done sooner or later. And here I'd been worried *she* wouldn't want *me* after killing her brother, regardless of what he'd done, regardless of her request. She probably never wanted me in the first place. Tonight had been all part of the act, or a delaying tactic due to second thoughts. The bile rose again, and I swallowed it down.

I was an idiot.

"Why?" My voice sounded ragged. I raised it to be heard over a new clamor outside. "Why do you want me to kill you? If you wanted to die, why didn't you kill yourself?" Why put me through all this?

Jaren picked up the knife I'd dropped. I didn't even realize I'd lost it until now. He handed it to me and sat in the opposite chair. "Suicide condemns me to eternal punishment."

Like I couldn't have seen that coming.

"The rest is hard to explain."

Rage replaced hurt and disappointment. I gripped the handle of the blade until my knuckles whitened, not because I intended to use it. I wouldn't give him the satisfaction. But it gave me something to crush my fingers around. "I suggest you try."

Jaren exhaled, resigned. "If I live, thousands, perhaps millions, will die."

I snorted with disbelief, sheathed my weapon in one violent shove, and stood to pace in front of him. "How?"

"I have something a lot of people would kill for." Jaren dug his toes into the thick carpeting. His hands clutched the armrests.

Talk about an overinflated sense of importance. "You mean your inheritance? Lissex is a rim world. Nobody off the planet, probably nobody off Triumph cares that you are going to rule your little island and be the decision-maker around here!" It took everything I had to keep from shouting. Shouting would bring the guards.

He looked at me, searching my face and seeming to come to a decision. "It has nothing to do with property or politics."

The noise from outside swelled into an uproar that drowned out his next words. The tone of the voices sounded commanding, and an authoritative male barked orders in crisp, precise phrases I couldn't quite make out. Others responded, and a cacophony of argument and scuffling ensued, coming from just below Jaren's window.

At first I thought someone had spotted my climbing wires, despite their thinness. Then a heavy black cylinder flew through the double-paned opening, clanged, thudded against the carpet, and rolled across the floor.

Without knowing why, I threw myself at Jaren, knocking him over backward in his chair and tackling him to the carpet. We ended up behind the couch when the flash bomb exploded, filling the suite with glaring white light.

The couch's protection prevented complete blindness, but even so, I blinked furiously from my perch atop Jaren's chest, and tears poured from my oversensitive eyes. Behind me, I heard metal scraping on stone. I turned, and despite the pain from the glare, made out grappling hooks on the windowsill.

I jumped to my feet, dragging Jaren up with me, and scanned the room. "Grab some shoes!" That would take precious seconds, but he'd be even slower barefoot once I got him out of the suite.

He flew to the bed, pulled slip-on sandals from beneath it, and yanked them on in two quick jerks.

"Come on!" I yelled from the door, but he hesitated, then dug into the top drawer of his dresser and removed two pairs of sunglasses. He tossed one to me. I nodded and put them on. The world dimmed to a manageable brightness.

I drew my pistol from my thigh holster, holding it at the ready. Then I slammed open the bedroom door, hoping to take the hallway guards by surprise. I turned right, then left, aiming the gun up and down the corridor in two quick motions. Jaren skittered into the hall behind me, staring in surprise.

There was no one there. Footsteps pounded down the stairs. They must have been headed out to assist the security on the grounds.

At the head of the stairwell, Jaren took a step toward his sister's room, but I caught him by the sleeve of his robe. "They're not after her." In spite of Kila's betrayal, leaving her behind twisted my insides into knots, but my practical side won out. "If you want to live—" I caught myself. Jaren rolled his eyes at me. "If you don't want whoever it is to get you, then we need to leave, now."

I don't know what motivated me to help him. Maybe I was determined not to let him satisfy his death wish in this new conflict. Whatever the reason, we hurried down the stairs together.

Halfway to the first floor, we came up behind his bodyguards. All their attention was focused on a group of camouflage-wearing military types trying to battle their way up. I recognized the sergeant from the squad of mercs I'd fought earlier in the day. He spotted me as well, and renewed his assault on the guards between us with increased vigor.

For party-colored house protection, I had to admit the T'ral guards fought well. They leaped into the fray without hesitation, and though it required both guards to take down one merc, I admired their courage. More T'ral security poured through the front doors and into the entry hall, swinging shock sticks and carrying stun pistols. Nonlethal weaponry, of course. Their religion would discourage the use of killing force. They launched into the struggle with the mercs, trying to haul them off the stairs but effectively blocking our escape route.

I had no such concerns. My work clothing blew my cover. I shot two mercs with my pistol, one in the chest, another in the head. When I turned to Jaren, he'd paled. The young lord stared at me with wide-open eyes.

"Your sister hired an assassin, not a pacifist," I growled.

Below, more activity erupted. Kila's father burst through the banquet hall doors, took one look around, and ducked back inside. I heard more shouting from within.

Above, the sound of boots stomping on carpet came from Jaren's room. I took a deep, cleansing breath. No matter how good I was, I couldn't shoot them all. I holstered my weapon, seized the banister with both hands, and swung myself over it to drop in a feline crouch on the floor below.

"Jaren, jump!"

He obeyed my command, landing with less grace and more noise. I grabbed his arms to steady him.

"Jaren! Cor!"

Kila's pale face appeared at the upstairs railing, hands gripping it for balance in her semidrunken state, as two men and a woman swarmed out of Jaren's suite. The new arrivals looked from Kila to us, decided we were the better targets, then made for the stairs to pursue. Kila's expression showed chagrin at giving us away.

Gun in hand once more, I glared at my former friend with pure hatred. She probably couldn't see it behind the dark glasses, but the grim set of my jaw and the tightness of my mouth backed her up a step. I turned and shoved Jaren through a door at the far end of the entrance hall.

I'd found the kitchen, and Jaren and Kila's parents, and the priest from the village, along with a number of servants cowering behind a central island of long metal cooking surfaces and storage cabinets. Three cups of unfinished tea rested on a glossy wood table, and a candle of Therix wax burned beside them. The narcotic smoke wafted through the room, and I wondered, very briefly, what the trio discussed under its haze.

Shaking myself from its influence, I scanned the rest of the room. No exterior doors, but the rear wall boasted a floor-to-ceiling window, and I blasted it with one shot from my pistol. Glass blew outward into the yard and clattered on some stone surface, a walkway perhaps. The men ducked as a few bits of debris showered them. Lady T'ral screamed.

My patience ended. I'd been teased, frustrated, betrayed, half blinded, and now I had paired up with the number-one target on Lissex. "Can you draw any more attention to us?" I shouted, waving the gun in her direction. I must have looked insane to her in my assassin gear and Jaren's sunglasses. She covered her mouth with one hand to prevent another shriek.

"Corianne." Jaren wrapped gentle fingers around my forearm. I almost backhanded him.

"What?" He didn't release me. He was either incredibly brave or incredibly stupid.

"We should leave."

His composure surprised me, keeping cool under pressure. Maybe his unwavering religious faith kept him on an even keel. Or maybe he wanted the crazy lady with the gun as far from his parents and the preacher as possible.

The buzzing in my head began anew, and a calming sensation doused my fried nerves in soothing relief. At first I thought the Therix candle was getting to me. But there hadn't been a candle in his bedroom that I remembered. I blinked at Jaren, really seeing him for the first time tonight. "It's you." I felt my eyes widen. Puzzle pieces dropped into place, forming a solid picture. Kila's humming. The healing of my injuries, past and recent. My affection for her. "Just how much can you—?"

His father stepped in front of us. "My son has a mission to fulfill, a role in the order of things. If you think I'm going to stand by and let you take him—"

Jaren interceded. "She's on our side, Father. I can't do anything if they capture me. She'll keep me safe."

"She's an assassin."

Oh, very good, Lord T'ral. A little late to the party, but not unfashionably so.

"If she wanted to kill me, she would have done it by now." Jaren headed for the broken window. His mother watched him and burst into tears.

"You should not accompany her," the preacher said to our departing backs.

Jaren hesitated, and I resisted the urge to shove him out the opening. I didn't want to fight him all the way to, well, wherever we were going. He'd either go with me by choice or not at all. After a moment's consideration, Jaren shook his head and climbed out, waiting for me beyond the sill.

"What if she wants to use you? Control you?" the religious leader tried one last time.

One foot over the threshold, I turned to him. "I don't. And that's all the reassurance I have time to give you right now." I followed Jaren into the night, ignoring his mother's despairing wail.

Chaos continued to reign outside. Teams of guards and invaders jogged about the grounds in groups of three and four, patrolling, searching. Wherever they met, conflict ensued and created unintentional distractions for us. In addition, a healthy fog rolled in off the water. I removed my sunglasses, no longer needing them in the darkness, and tucked them in a jacket pocket. Jaren hung his off his robe tie.

"I take it boats are the only means of transportation off the island? We have to get to your family's yacht." I leaned in close to him, uncomfortable with his audible mind control but not wanting to be overheard.

"We try to keep things simple," he said, no trace of apology in his tone. No buzzing in my head, either. Apparently he could turn his power on and off. "There's a spaceport on Paradise, on the far side of the main island, away from Wayfarer's Wharf, if you're thinking of getting me off-world."

That meant another day and a half boat trip, and that's if we went directly, but what choice did we have? I nodded. Taking Jaren by the sleeve, I pulled him toward the gate.

A light sprang on at the side of the house, illuminating a small garden trampled by booted feet. In the glow, I spotted the preacher, arms raised and head turned toward the heavens as if seeking divine guidance or aid.

He'd better be. A team of angry mercs surrounded him.

They didn't shoot him. He wasn't their target, after all. Instead they watched as he lowered his hands and gesticulated around the grounds, maybe ordering them to leave the premises.

Unfortunately, he ordered them to leave in our general direction.

I grabbed Jaren's sleeve, tugging him toward the perimeter. The mercs hadn't seen us in the shadows, and their entry had ripped down the fencing in several places. I chose a flat section, and we climbed over it, trying to make as little noise as possible. Every creak and groan ramped up my pulse rate.

Once beyond the property, I held us off the main path, creeping between the bushes and shrubs that lined it. The fog shielded us from attackers, but also made the going difficult, and we both tripped several times, almost tumbling headlong down a steep hill.

In town, we took backstreets, angling our way toward the docks. Pockets of local resistance had sprung up. Shopkeepers and residents barred more mercs from trying to get to the T'ral mansion. Their willingness to lay down their lives in the face of a superior force impressed me. As I watched, an elderly man was taken out by a single blast from a pulse rifle. His wife carried on the fight, stepping over him and swinging a makeshift club of broken shutter. Jaren made a move to assist, but I yanked him into the shadows and slammed him up against the stone wall of a small eatery. His eyes were wild.

"I have one gun," I told him in a harsh whisper. "The charge is low. You can't save everyone. Best thing you can do is escape and draw the battle away from here. When they figure out you're gone, they'll leave."

He looked from me to the dying man and back again. In the dim yellow streetlights, his skin had gone green. He nodded shakily.

Heading away, I softened my hold on him but didn't release. "Is everyone on this island a Believer in the Givers of Life?"

"Everyone. And most on the other islands as well."

We came within sight of the boardwalk. The fog cleared a bit, and I could make out the T'ral yacht bobbing in the first slip. "I thought the Believers were nonviolent."

The stricken expression on his face tore at my heart. "They're allowed to commit violence under one circumstance—in defense of the Chosen. In defense of *me*." He gagged on the last word, spitting bile onto the wooden boards as we crossed to the boat.

I sniffed the air, smelling smoke, and turned to see several waterfront shops on fire. The flames danced and shimmied, reflected in the calmer water of the bay. Shattering glass and gunfire destroyed the peace of the sleepy village. Such an incredible waste of beauty and lives.

When we reached the yacht, Jaren broke away from me, grabbed one of the lines, and swung onto the deck. "I'll go below and get the engine started," he called.

A moving shadow emerged from the central cabin.

"Watch out!" I leaped, landing on the deck in front of him, between him and the new threat.

Light flashed, and the ripper blast caught me in the left side. I fired back, and a groan rewarded my efforts. Searing white-hot pain doubled me. I gripped the wound, feeling warm, sticky wetness gush over my fingers.

Jaren caught me as I staggered, wrapping his arms around me and leading me to the cabin. "There might be more of them," I protested. The weak tremulousness of my voice scared the shit out of me. A roaring in my ears and sparkles at the edges of my vision warned me I would soon lose consciousness. The shot must have hit some major organ. Please let it be the spleen. I might survive if I could get some medical attention somewhere.

"Then we're dead, regardless. You can't run, and I'm not leaving anyone else behind."

We stepped over the body, and I recognized the first mate from the *Regiment 1*. He wasn't singing little ditties now. So, this had been Captain Vargas's interest in Lissex. They must have used the other pods to reach the surface and come in right after I had. I'd caught this crewman in the chest with my laser. He died before he fell.

I might not be far behind. Looking down, I saw a pool of blood forming at my feet that didn't come from the first mate. As Jaren half dragged, half carried me down the steps to one of the cabins, I found myself wishing I'd let Kila succeed in seducing me tonight. Maybe then I would have known if any of what she'd professed to feel for me had been real.

Jaren shouted orders to the yacht's onboard computer, bringing up interior lights, casting off lines and starting engines, but I barely heard him. He laid me on the bunk in the same room I'd occupied on the way out. With nothing else to concentrate on, the full agony of the wound hit my nervous system, and I couldn't suppress my cry of pain.

Jaren drew my hand from the injury, placing his own atop it and ignoring the gory torn flesh and flowing blood. He rested his other hand on my forehead, smoothing my hair and speaking in gentle tones.

"Let yourself heal, Cor. You're all right. Breathe. Rest."

I wasn't all right. I didn't know the extent of Jaren's skills, but I was dying. I wanted to tell him, but my mouth didn't work. The buzzing in my head resumed with a vengeance, deafening me so I could no longer hear his words, though his lips still moved. Nausea reared and I gagged, then rolled to vomit over the edge of the bunk.

The effort drained the last of my strength. I fell against the mattress with a groan and passed out.

Hours passed. The guards secured the T'ral household. Kila's parents came to tell her what happened, that she'd inadvertently brought a murderer home. They never suspected that had been her intention.

Through a constricted throat, Kila begged they leave her alone. One last look into her tear-filled eyes, and her mother and father departed her suite. She'd been duped by her lover, after all. She needed some time alone. Or so they thought.

He lived. Jaren T'ral lived. Despite their master's quietly hired mercenary reinforcements—they took some satisfaction from that—he'd lived and escaped. And now, one needed to return to He-Who-Had-Created-Them and pay the price of failure.

Within Kila's body they battled, the larger of the two ephems enveloping the other, compressing its companion until the girl doubled over from the abdominal pain. She retched and expelled the weaker entity along with her vomit while the other remained inside, wrapped around her intestines, clinging for its life—or what passed for life.

Kila trembled from stress and emotion, seated there on the cold flooring of her suite's bathroom. Cor left her. Jaren left her. And yet, a part of her thrilled to the knowledge her brother survived.

But what did Cor intend to do with him? The assassin hated her. That much she'd seen in Cor's expression when they parted at the stairs. Maybe she would eventually take out her revenge on Jaren. Maybe he'd end up dead after all.

It was what she wanted. It was what she dreaded.

How could doing the right thing, what Jaren himself wished for, hurt so much? And losing Cor....

Kila reached an unsteady hand to activate the suction system, flushing her regurgitated dinner and the unseen ephem down into the plumbing and out of the T'ral mansion. The second entity read her thoughts and soothed her strained digestive and nervous systems, triggering her body's release of endorphins. It waited until she flung herself on her mattress and slept, then nudged her subconscious.

The fates of worlds were at stake. She had failed, but she could not give up. If Cor refused to assassinate Jaren, perhaps someone else would carry out the assignment.

In a dreamlike state, Kila rose, packed toiletries and a change of clothes in her carry sack, and departed the mansion in the glow of early dawn.

The grounds lay in shambles, scorch marks on the healthy green grass, flowerbeds trampled, stone walks cracked from the weight of too many heavily armored men. The attackers had knocked down the perimeter fence in numerous places, the metal bars bent and mangled, flattened against the ground.

During the night, emergency personnel from the village had removed wounded house guards, much to the entity's disappointment. It could have used a snack to recharge itself. A skeleton team of protectors stood sentry at the remains of the front gate, useless as that was. They never saw Kila step over a strip of fallen fencing and make her way toward the smoldering town at the base of the hill.

From there, she proceeded to the wharf, ignoring those who called to her, inquiring after her brother and the rest of her family. The Triumph *wasn't the T'ral's only vessel. They owned several other, slower yachts, and she selected the* Tempest *and got her underway with a minimum of conscious thought.*

Only after the island receded into the distance and appeared as a mere shadow on the horizon did the ephem release her Will. Kila swayed on the Tempest's *deck, taking several minutes to get her bearings. She convinced herself her conscience had driven her actions, sending her after Cor to make amends, to try to salvage their relationship if she could.*

CHAPTER 17

THE *TRIUMPH*'S engines hummed, vibrating the mattress beneath me. The waves rolled outside the window, and the smell of salt air carried on the morning breeze. Hazy sunlight lit the room. Then the events of the past two days flooded back to me and I groaned into my pillow.

I was alive. That was something, I supposed. And I'd saved the Chosen, at least for now. I huffed out a breath. The importance of that remained to be seen.

I pulled away the thin sheet covering my upper body. At some point, Jaren removed my jacket and shirt, and I could now see the extent of my injury. I blinked at the half-healed wound forming an impressive scar across my abdomen. Either I'd slept a lot longer than one night, or Jaren's powers far exceeded calming and soothing techniques.

The subject of my musing chose that moment to enter, bearing a tray of dried fruits and a glass of water. He'd changed clothes. I supposed the family kept a shipboard wardrobe. Now he wore loose-fitting beige shorts and a casual white shirt. The color choices made him appear even paler, or maybe that was simply stress.

He noticed my appraisal and gestured at himself. "Sorry. I didn't find anything onboard that might fit you."

I waved off his apology.

Jaren handed me the tray and checked my wound, nodding with satisfaction. He sank into the chair he'd dragged to the side of the bed sometime during the night. Dark circles beneath his eyes told me he'd likely slept in it. "Now you see why I wanted to die."

I shook my head. A wave of dizziness blurred my vision, and I closed my eyes for a moment. "I see why you'd need to hide."

"There's no place to hide. No place I'll be safe. The Givers of Life have many followers, on every settled world. They're fanatical, bound to the Generational, and take what it says quite literally. They believe once I come to power that they have the right to not just defend me, but to conquer worlds on my behalf, to force others into peace. The ultimate protective effort." Jaren gave a humorless laugh. "Every few hundred years or so, one of the Chosen appears. Wherever the Believers congregate, warfare erupts. In the past, it has ended rather quickly." He paused, studying me. "Maybe religions don't interest you—?"

I neither agreed nor argued.

"But even hidden, they would fight on my behalf unless I faked my death first, and sooner or later, my location would be revealed." He spread his hands in a helpless gesture. "I'm driven to heal others. Suffering makes me ill. It's not something I can shut off."

I considered all that, picturing the simple Believers attempting to subdue armies. They'd be slaughtered. I forced myself to nibble a piece of fruit from the tray. "I thought it wasn't even supposed to be 'on' yet. Twentieth birthday? Ceremony?"

Jaren's mouth quirked, and he cocked his head. "It's biological. Some want to call it magic, but it's a recessive genetic trait, miraculous, but it follows its own time line. Do all women begin their cycles at a set age? Do all male voices change at a specific hour in their lives? Twenty is an estimate. I actually came to full power a couple of months ago, though only you, I, and Kila know, and I hid the early indicators for years. It's all about what the Believers believe. For example, they don't know about Kila. She has it, too, though to a lesser extent. The Generational's scribes didn't account for twins. And so she is safe. They aren't looking, so they don't see."

Like I hadn't seen. She'd played my emotions to suit her needs, and while I now understood her reasons, it didn't hurt any less or take away my anger. "And what, exactly, is *full power*?" I spat the question, and all the bitterness in my voice twisted my face into a snarl.

Jaren reached to place a hand on my shoulder. I feared unnecessary motion would hurt, so I let it stay.

"We're audible healers. I can calm nerves, eradicate disease, close wounds. Essentially, I can give a body the strength to live, despite fatal injury, though it does have some side effects, I'm told."

Yeah, ear buzzing and nausea. I nodded and used more fruit to remove the remains of the bad taste in my mouth.

"Dead, however, is dead. Once life leaves someone, I cannot bring that person back. I'm not one of the gods." He snatched an orange-colored piece from my tray and continued. "Kila's talent works through music, not words. Don't ask me why. She can relieve stress, begin the healing process of nonlethal injuries, and reduce pain in old physical damage that's already mostly healed."

Hence the reason my leg and arm no longer bothered me. I hadn't had trouble with dusk vision since I'd befriended her, either, though I didn't make note of it until now.

Jaren's fingers tightened on my shoulder in a gentle squeeze, forcing me to meet his gaze. "She can't create feelings where there are none. Neither of us can." He smiled, guessing my thoughts perfectly. "We might unconsciously enhance what's already there, but we don't originate affection."

Jaren turned to the window, looking out across the waves to the distant horizon, and I knew he worried about his sister.

What he said helped, but not enough. "She lied to me. She used me."

"She loves you," he said firmly. "And she loves me. We talked about finding someone to assist in my death, but I never thought she'd have the strength to do it. When she came back with you, I truly believed she'd found her Bond mate. Hiding the truth from us both must have torn her apart. But it had to be done. You never would have believed her."

He was right. I wouldn't have. Not without seeing Jaren's miraculous acts. I still didn't understand why he needed to die, though. Why he couldn't change his identity, take on a new persona, of a doctor, perhaps. Surely his ability could be hidden behind placebo pills, fake devices, something.

He stood and paced the room. "And you have to see how important it is. Outsiders who suspect the legends are true have already destroyed my home, killed my friends. Armies will go to war to possess me. Can you imagine? I could heal hundreds of soldiers."

"Only one at a time."

"Perhaps. But it would still give one force an incredible advantage over another. And think of what scientists would do. If they get a hold of me, they'll take me apart trying to find what makes it work. And then there are the Believers themselves and their refusal to interpret the Generational any differently. They'll all die and take thousands with them in the process." He threw up his hands in exasperation. "It's better for everyone if you just kill me. Let them worry about it again in another few hundred years." Jaren stopped and stood over me, staring down with pleading eyes. "Everything I know of the Guild says they kill for the betterment of humanity. I'm a threat. Assassinate me and save the others."

"What do you believe?" I asked him.

"What?"

"You refer to the Believers as fanatics, yet you are their Chosen, raised in this religion. What do *you* believe?"

He paused, lost in thought. "I believe that peace cannot be forced, that the forcing drives the targets to greater acts of violence. Peace must be a choice."

I leaned forward and set the tray at the foot of the bed, then swung my legs over the side. The movement caused a dull ache and an odd pulling at my waist, but I could manage the minimal pain. Fatigue from blood loss made me want to curl up under the blankets, but I stood and faced him instead. "I kill evil people. I kill those who intend harm toward others. I will not murder you. There has to be another way."

Jaren went to the bedside table and opened the single drawer. He removed a modern copy of the Generational with its plastic pages and cartoonish colored images. This he tossed on the bed, knocking over my glass of water and letting the liquid soak the sheets. "Kila thought so too. Even she gave up. I wish you better luck." He stood and left the room, shoulders slumped, utterly defeated.

Free of Kila's corporeal shell, the second ephem soared on the ocean breezes, reveling in the feel of complete lack of inhibition, recognizing its fleeting nature. Experiencing life through the Kila-host felt good, too, especially when the assassin touched her. Especially then. Tasting, smelling, hearing all had their own pleasures as well, but it missed the ability to fly, to go places the human body could never go without mechanical aids.

Its destination dampened its enthusiasm, however.

The island in the distance, just a few kilometers from Triumph, could hardly be called that. More like an oversized sandbar, it held a small dock with a traditional sailing vessel tied to its moorings, a grove of trees, and a single house built of dark atchet wood. Six shallow graves lined the gray stone walkway leading to the vacant porch—the final resting places of the architect and builders who'd constructed the home and dock. Its owner named the isolated locale Dreadmore—he had a flair for the dramatic—and its name wouldn't be found printed on any map.

The ephem drew within half a click of the residence and hovered, sensing the energy barrier that shielded and protected the home from view and attack. Crossing the barrier hurt, in every sense such an entity could feel pain, but no other avenue of entry existed. He-Who-Had-Created-It already sensed its presence, and once detected, He would retain little patience for delays.

Resigned to its fate, the ephem passed through the shielding, flowing with the invisible electrons, clinging to its cohesion with all its strength as the energy attempted to tear it apart. As it had within the assassin's skull, it lost a bit of itself, weakening its overall strength. On the opposite side of the shield, it reformed as best it could and flowed toward the forbidding house.

Any human approaching the structure would assume it abandoned. Not that its owner allowed it to deteriorate, but it simply looked empty. Thick shutters covered the windows on every side, and the front and rear doors lacked the traditional viewpanes that adorned most entries on Lissex.

None of these proved a problem to the entity. It seeped beneath the front entrance and wafted down a long, dark hallway where hastily discarded sailing gear lay strewn to one side, still wet with spray. The master had arrived only shortly before.

The ephem slipped into the study at the back of the house. No bookcases lined the walls, no desk dominated the room, no easy chair reclined against the wood paneling. Instead, ancient oil lamps hung in each of the four corners, flickering in the darkened interior. Intricate artwork in pitch-black ink wound its way from the base of each lamp, wandering through curlicue patterns and almost-words of the old tongue until they touched the floor.

There, the designs changed to sharp angles, jerking and thrusting their way to the dead center of the otherwise empty space. The four lines met in a single point, a pinprick of deep red, and upon that point knelt He-Who-Had-Created-It, spine arched and head bowed.

An intruder might mistake Him for a corpse, so motionless did He remain.

His arm rose as if of its own accord, seemingly detached from the rest of His body. No other part of Him so much as twitched. The palm extended up and back, beckoning to the ephem hovering in the doorway, uncertain.

The ephem felt true fear for the first time since its humanly existence, far worse than during its battle with the assassin's Will. It hesitated.

"Now!" He commanded, curling His fingertips.

The entity was helpless to resist that pull of power. Sucked in by an invisible force, it was drawn across the room in a thin line of vapor-like smoke, curling around His head and entering through His open mouth.

He drained his creation of power and expelled the ephem on an oath of disgust, leaving it hovering before him in a cloud of mist.

"Jaren T'ral lives. You have failed."

Mumbling words in the founders' tongue, He stood on skeletal limbs much more obvious without his flowing white robes. He pointed one bony finger first at the entity, then at the red dot between his legs on the floor. An inhuman undead shriek sounded from the ephem as it split into four equal parts, each in turn pulled into that red dot, that spot of His blood, and shooting off along the painted lines in four separate directions ending in the searing flames of the oil lamps.

I spent the next half day poring through the religious text, reading it from cover to cover. Egotistical to think I'd spot something Kila hadn't. She'd had a lifetime to study its meanings. But I felt too weak to get out of bed, and Jaren had sunk into a deep depression, avoiding me except to deliver meals, so I had little else to occupy my time.

In one short burst of conversation, he informed me he'd charted a somewhat convoluted route to Paradise, keeping out of the primary shipping lanes to make us less traceable. It added hours to our passage but was probably safer. He'd also shut down all systems except the engines to minimize our heat signature. If pursuers did try to track us from a flying craft like an atmospheric shuttle, they'd have a hard time honing in on our location in the enormous oceans of Lissex.

This worked fine until the wind picked up, whipping the sails against the masts and rocking the small vessel from side to side. No support systems meant no stabilizers. With some effort, I put on my torn shirt and jacket. I tried to ignore the pounding headache developing and went topside, clinging to every handhold and rail to prevent myself from being thrown to the deck.

Dark clouds rolled in from the east, and a curtain of rain fell in the distance, not yet at our location, but heading our way. Stinging spray lashed my face. The waves tripled in size, some crashing across the deck and making footholds tenuous. I took the grip soles from my jacket pocket and slapped them on the bottoms of my boots, then made my way to the main mast where Jaren stood.

Wind had torn the sails loose from their furled position. Two had ripped, strips of them hanging along their white lengths. The young lord struggled with several ropes and a winch, and I could see him trying to reel in the sails and secure them before further damage occurred.

When I moved to help, he waved me off to one of the other masts, showing me with hand gestures and arm motions what he wanted me to do. Though I nearly whacked myself in the head with the boom, I got the general idea. The rain hit, drenching my hair and pants and running off my jacket and down my collar. The sky turned black as night, and lightning flashed, arcing across the sky in a spectacular display.

I hauled in the sail and secured the lines as well as my desert-raised brain knew how. Jaren fastened his own in place, and we met at the third and final mast to work on it together. I made the mistake of looking over the rail at the rolling waves, noting the rise and fall of the yacht as it bounced and rocked. Holding the mast for support, I closed my eyes and fought the vertigo in complete misery. My side ached, and my head spun.

Jaren wrapped one arm around my midsection, palm flat on my churning stomach. He pressed the other to my forehead, and his chilled touch eased the pounding. "You're not seasick." He spoke directly into my ear to be heard over the storm. Thunder rumbled, and a lightning bolt hit the water off the starboard side, sending up a spray of foam.

The buzzing made everything much worse, and I doubled over. The healer-induced nausea caused me to dry heave, coughing my throat raw.

"You're not seasick," Jaren said with authority.

I wanted to yell at him to shut up, but I choked instead. Rain plastered my hair to my face. The boat rocked. The thunder boomed.

The nausea ceased.

"I'm not seasick," I echoed him.

He smiled. "Let's secure these sails."

When we finished, we headed across the deck to go below. A wave and a gust of wind caught us simultaneously, tossing me to the deck and throwing Jaren against the railing, sending him halfway over it. I watched him hover there, suspended above the furious sea. The indecision etched itself in his features. It would have taken so little to release the rail, to jump.

I held my breath. No way could I rise and reach him in time. Suicide violated the rules of his religion, but if he changed his mind, there was no preventing it.

I found myself wondering what Kila's punishment would have been if I'd succeeded in killing him and the Believers discovered she hired me. Then again, with her pious innocence, who would believe her capable of such an act?

Centimeter by centimeter, Jaren eased himself off the barrier and backed away from it like a sinful temptation. No fear haunted his eyes when he turned to face me, only determination. He reached out a hand to help me up, and I grasped it.

"Where's the body?" I shouted over the gale. I'd paused at the head of the stairs. The corpse of the *Regiment 1*'s first mate was missing.

It took him a moment to register my question. "That one, I gave to the sea."

KILA PROGRAMMED the *Tempest* to take the most direct route to Paradise, pushing its engines to their highest possible speed and beyond. The auto-captain warned her, in its patient but firm computerized voice, she might burn out the mechanisms, but she had no alternative. She had to head off Jaren and Cor before they left Lissex. Otherwise she might never find them.

Her parents told her of Cor's apparent intent to protect her brother, but she had no idea where the assassin might hide him, and if there was one thing assassins were good at, besides killing people, it was hiding.

When she docked at Wayfarer's Wharf, the first thing Kila did after securing the vessel was scan for the *Triumph*. Not there, and it should have been. A wave of fear swept over her. Weather analysis detected a violent storm to the east. The auto-captain avoided it, skirting its edge so she experienced nothing more than a little drizzle. But if the *Triumph* had gone down in that squall….

Tears formed at the corners of her eyes while a fist closed around her heart and squeezed. She couldn't bear to consider losing Cor without ever having the chance to apologize for lying to her.

No. Jaren was an adept sailor, and Cor had proven herself resourceful time and time again. She brought up a meteorological graph of the inclement weather system. The storm registered as a class two, not a hurricane. She was being silly.

Kila tried to get a grip on her frayed emotions, to think things through. Cor wouldn't plot a direct course to Paradise. Too obvious with so many searching for Jaren. Kila had seen the hunters, flying low in their atmospheric craft, buzzing back and forth over the ocean, returning to Paradise to land and refuel, only to head out again.

And the boats, some of the fastest she'd ever encountered, hulking metal military vessels in dull grays, their steel hulls uniform and featureless except for the weapons extending through small portholes on their sides. One brazenly halted her, commanding Kila over radio channels to appear on deck so they could see her. Once they made eye contact, they let her go. They'd detected one life-form aboard, and she wasn't Jaren.

What if one of them captured the *Triumph*?

Kila shook herself. She'd make herself crazy thinking along those lines. No. She had to trust Cor and Jaren would arrive on Paradise, maybe by a more indirect route, maybe without docking at Wayfarer's Wharf at all, but they'd get there. The problem was, how could she possibly intercept them?

Inside, the ephem swelled with a sudden surge of power and knew He had sacrificed the other, channeling its energy into the one remaining entity. With this much strength, it could more easily control the girl.

To test itself, it nudged Kila's consciousness, guiding her off the deck and onto the pier. There, it took a long, slow look through her eyes, searching for the Triumph....

But it spotted something else. Or rather, someone.

Evil knows evil. Darkness gravitates to darkness. And the woman dangling her legs over the edge of the dock, black boot bottoms centimeters above the water's surface, gave off the vibes that could make even an unemotional ephem vibrate with suppressed excitement.

Kila's human eyes had insufficient strength to identify the indelible ink markings on the woman's bare forearm. The redhead wore the tattoo openly, leather vest leaving her arms naked from shoulder to fingertips. But through Kila, the entity recognized the Guild brand.

Another assassin meant renewed opportunity.

Kila turned her steps in the woman's direction. Tears welled in her eyes and fell, rolling down her cheeks before she knew she'd shed them. She hovered over the Guild member until several drops landed on the dark leather pants clinging to muscular thighs. Cosmetically altered lavender eyes turned to glare up at Kila.

"What the fuck you cryin' about?"

Her throat threatened to close, but Kila forced the familiar words out. "I want to hire you to kill my brother."

"And who the hell is your brother?" The woman was amused now, a smile quirking firm lips between sharp cheekbones. The hint of a chuckle bubbled beneath her words.

"Jaren T'ral. He raped me." No time to mince words, to build up, to earn trust. Not if she wanted to catch Cor.

All trace of the assassin's humor evaporated in the Lissex humidity.

"WHAT DID you think of? What made you decide not to just let go and fall overboard?" I asked, grasping a mug of hot tea while I sat across from him in the galley. I didn't need to clarify further. Jaren took a long swallow from his own steaming cup and set it down with a clink muffled by a coaster. The ship continued to rock, though I hardly noticed, and he retained his hold on the cup to keep it from sliding across the table. "Kila, my parents, friends I went to school with."

"Not your religion."

He flushed a deep shade of red. "No."

I didn't press the issue. I wasn't trying to disillusion him further than he already was. The foundations of the Givers of Life seemed sound. They'd simply become misguided somewhere along the way. I just wanted him to see he had many reasons to live beyond, "My gods told me I have to."

Lightning flashed outside the galley's porthole, and thunder rolled in a long bass rumble. I stood, using the back of the chair for balance, and reached for another self-heating pouch of tea from the cabinet. Breaking the seal, I let the chemicals mix in its lining. In a minute, steam rose from the inner compartment. I refilled both our cups. "Tell me about the origins of your religion. It sounds like you once had military defenses, an army of protectors."

Jaren smiled in a condescending manner, then erased it at my dangerous look. "Sorry. It's that everyone I know was raised on the history of the Givers of Life. I'm not used to outsiders." He folded his hands on the table. "Our beliefs are thousands of years old. The Generational Kila carried wasn't an original text. None of those were preserved. That one's only a few hundred years old."

"Still seems like a valuable artifact to carry around on her travels," I interrupted.

"She always believed the older the text, the less lost in translation to modern-day speech."

I nodded, and he went on. "Our precise origins are unknown. The religion didn't evolve on Lissex. We traveled from some other world described as a harsh environment with little moisture." He laughed and indicated his soaked shirt and shorts. "I could have used a little less moisture today."

I chuckled with him, wringing out my shirt and leaving a wet spot on the floor. His smile reminded me of Kila's, and an ache unrelated to my injury wrenched my insides. I wondered if her home survived the onslaught, if she was safe and unharmed.

"According to scripture, an earlier Chosen left the sacred temple for reasons unknown and was killed by nonbelievers. The gods punished the Givers of Life for not protecting him, making the temple disappear beneath the planet's surface. With their place of worship gone and their leader dead, our ancestors had nothing to hold them there, so they left."

I froze with my cup halfway to my lips and stared at nothing. The liquid within sloshed around as the boat rocked, but I ignored it. A prickling sensation unrelated to Jaren's powers began at the base of my neck, crawling into my head and down my spine until I shivered.

It couldn't be. It was too much of a coincidence.

Then again, if there could be audible healers and Chosens, why not send an assassin to lead one home? Until now, I never really believed in Fate. I might need to reconsider that position.

And I thought my life couldn't get more complicated.

Jaren left the room, catching himself on the doorframe on the way out. He returned with a towel and wrapped it around my shoulders. I drew the edges closed over my chest. To him, I must have seemed dazed, but a plan began to form.

"In this temple, you'll be safe?"

He watched me, studying my eyes, gauging my sanity. His words came slow and measured. "According to legend, yes. Dark forces pursue me." The corner of his mouth twitched. "Your typical evil entities, not our mercenary friends. We call our demons ephems." Jaren's half grin showed his skepticism about the accuracy of the legends. "Outside the temple, they could conceivably defeat me, but an undefeatable army awaits my return. I'd be untouchable there. Unfortunately, we lost those records. We have no idea where the temple was or the world of our origins, for that matter. It might lie beyond the settled worlds, in some distant galaxy reached through a wormhole for all I know. Cor, you're pulling on threads instead of weaving the blanket. Historians have tried to find the temple of the Givers of Life for centuries."

"Yes," I told him. "But they never asked a bringer of death where it was."

A flash of lightning lit the darkened afternoon sky, and thunder growled its response.

THIS REST house where the assassin rented a room lay in a part of Wayfarer's Wharf Kila avoided when she came here. The same collage of pastel colors decorated each building, but here the storm-weathered, paint-chipped, hurricane-damaged shutters hung unrepaired; half-dressed innkeepers doubling as prostitutes lounged in doorways or on ratty rattan recliners.

Despite the warning signs, Kila followed her guide, hurrying to keep up with the assassin's brisk pace and muscular limbs. Yesenia, she'd called herself, told her they'd talk business somewhere more private than the sunlit docks.

Beyond the threshold, dim lighting hid the shabby furnishings from prospective renters. A rickety stair led to the second floor, and they entered the third door on the left.

When Kila turned to plead the particulars of her case, she found herself flattened on the room's narrow cot, the weight of one of Yesenia's elbows digging painfully into her spine. She squeaked in fear and surprise, but the pillow muffled the sound.

The elbow switched to a knee. Callused hands gripped her own, wrenching her arms at painful angles behind her until her wrists met. Something cold, tight, and metal bound them together. Yesenia jerked her upright so she knelt on the mattress, a ripper pointed at her head.

"You know her," the assassin accused. Her voice grated in the silence.

"Who?"

Yesenia struck her across the face with the barrel of the gun. The blow snapped her neck to the side, and the tender flesh bruised and swelled around the point of impact.

"The Core of Sardonen. She's here on Lissex. I've tracked her this far. That's how you recognized the Guild brand, isn't it?"

When Kila failed to answer, the woman's eyes flashed with a maniacal glint that had Kila reeling as far from her as she could manage in the small space.

"Isn't it!"

"Yes. Yes, I know her. She didn't finish the job. She ran off with him."

Yesenia paced the length of the room, five steps across and five back, muttering to herself. "She didn't run off. And Jaren T'ral is no rapist." Stopping midstride, she faced her young captive. "You T'rals are leaders in your religious community. And I've heard a few things from the mercs in town. Whatever you and the Chosen are up to, it doesn't involve violent sex acts, and I couldn't care less why you really want him dead. You know where Cor Sandros is. And you're going to lead me to her."

CHAPTER 18

THE STORM ended in the middle of our second night at sea. Without the seasickness, I slept like the dead and awoke stronger and more refreshed with my ripper wound almost unnoticeable.

We agreed to land the boat on the beach along the east side of Paradise. This put us away from the village of Wayfarer's Wharf and equally distant from the spaceport and landing field on the island's north end. Though the larger island also tried to maintain its quaintness, it had roads and aircars. We'd be avoiding those. It meant a long hike of more than a day to reach a ship to get us off-world, but it would make locating us more difficult for our pursuers. And I had no doubt we were being pursued. Near-immunity from physical harm wasn't something humans relinquished easily.

We ran the *Triumph* aground in the midst of a glorious sunrise that turned the sky a pastel montage of pinks and oranges and yellows. Standing on the beach, I caught Jaren's sad expression as he gazed at the vessel.

"If we leave Lissex, I'll never see her again. I'll never see any of this beautiful world again."

I sighed and moved to stand beside him, resting a tentative hand on his shoulder. Comforting wasn't my strong suit. "I wish I could tell you Sardonen was just as lovely, but it's as harsh and uninviting as your Generational describes." I thought about that, recalling stolen moments with Micah when we did survival training in pairs. "At night, though, in the empty desert, with no cities for kilometers, the stars are more brilliant than I've seen them from any other world. I guess there's beauty everywhere, if you know where to look."

Jaren laughed. "An assassin poet." He glanced sideways at me, lips curling up in a smile that reminded me of his sibling. "I understand what Kila sees in you. Your aggression is tempered with empathy. Your willingness to take life is complemented by an appreciation for it."

He turned to take one last look at the sunrise. Despite the absence of scrutiny, I blushed and turned to stalk across the sand. He had to run to catch up.

We hiked for several hours in companionable silence, leaving the beachfront and crossing through farmland.

At dusk, Jaren approached a rustic farmhouse and requested lodging for us. Better him than me. In my assassin gear, with the tear in the shirt, I'd scare off any offers of hospitality. At least I'd run the clothing through the *Triumph*'s cleaner and removed my own bloodstains.

The farmer and his wife, an elderly couple with graying hair and gentle smiles, fawned over Jaren when we entered. They knew his identity, which made me nervous, but when he asked for their help and silence, they were more than willing to comply. They even attempted to give us their bed for the night. We refused, of course, electing to sleep on rolled-out mats on the floor of the gathering room.

Jaren attempted to use their communication system to gain word of his family. I wouldn't allow him to contact the T'rals directly. Instead, he managed to connect with a childhood friend. From her he learned his home still stood. The fire brigade contained and extinguished the town blaze. The invaders left as soon as word spread of our departure, and his parents were fine.

Kila, however, had disappeared.

"You don't think they discovered her talents…."

Jaren turned from the viewscreen, which had gone dark at the end of his communication. "More likely she's coming after you. Her skills hold much less value. A military group wouldn't benefit from them. But she'll want to make amends, explain herself to you. The question is, will you accept her."

I refused to answer. My feelings needed to sort themselves out first. "It's too dangerous," I argued instead, pacing between the bedrolls.

The young lord smiled. "For her? Or for you? Danger has never bothered Kila. Since we were children, she always stormed headfirst into everything, took unrealistic chances to achieve her goals, and let nothing stop her."

That sounded like a good way to get herself killed, but I kept my thoughts to myself throughout the sleepless night spent on the farmers' floor.

In the morning, the farmer's wife, Hena, served heaping bowls of thick porridge and a pink juice that tasted tart and sweet at the same time. I settled in at the wood table, relishing the last few minutes of calm I'd likely see for the extended future.

Ric, the farmer, entered carrying a high-powered pulse rifle and wearing a military-grade blast helmet.

My chair crashed backward in my haste to stand and draw my pistol. Ric turned toward me, swinging the rifle in my direction. Only Jaren's hand on my wrist prevented me from killing the simple farmer then and there. I couldn't see Ric's eyes through the polarized shield of his headgear, but the dark plastic faced me, then angled down at the rifle he held, then at the gun in my hand. Very slowly he raised a glove to his visor while he lowered the rifle. My heart started beating again. He lifted the shield to reveal sheepish eyes and a reddening face.

"Sorry. Didn't mean to startle you. Just wanted to let the young lord know we're prepared."

Jaren wouldn't meet my eyes. "Prepared for what?" I asked, still fighting the adrenaline rush.

Ric puffed out his chest, twirled the rifle twice, then slammed the butt on the wood floor, coming to a rigid full attention. Impressive for an old man, but gods, I hoped the safety was on that thing.

"He's been training with the boys, our two sons," Hena said, patting her husband's arm. She seemed oblivious to the fact the man had almost died a minute before. "Thinks he's joining the Peacemakers force."

"I *am* joining the force." He humphed and leaned the rifle against the wall, then stomped in heavy boots out of the room.

Jaren was right. If old men were this determined to throw away their lives in the name of the Believers, I could only imagine how enthusiastic the teenagers and young adults would be. The battles would be bloodbaths.

Before taking our leave, Jaren thanked our hosts by healing the woman's arthritic pains and the man's pronounced limp from a farming equipment accident.

"Won't that make it easier for him to fight?" I remarked once we were out of earshot.

"He was kind to us, and he hurt. Should I have let him suffer? Besides, if you're right about the temple, no one will need to go to war."

Yeah, that was a big *if*. An *if* that had me willing to walk myself into a den of people bent on killing me, not to mention I'd be bringing in outsiders—another major Guild rule violation, also punishable by death. I was placing a lot of stock in this *unbeatable army* the Generational referred to. Genetic recessive healing traits I could deal with. Magical hidden armies were a bit of a stretch.

I had to be out of my mind.

Throughout the second day, roaring engines overhead interrupted our pleasant hike. They startled the herd beasts in fenced fields grazing on the tender grasses. I recognized some from the pictures of Kila riding them, and my chest tightened. Dozens of ships were arriving on Lissex, military vessels from the look and sound of them, all bearing those who would use Jaren's skills for their personal benefit.

"Why now?" I asked him, watching an X9 Cruiser pass above us.

"Hmm?" Jaren stared after the ship until it dropped behind some low hills.

"Why not capture you a year ago, or two years, hold you until you developed? Why wait?"

His expression turned sheepish. "My fault. The Generational, as I said, is interpreted widely, and levels of devotion vary between households. Some adhere strictly to its guidelines. Others loosely follow its doctrine. It gives estimated time frames for the appearance of a Chosen in my family line, but those times are generations apart, and people forget, lose track. Besides, which measurement of time does one use? One assumes we should go by the yearly rotations of our religion's world of origin, but we don't know where that is. So, people guess. People reinterpret. They wonder if the Chosen is simply an intelligent man with medical skills, if the 'gift' is an exaggeration of something a lot more realistic.

"Every hundred years or so, a resurgence of faith occurs, brought on by poor economic times, times of war, an outbreak of disease, or just a general consensus that we've strayed too far from our beliefs. Congregations make preparations for the Chosen's return. The devout build ships. Pilots and fighters train in secret. Every male child born into any branch of my family is assumed to be the Chosen and watched for signs of the talent. I tried to ignore early indications of my power, pretend coincidences. Then, about ten months ago, Kila and I were walking down the hill from our home to the village." His brows knit together in remembrance. "She tripped, fell, and shattered her ankle. She was in so much pain."

His tone pleaded. For what, I wasn't sure. Forgiveness, maybe, but who was I to judge?

"I healed her without thinking. I could have gone for a physician, but I healed her. It was hard, a lot more exhausting than now, and if she'd broken something more serious, like her neck, I would have lost her. I wasn't strong enough then." Jaren stared down at his hands, grimacing as if they were enemies. "She tried to stifle them, but her cries brought witnesses. Word spread, gradually at first, but it spread. People were already looking. The timing was right." He looked up at me. "It takes time for a story like that to travel, to be verified and believed by outsiders, but there were plenty of outsiders who wanted to believe. Now they are here, determined to use me, dissect me, destroy me."

By sunset, the landing fields came into view, and we skirted the edges of the circular slabs of concrete, keeping low in the surrounding tall grass and scoping out each shuttle and private starship. The area bustled with activity, crews doing external maintenance to their ships, refueling, and bringing in supplies and goods for their return voyages. Several squads of soldiers practiced formations and drills in the shade beneath their vessels. Even at a distance, I could see some damage on their hulls and wondered if the people of Lissex were trying to prevent some of these from landing. I kept us as far from those ships as possible.

In the distance, I spotted what looked like rows upon rows of low, domed structures. "What are those?"

"Hangars," Jaren said, spitting into the grass at his feet. "Shielded hangars, housing our warships."

I blinked. They resembled produce storage facilities. Clever. "What kind of ships?" There were dozens of those domes, extending beyond my range of vision. Maybe hundreds.

"RS Annihilators."

My eyebrows rose. The entire perception I had of the Believers changed with that pronouncement. I swallowed hard. Annihilators were quick and compact, with high-energy-output weapons and fantastic maneuverability. "How did your people afford them?"

"You'd be amazed what religious devotion will get people to donate—time, expertise, money. Believers come from many worlds, not just Lissex. And here we also have a wonderful climate and a healthy tourist trade."

Each of the large hangars might hold two or three of the ships. If the Believers had the skills to fly them, they wouldn't be the ones getting slaughtered.

Jaren watched my expression. "I hope you know what you're doing, keeping me alive."

Yeah. Me too.

We didn't know whom to trust. We couldn't book passage. That would reveal us to strangers and potential enemies. Lissex exported almost nothing off-world, so any ships on the actual landing field belonged to outsiders.

Our only option was to steal one.

"Can you get us to the Annihilators?" I didn't know if I could fly a warship. My piloting experience was limited. But I was willing to try.

Jaren gave me a sheepish look. "I'm afraid not. Father has overseen preparations for the crusade to other worlds. I wouldn't get the access codes until after the official ceremony."

I started to speak, but he cut me off.

"And no, even then, I wouldn't be able to stop them. They aren't following me, remember? They're following our gods."

Which brought us back to these ships on the landing field not guarded by religious fanatics and high-tech security.

A shuttlecraft with a familiar shape and configuration of engines caught my eye from the far side of the landing area. Waving for Jaren to follow, I scouted it, affirming its name as the *Protector*. The Guild owned three ships, including this ship, for the use of the Guild, and only under unusual or very important circumstances. Most of the time assassins took public transports between worlds. The practice drew less attention. We, *they*, kept the *Protector* and the other two in a hangar in Weathered Palms on Sardonen when not in service. Had the Guild joined the hunt for Jaren? I didn't think the contract on me would warrant use of the *Protector*. Then again, the others thought I caused three deaths among them—Micah, the unknown driver of my aircar, and Alek.

And damn my former lover for forcing me down this path.

I shook my head, freeing it of images of Micah and Alek's brutal deaths. Whenever I closed my eyes, most often at night, I could still see the blood pouring from Micah's sliced throat and Alek's body contorting at unnatural angles as vacuum sucked it into space.

Shivering despite the warm evening, I pondered how best to take the shuttle. The *Protector* carried two people, though its systems could support up to four in a pinch. I had to assume I'd have two masters to contend with. Not good odds, considering Jaren would be of no help except to heal my wounds after the fact, if I survived long enough.

It was still our best bet. I knew how to fly the *Protector*. Every Guild member did. The ship's security would respond to my palm print and retinal scan, assuming the Guild hadn't deleted them. It was a big assumption to go on, but any other vessel would require hot-wiring, and while I'd done some circuitry work on doors and windows to get to targets, I had no idea what to do with a shuttle. A mistake could cause a vital system to fail, like life support or the Weiss-space drives. Not a chance I would take.

If I couldn't get access, I'd have to force the pilot to let me at the controls. That would not be fun.

Shadows lengthened, stretching dark reflections of the various ships across the concrete surfaces and the fields around them. The *Protector*'s boarding ramp was down, which meant the occupants were inside or close by. I had to assume the former.

I waited for the sun to set. Jaren and I shared some jerky the farmer's wife packed for us. We chewed the tough, stringy dried meat in silence and watched the rays disappear below the horizon. Raising a palm outward to my companion, I indicated he should stay put. After all we'd gone through, I wouldn't let him get caught in crossfire. Then I drew my pistol, which I'd recharged on the yacht, and approached in a low crouch.

I made it behind and beneath the ramp, where I caught my breath and extended my legs to stretch them. So far, so good. No alarms echoed from within. Travelers knew Lissex as a peaceful world despite recent events, so the pilot might have kept ground scanners off.

Leaning out, I peered into the darkness at the top of the ramp and detected no movement within. I pictured the layout of the *Protector* in my head, the central sitting and eating area with a food processing unit, the rear compartment with two bunks, the floor hatch leading to the engines, and the forward cockpit. Not many places to hide, but I neither heard nor saw any signs of life.

Then a faint scuffling reached my straining ears. At first I thought it might have come from an animal in the tall grass, but I heard it again, and I pinpointed its origins in the *Protector*. It came closer, accompanied by a muffled voice. I had no idea what in all hells was going on in the ship, but I was about to find out. I pointed my pistol at the dark opening, keeping most of my body off and behind the ramp, and waited. If I could pick off one of them before they spotted me, I'd even the odds. I aimed low, hoping for a crippling, not killing shot. I didn't need any more former friends haunting my nightmares.

The first figure stepped to the ramp's head, a shadow against shadows. My finger tightened on the trigger.

Always confirm your targets. Micah's teachings flooded back to me, the constant repetitive drills with holographic simulations replaying in my head. In the underground temple, we trained with headsets and retinal projectors. The computer gave us a figure to hunt, then told us where to find the target, all the while popping out children—huh—old ladies, and other innocent bystanders in our paths. If we shot one, the victim's death was realistic enough to cause nausea, and the user of the device received a nasty shock from the system.

Under these circumstances, waiting could get me killed.

My hand shook. I'd never had this problem before. I wondered if Jaren's passivity affected me somehow.

The figure took a step onto the ramp. She had a slight build and long, flowing hair. Another step brought her into the glow of the landing lights on the underbelly of the shuttle.

I jerked my arm up and away, releasing the trigger as if burned. Kila.

Uncomfortable tingles made my muscles twitch, psychosomatic memories of training shocks I'd received. Thank Fate for Micah's incessant drills. My heart pounded. My breath came in panting relief.

Then I saw the figure behind her and readjusted my aim.

Yesenia shoved Kila forward, one hand over Kila's mouth, the other with a gun, a ripper, pressed to her spine. I knew the master assassin well. She'd envied my skills. Beating me became her goal in everything. She never succeeded, but she had an inflated opinion of her abilities and wore her Guild brand openly at all times. I could see it now, with her sleeveless vest revealing her arms completely. Outside the Guild, she drank heavily and slept with anyone willing. Her tolerance was great, and her performance never declined, so everyone overlooked her vices, but I knew Micah had several talks with her once he became Guild Leader. I suppose I shouldn't fault her for the alcohol and narcotics, given my recent history, but I never did those things prior to the Guild kicking me out.

She must have spotted our approach on the shuttle's scanners. Now she held my friend as a human shield, using a ripper of all things. The act wasn't a minor transgression. It violated Guild law. It endangered an innocent and employed an outlawed weapon.

"Let her go, Yesenia."

She located me quickly. I watched her eyes dart from my face to my gun and wondered if she'd lost her mind.

Yesenia released Kila's mouth, switching her grip to her shoulder, and Kila gasped, sucking in a lungful of air. "Cor!" she cried when she could breathe. "Cor, I'm sorry. This is my fault." Tears flowed down her pale cheeks. Shadows under her eyes suggested she hadn't slept in days.

"First-name basis, tears, good. You mean something to each other." Yesenia smirked. "I came here looking for Alek, hoping he'd lead me to you. This little rich girl approached me on the docks at Wayfarer's Wharf. She thought she'd hire me to kill her brother, a *rapist*." Yesenia spat the final word. "Then she said her last assassin had refused to do the job and teamed up with her brother." She shoved Kila all the way to the foot of the incline, and I backed off, sliding under the *Protector* and keeping the ramp between us. The two women differed only slightly in height. Unlike with Derrick Vargas, who'd towered over Kila by a head, I couldn't make the shot without hitting my friend.

Yesenia's angular face twisted in a smug grin. She shook her head, throwing back bright red hair that fell below her shoulders. "It didn't take me long to figure out that first assassin was you. None of our current members had assignment on Lissex." She paused. "Whatever happened to Alek, anyway? He turn up?"

"He's dead." I showed no remorse. The method sickened me, but I hadn't actually killed him. It was Vargas's shot that punctured the bulkhead on the *Regiment 1*.

"You slice *his* throat too?" Yesenia's face reddened with anger. Her tone dropped to an angry growl, and the grip on Kila's shoulder tightened until Kila squeaked with pain. The Guild trained assassins to remain detached and dispassionate. With me, she'd made it personal.

Emotions caused mistakes. Maybe I could use her feelings against her. I shrugged in response to her inquiry. Kila stared at me but said nothing.

"You fucking bitch!" Yesenia let loose a single blast from her pistol. I ducked farther behind the open ramp as the beam burned a black line across the gray concrete at my side. I smelled the acrid stench of melted stone and tar. Yesenia coughed, and the distraction seemed to sober her. I watched the flush fade from her cheeks. She took a ragged breath. "Unlike you, I did my research. I've been tapping into the local comm chatter for the last several days. The T'rals are fanatical religious pacifists. Jaren T'ral is their Chosen and a harbinger of doom for all nonbelievers, if you follow all that shit—something you didn't figure out until later." She straightened with pride. "I'm betting she wants him dead to save the universe or some crap like that. And then the *Core of Sardonen*"—she twisted the title into a taunt—"broke another contract." She circled the ramp, pushing Kila ahead of her, but I mirrored her steps, always keeping the metal barrier in the way of her line of fire.

"You can't break a contract forged on false accusations," I reminded her. "She gave me the same lie about rape. That lie voided the agreement." Kila looked away from me, staring at her feet.

Yesenia ignored my words. "Made sense you'd come here. You'd have to, to get off-world."

Throughout the confrontation, I wondered what Jaren was thinking or, worse, what he might be up to. Seeing his beloved sister in Yesenia's clutches had to be driving him mad. It didn't do much for my sanity, either. Worse, I couldn't see a way out of this, short of self-sacrifice. Yesenia intended to drag me to Sardonen for public Guild execution. To save Kila, I'd let her, and the shock of awareness formed a pit of ice in my stomach.

I really loved her. Enough to die for her.

"You wouldn't have killed him, anyway, just like you won't endanger her." Yesenia pressed the barrel of her gun deep enough into Kila's spine it forced her back to bow inward. My fist clenched at my side. "It's a good thing the Guild got rid of you. You were too soft to do the difficult jobs."

"Too soft to kill children, you mean." My voice carried despite the softness.

Yesenia's eyes widened as if she'd had a sudden thought. "Oh, I almost forgot to tell you. You've been pardoned! That's right. The masters looked into your final assignment. They admitted Micah's mistake, deemed everything afterward as self-defense. The majority ruled to cancel the contract on you. You're even welcome to return, if you like."

My thoughts whirled. I could regain my status. If I forgot about Jaren, about Kila, I could go home without risk of retribution.

Too bad forgetting about Kila would be impossible.

It had to be a trick, telling me what I most wanted to hear. Otherwise, why would we be engaged in this conflict? I darted back, taking a chance on the quick break in cover to move behind one of the *Protector*'s landing struts. This placed me closer to the edge of the concrete circle, closer to the tall grass.

I risked a glance over my shoulder. Not close enough. I'd have to cross a space of three meters to lose myself in the thick growth of plant life. A rustling came from the grasses, and I knew Jaren had shifted his position to right behind me, though I couldn't spot him in the darkness.

"If I'm forgiven, why are you trying to kill me? Why was Alek?"

"You killed Alek before the decision was made." Yesenia's eyes flashed with hatred. "And *I* haven't forgiven you!" She fired another random shot, this one boring into the grasses and setting some alight.

The rustling behind me intensified as Jaren scrambled to avoid the blast and the smoldering plants. If I didn't end this soon, someone I cared about was going to die.

"I don't give a fuck how the majority ruled. You killed Micah!"

Micah. It all centered around Micah. I hadn't noticed a particular friendship between the two of them. The only times I ever witnessed them spending time together were during practices, group meals… and when he took her off for his private counseling sessions. He'd escort her into the tunnels. When they returned, she seemed calmer, more composed. Eventually, I thought he might convince her to stop the drinking and the drugs. Maybe he hadn't been the one doing the convincing.

"He cared about me, listened to me, tried to help me." Yesenia's gun arm shook. "You think he broke off with you because he became Guild Leader?"

I closed my eyes. It might all be lies, but I didn't want to hear this.

"He broke off with you to be with me! And he was, up until the night you killed him!"

Something broke inside me. It hurt, but not as much as I feared it would. Too much time had passed. What I'd felt for Micah had faded to be replaced by bitterness toward him and feelings for another. And now I didn't need to experience guilt about those feelings. I saw Yesenia in an entirely new light. I gave her a look filled with pity. "I didn't kill him. He killed himself to both save face and not have to publicly execute me," I said softly. "To give me a chance to escape." And I desperately wanted to believe doing so meant he'd loved me, at least a little bit, even then.

She never had him. Not really. He had me. Then he had the Guild. He used her.

"Liar!" Yesenia screamed and fired again. The beam ricocheted off the landing gear and scored the underside of the *Protector*. A panel blew open, and sparks flew from the circuitry within. I heard the sizzling as wires flared and fried. Another blast created a flaming streak through the grasses, lighting that strip of field. Seedpods popped, and the smell of cooked vegetation filled the air. At least now I understood the ripper as her weapon of choice. She'd gone rogue, stolen the ship. And she didn't give a damn how much pain she caused me… or anyone else.

Yesenia lost it, unable to hit me, firing wildly and in random directions, then alternating pointing the weapon at Kila's back and head. The gunfire drew attention from some of the other ships' crews, and I saw ground lights springing on and pilots coming down their ramps to stare at us across the spaces between the landing disks. Some ducked back inside their ships. On the far side of the field, a platoon of uniformed men and women broke into a jog toward us.

Kila squeaked a terrified cry as the crazed woman wrenched her from side to side, oblivious to the activity beyond our personal struggle. "Step out or I'll kill her," Yesenia shouted. "You want her death on your head?"

I didn't. And watching her eyes, I believed her. She had her pistol in contact with Kila's temple. If she fired now, it would blow out her brains.

I shifted to step from behind the landing strut. The rest of the universe could fuck itself. I wasn't letting Kila die. Kila sobbed, and it tore at my heart.

"Cor!" Jaren's fierce whisper came from the grass, halting my motion. "Cor, shoot her!"

I looked for an opening, something I'd missed, but saw none. Kila's body blocked my aim. "There's no shot," I hissed, hoping he could hear me. "No choice."

"Just shoot!"

Then I understood.

Every doubt, every uncertainty I'd ever faced about my skills resurfaced in that moment. If I missed my target, even by centimeters, all our efforts would have been for nothing. I'd never forgive myself. Jaren would never forgive me.

And Kila would be dead.

"I have faith. Kila has faith."

I couldn't do it, couldn't cause her this pain, couldn't take this chance. The squad of soldiers jogged closer. Some had their weapons raised.

I had to.

I shifted my aim, watched Kila's eyes widen, saw her body tense as she braced herself. I caught her reassuring smile and nod, but it didn't help. In the split second before I pulled the trigger, I think Yesenia realized my intention. She opened her mouth to protest.

I fired.

The beam pierced Kila's shoulder, passed clean through, and hit Yesenia in the same spot. The older woman shrieked and fell, the gun slipping from her grasp. Kila made no sound, but crumpled in a heap, curling into the fetal position.

I couldn't move. My legs trembled, then buckled, and I came down hard on the pavement. The rough surface tore my pants at the knees and the skin beneath. I crawled to Kila on all fours, ignoring Yesenia, who writhed and moaned. Visions of Micah overlay my view of Kila. I swam between memory and reality.

Jaren burst from his ground cover, rushing to us while keeping low. His efforts to maintain anonymity failed. I heard shouts from the approaching forces, and someone used a vocal enhancer to order us to stay where we were. Another fired a warning shot that hit the ground a meter from where I knelt.

It jolted me from my disorientation and shock. "Take her!" I ordered Jaren, waving a hand to the *Protector*'s ramp.

Jaren scooped his sister into his arms. I tried to block out Kila's cry of pain and the subsequent gasping sobs. They disappeared into the shuttle.

Gritting my teeth, I stood and seized Yesenia under both arms, paying no heed to her protests or screams. More ripper bolts landed all around me as I dragged her off the concrete circle and left her in the tall grass, out of range of the soon-to-fire engines. We didn't have time to heal her, and I wasn't risking taking her onboard. But she didn't deserve to be fried in a starship's ignition flare. Her wound gaped, covering my hand with blood, but the arriving soldiers could treat it, if they didn't kill her first.

Yesenia's hoarse curses followed me all the way up the ramp and into the shuttle.

The ephem raged against Kila's innards, ripping and tearing at flesh and muscle, nerves and bone. It stretched the injury, piercing the lung, flooding it with blood. It fought to undo each collection of cells Jaren healed, wearing upon the Chosen's strength, testing the young lord's stamina and straining it to its limits. If the assassins would not do the job, perhaps killing Kila would convince Jaren to break with religious faith and end his own life, eternal damnation, well, be damned.

Jaren would not be defeated. He focused his talents, clotting the bleeding, closing the sundered skin, willing the heart to continue pumping, though it stuttered several times. His power drove back each of the ephem's onslaughts, and when Jaren lost ground, he gave of himself, risking his own health to assure his sister's.

The ephem poured every bit of its energy into a final assault, relishing Kila's weakening screams of torment. It had him. It had Jaren T'ral. It didn't need the Chosen to kill himself with a gun or blade. It would drain him of all his essence, here and now, and leave him a lifeless husk on the shuttle's deck plates.

The ephem sensed it as the Chosen reached for more power, finding it in the body of Cor Sandros and drawing it into himself. He took only what he needed—not enough to incapacitate the assassin, as that would result in all their deaths. But he gained a sufficient amount to save his sister.

Through Kila's eyes, the diminished ephem watched Jaren collapse against the bulkhead, sinking onto the cot attached to the wall while his sister's breathing evened and her heart rate strengthened. The wound closed in a nasty scar that would remain for some time as a reminder of how close she'd come to death, but for now, death was cheated.

CHAPTER 19

I SLAMMED my palm against the ramp retrieval system, not waiting for it to seal in place behind me. Jaren had Kila in the rear sleeping compartment, and the door stood open. I heard his soothing tones, though I couldn't make out the words. Kila's screams rubbed my emotions as raw as her vocal cords. I wanted to go to her, be with her, but I had other duties to perform or none of us would escape. Exhaustion pulled at me, muscles aching with the strain of continued use and tension.

I shook it off, thrust it aside, boxed it into a sealed corner of my tired mind as I'd done on many assignments for the Guild. I could collapse later when the job was done, when we were all safe.

"Make sure you're strapped in!" I called, hoping they heard me. I charged to the cockpit.

At the entry, I hesitated, then pressed the secured lock panel and held my breath. If the Guild had reinstated me, then my ID should be on file. If Yesenia lied, knockout gas would flow from the overhead ventilation system. I knew where the breather mask storage was, but losing consciousness would become the least of my problems. If I triggered the security system, I could grab Yesenia and force her to use her own hand for access, but I'd have to fight my way through the approaching military contingents. An agonizing moment passed while the computer compared my palm print to its records. The air hissed out of me as the hatch slid aside.

I threw myself into the pilot's seat. The first switch I flipped brought up the retinal scanner, and I stared into its red light until it satisfied itself I deserved access. The board lit up in greens and reds. The shuttle rocked, and the hull clanged with ripper bolt impacts.

I scanned the controls, experiencing a few seconds of panic while I drew a blank on how to initiate liftoff. I hadn't flown the *Protector* in years, and then only a handful of times. Most flight training was done in simulators. Then Micah's training came back to me and I sighed. Devoted or not, stubborn bastard or not, he continued to save me even after his death.

Skipping preflight protocols, I fired up the repulsors and channeled power to the main engines so they would warm while we left the atmosphere.

The shuttle shimmied as it rose. Radio signals poured in, some from the control center—a low, flat-roofed building on the far side of the landing field. The gunfight they could ignore, but I was launching without clearance or authorization. Other messages from the surrounding vessels threatened to shoot us down if we tried to take off. That was a bluff. If they wanted us, they wouldn't destroy us.

The hull pinged again as more ripper fire connected with the metal. They could, however, disable us. Shields were meant for use in space, not in atmosphere or on a planet's surface. Activating them would repel with violent force anyone and anything within a hundred meters.

I switched them on anyway.

Through the forward viewport, I watched as the unseen energy flung bodies backward, weapons, helmets, and other pieces of equipment flying free and scattering the ground where they fell. The small transport ship on the next pad rocked, then rolled on its side and over, landing struts reaching for the sky like the legs of a dead insect.

I retracted our own landing gear and opened a channel to control. "Get everything out of the way," I ordered, cutting off the tirade from the Lissex operator. "If you want the Chosen to survive, you'll clear us a path." Maybe that announcement did us more harm than good, but anyone who saw us board knew whom I was carrying already. I could only hope the frazzled male voice on the other end was a Believer or at least sympathetic to them. A flick of my finger closed the connection. The red light over comms ceased to flash.

The *Protector* lifted unsteadily, rocking from side to side instead of rising straight up. At first I blamed my novice flying skills. Then an alarm wailed, and another red light blinked in a steady pattern.

Nothing in my life was ever easy.

I ran a diagnostic of the ship's systems. One of the four repulsors had failed. External scans located an open panel beneath the ship, the same panel Yesenia had blown out in her wild shooting spree. We could still lift, but it wouldn't be pretty.

I activated internal comms. "Better brace yourselves. It's gonna be rough." I winced, thinking of how each jolt and shift would aggravate Kila's injuries.

As gradually as I could, I increased power, and Lissex dropped away beneath us. Flares of light below suggested other ships prepping for pursuit, but we had a good head start.

The *Protector* burst from the upper atmosphere, and I shut down the repulsors and lit the primaries. The sudden thrust from the more powerful engines pressed me against my seat. I thought I detected a wail from the rear compartment, but it had to be my sympathetic, overactive imagination. The cockpit door should have blocked any sound emanating from the sleeping area.

I ran a quick scan of the ships in orbit, surprised by the number of them. A dozen or so vessels circled Lissex, some equipped with powerful laser cannons and bristling with missile launch tubes. A few were engaged in combat with each other, ships sent by warring worlds who wanted to secure Jaren's abilities for their own use. Others moved to intercept our course, probably alerted by scouting parties on the surface. But for the most part, our path was clear, and I silently thanked the flight controller in his little office on Wayfarer's Wharf.

Smaller size meant fewer weapons and weaker shields, though the Guild put the best available technology on the *Protector*. It also meant greater maneuverability, and I dodged the few vessels crossing our trajectory, my hands blurring over the controls while I compensated. The blasts that hit home rocked us, but the shields held and we suffered no damage. I checked the diagnostic computer. They were targeting to disable us, not destroy. They still wanted Jaren.

I reached to bring up astrogation charts on the screen embedded in the console. Anyone who brought up the *Protector*'s registry could make a good guess at our destination. We had to outrun our pursuers to Sardonen, ditch the shuttle, and lose ourselves in the desert wasteland. After plotting the most direct route, I activated the Weiss-space drives. The viewscreen before me became almost blinding as the whiteness of the alternate dimension enveloped our little shuttle and hid us from eyes and scanners alike.

My first thoughts, now that we'd found temporary safe haven, were of Kila. What if Jaren's powers failed this time? What if she'd died of blood loss before he could heal her?

I stood from the pilot's chair and just as quickly fell back into it. The adrenaline rush had entirely worn off, and I felt mentally and physically drained. Other than a few stolen fruits and vegetables from farmers' fields,

I hadn't eaten since this morning, and worries over Kila's whereabouts kept me tossing and turning throughout the previous night.

I willed my exhausted limbs to obey my commands and stood again, locking my legs in place, then moving one foot in front of the other. The walk to the rear compartment seemed as long and unending as my march in the Guild hall between silent ranks of master assassins to receive my wrist brand. The tattoo burned my skin like fire, each needle insertion a reminder of what I'd become—a taker of lives.

When I stepped over the threshold of the sleeping area and stared down at Kila's slack pale face, I feared I'd taken another one. I grasped the doorframe for support, clinging to it until I saw her chest finally rise and fall. Then I blew out a breath and sagged, letting Jaren guide me by the arm to the room's solitary chair, a slab of plastic that folded down from the bulkhead. He patted me on the shoulder, but I took no comfort from the gesture.

Breathing or not, Kila looked terrible. Newly dried blood stained a third of her white peasant blouse. Some matted in her long hair, caking the strands together in clumps. The shadows around her eyes were dark as bruises. I had the strongest urge to rinse her hair, to change her shirt, to remove all evidence of the trauma her body had suffered at my hands.

As if sensing my arrival, Kila moaned and shifted. Her eyelids fluttered, then opened, and she stared around the room. From the way her gaze wavered, I suspected delirium, and I took one of her hands in both of mine, pressing the chilled flesh in what I hoped was a reassuring manner.

"I never knew it hurt so much." Her voice was so weak I almost missed her words.

I'd been shot many times. I knew what it felt like. It burned through skin, severed nerves, arteries, muscles, and seared bone. Every wound I'd ever received ached in sympathy. Something within me shattered. My eyes filled with tears that ran unhindered down my face. "Gods, Kila, I'm so sorry," I whispered. "Gods…." I wanted to say so much more, but my throat tightened beyond speech. I couldn't look at her, couldn't face what I'd done, but a tug on my hand brought my attention back.

She smiled.

I saw tightness around her lips, and her forehead creased with pain, but I couldn't mistake her smile.

"I thought you weren't a Believer," she said softly, fingers snaking from my grasp to wrap around mine.

I forced a grin onto my own face. "You're alive. What choice do I have?"

Her smile faltered, replaced by uncertainty. "You forgive me, then?" I felt a tremor in her fingers, and her eyes closed as if she feared my response.

I'd trusted Micah. I'd trusted her. Both betrayed me in one way or another. I wanted to speak them, but the words of forgiveness died in my throat.

I took a deep breath. "I understand why you did what you did."

Her breathing deepened and evened out. Maybe it wasn't quite what she wanted to hear, but the smile returned, and she carried it into sleep.

Weak, all of them, weak and vulnerable, and the ephem equally incapacitated. If only there had still been two instead of one, they could have defeated Jaren the night before. They could possess the assassin now. They could destroy them all!

But not like this.

The entity was a mere wisp of ether, a tiny spark of energy coiled upon itself in Kila's innards. It had come so close to complete dissipation, nonexistence. The healing force had nearly scattered its atoms for the world of death and demons to reclaim them.

At least there, it wouldn't be so alone. Eternally damned and tortured, yes, but no longer lonely.

Who knew an ephem could experience loneliness?

It thought of returning home, to He-Who-Had-Created-It, but that would have the same result.

Instead it waited, rebuilding itself, drawing from Kila's life force in tiny, unnoticeable amounts so as not to cause her distress and draw Jaren's attention, one strand of power at a time.

Somehow, it would finish this.

Piloting a tiny shuttle through Weiss-space bored me as much as being a passenger. My duties were few. Every six hours or so, I double-checked we maintained the proper heading. The computer would alert me if any problems arose, but I found myself in the cockpit more often than necessary. I had little else to occupy my time and my thoughts.

My nights were filled with new nightmares, dreams of my return to the Guild, Yesenia lying about their forgiveness, their judgment and punishment. I'd try to reason with the new leader, whoever he or she might be, but it would work as poorly as it had with Micah. Then they'd kill me.

Other night terrors involved a replay of shooting Kila, over and over again. I awoke in cold sweats, shivering and hyperventilating and glad I'd slept in the cockpit.

In the middle of day two of our four-day journey, I caught Jaren by the sleeve in the central sitting area. "She's really all right?"

I'd washed the blood from her hair using a small bowl of warm water and some shampoo I found in a cabinet. She now wore one of Yesenia's shirts, and I could tell from her expression when I helped her into it that putting on the clothes of a woman who threatened to kill her didn't sit well, but it was clean and it fit. She seemed to be getting stronger, but I'd recovered much faster.

Jaren seated himself on one of the foldout benches and indicated I should join him. "As I told you the last four times you asked, she's going to be fine." His voice held no reprimand. He merely stated fact. I'd never known anyone so patient.

"I was up and around in a day."

"You're stronger, Cor. You've had physical training, conditioning. And...." He trailed off, breaking eye contact.

"And what?"

Jaren covered my hand with his own. "Well, you did more damage than you intended." I felt the blood drain from my face. He hurried to continue. "It's all fine now, I promise. You caught her lung, and I probably made it worse when I picked her up and carried her, but I assure you, she's healed."

"If you say so."

We spent the rest of that day in uncomfortable close quarters, nothing to say to each other, really, and nowhere but the cockpit and seating area to go if we didn't want to disturb Kila. Just as well, since my actions put me in a terrible mood and I didn't want to take it out on Jaren.

Each time I dozed off, I dreamed about Kila. Sometimes we made passionate love, and I awoke frustrated and unable to satisfy my body's increasingly demanding needs.

Other times, in the midst of our lovemaking, she would scream in agony, and I'd watch while her flawless skin rose into blisters and burned, leaving white bone beneath. In my hands, I clutched a recently fired weapon.

On day three, the subject of my every waking and sleeping thought appeared in the hatchway to the rear compartment. Kila did look better. The color had returned to her cheeks, and the shadows around her eyes had lightened. Her smile was no longer strained. She glanced at Jaren lounging across from me, then crooked her finger in my direction, beckoning me inside.

"Ahem, well, I think I'll go and have a meal, um, in the cockpit. Chairs are more comfortable." Jaren stood and headed in that direction, without fetching any sort of bowl or eating utensil. The red in his face crept down the back of his neck.

"Don't touch anything!" I called after him.

He winked and sealed the cockpit hatch.

CHAPTER 20

KILA HAD the lights dimmed in the cabin. I suspected she didn't want me to notice how weak she still was, but I could see how she held herself, the tentative way she moved to let me enter.

She'd made her bunk, changed the sheets and turned the covers back. Her intention was clear. I worried she might not be up to it. "Kila, maybe this isn't the best time—" Besides, if the Guild did elect to kill me, strengthening the bond between us would be cruel.

The force of her body slamming mine against the bulkhead surprised me. Her hand snaked behind my head, and she brought my face down for a fierce kiss that stole my breath.

"I'm entirely sober," she whispered, her lips brushing mine when she spoke. I felt and heard every syllable as her mouth moved. "Do you want me? Will you stay?"

I nodded dumbly, transfixed. The possible future was forgotten. There were no words. My arms went around her tiny waist, pulling her closer a few centimeters at a time, cautious of how much pressure I applied to her injury. With her full length pressed against me, I could feel her heat. It warmed my soul.

She kissed me again, her tongue teasing between my lips, and my pulse raced in response. Her breath smelled sweet, like the fruit tea I'd brought her that morning. With her good hand, she tugged at the sleeve of my jacket. "Take this off," she demanded.

I complied, shrugging out of it and letting it fall to the deck plates. The fasteners jingled against the metal. While I watched, her fingers went to the tear in my black shirt. She pulled the fabric aside, then sucked in a breath at the scar beneath.

"Jaren told me you'd been hurt protecting him. I didn't know it was so bad."

I raised and lowered one shoulder. "It's healed."

"It's terrible." She ran one fingertip from the top end of the scar to the bottom, just above the waistband of my trousers. Part of me wished the wound extended farther.

I shivered at her touch but felt no chill. On the contrary, a warmth was building, beginning in my abdomen but heading lower fast. I massaged her back through her shirt—Yesenia's shirt—and tried not to dwell on its owner.

The scar didn't hold her attention for long, and her hand slipped up my rib cage, then beneath my breast. Except for around the rip, the material of my top fit snugly. I didn't normally notice or care about such things, but I'd always liked the attention men gave me when I wore this particular shirt, turning average cleavage into something to be appreciated.

Judging from the way Kila's finger now traced around first one breast and then the other, certain women could appreciate my choice of attire as well. She paid special attention to the undersides, something I never knew I liked so much, but my response was immediate and obvious. I'd just discovered another advantage to the shirt's material. Close-fitting meant close-feeling.

Kila giggled against my lips, and I broke our kiss to draw back and look in her face. Her beatific expression made my breath hitch. "What?" I asked when I could speak.

"I love watching your reactions. It makes me feel powerful."

"You *are* powerful," I assured her, stroking her hair. She smelled of flowers. I wondered where she'd gotten the scent. Yesenia didn't strike me as the flowery type, but who was I to judge? I felt like a walking contradiction, a controller completely out of control of the current situation.

"I'm not as powerful as Jaren. I couldn't have saved you." She leaned her head on my arm.

I cupped her chin in my hand, tilting her head up and forcing her eyes to meet mine. "That's not the kind of power I was talking about. And you've already saved me."

Kila blushed and then focused. "I'd like to see more of you, but I'm a little incapacitated at the moment." She inclined her head toward her shoulder wound.

I nodded, surprised and pleased her discomfort with nudity had vanished, and she stepped away so I could reach behind me. The snap of the catch on my back holster echoed in the small space. I eased it to the deck, afraid of jolting the weapon within. I pulled my shirt up and off. It joined my jacket on the floor.

At first Kila's expression remained completely serious, but as she seated herself on the edge of the bunk and watched me, her heavy-lidded eyes and the parting of her lips suggested she enjoyed seeing me reveal myself to her one piece at a time. I smirked, suspecting she'd used her injury as a mere excuse to get me to put on this little show for her.

Slowing, I decided to tease her as punishment. Off came one boot, then the other. I tucked my socks and knife inside one. It felt a little ridiculous, unfastening my belt and drawing it through the loops instead of just yanking the trousers down to step out of them. With Micah and definitely with Vargas, sex had been hard and fast without preamble. It was pleasurable, with Micah at least, and I'd held true affection for him and thought he'd had the same for me. But initially it had been born out of desperation and a need to assert our continued existence among the living. This felt completely different.

I glanced at Kila, worried I might be embarrassing myself. Her tongue darted out to moisten her lips. Her eyes sparked like struck flint.

I kept going.

When I stood in nothing but undergarments, I stopped. The heat in her eyes pleaded, but this would not be rushed. "Now you." With one finger, I beckoned her to me.

She came without hesitation, delivering herself like a gift for unwrapping. I pulled her shirt from the waistband of her skirt, removing it from one arm, then over her head before drawing it gently off the injured shoulder. I tossed it on the opposite bunk and studied her wound.

Kila's injury hadn't had much time to heal. With Jaren's help, it had closed, and a scar covered it, but it looked raw and painful. I couldn't resist bringing my lips to the upper end and pressing them gently to the damaged skin. I traced the length of the scar with soft kisses while Kila trembled at my touch. I continued to her breasts. A bit of wrangling with her bra ensued, and she giggled at my ineptness. Taking off my own was one thing. I'd never had to remove someone else's before, and I finally understood all the trouble men had with mine. At last the damn hooks popped and I got the restrictive garment out of my way, leaving her exposed to my lips, tongue, and hands. My explorations were tentative at first, but I gained confidence with each soft gasp and sigh.

"Not... fair," Kila panted.

"Are you complaining?" I mumbled, teasing her nipple with my teeth.

"Noooo… ooooh…."

I smiled against her skin. My hands went to the elastic at her waist. I eased the fabric over her hips and down past her thighs, where it stopped clinging and dropped to pool on the floor. She kicked off her own shoes, turned me, and edged me toward the bed.

When the backs of my knees touched the cold metal of the foot of the bunk, I sat. The single-width cot creaked and squeaked, and Kila gave a throaty laugh. "Romantic," I said, lips quirking upward.

"Very." She was utterly serious. With her legs, she pushed my knees apart and stood between them. Leaning forward, she bent me back until my heated skin reclined against the cool sheets. I inhaled, and the scent of her wrapped itself around me. I closed my eyes and reached, but my hands found empty air. Then I felt a tug on one of my last two articles of clothing, and I raised my hips to accommodate her. "Lights out!" she called, plunging the cabin into absolute darkness.

"Kila…." Not entirely sure I liked this, I waited. My innate paranoia kicked in, and the vulnerability of my position rang alarms in my brain, but I willed myself to remain still.

Gentle hands rested on my knees. Her voice carried from the foot of the bed. "Do you trust me?"

I'd never trusted Vargas. Not completely. Not enough to go weaponless into his quarters. Not enough to let him turn the lights off while we had sex. Micah, I'd trusted, but he was Guild. And even he lied to me in the end, using the Guild rules as an excuse to go be with someone less demanding on his emotions. I didn't answer Kila's question, but I didn't pull away.

I felt warm breath, then pressure, then teasing pleasure wherever her lips and tongue touched me. Desire for completion warred with never wanting it to end. My hands gripped the sides of the cot, wrapping themselves around the metal bars beneath it. I moaned, and the sound of my own voice heightened the intensity. When she stopped, I almost screamed. Instead I waited in the heavy silence, biting my lower lip while I willed my heart rate to slow.

"Do you trust me?"

I understood now. She needed me to trust her. She'd lied to me, and though she'd asked for forgiveness, I hadn't said I'd forgiven her. And still, I couldn't speak the exact words she wanted to hear. Her soft sigh brushed my inner thigh, and I shivered in the darkness.

Fingers replaced lips, and I writhed on the bunk, making it creak and groan beneath me. Her touch ranged from featherlight to driving hard. I gasped for breath, my hips lifting off the damp sheets, but I couldn't quite reach where I needed to be so desperately.

"I'll never lie to you again," Kila whispered. I almost didn't hear her over my own low growls and moans. "Trust me, Cor." Her fingers slid from me, and I felt her slip her hands under to raise my body to a better angle.

"Gods, Kila, please…." No one had ever driven me to such heights before. I couldn't believe I was begging, but there it was.

"Trust me, Cor." Her lips closed over me again. This time she hummed that simple little tune, the vibrations carrying through to the center of my pleasure.

My brain shorted out. My ears roared with white noise. Flashes of lightning went off behind my scrunched-shut eyelids. I bucked and heaved, but Kila never lost contact, and finally she eroded my resistance, collapsing my mental and physical barriers so I gave all I had and everything I was to her.

I sensed her waiting in the darkness and knew what she waited for.

Leap of faith, Cor. Leap of faith.

"I… trust… you," I panted as she crawled up beside my limp form, and I struggled to refill my expired lungs with oxygen. And I did trust her, with my life and my heart, gods help me. The painful shadows of Micah faded into a muted background, hidden by the afterglow of new romance.

Kila curled into the crook of my shoulder, head against my breast. "I could tell." She laughed. Then, more seriously, "Thank you."

I stroked her long hair. "I'd like to return the favor, but…." Sleep was already claiming me, and I could barely complete a thought, much less a sentence. Normally I had more endurance, but the stress and worry of recent days wore away my stamina, and additional strain would soon follow, no doubt. Besides, I sensed the exertions had tired Kila as well. She sounded pleased but weary.

"Rest, Cor." I heard the smile in her voice. "I'm more of a morning person, anyway."

I drifted off to sleep and dreamed of what the morning might bring.

In my nightmares, I stood upon the altar in the Guild temple, my clothing and then my flesh removed in strips from my body while masters and apprentices took turns peeling away each piece.

When I woke, shivering in my cold sweat, I wrapped my arms around myself to prevent my shaking from awakening Kila. My teeth clenched upon my lower lip to stifle the sobs distending my throat.

Sex might drain energy, but it created it as well. While the two women wore themselves out with pointless fucking, the entity sapped bursts of strength from them, flowing between them freely as their thoughts focused elsewhere.

It took more power from Cor, the stronger of the two, but could not remain within her. Once fully rested, her Will would thrust the weakened ephem from her body.

No. Better to stick with the girl. She had much less sense of self, much less confidence in her worth.

An opportunity would present itself. The ephem was drawing closer to something. It could sense it, a tremendous source of power, and they were approaching it fast. If the entity could tap into that source, nothing would be able to resist its influence.

CHAPTER 21

KILA AND I didn't see much of Jaren over the next half a day. At some point, he tapped on the sleeping compartment hatch, requesting entry, and Kila groggily waved him inside. I managed to yank the covers over our naked bodies before he crossed the threshold, and didn't check to see if he blushed before crawling into his own bunk.

After that, though, it became all business. A half day out from Sardonen, I disassembled, cleaned, and reassembled my one remaining laser pistol, then charged it. I found another and a thigh holster among Yesenia's things that could be adjusted to fit me and cleaned that gun as well. I also discovered a second ripper and spaced it, along with several fragmentation grenades and a vial of extended time-release poison, all banned by the Guild.

Kila scanned my heavily armed figure from top to bottom, a scowl marring her beauty. "You enjoy confrontation."

The statement caught me off guard. I stopped retightening the thigh holster, holding both ends of the leather in my hands, and looked at her.

"*Enjoy* isn't the right word, but I won't deny it gets my blood pumping."

Her frown deepened.

"Look," I said, pushing the piece of metal through the hole and releasing the holster to lie tight against my leg, "people can't always fight for themselves. They don't have the strength, the training, the aptitude. If something I'm good at, something that, well, yes, excites me, happens to help others, then…." I shrugged.

"Then it might as well be you?" Her tone sounded bitter.

"Might as well." I took a seat. Time to change tactics. "What is it about me that attracts you?"

She blinked. "Well, you're— You're—"

"Dangerous? Exciting?" I leaned against the backrest.

Kila blushed. Her voice grew soft. "You're a lot more than that."

"But that's part of the appeal, my nature. It didn't repulse you, though by all the teachings of your religion, it should have."

She paced the length of the small compartment. "And now that they want you back, you'll return to it, permanently, despite all they've done to you?"

Ah, the heart of the conflict. I stood and captured her hands in mine, made her stop and face me. "They've done a lot *for* me. I don't know what's going to happen when I meet with the Guild, but I know what I *am*. If this works out, Jaren will stay in the temple."

Her eyes glistened with unshed tears.

"*I* intend to stay with *you*," I told her. At least for as long as I was able. "If that is with Jaren, with the Guild, so be it. If not...." I spread my hands in a gesture of surrender to her.

She wrapped me in her embrace, and we remained that way until the ship chimed its final approach to the desert world.

Minutes before arrival, I programmed the onboard computer to run us dark the minute we dropped out of Weiss-space. Then I leaned back in the pilot's chair to wait. Kila and Jaren strapped themselves into their seats in the central section of the shuttle.

A subtle tremor rippled through the *Protector*, and the view outside the forward screen went from what looked like white fuzz to the usual star field. The white-yellow glare of Sardonen almost blinded me before I turned away and polarized the screen. It had been too long since I'd seen Sardonen's surface from space.

Proximity alarms sounded, and I slammed my palm over the control to shut them off. I didn't want to risk a scan someone might detect, so I counted with my own eyes. At least five vessels in orbit. Three obvious warships. I had to assume those hunted us.

They couldn't have gotten here faster from Lissex. These had to be new ships, contacted by their allies to attempt interception, all different designs from different worlds, all spaced nicely apart with lots of emptiness between them. Antipathy and competition worked in our favor. Operating in concert, they could have boxed us in. Three craft working independently would be hard-pressed to catch us.

Wide spacing also meant lots of gaps in their scan radius. At least the closest one should have registered our arrival in the same way the *Protector*'s alarms went off, but it might not have had time to observe details before I angled us away. I used the curvature of Sardonen to block the rest of their signals and dropped us into the atmosphere on the far side of the planet.

Prolonged shuttle operation in atmosphere violated a number of safety regulations, but at the moment, I didn't care. The plan was to ignore flight control at Weathered Palms and put us down next to the Guild stronghold. After all, once Jaren established himself in the temple, it was unlikely our presence would remain a secret anymore.

So much for planning.

A strong vibration in the frame shuddered through the *Protector*. More alarms and a high-pitched whine from the engine compartment followed. The shaking made activating anything difficult. My hands kept missing the controls, but after two tries, I brought up internal and external diagnostics and expounded a string of curses that would have impressed a slaver.

I opened shipboard comms. "Pull those straps tight! We're making a forced landing." Which translated to, "We're going to crash, and I hope we live through it."

"Are we under attack?" came Jaren's voice.

I shook my head once, before I remembered he couldn't see me. "Cascade failure from the damage we got during our Lissex escape. One engine gone, repulsors offline, landing gear nonfunctional. And unless you can heal metal the way you do people, I need you to shut up so I can concentrate." I heard the click as the channel closed.

I'm an assassin, not a fucking daredevil pilot.

"Today," Micah would have said, "you are both."

My stomach lurched as one of the compensators failed and the shuttle took a nosedive. I hit the sequence to switch primary systems to manual. The computer couldn't handle the delicate and frequent adjustments necessary to get us down safely. Quite frankly, neither could I, but if I was going to die today, I wanted to control my destiny.

And Kila and Jaren's as well, a little voice reminded me. I told it to shut up too.

The powerful desert winds I remembered all too well buffeted the little craft, knocking me around in my seat and raising bruises despite the padding. I shot a quick look at our trajectory and the location of the Guild hideaway. We were off target by kilometers, and I fought to keep us gliding for as long as possible in the right direction.

Sensors registered fire in our second engine, followed by more alarms. Smoke poured through the ventilation system, and I coughed while straining to see through the forward screen.

No more time. If I didn't get us on the ground soon, the shuttle would explode with all of us aboard. I picked a flat spot between two large dunes and said a quick prayer to whatever gods the Believers worshipped that Jaren would be able to repair any physical damage our bodies sustained. Of course, if Jaren himself were injured or killed that fallback would vanish.

I tried to keep us flat and even, hoping to skim us in over the soft sand, but at the last moment, a gust of wind caught us. I overcompensated, and we slammed nose-first into the desert floor. The impact threw me forward with so much force one of my restraints tore free and my head made contact with the console.

WORST THING about dreams or unconsciousness: they always brought up things best left forgotten.

"This time, I win." Yesenia's body hovered over mine, her weight pressing my spine against the stone floor of the Guild hall, her stinging sweat dripping into my eyes.

We'd fought long and hard this session, the apprentices and Micah looking on while we *demonstrated* proper hand-to-hand combat techniques. Only it never amounted to a mere demonstration when Micah paired me against Yesenia. With her, it always felt personal.

Both of us bore the marks of a true fight; the back of my head throbbed where I'd made contact with the stone, and my right knee ached from a painful kick and near dislocation.

Yesenia had one blackened eye, its lid swollen and holding it closed so she glared at me like an angry cyclops. I'd split her lip with a right cross, and the red stained her front teeth. Her raspy breath belied several broken ribs.

Fighting Yesenia was pointless. She had skills, but I always defeated her. Her shorter stature gave her less reach, and though she moved fast, I had the greater agility.

Sometimes I wondered if Micah got off on watching us battle each other. One thing I knew for certain.

She hadn't won.

I reached up, grabbed a fistful of her auburn hair and yanked it out by the roots, then rolled us both while she screamed. I jammed a finger into her good eye, not deep enough to blind her—I had some restraint, even with Yesenia—and broke away from her twisting form.

Both were dirty moves, without honor, but she wouldn't have hesitated to use them on me, and I'd grown tired of these games.

This was the third time this week I'd fought her. The third time I'd take her down. Maybe she initiated these bouts, asked Micah to assign us together. She tripped me in the corridors, intentionally bumped my arm at the dining table, muttered curses and threats just loud enough for me to hear. We were supposed to be comrades, but she never missed an opportunity to antagonize me. And I never, ever rose to her bait.

Here, all bets were off.

I raised my hand, the heel of it poised to strike a knockout thrust to her jaw, when Micah called a halt to the exercise.

Despite her obvious position of defeat, I could see in her expression Yesenia wanted the match to continue. Her glare burned with a hatred I did not understand at the time—a desire to do more than win. I saw lethal anger there.

Micah gathered the viewing apprentices into a cluster to expound upon the successful and unsuccessful choices we made in the session. Our custom dictated the winner assist the loser to her feet, and warily I extended my hand to my opponent.

Yesenia spat on my fingers, bloody drool running over the tips. One arm clutched around her midsection, she righted herself and moved to the corridor archway. Over his shoulder, Micah watched her go. Then he excused himself and followed. At the time, I assumed he planned to provide medical assistance.

Yesenia shot me a look of victory. "I still win." Her words garbled around a broken tooth, but I heard them.

I didn't understand them until much later.

Maybe I'd moved on from the pain Micah had caused me, but if she'd survived, Yesenia would need to be dealt with, sooner or later.

WHEN I came to, the cabin was silent except for the occasional pop and sizzle of a circuit in the control panel. I groaned, and the sound echoed in the confined space. Or maybe my ears weren't working right. Not sure. Bigger things to worry about. No alarms sounded, though I didn't take that as a positive sign. They'd likely been damaged in the crash. Flashing red lights from the console glowed eerily through the thickening smoke.

I raised my cheek off the controls and tried to look out the forward viewport, but sand covered it from bottom to top. A surge of panic set my heart racing. Living in the Guild catacombs, amidst frequent earthquakes, I had repeated nightmares of live burial. Now I got to experience it awake. I had no idea how deep we might have driven before our momentum ceased. We could be under tons of packed sand, hardened by the heat of the shuttle's exterior.

I attempted a couple of deep breaths to calm myself but coughed on the smoke instead. Standing, I held on to the pilot's chair for support. The room spun, and my head pounded. A tentative touch, and my fingers came away sticky with half-dried blood. Depressing the comm switch brought no response. Only static erupted from the speakers.

Fear gripped me. I scrambled for the hatch, a small part of my rational mind noting the upward angle of the deck plates. With a little luck, our tail, including the ramp or at least the overhead escape exit, would be above ground level. I pressed my palm against the opening mechanism, afraid of what I might find of my companions on the other side. I heard a loud grinding. The door slid open about two centimeters and then stopped.

I slipped my fingers into the crevice and pulled at the opening, muscles straining with the effort. Another set of hands touched mine and I jerked away.

"Kila?" I called.

"No. Jaren."

He moved lower, and I went higher, and between the two of us, we managed to get the hatch open enough for me to step through. Oddly enough, less smoke filled the seating area. There must have been a direct shaft between the engine compartment and the cockpit channeling the smoke up front. I took a breath of fresher air and surveyed the damage. Anything that hadn't been tied down or locked in a cabinet lay strewn across the deck plates. Sparks flew from the food-processing unit, threatening to start a second fire in here.

Kila stared at me, pale and wide-eyed, but I didn't see any new injuries. She hadn't unfastened her restraints but remained trembling in her seat. I went to her first and disconnected her safety straps, then pulled her against me for a quick hug of encouragement. Yesenia's desert gear looked out of place on Kila, but the clothing fit, and the lighter fabrics and camouflage colors would be more practical on Sardonen than Kila's wardrobe.

"You're hurt," she mumbled against my side where I held her. She pulled away. "Jaren!"

I waved off her brother with one hand. He seemed to be handling this better than his sister. Maybe it was shock. "No time. There's a fire somewhere. We need to get out and put some distance between us and this shuttle, fast. Besides, if one of the orbiting ships registered the crash, we won't be hard to track."

I rummaged through a pile of survival gear that had fallen from a bin and removed two packs. "Shove everything you can in these." Once they got moving, I went to the entry ramp and tried to open it. The mechanism inside the door whirred and screeched, and the ramp lowered a centimeter, letting in a small trickle of sand, then stopped. Just as well if we were buried. I turned to my companions, who each wore one of the packs. "Breathers," I ordered, pointing to a sealed compartment. "There should be two. I registered a pretty bad dust storm as we came in. Might still be going on."

"What about you?" Jaren asked, fitting the oxygen mask over nose and mouth and sealing the goggles to cover his eyes.

I tied a handkerchief over my face and put on Yesenia's sunglasses. "These will have to do. The *Protector* is a two-person vessel, not stocked for three." I grabbed the access bar to the overhead escape hatch, took a deep breath, and pulled.

The seal released and the square metal door swung downward. Sand poured on top of my head and formed a sizable mound at my feet, but I could see sky through the opening. I shook the granules from my hair and eyes and stared up. Darkening sky. Good and bad. Cooler temperatures but more predators.

A small explosion sounded from beneath us, and a rumble shook the deck under our feet. We exchanged looks, and then I hauled Kila to the pull-down ladder and shoved her upward, both hands on her ass. "As soon as you're out, get clear. If there's a rock outcropping, get behind it!" I shouted after her, hoping it wouldn't be the last time I got to grab her there. I turned to Jaren. "You next."

He hesitated and opened his mouth to argue but snapped it shut at my look.

"This is all for nothing if you die here."

He started up the ladder, and I fell in behind him. "That's what I wanted," I heard him mutter when he reached the top.

"You still want it?"

When he turned to look down, his expression through the transparent breather mask showed genuine surprise. "No, not at all."

I'd given him hope he might live his life without starting an interstellar war, and my determination to get us through this increased tenfold. "Good. I'd hate to think—" A wave of dizziness caught me off guard, and I almost lost my grip on the rung. I clung to it one-handed, the other going to my forehead while the world spun around me. Nausea and an overwhelming desire to sleep followed close on the vertigo's heels.

"Cor!" Jaren reached down and caught the shoulder of my jacket, then drew me upward.

The shuttle rocked with another minor explosion, one of the fuel tanks most likely, and a deck plate burst from the floor. Steam poured out of the hole, and I swung myself to the opposite side of the ladder to avoid having the flesh melted from my body.

Somehow, Jaren retained his grip and continued to pull. Kila's face appeared beside his, and more hands caught hold of me. It took both of them to drag me through the opening. The three of us tumbled down the side of the *Protector* and landed with soft thuds on the sand below.

The wind picked up, and with the swirling sand, I could hardly see in the twilight. Each of the siblings grabbed an arm and dragged me, half walking, half stumbling, across the dunes. We dropped behind an outcropping of jagged black rocks, our backs pressed against the rough surface, our breaths coming in harsh gasps. Jaren and Kila were winded from the exertion. I actually couldn't draw a good lungful of air, even with the protective handkerchief over my mouth.

Jaren pulled off his oxygen feeder and slipped it under my facial covering. I heaved a few breaths before nodding and pushing it back at him.

The shuttle chose that moment to explode, and we huddled together, shielding our heads with our arms while debris rained down around us. I leaned over to protect Kila's body with my own and caught her faint whimper despite the noise.

This was only the beginning.

Once things stopped going boom, Jaren gave my head a quick healing, and we set out across the sand. I ended up taking Kila's goggles and giving her the sunglasses. Jaren could lead her. I was the one who knew where we were going, sort of, so I needed to see.

Pausing, I consulted the GPS Kila had tossed in her pack. Not like it could give me precise directions. The Guild stronghold wasn't on any map. But at least it told me we headed west, which was where we wanted to go.

After about an hour, twilight turned to full dark. The wind died down—thank any and all gods. We removed our protective eyewear, and Jaren and Kila no longer needed the breathers, but the cold bit through our insufficient clothing. Exhaustion showed in my companions' faces and I'm sure mine as well. I suspected I looked the worst. Even with the concussion healed, receiving the injury plus the vomiting that always accompanied Jaren's ministrations drained me. The siblings kept shooting me concerned glances and exchanging looks.

I opened my mouth to tell them to quit it, when I tripped and ended up face-first in the sand. Staying there didn't seem like such a bad idea.

"We should stop," Jaren said, pulling me to a seated position. "You have to rest after a healing. The process draws from your reserves."

I spit out a mouthful of sand. "Is that how it works?"

He cocked a grin at me. "Far as anyone can tell. I just help things along."

I allowed myself to rest a moment while I considered our options. We hadn't put nearly enough distance between ourselves and the shuttle for my comfort. In fact, if I strained my eyes, I could still make out the flames from the explosion flickering in the distance. However, the sandstorm would have erased our tracks, and I already knew from prior experience with all the wildlife, scanners became useless.

I could hear that same wildlife now, hissing and spitting in the darkness—Sardonen sand lizards trying to decide if we'd make a good meal or were too dangerous in a pack of three to take down. "We need shelter. Some of the rock formations have caves."

"Like that one?"

I followed where Kila pointed. An outcropping of large stones loomed about a third of a kilometer away. At least that was my guess. Distances could be misleading in the desert. The moonlight cast odd shadows over the rocks, but I thought I could see a darker area at the base that might be an opening.

Nodding, I let them pull me to my feet, then swayed where I stood. No more taking point for me. Jaren threw one of my arms over his shoulders while Kila took the other, and the three of us trudged our weary way across the dunes.

The temperature dropped another ten degrees before we made it to the cave mouth. If I'd had a scanner, I would have checked the interior for life-forms. Without one, we had to take our chances or freeze.

We hadn't gone more than three steps inside before a low hiss greeted our entry. Jaren extended a flashlight outward. The beam bounced off a pair of angry red eyes.

Chapter 22

"Nobody move," I whispered.

It heard me anyway, and the hiss intensified in volume. The four-foot-long lizard crept toward us. We could make out its pointed snout, gaping jaw, and jagged yellow teeth. A thin line of drool dripped from its mouth. Several of the teeth were chipped, and one was missing altogether, indicating the advanced age of the beast. That meant it might be slower but presumably more experienced and intelligent to have survived this long in such a harsh environment.

I lifted my arm from around Jaren's shoulders, slowly reaching down to Yesenia's confiscated holster and pistol hanging on my thigh. The lizard growled, low and deep in its throat. I never knew they could growl. Then again, if I'd ever gotten close enough to find out, I probably wouldn't have lived to share the discovery. The beast's throat muscles distended. That I recognized.

"Watch out!"

I pulled the others back as it fired a warning shot of venom. The yellow liquid spattered the sand where we'd stood. Wherever it made contact, the granules sizzled, and a tiny curl of smoke rose from the ground. If it touched skin, it would first burn like acid, then sink through the epidermis to the blood vessels. Once in a human's system, it placed its victim in a state of euphoric bliss, making the lizard's dinner docile while it ate the subject alive.

"I think the gun is out," Jaren muttered out of the corner of his mouth. We'd frozen in place again. Kila trembled under my hand.

"No shit," I whispered back. "Any other ideas?"

"One." Without moving, Jaren began speaking to the beast. "You don't want to eat us. You just want to go away, find some other nice, comfy cave to sleep in tonight and leave us this one."

I rolled my eyes. Under any other circumstances, I would have burst out laughing, but not here and not now. The lizard's back arched, and it hissed again. It took a few steps toward us.

"I don't think it understands Standard."

Jaren ignored me, continuing to reason with the creature in that soothing tone of his that made my head spin when directed at me. Even without being the target, my hearing fluctuated, Jaren's voice rising and falling in volume in my ears. My peripheral vision blurred. I saw no indication it had any effect on the predator. The lizard moved again. Soon it would reenter spitting range.

At first I thought the soft humming signified a new threat, and my muscles tensed in anticipation of an attack from my left. Then I realized the source—Kila. I risked a quick glance down at her. She closed her eyes in concentration and increased the volume of the simple little tune.

The sand lizard swayed, and it blinked in quick bursts. The rigidity of its body relaxed in a ripple that traveled from snout to tail. The creature shook its head in apparent confusion, spattering spittle everywhere and sending up tiny clouds of acid-smoke. Then it tucked its tail around itself like a wrap. In a resigned fashion, it stalked from the cave and disappeared into the night.

I let go of Kila, and she and Jaren sagged against each other. After searching the rest of the cave for wildlife, I rummaged around in the pack on his back and came up with a palm-sized mini-shield generator, which I set at the entrance. A remote activated the repellent field, producing a low hum. Anything that touched the invisible screen from either side would get a mild shock and set off a beeping alarm. It wouldn't stop a determined human, but it would send most animals scurrying and alert us either way.

I'm not sure which of us was in the worst shape, between using the healing power and being healed. It took all our efforts to make the frigid space comfortable enough for sleeping. Not wanting to risk a fire that might be seen from outside, I warmed a few stones with my laser set on low power. I wouldn't call our makeshift home cozy, but it raised the temperature to a bearable level. Jaren spread out the two thermal sleep sacks, and Kila heated some tea and soup in their self-warming pouches.

We ate in silence, and I hadn't noticed I'd dozed off sitting up until Kila tugged on my sleeve. I'd finished the soup, but the tea spilled from my slack hand and soaked into the dry earth.

Smiling, she drew me down beside her, wrapping one of the padded sacks around us while Jaren took his to the opposite side of the cave. I appreciated his attempt to give us some privacy, but it wasn't that large a space. Besides, I didn't possess the strength for anything amorous tonight.

Her hair brushed my face as she lay with her back to my chest. "I told you, you were powerful," I whispered. "You saved all our lives tonight." Despite the obvious drawbacks, it had to be tough living in her brother's shadow, but Jaren hadn't been able to deter that sand lizard.

"Mmm. I did, didn't I?" Her voice sounded sleepy and a little sultry, and my stomach did a flip.

Calm down, Cor. No matter how much you want her, your energy is spent, and her brother is five meters away.

I wrapped my arms around her and settled my head on my folded jacket.

Exhausted as I was, sleep refused to come. I tried to lie still so as not to disturb Kila. She'd drifted right off, and her breathing came heavily and even. But all my body wanted was to toss and turn.

This night might very well be my last.

By tomorrow afternoon, assuming nothing else interfered, we'd reach the Guild hideout. I'd explain the situation to the new Leader, whoever he or she might be. Mystical armies aside, my fate would be in that person's hands.

I had many regrets, but revisiting the events of the past few weeks, I wouldn't alter my actions. Jaren deserved a life, and his and Kila's wondrous abilities needed to be protected. But I hated myself for building the relationship between Kila and myself, for leading her to believe we might have a future together.

Assassins died young, and I was ensuring my life expectancy would be especially short.

In the earliest hours of morning, I awoke from uneasy dreams. Kila's warm body pressed against mine. She'd turned at some point and lay facing me, the top of her head tucked under my chin. I waited until my breathing regulated and my heart rate slowed from the nightmares. Then I listened as Jaren stood and crossed the cave. I heard the hum of the repellent field die, then reactivate, and assumed he went outside to relieve himself.

I slid my hand down Kila's body, rough calluses against her smooth skin. The waistband of Yesenia's camouflage pants put up a bit of a barrier, but I managed to slip my fingers inside. She wore nothing beneath. A silly grin spread across my face, and I tried to will it away, but it remained. Encouraging her further was wrong, dead wrong. But on this possible last morning, I couldn't resist touching her one more time, and here, behind the repellent field, we were safe enough for a brief indulgence.

Kila moaned in her sleep, or half-sleep, as my hand explored the softest parts of her. She shifted closer, pressing her hips against mine, begging my fingers to enter. "Shh," I cautioned, obliging her needs while smoothing her auburn-blond hair away from her face with my other hand. I enjoyed watching her expression shift from confusion to pleasure. Her eyelids fluttered.

She sighed, then gasped as I located a particularly sensitive spot.

"Cor...." My name shuddered out of her on a ragged breath. My own arousal increased as her hips moved rhythmically in time with the motions of my fingers, but I fought it down. This wasn't about or for me. It was for her, all of it, everything.

The fabric of the sleep sack whispered and rustled around us as Kila's movements became more rapid, more desperate. With a gentle nudge, I urged her to roll onto her back, but she shook her head. "I want to be... this close to you... when—" She gasped again, then bit down on her lower lip to stifle a moan.

My soft chuckle disturbed wisps of her hair. They fell across her cheeks and forehead. "What's the matter? Can't do this quietly?" I made it a challenge and used my thumb to tease her without mercy.

A whimper rewarded my efforts, a whimper that rose in volume when I drove my fingers deeper.

"Your brother's outside, but if you're too loud...," I warned, leaning forward and closing my teeth gently around her hard nipple through the thin fabric of her shirt. My tongue drew wet circles over the material.

That did it.

"I... don't... care... ooooh." Kila pressed her lips against my shirt to stifle the rest of her cry, but too late. Jaren returned as she released, and I shot him a sheepish grin over Kila's shoulder. The redness in his cheeks gave away his embarrassment at overhearing us.

"I'm thinking we should cover as much ground as possible before the sun gets high," the young lord said, shifting the focus and gesturing at the cave mouth. A thin beam of light spilled in through the opening. Dawn had arrived.

Kila growled something unintelligible, yanked my jacket from beneath my head, and hurled it at him without looking. It managed to hit him in the face anyway, and he tossed it back while packing our survival gear in the knapsacks.

Despite the early start, it didn't take long for the temperature to rise, and by full daybreak, the heat drained us. I recognized some of the rock formations and knew we would walk the rest of the day to reach the stronghold. We'd drunk most of the water in the two canteens we'd brought. Kila's hair stuck to the back of her neck, despite tying it up in a long tail, and weariness showed in every heavy step she took. Jaren seemed to be focusing all his concentration on putting one foot in front of the other. He kept his gaze fixed straight ahead and didn't waste energy on idle conversation. Both the T'rals stumbled often, and I walked close to Kila, ready to catch her if she passed out.

I fared a little better, having spent many years living in the Sardonen desert, but in the evening, when the outcropping hiding the entrance to the Guild fortress came into view, even I was almost grateful. Almost.

We walked past several aircars hidden under camouflage netting before reaching the rocks. One of them was a burned-out heap, half-buried in the sand, and I recognized my own vehicle stripped of all usable parts. Nausea twisted my gut as the memories of that horrific night flooded back to me, and I felt Kila rub my shoulder, following my gaze. She didn't know all the gory details, but she knew *me*, was synched into my emotions, and tried to provide comfort. I loved her for it, and it hurt even more.

The closer we got, the worse it became. Maybe it was the heat after all, but my vision swam with images of Micah's slit throat, the crash of the aircar and the driver's subsequent death, the blade protruding from my thigh while blood ran the length of my leg. When we stood at the holographic rock face disguising the cave opening, I froze.

This was it. I'd come full circle, and it had been a damned vicious one at times.

Kila and Jaren exchanged concerned looks while I took several deep, calming breaths. Their presence helped, reminding me of the good I'd found along the way, as well as reminding me of what I had to do. Suicide wasn't in my repertoire, but I took the final step forward and walked through the illusion of the wall.

No alarms sounded, but they wouldn't have. An intruder would trigger silent signals sent to a flashing alert light in the central chamber. A *friendly* entering the tunnels would not. No way to know which one I was these days until I got there.

I heard Kila's sharp gasp from the other side of the hologram, but I could no longer see her or her brother. With a word, I shut the hologram down, knowing for certain the twins would set off the alarms if they passed through it. "Come on!" I beckoned once they could see me again. They joined me in the corridor. I reactivated the camouflage holographic display.

Jaren turned to admire the image from the back. "Excellent quality. Expensive technology."

I favored him with a wry smile. "The Guild doesn't work for cheap."

He opened his mouth to say something else, but Kila's shriek grabbed our attention. We turned to see her with one hand over her mouth, staring at the walls of the tunnel.

She'd spotted the skeletons.

I'd meant to warn them both about the ritualistic burial methods of assassins, but with all my personal demons, it slipped my mind. I wrapped my arms around her while Jaren studied some of the remains. He didn't seem disturbed as much as curious. "Victims?"

"No. Guild members. It's how we bury our dead."

"It's barbaric," Kila muttered against my shirt.

"It's tradition. You of all people should understand that. I'm not a fan, but it's the way we do things." I caught myself. We. Like I belonged to them once more. Well, I did, if Yesenia was to be believed, at least until the new Leader spotted my companions and got a hold of me. Part of my macabre imagination wondered if the skeletal remains would become the Generational's magical army, if Jaren would resurrect them somehow. It didn't make sense, really. The Givers of Life occupied the temple before these tunnels had been excavated and used by the Guild. The writers of their sacred text would have known nothing of what was to come, unless prognostication was among their talents.

Jaren ran his hand over some of the bones, eliciting a grimace from Kila. "They're small, not fully grown. Many of them were young, in their teens," he commented, glancing at me over his shoulder with a questioning expression.

I shrugged it off, though it bothered me as much, if not more, than it did him. "That's when mistakes are most likely to be made. We apprentice to the Guild in adolescence. Those who survive the training become masters. Those who don't serve as a reminder to show care and caution."

He nodded. "A method behind this madness. I've found the more I study the Generational, the more I understand the reasons our ancestors had for their rules. A purpose. Only times change, but the text does not. Any religion, and I would almost count the Guild as a sort of religion in its own way, must evolve in order to survive."

"I suppose."

We walked along the dim corridor, Kila close beside me and Jaren examining the walls. "The bones are hundreds of years old, perhaps older. The Guild must have moved in not long at all after the Givers of Life abandoned Sardonen." He paused next to a protruding skull. "From the looks of these, though, the assassins themselves all died prior to middle age." He pointed. "Wear and tear on the teeth is minimal." At my raised eyebrows, Jaren shrugged. "I studied medicine to better understand my abilities."

I felt Kila's eyes on me. I couldn't look at her. If she hadn't realized what she was falling in love with before, it had to be obvious to her now. Even if the Guild didn't punish me for what I was about to do, our life together wouldn't be lengthy. That is, if I rejoined the Guild. Her hand slid into mine and squeezed. My heart constricted.

Only our arrival at the temple entrance stopped me from grabbing her and crushing her to me. Noise spilled out of the primary chamber: clinking mugs, clattering dishware, rumbling conversation—nothing out of the ordinary, so my entrance had not set off the warning system. The smell of cooked meat started my stomach growling. Zibrin roast, a rare mammal on Sardonen and a delicacy. Vegetarianism got old for me fast. I glanced at my watch. Time for the late-evening meal, then lectures, training, meditation, and sleep. The memory of my old life seemed so distant it felt like a tale told to me by someone else. I'd loved the routine, knowing within these walls exactly what I'd be doing at any given hour of the day, knowing exactly where I belonged.

The warmth of Kila's body pressed against my side. Now I belonged somewhere else, but I couldn't turn back.

"This would be a great time for that undefeatable army of yours to show up," I said, disengaging myself from Kila's hand and straightening my jacket. I smoothed my hair into place and brushed away the sand that had collected on my trousers.

Jaren offered a helpless shrug. "Myth and legend, remember? Besides, I thought the Guild invited you."

It did. It just didn't invite the two of *them*.

"Wait here," I told the T'rals. Time for some fast-talking.

I stepped into the temple's main chamber.

Power. Power everywhere. In the walls, the floors, the ceiling. In the very stone itself, it surged and flowed. It rose up from the core of the planet, seeped into every organic structure, infiltrated every cell. It regenerated and propagated. In certain bloodlines, those with the genetic code to unlock it, those like the T'rals, it bound with DNA and passed itself from generation to generation. It lay dormant, waiting for the right mix of genes to set it loose.

Just as the entity lay waiting.

Here, within one of the accursed T'rals, it could tap into that power. The ephem tasted the energy flow, testing its compatibility. Neither good nor evil, the source could be used by both, and the entity drank heavily. The resurgence of its strength made the ephem giddy with euphoria, and its cavorting about Kila's body sent the girl stumbling against the corridor wall.

Her brother hastened to steady her, urging her to lean and rest, blaming the heat.

The heat had nothing to do with it.

CHAPTER 23

ASSASSINS ARE notably perceptive. All conversation and movement ceased the moment I stepped into the great chamber. Heads turned; some hands dropped to their weapons below the long wooden tables. There was plenty of space between us. The eating area rested at the far end of the room, at the base of six steps leading up to the old stone altar.

I made no sudden moves. Instead, I looked casually around the large space, noting subtle changes, the repairs to the damage I'd caused in my acrobatic escape all those months ago. They'd excavated a few more hallways leading off the main room. I remembered Micah debating the merits of expanding the usable space versus the dangers of potential cave-ins. Whoever the new leader was, he or she must have decided the Guild needed a bigger area in which to operate.

My eyes went to the head of the main table, the one closest to the altar steps. Benn. A small glimmer of hope sparked in my chest. Benn trained with me, graduated to master a few days after I did. He alone hesitated when he discovered me with Micah's body. My reacceptance into the Guild surprised me less now.

Benn admitted to mistakes and listened to reason. He also played by the rules to the letter. The spark of hope burned out.

He stood, hands away from his sides and palms turned toward me so I could see their emptiness. "Welcome home, Cor. Come in and join us." His smile seemed genuine.

A shiver of memory passed through me. The last time a Guild Leader invited me in, he tried to take my life, and the last time I'd seen Benn, he'd done the same, however reluctantly. The presence of Jaren and Kila behind me felt like boulders crushing me beneath their weight. Other masters and apprentices smiled as well, some raising their mugs, others inclining their heads in respect. My heart twisted. The outcast daughter had been allowed back home only to arrive and find the door locked.

A frown replaced the smile on Benn's face. "You're among friends, Cor. Surely Yesenia delivered our message or you wouldn't be here."

Anger replaced sorrow, and my fists clenched at my sides. "Yesenia went rogue." My voice echoed in the stunned silence that followed. "She tried to kill me. With a ripper," I added for good measure. "I spared her life, but I doubt she'll be back." I opted not to mention Alek. No point in adding more fuel to this fire. If he'd gone after me prior to my redemption, he'd only been upholding Guild law.

Benn studied me for a long moment, judging the truth of my words. He nodded sagely. "Yesenia expressed concerns over your reinstatement but hid any real opposition. I knew about her competitive animosity toward you but had no idea of the extent. For that, I apologize." For a man of thirty-two, he possessed a remarkable amount of wisdom and dignity. The early-graying hair and impressive two-meter height didn't hurt either. I'd flirted with him on occasion, just for kicks, but never got anywhere.

Rule follower, I reminded myself.

And I hadn't really wanted to anyway. I'd been loyal to Micah. Resentful heat burned in my chest. Wasted years. Wasted tears.

My gaze fell upon the place beside the firepit where his body had lain. Traces of bloodstains marred the light-colored stone, but those had to be my imagination, impurities in the rock's composition. Surely the Guild would have removed all reminders of his death. I thought of the skeletons in the corridors.

Then again, maybe not. He might even be among them.

Squaring my shoulders, I gestured behind me for Kila and Jaren to enter. Now that I knew they hadn't set all this up as a trap, it was time to get everything, and everyone, out in the open. "Guild Leader Benn Narsus, meet Jaren and Kila T'ral of Lissex." I kept my hands where everyone could see them, closed my eyes, and waited for the firestorm to hit.

It didn't take long. Chaos erupted as masters and apprentices alike sprang from the long benches, sprinted across the room, and, with weapons drawn, flanked all three of us. Benn approached behind them at a sedate pace, but a cloud of anger transformed his features.

Kila squeaked as two assassins pointed lasers at her while a third held a knife at her throat. I took a step in her direction, even though I knew they wouldn't harm her, and got an elbow in the gut for my efforts. The pain doubled me, and I glared at the apprentice teenager. Jaren remained calm, holding his ground despite the sudden uproar, looking every bit the religious leader he'd been born to be. He and Benn appraised each other, neither breaking the intense gaze. In this place, they were both home.

When they finished sizing each other up, Benn gestured to the teen assassin. The boy disarmed me, knowing exactly where to look for each weapon, even the concealed ones. Guild trained. Guild predictable. Losing them felt like losing limbs.

Benn seized my forearm. "I will speak with you privately, now." It came out as a low growl. He raised his voice to the Guild and gestured at the T'rals. "Keep them here, watch them!" His eyes wandered over their gaunt, tired, frightened faces, and his tone softened. "Feed them." Then he dragged me into one of the new corridors leading from the central chamber.

Muttering under his breath, Benn hauled me to another archway and a room I'd never seen before. And it was a room, not a cave. The ceiling above showed cracks but held, and several wood pillars had been brought in to shore it up. I realized this was more of the buried temple and wondered what it had been previously used for. Now it held a simple desk, two chairs, some storage boxes, and a cabinet housing weapons.

A part of me considered going for them, but I'd never get to those shelves before Benn would have me. He probably had it locked anyway. Apprentices were always getting into things they shouldn't. I had.

Benn shoved me into the seat in front of the desk, while he perched on the corner of the polished surface. I felt like a student summoned to see the principal, although most schools didn't execute wayward adolescents.

"Do you have any idea what you've undone? How hard I worked to arrange your return? How many files of bylaws I searched to find a loophole for you? Do you?" His fury threw him into motion, and he stood to pace back and forth in front of me.

I wasn't sure which question he wanted me to answer. Probably none of them. I stayed silent.

"I thought I knew you, Cor. You were steady, dependable, and you cared. It's what earned you that ridiculous title."

I bristled at the insult, shoulders stiffening and jaw tightening. The Core of Sardonen. Yeah. I never thought it was ridiculous, though. I actually kind of liked it, though I never admitted that little egotism to anyone.

"I knew, *knew* you had a good reason for leaving a contract unfinished, and when I researched the target and found his age…. We don't kill children." He sat down again with a huff and looked at me. "You'll know that I sent someone after his guardian. *That* contract did get completed. The boy is living with an aunt and uncle now, until he is of an age to make his own decisions. He's doing well."

"I'm glad to hear it." Benn would make an excellent leader, one to go down in the Guild historical records if he survived long enough. I could feel it.

"Micah screwed up. That became clear. But rather than admit that in front of the Guild and step down as Leader, he decided to blame and punish you." Benn raised one eyebrow. "And we know how that turned out, don't we?"

No, he didn't. "Micah didn't go after me." My throat closed over the words, despite his betrayal with Yesenia. "He went after himself. He used my knife. I didn't kill him." I looked down at my empty hands, my memory flashing on them covered in my former lover's blood.

Benn shook his head in apparent disgust. "So, he couldn't admit a mistake to save his own life and restore yours. Figures. And instead, he marks you with a double death sentence, one for unfulfilled assignment, and a second, public execution for killing him. I know you were devoted to him since your rescue in adolescence, but he was an egotistical bastard and a fool."

I blinked. By now I'd figured all that out and come to terms with it. But in my previous experience, Benn spoke ill of no one. And Micah hadn't done *everything* wrong. "He gave me a chance to escape. He didn't know you and the others would show up so quickly."

"He could have just let you go. But no, he didn't want to lose face in front of the Guild." Benn threw his hands up in frustration. "Enough arguing about the past." His blue eyes bore into mine. "Let's talk about the present. I have your unfinished contract declared void due to its inappropriate nature. That negates anything else you were forced to do in your own defense, like killing Micah or, I'm guessing, Alek, since we haven't heard from him. Wouldn't have sent him at all, but it was expected. I tried to recall him after the repeal of your sentence."

"I didn't kill Alek either, but yes, he's dead," I admitted, wishing I could sink deeper into the chair. The wood was unforgiving.

"I do all that, and you dance your way in here with two outsiders. Cor! You've left me no choice. You've exposed our hiding place, endangered the entire Guild, and saddled us with keeping them here and caring for them for the rest of their lives!"

Which had been my intention. They'd be safe. I'd be dead, but Kila and Jaren would be safe. A sad smile tugged at my lips. Benn looked like he wanted to smack it away. His hand clenched into a fist, but he restrained himself with a cleansing breath, chest expanding and contracting. I considered telling him my reasons, but he would never believe me, not without some sort of demonstration of Jaren's power, and I doubted he'd give me time for that.

"There's no loophole for this."

I had to try. "They needed protection." My fingers dug into the arms of the chair. "It was the right thing to do."

"Hells, Cor, I don't want to hear it. Let them hire protection. We're assassins, not guardians, not nursemaids or nannies." He reached behind his desk and pressed something. "I can't help you this time." A low chime sounded in the corridor outside the makeshift office.

Right. Tradition and technology in perfect balance.

A pair of masters arrived to escort me back to the central chamber. Benn trailed behind us, and I saw him over my shoulder, head lowered, spirit deflated, thoughts known only to himself. I understood his anger, though I'd hoped he'd hear what I had to say before carrying out my punishment.

It occurred to me this moment presented my best opportunity to attempt escape, now, while only three guarded me. Three masters.

Suicide now or public execution. Here, Kila and Jaren wouldn't have to watch.

It ended in seconds.

I brought up both fists, connecting with jaws on either side of me, and at least one cracked. But Benn had me from behind, and I was still weak from our desert trek and other injuries I'd sustained. His massive hands grasped my wrists, twisting them painfully over my head. The movement forced me to my toes to avoid further agony and the dislocation of both shoulders. He whirled me to face him.

I expected anger but saw sadness and mild surprise instead. "I wondered if you'd fight. Didn't think you would. You know you broke our laws, and you knew the consequences." He lowered me enough to place my boots flat on the floor but didn't release me.

"Do this here," I begged him. The idea of pleading galled me in the past, but it didn't faze me now. "Take that knife off your belt and end this." I choked on a half sob and saw his blink of shock at my emotional weakness. I didn't care. "Please don't make them watch." A single tear rolled down my cheek. "Please...."

The other masters shifted in embarrassment and disgust. One held his jaw and glared. The other avoided my eyes, but I could tell I'd affected Benn. He stared a long moment at the blade in its sheath at his side. The silver grip gleamed in the hanging overhead lights. Then he steadied himself, muscles tensing and shoulders pulled back.

"No, Cor. Your decision, your punishment, your fate." He let go of one of my arms, retaining his grip on the other and leading me into the grand chamber himself.

I located Kila by her gasp. She stood at the central fire, warming her hands, but turned to face me when I entered. Her stricken expression chafed at my already raw emotions, and I knew the stress and fatigue showed through my features. I was too damned tired to hide them anymore.

Until that moment, she'd probably thought I'd talk us through this or fight my way out of it. The way I'd been removed from the chamber, she had to suspect I was in serious trouble. Having me hauled back in like this confirmed it.

Jaren stood beside her, one hand on her shoulder. He, too, looked concerned. "Cor, what's going on?" I saw they'd discarded their packs, though their breathers and glasses still hung from their belts. No one guarded the T'rals. Where would they go? They were guests, permanent ones, and any Guild member could overtake them in a heartbeat if they chose to run.

"You are not permitted to speak," Benn reminded me in a low undertone.

Or what? If I decided to talk, what would Benn do? Kill me? Didn't matter. I wouldn't have been able to get words out, anyway. And what could I say to them?

Benn marched me to the marble altar on its raised dais at the end of the room. We stood behind it. From here, in this acoustically perfect spot, every ear would hear his words. At least this particular ritual didn't involve stripping me naked. If this were for killing Micah, that's what would have been done to me—complete public humiliation. Didn't really make much difference, though. I felt plenty vulnerable enough without the removal of my clothing.

"Corianne Sandros," he began, voice resonating throughout the chamber, "you have revealed our location to outsiders and thereby endangered us all."

Two masters moved to stand beside Kila and Jaren, in case the benevolent twins decided to break with years of religious indoctrination and try something foolish. They needn't have worried. Kila clung to her brother. I think she would have fallen if she let go. She stared at me, horror evident in her eyes. I wrenched my gaze from her, locking it on a bare spot on the far wall. I would not watch her watch this.

"The penalty for this act against the Guild is death."

No surprise there. The penalty for almost every act against the Guild was death. We were a brutal bunch.

Kila sobbed openly now. I wished someone would deafen me.

"Do you deny these actions?"

Stupid, pointless question. I led them in here, presented them by name. I was tempted to spit and roll my eyes, but I simply said, "No."

I heard the whisk of Benn's blade drawn from its sheath, metal scraping on leather. The hand he moved to my shoulder surprised me with its gentleness. He removed my jacket and laid it on the marble, then turned me to face him, presenting our profiles to the watchers below the dais. From the corner of my eye I caught expressions of both anger and sadness—those who continued to oppose my return and those who supported it and regretted this act.

Benn raised the knife so the tip of the blade pointed down at my chest, right over my heart. I felt faint, and darkness encroached on the edges of my vision. I grasped the altar with one hand to steady myself. My pulse pounded in my temples.

"Do you yield to the law of the Guild?" Even at a whisper, his voice carried.

The collective assembly held its breath.

"I yield." Ritual spoke for me, words I never thought I'd have to say.

Oh hells, I'm going to die.

Benn lifted the blade a little higher to bring it down with enough killing force that I wouldn't suffer long. I saw it begin its descent and closed my eyes.

"Stop, you bastard! No one kills her but me."

The voice came from high above us, drawing all our attention upward. My eyes flicked open to see Benn distracted as well, but not enough to stop his arm's progress. The sharp metal caught me at my shoulder, slicing through my shirt, drawing across my breastbone in a deep diagonal gash. An equally fatal wound, but not as quick and humane as the one he'd planned.

Oh gods, it hurt.

Kila's scream echoed in my ringing ears as I sank toward the stone floor. I would have fallen harder, but I held on to the altar and eased to my knees. I wrapped my arm across the wound, feeling warm stickiness soaking through the fabric of my shirt and sleeve, trying desperately to hold my lifeblood in and failing. "Dead is dead." Jaren's words came back to me. "Once life leaves the body, I can't bring that person back." My life was leaving my body fast. My vision blurred, but I fought the pull toward unconsciousness and relief from the pain, aware of frantic activity all around me.

Kneeling as I was, my eyes just cleared the marble surface of the altar, and I watched Guild members draw their weapons and point upward. The voice above had been Yesenia's. Everyone recognized it, though no one could see her through the narrow opening around the ventilation shaft. She must have used some kind of ocular enhancement tech to watch the proceedings.

I wondered briefly how she'd gotten so close without detection. Then again, she was considered a full-fledged member. The Guild's equipment would have accepted and ignored her approach as valid. We didn't have contingency plans for attacks from within our own ranks, something that would need to change if any of us survived.

A figure crouched beside me, Benn, and I scrambled backward, torn between survival instinct and the desire to be put out of my misery. "Let me finish it, Cor," he said, softly. "It wasn't my intention for you to suffer."

"Yesenia—" I managed through gritted teeth. "My friends...." I had to stop talking. There wasn't enough air left in my lungs to produce sound. My heart pounded, and with each beat, more blood poured through the open gash. The smell made me gag. I tasted it in my mouth and spat it at Benn's feet.

"You have my word they will be protected."

In my backward crawl, I'd cleared the altar and could see Jaren and Kila surrounded by armed assassins. They were innocents. To allow harm to come to them, especially from a former Guild member, would be a great dishonor. Benn would keep his word.

I pulled my arm away from my chest. It stuck, bloody fabric to bloody fabric, and took almost more strength than I had. Exhausted, I let my head fall back against the nearby wall. My shoulders slumped. I waited for the inevitable last strike.

Something dark and heavy dropped through the ceiling aperture.

In my dizziness, I could barely make out the shape, cylindrical, a canister of some sort, black and metal. It hit the stone floor with a clang, bounced twice, then rolled toward the group of assassins clustered at the base of the dais steps, toward Jaren and Kila. The seal popped, and a bluish gas poured into the room.

Those closest to it scattered but fell to their knees, coughing and wheezing, before they could escape from the chamber. Kila and Jaren went down as well, lost to my sight in the swirling blue mist and the throng of gasping assassins.

The first wisps of the poison reached my nostrils then, and the sickeningly sweet smell sparked memory. Issiumoxide. Illegal everywhere. Tortuously lethal in both liquid and vapor forms. It ate away a victim's lungs from the inside out.

Yesenia might just get to kill me after all.

Panic seized the ephem. If the host expired while the entity remained within it, the entity would also cease to exist. The ephem would have willingly sacrificed itself before, when it tore at Kila's innards, because killing her would have spurred Jaren to suicide. But then it would have succeeded, and He-Who-Had-Created-It would reconstitute its form, giving it new existence, a new and higher purpose. If Kila died now, it would fail. It would become one with nothingness for eternity.

Testing its new strength, the ephem pulled at Kila's arm, forcing her hand to her side where the breather mask hung on her belt. When her fingers closed around it, her own Will took over, and she slipped it over her face to draw breath after breath of untainted air.

Jaren also found his mask, and the entity caused Kila to stumble against him in a failed attempt to jar it loose. Her brother gave her a grim smile, steadying her with one hand and reaching to help one of the fallen assassins with the other.

No. She needed a weapon, something definitive and faster than even the poisonous gas.

The entity guided her to the closest writhing body, her hands searching its tunic for concealed knives, but the teenager fought her, honor discarded as he sought to wrench her breather from her face.

Darting out through an ear, the ephem mixed with the poisonous gas. It flowed into the struggling young assassin, drawing in a greater concentration of the toxin, filling the teenager's throat and constricting it.

The lithe body thrashed and convulsed, lips turning blue, eyes bulging, tongue lolling. The heart thudded against the rib cage, lungs burning for oxygen. The throat jerked in pulses as coughs began in the chest and failed to expel the ephem. Then the flopping teenager fell still. The entity within sucked his life force dry.

Kila's mask filled with condensation as she breathed rapidly in and out, eyes wide in horror. She staggered away, standing upright to avoid more desperate, clawlike fingers, and the ephem rushed from the corpse to rejoin her.

All around Kila the Guild lay dying, but only the one young man had yet died. She needed to take a weapon from someone focused on anyone besides herself and the life-giving equipment she wore. Someone like Benn.

He crouched next to Cor, speaking to her in words Kila could not make out now that he'd moved off the volume-enhancing tile behind the altar. He still held the knife.

Using Kila's own desire to be with Cor against her, the ephem spurred her into motion toward them. It would use this vessel to take the weapon. It would use its enhanced strength to finally force Kila to murder her brother. And then, if the virtuous, meddling Core of Sardonen continued to draw breath, it would use her lover to end her life as well.

CHAPTER 24

BENN STARED at me, the horror of the attack evident in his eyes. Issiumoxide had no antidote, and even if it did, none of us could get to it in time. He prepared to stab me anyway, likely planning on using the knife on himself next in order to spare us both the slower death by gas. I raised a shaky hand, holding him off with no more than my pleading expression.

He hesitated. "You're delaying the inevitable, Cor." Benn's voice was raspy. He coughed, and bloody spittle collected on his chin. "We all go together?"

Below, several apprentices writhed, faces twisted in agony. The masters tried to remain stoic, but panic showed in their eyes while they hacked and wheezed. The cluster dispersed enough that I could spot Kila and Jaren. Thank the gods, they'd gone for their breathers when the gas canister popped. Jaren held a dying assassin, no more than sixteen, desperately trying to save the young girl. I could see his mouth moving behind his clear mask. Kila headed toward me, on her feet and staggering between the bodies. Some of them clawed at her legs, probably attempting to bring her down and take her breather. Not honorable but understandable. One caught her, and they fought for it, Kila's unpoisoned strength barely a match for the assassin's training and skills. Then the assassin went into convulsions and fell still. I didn't have time to wonder why he was more susceptible, only to note he was, and to experience a mixture of relief and guilt he hadn't taken Kila with him. But there would be others. I had to act fast.

"We don't have to go at all," I panted, returning my attention to Benn. Blood soaked the collar of his tunic. It oozed from the corner of his mouth. "Get me onto the square." I nodded toward the concrete space, darker than the surrounding squares, behind the altar.

Benn looked at me like I'd lost my mind. Maybe I had, but the Guild Leader was willing to grant my last request. We were all dead, anyway. He caught hold of my shoulders, wincing at my cry of pain, and crawled with me on hands and knees until I toppled on the cold gray surface. Lying there, my cheek pressed against the stone, I tried to speak.

A stream of red pooled on the floor by my lips. On my second attempt, I managed to whisper.

"Jaren, come to the altar." Despite the weak volume, the acoustics carried the command throughout the room. I prayed to any god that would listen he'd understand and obey me.

Benn lay beside me, his blood mixing with mine. His eyes closed. His breathing grew more labored. He passed out.

I was seconds from joining him when Jaren grabbed me, pulled me into his lap, and seated himself in the dark gray square. Thank the gods he was quick on the uptake. I closed my eyes and listened as he spoke, listened with every fiber of my being.

"Breathe!" Jaren commanded. "All of you, breathe. Inhale. Exhale. Expel the poison."

The power hit like electrical current. Jaren's words resonated throughout the chamber, bouncing off walls, reverberating and echoing. It was as if the room had been fashioned specifically for the use of his vocal cords. Every Guild Leader had spoken from this very spot, and none of them sounded like this.

The sound waves flowed through and around me, my body tingling in response as he repeated his demand for continued respiration from his captive audience. Gone were the head buzzing and the nausea. The walls themselves complemented his genetic gift, honing and fine-tuning it for maximum efficiency.

All around me I heard relieved gasps as lungs repaired themselves. My next breath still hurt, however.

"Jaren…."

He turned his face to me, eyes wide with surprise at the effect he had on everyone around him. He'd known the legends, memorized the scripture, but seeing the reality visibly shook him. Concern replaced awe as my hand clenched on his arm. I'd lost too much blood. His figure became hazy in my sight.

"Shit," he whispered, and it carried throughout the room. If I'd had more strength, I would have laughed. I guess we were lucky we didn't all crap ourselves, but apparently he had to have intent behind his words for them to command our bodies. Jaren raised his voice and spoke with authority. "Heal, Cor. Seal the wound."

I grimaced as the edges of the gash across my chest drew together and closed. Leaning against him, I listened to his soothing tones, though the words faded to an incomprehensible mumble, something about letting my heart beat and the occasional reminder to breathe. The world became a warm blanket wrapping around me and soothing away all aches and pains.

Damn the woman. Damn the T'rals. Seated upon that space behind the altar, the Chosen controlled every ounce of power within the room, including that which made up the entity itself. A shiver vibrated through the ephem, knowing Jaren could have destroyed it with no more than a thought. As it was, the residual energy bound the ephem, prevented it from taking further action. It raged and seethed in helplessness but could do nothing else.

This was what He-Who-Had-Created-It feared and sought to prevent. In this place, the Chosen controlled all, and someday Jaren would comprehend exactly what that meant and how much power he truly could wield.

The entity held itself as still as possible, drawing no attention. It would wait for Jaren to move or to learn. One meant victory, the other, annihilation.

When Jaren stopped instructing and asked a question, I missed it the first time.

"Mmm?"

"The canister," he repeated. "What should we do with it?"

We? I blinked, wondering how long I'd drifted in semiconsciousness. Kila knelt beside us, both her hands wrapped around one of mine. Dried tears showed on her cheeks beneath the breather mask. Her arms had scratches from someone pulling her down, and her pants were torn to strips at the cuffs. She tucked a stray strand of my hair behind my ear and offered a smile. My thoughts cleared.

"Put it in the fire. The ventilator will draw the rest of the gas out and disperse it. It's not effective outdoors. It dissipates too fast."

Kila released me to tend to it. I turned a wicked grin to Jaren.

"Hope Yesenia has a breather of her own." She was about to get a face full of poison. "Bitch."

Jaren's eyes widened at my ferocity. Having seen my gentleness with Kila and my willingness to sacrifice myself for them both, he must have forgotten what I truly was. I felt him tense and wondered if he'd call

a warning to the rogue assassin before Kila sent the remains of the gas
her way, but he clamped his jaw shut. So, there were limits to his need to
heal all humanity. Good. I no longer counted Yesenia as human, either.
Maybe he was thinking of the greater need, allowing one to die to protect
many, like he'd tried to do with himself, like I did every time I went
on assignment. Not so much difference between assassin and Chosen,
though I wouldn't point it out to him.

And speaking of assassins, I'd be damned if I'd trust Yesenia's
death to the Issiumoxide.

Using Jaren's shoulder for support, I raised myself to a seated position.
Benn sat a meter to my right, staring about the chamber at his Guild like
he was seeing ghosts. Some of the masters gathered in a circle around the
two of us, but they kept a respectful and perhaps fearful distance. A couple
moved the body of the dead teenager from the room.

I felt my hands clench into fists.

"How much strength can you give me?" I asked, getting on my
knees in preparation to gain my feet.

Jaren paused, considering my question. A metallic clang and loud
pop from the area of the firepit signified Kila's disposal of the canister.
She returned to stand behind me, and I leaned against her legs.

"I'm not certain," he admitted. He closed his eyes as if directing
thought inward, then opened them again. "When used here, the power
doesn't drain me. Interesting."

"Jaren," I urged, glancing toward the ceiling for emphasis. The last
wisps of gas disappeared through the opening. Yesenia might make her
next move at any moment, and given this failure, it was bound to be
spectacular. Crazy people didn't quit.

"Right. Let's find out." He placed a hand on my shoulder. I felt his
firm grip through the fabric. "Prepare yourself."

I had no idea how to do that or what to expect, so I exhaled, tried
to relax all my muscles, and nodded once. With everyone watching, he
spoke words I could not understand, a long string of syllables interspersed
with unfamiliar consonant combinations, some of which grated on his
vocal cords and roughened his melodious tone. Definitely not Standard.
Ancient Sardonen, perhaps? Something he'd learned in his study of the
Generational?

The power surged into me. My body jerked in a spasm that
snapped my teeth together and straightened my spine into an iron rod.

My shoulders rose and fell as I heaved in breath after breath. I felt supercharged, synapses firing, touch, smell, sight, hearing, all intensely acute. My heart pounded, blood flooding my veins and arteries to the point where I feared they'd burst. The overwhelming need to move drove me to my feet, and I stood, fists clenched at my sides, legs braced apart, muscles rippling with energy and a desire to unleash it upon something, or in this case, someone.

I can only imagine what I must have looked like, face flushed, hair tangled and matted, shirt torn and soaked with my own blood. I cast about for a weapon, panting like a wild beast just released from a cage and uncertain of which captor to kill first. My pistols and knives lay across the room on one of the docken-wood tables, and I made a move toward them. Everyone, including Jaren and Kila, got out of my way. Kila's hand covered her mouth, shock and fear at what she saw in my expression apparent in hers. I couldn't blame her. This sudden power scared the shit out of me, but I would use it, and only a fool would try and stop me.

I'd never taken Benn for a fool, but my next step brought me up against his chest, as he stood between me and my weapons. He looked as haggard and drained as everyone else after the recent ordeal except for me, Kila, and Jaren, but that wouldn't prevent him from interfering if he thought it was the right thing to do. Dropping back into a fighting stance, balanced on the balls of my feet, I met his intense gaze head-on.

"Fuck your rules and rituals. I do not yield." *Your* rules, not *ours.* The words came out in a low growl I barely recognized as my own voice. No one else moved. The chamber fell utterly silent save for the crackling flames in the firepit.

To my astonishment, Benn smiled. "You found your loophole."

I blinked, mind racing back in time to the hours I spent poring over Guild law, training to become a master, and it came to me. Life debt. That's what I had here, and so did Jaren. A life debt with the whole fucking Guild.

A life debt overrode everything, every transgression. The Guild was now honor-bound to protect and defend us.

Holy shit.

The thought made me laugh, earning further incongruous looks from the assembly. This was some holy shit, indeed.

"I'll need explanation for all this," Benn said, easing out of my path, making no sudden moves to provoke me, "but for now, go kick her ass."

I jogged to the table and collected my gear, slamming the pistols into thigh and back holsters, both Yesenia's, and sliding the knives into each boot. The way my pulse pounded, I felt I could take Yesenia out with my bare hands, and with her barely healing shoulder wound, that likely wouldn't take much. My comm lay on the table too. I waved it in the air at Jaren, and he pulled his off his belt and held it up to show me he still had it. I slipped mine into my pocket.

On my way out of the chamber, I stopped in front of Kila, cupping her chin and forcing her to meet my eyes. Her initial flinch at my touch hurt me more than I could have imagined. I'd come a long way from the person who wanted everyone around me to shudder at a lot less than physical contact. "I'm still in here," I assured her. "But this needs to be done."

A hesitation, then she nodded. "I know." She reached up to kiss me lightly. Her lips brushed the skin of my flushed cheek. "Just try not to want it so much." She turned away.

Then I was running for the surface, navigating the maze of tunnels, slowing only to check my corners before rounding them. I didn't think Yesenia would risk coming underground. Being older, I knew the passages better than she did, every twist and alcove. No, she'd stay topside and level the playing field.

Kila's words haunted me as I ran, repeating in my head over and over. She was right. I *wanted* this. I wanted to kill. The shiver that passed through me came from more than the absence of my jacket. Too many steps down this road could lead to my moral destruction, but, as Micah had always taught, recognition was half the map to finding my way back. Kila would provide the other half. Something for later consideration. I had other concerns right now.

I cut the last corner a little too close, scraping my knuckles on a broken femur protruding from the stone wall. I felt the skin tear and the welling of blood, but when I glanced at it, the gash was already closing.

Oh, this was going to be fun.

As I passed through the hologram of rock, the night air hit my skin and cooled some of the fire burning within me. I stood under an endless sea of stars untainted by man's artificial light sources. The full moon, low in the sky, lit the desert floor, drawing every rock, every object in dark outline, including Yesenia's aircar.

She hadn't bothered to conceal it beneath the available camouflage netting and heat sensor deterrents. It sat out in the open for anyone to see. After all, if she planned on killing everyone, what point was there in continuing to hide the Guild's location?

I snorted. The rogue assassin left the Guild far more visible than I had by bringing in Kila and Jaren.

Keeping my back to the rocks around the tunnel entrance, I skirted the outcropping and made my way toward the flat expanse, where the ventilation shaft expelled the Guild's smoke. I'd fully intended to behave in a manner befitting my profession, sticking to cover until the last possible moment, sneaking up on her if I could, but when I spotted Yesenia kneeling next to the aperture, fumbling in a large knapsack with her one good arm, I snapped.

Somewhere along the line, my gun found its way into my hand, and I raised it now. I stepped from the concealment of the rocks and strode toward her at a brisk pace, avoiding several steam geysers and closing the gap between us. In twenty strides, I'd brought myself within range. She spotted the motion, rising with her ripper drawn.

She'd been using a small hand lamp to fiddle with whatever equipment she carried, and it lay at her feet now, discarded. The lamp's failing battery made the light flicker, but I could make out what looked like an explosive device.

"Always have a backup plan," Micah had instructed. She'd learned his lessons as well as I had. After all, she, too, benefited from his *personal* tutoring.

The Guild's survival must have stunned her, but she'd chosen a much more direct method of annihilation this time, and she had the right plan for success. If that bomb went off in the audience chamber, it would kill at least half the assassins present, putting them beyond Jaren's abilities to help. It would also bring the ceiling down on everyone left alive, potentially disabling Jaren if he weren't blown to bits. She'd have her revenge on them all for reinstating me. Ironic, since they'd decided to kill me for something else, but Yesenia's sanity left her when Micah died.

The others might have evacuated the main room of the temple, but I doubted it, given Jaren's newfound connection to the place. I certainly couldn't depend on it. In that chamber the assassins had immortality. With that much power at my disposal, I knew *I* would never want to leave it. Disturbing thought.

Later, Cor. You need to lure Yesenia away from the explosive. Psychological evaluations could wait.

"How's the shoulder?" I taunted. One hung lower than the other.

Yesenia glared, but she didn't move to take the bait. She trained her ripper on my chest. My laser pointed at her head. I could fire, but it might set off the bomb. Never a good idea to use that much energy around a demolitions device.

Standoff. Again.

Overhead, two shuttles roared by, one coming from Weathered Palms, the other flying low over the dunes from the opposite direction. Judging from their configurations and camouflage armor plating, these were military vessels. Either they'd followed Yesenia from Lissex on whatever transportation she'd found to get here, or they'd traced her from the oasis city, or both. But they'd pinpointed her location, and by connection, the location of the Guild.

A lot of hostile company was about to come calling, and no one was available to answer the bell.

Priorities. Epiphany. It could not complete its mission for He-Who-Had-Created-It if its priorities were skewed.

It used the assassin to bring it to this seat of power, but now she interfered with its ultimate goal. The Core of Sardonen could not be controlled, and her insights set up barriers. It must destroy her before it destroyed the Chosen.

When Jaren moved from the altar to see to individuals' needs, those who suffered injuries when they fell or convulsed in the throes of the gas, his power weakened. The ephem reasserted itself over Kila's will. It drove her from the audience chamber, and in the aftermath of the assault, no one noticed her departure.

Kila didn't know her way through the maze of corridors, but the entity remembered, and when it faltered, the scent of Cor's blood and essence guided it onward.

Outside, it enhanced Kila's vision, allowing her sight to pierce the darkness and scan for her prey. When she rounded the rocks, she spotted her target and honed in.

Cor and Yesenia stared each other down, and the entity hesitated. The rogue assassin might do its job for it, but it made the mistake of leaving its work to others before, and Cor had Jaren's power within her.

This time it would wait to see the results, use Kila to commit murder if necessary, watch Cor's life drain from her body, and perhaps let Cor see her lover one last time as the light left her eyes. And when it allowed Kila to return to herself, that memory would stay with the girl and drive her to despair.

There could be no more mistakes. Already it felt the pull of its master's call. Soon it would have to obey, whether it succeeded or not.

CHAPTER 25

PUTTING ALL my faith in Jaren's power, I holstered my weapon and raised both hands in a gesture of surrender. "Come and get me." Let her think I was desperately trying to draw her away from her explosives, which, in effect, I was.

I knew she wouldn't approach, especially not with her injury, and she didn't disappoint me. "You're a bigger idiot than I thought you were." She fired the ripper.

Sometimes I wondered if I had some kind of death wish. Growing up surrounded by killing, it wouldn't surprise me.

The ripper blast knocked me backward, and the soft sand broke my fall. The unrefined energy tore open my chest with a shredding agony that wrenched a scream from my throat. I lay there, eyes closed, panting for breath, cursing the stupidity of this ill-conceived plan and clinging to consciousness by a thin wire. Beside me, a steam geyser erupted, singeing the hairs on my forearm, but I fought to remain motionless.

The wound closed. I shuddered at the strangeness of feeling blood sucking inward rather than pouring out, nerves and muscles and my very heart reforming and healing, my skin drawing together over the injury. Even the steam burn vanished, the redness fading to my normal ivory tone. The pain ebbed, then subsided. I held myself still and tried to slow my breathing.

Yesenia could not resist checking my body. In training, Micah instructed his apprentices to be sure of a target's death, no matter how fatal the wound appeared. Personal shields were rare, expensive, and often faulty, but not unheard of. It never hurt to be certain.

Until today.

When she stood over me, I swung a booted foot up and into her forearm, sending her gun flying across the sand. Her stunned expression brought a smile to my face as I leaped to my feet and slammed my fist into her nose. I felt the satisfying crunch of cartilage. She staggered backward, blood running over her lips, and scanned my torso with wide eyes, probably searching for some sign of body armor under my clothes.

I laughed and raised my shirt to show her the forming scar, then laughed harder as she paled. A small part of me distanced myself enough to view my actions from the outside. Showing humor made me sound insane, but I could not stop it.

"How? How did you…?" Yesenia shook herself and drew a knife off her belt, consummate assassin to the end. Before I could pull my laser, she threw the blade, driving half its length into my thigh.

"Aim's off," I scolded. The skin closed around the sharp edge, healing fast, and I yanked it free before the weapon became permanently embedded. Then I returned it to its owner, via her abdomen.

Yesenia doubled over the wound, sinking to her knees with a grunt and a string of curses. The landing shuttles drowned out whatever else she intended to say, both of them setting down near the outcropping of rocks hiding the tunnel entrance. So much for obscurity.

Pulling the comm from my pocket, I opened the channel. Static assailed my ears while I dialed down the volume. "Jaren, pick up."

It took several seconds. In the meantime, ramps lowered from the two vessels, and dark figures swarmed out of them. Yesenia wrapped both her hands around her own knife in preparation to remove it. Foolish. That would speed the loss of blood. But she was no longer thinking rationally, hadn't been for a long time. She must have loved Micah more than I ever had. A small part of me pitied her for half a heartbeat.

"I'm here, Cor," came Jaren's anxious voice over the comm. "You all right?"

"Fine," I assured him. "Better than fine. But we've got a lot of visitors. Tell Guild Leader Benn I'm going to need reinforcements, if anyone is able."

A pause. Shuffling and indiscernible voices. "Let me see what I can do." He clicked off.

I stood over Yesenia, looming like Death itself, watching her writhe and spout blood. I pictured the torture she'd planned for me and the others. Another kick drove the blade deeper into her gut before she could pull it out.

My fury exploded, a blind anger blocking out everything else, and I drew back my leg again, but when I swung it at her head, she grabbed for it and brought me down in the sand beside her. She yanked out the knife and thrust it into my forearm, then sliced me twice more along my rib cage before I drove the heel of my hand up into her chin. Her teeth clamped shut on a muffled scream.

No more curses rained from her mouth, only blood. I think she bit off the end of her tongue. She spit the bit of flesh into the dust.

While she fell back to regroup, I took stock of my injuries. My arm closed up until no more than a thin red line remained, but the cuts on my side seeped red that added more dark stains to my ruined shirt.

The power was fading. Fleeting invincibility.

Yesenia propped herself up on one elbow, but I stood and kicked it from beneath her. She grunted as she hit the sand. Images of Kila and Jaren suffocating from the Issiumoxide, torn apart by a fragmentation explosive, or crushed under a cave-in flooded my mind while I continued to strike her again and again.

I cracked her ribs, ground my heel over her fingers, and pummeled her face until it became unrecognizable and she ceased breathing. The rage urged me to continue, a desire to deface and damage beyond her death. I fought it like a physical thing, forcing it down, drawing it into myself, where it boiled and burned and tried to claw itself free.

When my vision cleared, I found myself on my knees beside her broken body, and when I saw the destruction I'd caused, tremors shook my limbs until I had to wrap my arms around myself to stop them. I could accept elimination of an enemy, but pure, uncontrolled destruction meant something else entirely. If I intended to continue using Jaren's power in the future, some sort of mental discipline would need to be developed. It was wondrous but dangerous in the extreme.

I crawled to Yesenia's abandoned explosive device and examined it. Every Guild member had basic demolitions instruction. Some even specialized in it, though I found that method messy and unrefined. I pulled the activator circuit, rendering it harmless. Then, with the little strength I had left, I threw the circuit across the dunes where the next sandstorm would bury it forever.

Kila's body strode across the sand, her steps strong and purposeful. The dead assassin's gun lay several meters from her body where Cor kicked it. Eyes focused on nothing, Kila wrapped her fingers around the grip, and she drew the weapon to her side.

Another figure moved in the darkness, oblivious to her, crouched there in the shadows, but well aware of Cor. It raised a pistol and pointed it at Cor's head.

No more waiting. No more chances. The entity would end them both.

Kila raised Yesenia's gun and aimed, but her arm trembled. Her aim wavered. Whether it stemmed from a lack of training or an unwillingness to comply, the ephem didn't know, but it would have to move her closer to be sure of the kills.

The sand muffled the girl's footsteps as she crossed soundlessly to stand behind Cor's new assailant.

Deep within Kila's soul, she raged against the entity's control. The ephem ignored her.

I didn't register the presence of another living being until the cold metal of a gun barrel pressed against my temple hard enough to leave an indentation. Ice formed in the veins of my neck. I resisted the urge to jerk away. Any sudden move might trigger a most unwelcome response.

"Stand slowly."

The voice was male, low and gruff. I obeyed its command, climbing to my feet while the power-high receded from my body. I felt its absence like the loss of a tangible thing and ached for it. It reminded me a little of palotrin withdrawal, and I inwardly groaned. The last thing I needed was a new addiction.

Once I was standing, the new arrival turned me to face him, hard eyes appraising me and the damage I'd done to my last victim. He wore military gear and fatigues, beige and brown splotches that would blend with the desert in daylight. His jaw bore several days' worth of stubble, and his pallor suggested he lived more on ships recently than a planet's surface. I recognized the insignia on his collar—crossed rifles and a grenade. He was a merc from the local unit that trained nearby, the same unit that saved me all those months ago.

I doubted I'd get sympathy this time.

The shuttles disgorged their occupants, and behind him dark figures milled about, scouting and searching, difficult to see with the shifting smoke and puffs of steam. A few engaged in combat with one another, rodents squabbling over the right to hunt Jaren, the largest piece of cheese. Half had to be the rest of this guy's team. The others I could only guess at.

A distant glow on the horizon indicated the approach of dawn, and it outlined the two vessels that landed, their underbelly searchlights scouring the dunes. Neither was an Annihilator, the ships favored by the Believers, so I doubted any of these folks were members of the Givers of Life.

"I know you," the merc growled. "You're Guild." He stared at the brand on my wrist, visible without my jacket to cover it despite the shadows and sparse light from the ships.

"What of it?" Exhaustion dropped on me like a block of stone. I'd strained my physical resources to the last, and I was so damn tired of fighting.

"You've got Jaren T'ral. Folks are offering big credits for him." His brows drew together in a thoughtful expression. It stretched his facial muscles in ways that seemed unnatural for this muscle-bound oaf. "We knew you were out here, you assassin types. Never located your base. Now you can show me where it is."

I shook my head, even that small motion taking a toll and spinning the landscape. "Not in this lifetime." Besides, they'd find it themselves, soon enough. All I wanted was to lie down.

"How about the next one?" The merc adjusted his aim, centering the laser pistol on my chest. My eyes focused on the lethal circular opening at the barrel's tip.

I shrugged. The fleeting power had left me with a kind of apathy I could not fight. If I did have some secret death wish, it was about to be fulfilled.

The gun fired, and I braced myself for the pain before my mind registered it produced the wrong sound. A ripper made that kind of low hum-whine. A second later, blood and gore from the merc's blasted skull spattered the front of my already disgusting shirt. Thank the gods he was taller than I. The remainder of the unfocused energy went over my head and dispersed in the fading darkness. All but headless, the body toppled, revealing his killer.

Kila stood behind him, Yesenia's discarded weapon clutched in both her trembling hands, a look of pure horror distorting her angelic features. She'd taken a life. Willingly. For me. And I knew she would never forgive herself.

Hells.

Encouraging Kila to kill the merc had been relatively easy. The entity convinced her conscience firing the weapon would save Cor.

Her heightened sense of moral values rallied against it, but only for a moment. Cor's life held greater value for her. But as the soldier's body toppled into the sand, the ephem detected exactly what that meant and recognized its fatal error.

Any force strong enough to make Kila betray the principles of her religion was also strong enough to defeat the entity itself.

The two consciousnesses fought for control over her gun hand, one trying to pull the trigger, the other resisting with all its strength. The weapon wavered, aim varying wildly, but at this close range, if it fired, it would find its target.

In her mind, Kila thought shock controlled her, emotional trauma over the life she'd taken. She could imagine no other reason for pointing a ripper at Cor. She pictured every moment they'd shared—Cor rescuing her from the slaver, then later, the pirate captain, and finally Yesenia, the two of them sunning themselves on the deck of the Triumph, *their lovemaking so intense and bittersweet, knowing how little time they might have together.*

Infused with her thoughts, the entity watched the images flow from one to the next, and it knew fear.

Kila gave one final wrenching scream that cut through the desert night and the distant sounds of skirmishes, causing everyone to fall still and silent. The ephem flew from between her gaping lips, mingling with the smoke of the assassins' fire and the steam geysers erupting nearby. Combined with so many other elements, it could not maintain its cohesion, and its atoms separated, scattering themselves into the darkened sky—a less-painful fate than its punishment for failure would have been.

Its last sentient view was of Kila as she drew back both hands high over her head and hurled the illegal, torturous weapon as far across the dunes as her slight muscles would allow.

I stumbled toward Kila, my boots heavier than granite. I caught her as she collapsed, and fell with her until we huddled together in the sand.

New movement from the rock outcropping drew my eye as assassins emerged from the hidden tunnel, weapons flashing in the morning sunlight. They swarmed the invaders, taking hit after hit and recovering almost instantaneously while they drove our enemies to their ships. Engines barely cooled from landing fired up again.

Jaren had found his undefeatable army.

The looks on the faces of the mercs, mouths agape as fatally wounded assassins stood up and retaliated, would have made me laugh if I hadn't been holding a shattered Kila in my arms. I smoothed her long hair, mumbled soothing noises, and tried to ease her violent shaking to no avail. Behind her, hardened men and battle-worn women screamed in terror, running from the immortals who pursued them.

She turned her tearstained face to me, her skin white as plaster in the dawning sun. "This one's really dead, isn't he?"

I glanced across the sand at the fallen merc, his brains spilled on the sand, blood staining the pale particles dark. There'd be carrion activity already if it weren't for all the humans and their struggles. "Very." Okay, that could have been said better. Sardonen krick beetles adored dead flesh, and the beaks and talons of a local species of hawk would render the body indistinguishable by midday. Having seen more than my fair share of death, this one was particularly gruesome.

Kila fixed me with a stare so intense I couldn't turn away. "So was that slaver, the one who tried to take me back on Deluge." It wasn't a question. I answered it anyway.

"Yes." Better to hit her with the full reality so she could absorb and recover from it all at once. Pain given in doses lingers too long.

She swallowed, and I wondered if she would be ill. "Thank you for sparing me until now."

My eyebrows rose. "Thank you for lying?"

She managed a sad smile. "Sometimes there are good reasons to lie." Meanings behind meanings.

I nodded acknowledgment of that statement.

BY THE end of the day, the Assassins Guild stemmed the flow of mercenaries, military personnel, and bounty hunters determined to capture Jaren to use for themselves or turn over to some employer for private benefit. Every time the power ebbed, the failing assassin would dash into the assembly room for a recharge. Jaren never tired, except in the amount expected at the end of a long, trying day. Within the temple walls, he was invincible. At last I understood the fears he'd had. In the wrong hands, especially if those hands discovered this seat of power, Jaren could have altered the fates of millions.

By the Generational's decree, with Jaren safely returned to the temple under protection of his unbeatable army, the Believers no longer needed to beat the rest of the universe into peaceful submission. Around sunset, the Believers' Peacemakers force arrived in their Annihilator ships. Jaren sent a broadcast via the Guild's comm system informing them of his status and instructing them to set up regular patrols around the temple area, turning the space above it into a no-fly zone. Others used ground transports brought in from Weathered Palms to sweep the desert in the vicinity of the sacred structure, discouraging any approach by land. Ships and transports not on watch duty parked outside the cavern entrance, and we housed the pilots while they rested and waited for their shifts, trying to ignore their fawning over Jaren T'ral, their Chosen.

The preacher—Speaker, I was informed, was the official title—from Lissex arrived on one of the Annihilators. He took on a sort of lieutenant's role, coordinating everything while Jaren caught a few rest periods. Self-serving or not, he was a natural leader, already had the respect of the Believers, and did a good job at organizing and scheduling, so I didn't argue his appointment.

Once we took stock of everyone and everything, we totaled our additional casualties at three: an apprentice who waited too long for a power boost and took a knife to the gut, a master who had his head severed from his body—no way to heal that—and Benn. We'd need to learn our new limitations better if this practice were to become policy.

At first we didn't even realize the charred figure belonged to our Guild Leader. And yes, he was *our* Guild Leader. *My* Guild Leader. I'd internalized my reinstatement when Benn sent me to kill Yesenia. Apparently, one of the mercs decided the only way to eliminate the seemingly immortal assassin was to douse him in engine oil and light him on fire. Gruesome and effective. We identified him by his knives and a metal armband he always wore. Witnesses later informed me it took him a long time to die while he burned and healed and continued to burn, staggering about blindly, searching for the tunnel entrance and his path back to Jaren. He never found it.

I shed tears for the short-term Guild Leader, and Jaren performed a service for his remains. He was a good man, willing to admit to mistakes and learn from them. He would have done well for the Guild.

Several of the assassins showed symptoms of the same apathy I'd experienced when the enhancements wore off. They moved on autopilot from task to task, their faces devoid of emotion or enthusiasm. A good night's rest erased those side effects, but only time would reveal the long-term damage that kind of power usage could do.

We located Benn's choice of successor on the computer in his office. Alek. With Alek already dead, by our laws, the present assassins voted, and we sent messages to those off-world on assignment. The results came in faster than I would have imagined possible.

I never considered myself much of a leader. Until I met Kila, I preferred to work alone. But the Guild had spoken. Guess when you help save all their lives, they feel a little beholden.

Big changes were in order for me and the Guild. Jaren had been right about religions and organizations like ours. It was time for us to evolve.

I began the very next day, using Speaker D'post as a historical resource and calling in teams of archaeologists and engineers from Sardonen and beyond. They brought heavy equipment to clear away the concealing rock and unearth the temple. The course of events revealed our secret. We might as well return the religious center of the Givers of Life to its original splendor, and splendor it was. The exterior proved to be constructed of the same marble as the altar in the assembly room. It gleamed in the bright Sardonen sun.

I doubled the size of the Guild, recruiting new apprentices and increasing the number of daily training sessions. If we were to continue to carry out our primary function while leaving a significant force behind to watch over Jaren, we'd need more trained assassins. I did, however, raise the entry age for apprentices. Children deserved childhoods, no matter how easy the young were to teach.

Jaren opened the temple to anyone who sought healing, holding daily services in the audience chamber while Speaker D'post moved among them seeking converts. Each applicant to enter had to pass through an extensive weapons screening prior to admittance. The Givers of Life charged no fees but encouraged donations. It didn't take long to discover healed people were generous people. With Jaren's permission, I hired several recuperated, loyal accountants to handle the wealth—and keep a quiet eye on D'post, though I kept that part of their job description a secret between me and the accountants. When he tried to order Therix candles, the requisition managed to somehow become lost. Three times. He gave up.

Most of the collected funds went to a variety of charities—mostly hospitals and medical research facilities. Jaren couldn't heal the universe. I also asked that a portion go to the group home where I'd spent several years as a child. The rest we used to fortify the Guild and the Believers. With the return of religious services, our eating, sleeping, and training areas needed replacement. Over the next many weeks, a dining hall and modern practice facility were constructed.

Gone was the idea of communal sleeping. We annexed dormitory housing for the apprentices and small apartment structures for the masters. The Guild still frowned upon relationships between its members, but Kila didn't belong to the Guild, and I planned to put that to a vote. Assassins, more than many occupations, needed outlets for tension and frustration.

Considering how little I saw of Kila, the distinction between Guild and not Guild didn't much matter, though.

The largest two apartments belonged to Jaren and me, as Guild Leader. My few possessions, along with Kila's shipped in from Lissex, were installed in the rather luxurious one-bedroom unit complete with a kitchen, living area, and sanitary facility. Well, compared to sleeping on a rolled-out mat on the temple floor, everything is luxurious. How the Guild managed to remain in the dark ages so long was a mystery to me. Maybe it was some kind of self-punishment for our deeds.

We had hardly shared that bed since the morning she shot the merc. Kila conspired to be up at odd hours, researching her antiquated copy of the Generational brought in with her belongings. My own schedule of overseeing construction, recruitment, and training left me little time for anything else. I missed her, despite her constant presence within comm's reach.

I knew she suffered horrible guilt over what she'd done to save my life. The few times we slept together she awoke drenched in cold sweat, trembling from nightmares.

"When does it stop?" she asked on one of those dark nights.

I lay beside her, willing my own heart to cease its pounding after her scream awakened me. An old-fashioned clock imported from Lissex ticked on the wall. That and our harsh breathing were the only sounds in the room.

I wished I had an answer for her. I knew exactly what she experienced. I'd been there. Still was. After my first kill, I saw that face again and again in my dreams. All my targets haunted me. A person would have to be a sadist not to be affected by killing. And she knew I fought my own late-night demons. She'd seen the results.

"It doesn't, does it?" Kila whispered, interpreting my thoughts.

"No," I murmured into her hair. "But time helps." Unless you keep doing it, like me. Then the nightmares mix and mingle. But that wouldn't be Kila's concern, just mine. I knew what she felt and hated that rescuing me had been the cause. Nothing I could say or do would take her pain, though I tried. That night I held and rocked her for hours.

I STOOD to the side of the altar, on Jaren's right, hands folded in front of me. Speaker D'post occupied the space to Jaren's left, a frown drawing his lips down along with the dark mustache adorning them. He hadn't approved of this ceremony. I didn't give a fuck what he thought.

Before the marble slab, Kila knelt, her lithe frame swathed in a single, simple sheet of white linen wrapped in intricate twists to cover her. The Generational lay open on the flat surface before us, though my angle of sight prevented me from reading the words within.

The rest of the assembly room waited in empty silence, the Guild dismissed after a long day of practice and a hearty meal. Torches in sconces lined the walls. I'd switched off the electrical lighting at Jaren's request.

Very surreal.

Outside, the wind howled. The newly excavated walls let in the sounds of desert storms much more loudly than they had while buried. The moans of each gust and the tapping of granules against the recently installed duraglass windows resembled night terrors seeking entrance.

Very pointless.

I could see from the set of Kila's jaw and the hardness in her eyes she didn't accept this ritual as cleansing her sins any more than D'post did. In private, he'd agreed she shouldn't be punished but didn't feel forgiveness was merited. I knew Kila would think the same. Amazing how well I'd come to know her in such a short time.

Jaren spoke the words from the text, some in Standard, others in ancient Sardonen. He'd grown fond of the ancient language over the past days, using it more and more and teaching common phrases to anyone who'd listen.

I didn't understand a word of it, and I'd grown up here.

"Kila T'ral," he intoned, and each syllable carried to the farthest corners, "you have taken two lives, the worst offense one may give under our religious laws. Is this true?"

A formality. Jaren and I discussed the circumstances surrounding the deaths in detail, searching for Kila's own loopholes so she might be forgiven in the eyes of the Believers, or at least most of them.

"Yes." So much weight in a single word.

"However, both were taken in defense of she who later became my Guardian, my savior. Is this not also true?"

Kila looked from her brother to me, carefully avoiding Speaker D'post's harsh gaze. I resisted the urge to reach around Jaren and smack him in the back of the head.

Kila sighed. "Yes." No belief there. She humored Jaren with her response, well aware of what he was trying to do. Justification. Understanding. Acceptance. Only Kila didn't feel she deserved any of it.

I knew, because in the dark, when I held her, she told me.

"Under Believers' law, the taking of lives in defense of the Chosen is permitted, encouraged even. By saving the Guardian, you saved me. I would not stand here today, in this place, to heal the sick and injured, if Cor had died on either occurrence."

Kila opened her mouth to argue, but Jaren stopped her with an upraised hand and a soft smile. "The decision of the Chosen is final." He turned a quick, intense glare on D'post, who would not meet his eyes, then returned his attention to his sister. "I absolve you of your guilt. The Givers of Life find you cleansed." He crossed in front of the altar, took Kila's hands, and raised her to stand before him. Then he hugged her. "May you find the strength within to forgive yourself," he whispered into her hair.

None of that mattered to Kila. She'd taken two lives, and she abhorred herself for it.

I had one idea of how I might reach her, but it would involve the biggest stretch of my life.

CHAPTER 26

GODS, THIS made me nervous. Good thing I skipped the last two meals.

I steeled myself and headed for the antechamber off the temple's grand assembly hall, boots echoing in the stone corridors. The workers unblocked access to the small room shortly after they began excavations around the structure. Jaren guessed the ancients used it for quiet meditation. Traces of wax and ash indicated the burning of candles. A stone alcove held chemically preserved books Jaren removed for his perusal. Kila claimed the space for her spiritual studies and solitude.

The late hour ensured privacy. Even the skeletons had been removed for proper burial outside the temple. New leadership, new era, new traditions. My fingers slipped into my jacket pocket, running over the velvet-covered container within, checking its presence, though I'd placed it there myself only minutes before.

Calm down, Cor. You're making yourself crazier than you already are.

Turning a corner, I saw flickering light spilling from the open doorway. We'd installed electricity in all the new areas, along with additional generators, but Kila preferred candles, said they put her in closer touch with her ancestors and the gods.

I slowed and softened my steps, not wanting to disturb or frighten her. In the entrance I paused, locating her on the far side of the room, seated at the single table in the solitary chair. It was a familiar scene, Kila hunched over the Generational, dried tears on her cheeks, one finger tracing the words within the book. Before, she'd cried for what she thought she had to do to Jaren. Now she cried for herself. The candlelight created a halo effect, lighting her gently in waves and shadows.

My heart ached for her. How could someone so beautiful be so sad?

"I think it's me," she said so softly I almost missed her words. I needed to work on my silent movement skills. My administrative duties took a toll on my practice schedule.

"What?" I stepped fully into the room, coming to stand beside the table. The light cast from the candles illuminated the pages of the ancient text, making the black-inked words seem to dance on the parchment.

She read from the scripture. "And one amongst them, an aberration in the blood, shall become a bringer of death. And unhindered, that aberration shall bring about the destruction of them all." Kila looked up at me, her expression painful to witness. "I think it's me." The simple sentence tore from her soul.

I couldn't breathe. Her words froze me in place. I'd referred to myself once as a "bringer of death" when I first discussed with Jaren my plans to lead him to the temple. "Maybe it's me." A few months ago, I would have scoffed at prophecy and mysticism. Now I took nothing for granted, especially if it was written in that book.

Kila's smile held no humor. "That's my Cor, always taking everything upon herself. No, it's not you. It says 'in the blood,' meaning in my family's bloodline. A relative of the Chosen."

I lay a hand on her shoulder. "It's not you either. I've never met anyone as good as you, except maybe your twin. You saved my life. Stop beating yourself up over it. This *aberration* could be anyone in your family, a fifth cousin, a lost branch you've never met. Kila, it's been hundreds and hundreds of years. Think of the possible spread of your genetics." Regardless, though, I needed to make some time in my schedule to continue my study of the Generational.

She placed her hand atop mine. "Thank you. I hope you're right."

"I'm Guild Leader. I'm always right." I paused, listening to the hoped-for giggle and reveling in it. "Except when I'm wrong."

That got a genuine laugh, the first I'd heard from her in weeks. The sound echoed in the small space, nothing like the audience chamber, but we both glanced at the ceiling, then each other, and smiled.

I pulled the long, thin velvet box from my pocket and placed it on the table beside the Generational. Kila wasn't the only one who'd been doing her research. I'd been picking Jaren's brain for days.

Taking a step back, I assumed the appropriate position—feet slightly apart, hands folded over my heart, head respectfully lowered with eyes cast down. My submissive posture reminded me of the first time we made love, when she took complete control.

I heard Kila draw the box toward her, velvet whispering over the wood. The hinged container creaked when she opened it. I caught her sharp intake of breath. It took everything I had to hold my gaze on the floor. I focused on the quake cracks running in myriad patterns across the stone and waited.

Choosing the Bond chains had been a lengthy process. I'd studied gemstones from Lissex, focusing on the symbolism and significance of each type. Every stone meant something different, and I wanted mine to convey the right message. The necklace closest to Kila, the one she lifted from the box while I watched her hands in my peripheral vision, was a choker of alternating gold and teal gems. Not quite the yellow and aqua of the T'ral family colors, but close enough. It cost me a huge portion of the savings returned to me by the Guild.

The gold hermizite represented unwavering trust. The teal briaz stood for love stronger than death. Considering my new appointment, ours would need to be.

My heart pounded, and I resisted the urge to wipe my sweaty palms on my pant legs. When I heard the soft click as she fastened it around her neck, I forgot to breathe.

The chair slid back and Kila stood, coming to take both my hands in hers, pulling them from my chest. Both of ours were cold. I think mine shook a little. Good thing I didn't need to fire a weapon right now. I'd probably shoot myself in the foot. Despite an almost overwhelming compulsion, I did not raise my head.

"You're asking me to take the Bond with you?" she whispered, incredulous.

My throat closed over the words. It wasn't that I didn't want to say them. I simply didn't know how. My exhalation of held breath was louder than I intended, and my face reddened as she giggled. Maybe looking back on this moment, I'd find this funny, but not now. She knew what I wanted. She wore the chain. She enjoyed torturing me.

"Yes," I managed somehow, eloquent as always.

"You're very nervous." A simple observation. I imagined her head cocked to the side, eyes shining with mischief.

"Yes." If my stomach muscles clenched any tighter, I'd turn inside out.

Her tone became serious. "You understand what the Bond means? It's for life. My people don't separate or divorce, even in the worst of times. We work through things as well as we can. Maybe not the best way, but it's our way."

With all we'd overcome, I couldn't imagine any personal quarrels we couldn't resolve. "I understand." Now I did look at her, even though raising my head at this juncture broke with her people's traditions. "Do *you* understand that life, especially for someone in my profession, might end tomorrow? That I don't intend to change who or what I am, at least not any more than I've already had to?" My lips quirked a little on that statement, with me thinking of how much my life had altered since meeting Kila and leaving my little subbasement apartment on Deluge. However, the question was dangerous and pivotal. It gave her an "out" I didn't want to provide, but I would not enter into this permanent relationship on false pretenses or inaccurate perceptions. I would love her to death, for as long as that might be, but I wouldn't lead a sheltered life.

Wind howled through the corridor beyond the chamber, another fierce sandstorm raging outside. Ominous accompaniment to my inquiry.

"I understand," Kila said, squeezing my hands. "Changing you would change the person I fell in love with." She released my hands and embraced me then in a quick grasp, as if she'd been resisting the urge to do so all along. Then she resumed her formal stance. "I will take whatever time we have together and cherish it."

I didn't think it possible to feel more for her than I already did. I was wrong.

She stepped away and removed the second chain from the velvet box. Mine was a little longer, designed that way to hang lower beneath my collar and not be so obvious to a casual observer. Letting my enemies know I had someone special in my life did not seem like a good tactical move. It hurt to realize I clung to my assassin's nature even here and now, but that nature kept me alive.

This necklace had alternating stones of deep green and blue, celathyst and unilite respectively. Celathyst signified steadfast loyalty. Unilite symbolized intense desire. I lowered my chin to my chest as Kila slid around me, her body brushing mine and eliciting delicious chills. Lifting my hair with one hand, she fastened the chain about my neck. It was lighter than I expected, not restrictive at all. She drew it centimeter by centimeter from where it had fallen down my shirt to rest on my breastbone and lay it over the black fabric for the universe to see. Well, what I did with it while away on assignment, she didn't need to know.

"We are Bonded." I spoke the final words to seal the ritual, a ritual I could live with for a change.

"We are Bonded," Kila echoed, pure joy and a touch of laughter in her voice. Her arms wrapped around my waist, and she laid her head on my chest. A sigh of contentment and relief left her.

Maybe there was a dark one out there, a "bringer of death." My mind flicked briefly to the odd weather patterns and increased number of sandstorms we'd experienced lately, and I shoved those thoughts to a corner and locked them there. Whatever evil awaited us, I knew with absolute certainty it wasn't Kila. And whoever it was, we would face it together.

ELLE E. IRE resides in Celebration, Florida, where she writes science fiction and urban fantasy novels featuring kickass women who fall in love with each other. She has won many local and national writing competitions, including the Royal Palm Literary Award, the Pyr and Dragons essay contest judged by the editors at Pyr Publishing, the Do It Write competition judged by a senior editor at Tor publishing, and she is a winner of the Backspace scholarship awarded by multiple literary agents. She and her spouse run several writing groups and attend and present at many local, state, and national writing conferences.

When she isn't teaching writing to middle school students, Elle enjoys getting into her characters' minds by taking shooting lessons, participating in interactive theatrical experiences, paying to be kidnapped "just for the fun and feel of it," and attempting numerous escape rooms.

To learn what her tagline "Deadly Women, Dangerous Romance" is really all about, visit her website: www.elleire.com. She can also be found on Twitter at @ElleEIre and Facebook at www.facebook.com/ElleE.IreAuthor.

Elle is represented by Naomi Davis at BookEnds.

ELLE E. IRE

THREADBARE

STORM FRONTS BOOK ONE

DEADLY WOMEN,
DANGEROUS ROMANCE

Storm Fronts: Book One

All cybernetic soldier Vick Corren wanted was to be human again. Now all she wants is Kelly. But machines can't love. Can they?

With the computerized implants that replaced most of her brain, Vick views herself as more machine than human. She's lost her memory, but worse, can no longer control her emotions, though with the help of empath Kelly LaSalle, she's holding the threads of her fraying sanity together.

Vick is smarter, faster, impervious to pain… the best mercenary in the Fighting Storm, until odd flashbacks show Vick a life she can't remember and a romantic relationship with Kelly that Vick never knew existed. But investigating that must wait until Vick and her team rescue the Storm's kidnapped leader.

Someone from within the organization is working against them, threatening Kelly's freedom. To save her, Vick will have to sacrifice what she values most: the last of her humanity. Before the mission is over, either Vick or Kelly will forfeit the life she once knew.

www.dsppublications.com

For more
great fiction
from

DSP PUBLICATIONS

visit us online.

WWW.DSPPUBLICATIONS.COM